RUIN THE FRIENDSHIP

MINNESOTA BLUE HERONS

ALICE DANIELS

This book is intended for mature audiences.

ISBN: 978-1-964971-08-7

Editing: Elle Lavendelle

Cover Illustration: Vera Osipchik

Typography: Willa Kay

ALICE DANIELS

CONTENTS

Content Warning | xv

1. Drug Store Vibrators | 1
2. Good Luck Charm | 8
3. Dottie Always Knows | 11
4. Never Say Never | 15
5. Pot, Meet Kettle | 18
6. Pancakes, Positive Tests, and Happy Trails | 25
7. Friend-zoned | 31
8. Hey Jude | 40
9. Unanswered Questions | 50
10. Falling Forward | 55
11. Little Bean | 61
12. And I'm a hockey player! | 67
13. Curly Girl Routine | 74
14. Long Story Short | 79
15. Buttery Salty Goodness | 84
16. Whatever It Takes | 92
17. Mommy Issues | 97
18. Operation Ruin The Friendship | 107
19. Ten Dates to Fall in Love | 109
20. The Size Of A Lemon | 112
21. More Than Friends | 115
22. Twinkling Lights & Hot Chocolate | 121
23. A Package Deal | 128
24. Share With The Class | 136
25. Practice Makes Perfect | 140
26. Christmas Cookies | 145
27. Plans Change | 152
28. Operation Ruin The Friendship | 158
29. Betting on Love | 161

30. Doing Things Backward ... 164
31. Ice Cream Makes Everything Better ... 169
32. Lydi-Bugs & Ladybugs ... 175
33. Hockey Shrines and Frozen Waffles ... 181
34. Patience Is A Virtue ... 187
35. Sparks Fly ... 193
36. Never Letting Go ... 202
37. Operation Ruin The Friendship ... 208
38. Le Château Whatever ... 211
39. The B Word ... 219
40. Bunny Hops & Forbidden Fantasies ... 227
41. Yours for the Taking ... 236
42. Millionaire Sugar Daddy ... 245
43. ZamBROnies ... 257
44. The Gang's All Here ... 259
45. Girlhood ... 263
46. Someone Special ... 267
47. Emotional Support Group Chat ... 272
48. Welcome Home ... 275
49. I Protect The Family ... 282
50. Crying Over A Onesie ... 285
51. A Little Ladybug Is On The Way ... 292
52. Biting My Tongue ... 304
53. Misfortune & Mama Drama ... 311
54. Disconnect ... 320
55. I Love You ... 324
56. Mustache Ride ... 330
57. Family Are The Ones That Show Up ... 334
58. Running Thoughts ... 340
59. Ready or Not ... 346
60. Room Seven-Ten ... 354
61. The Next Chapter ... 361
62. Namesake ... 366
63. Good Luck Comes In Twos ... 371
64. One More Chance ... 377
Epilogue ... 382

Acknowledgments 387
Also By Alice Daniels 389
About the Author 391

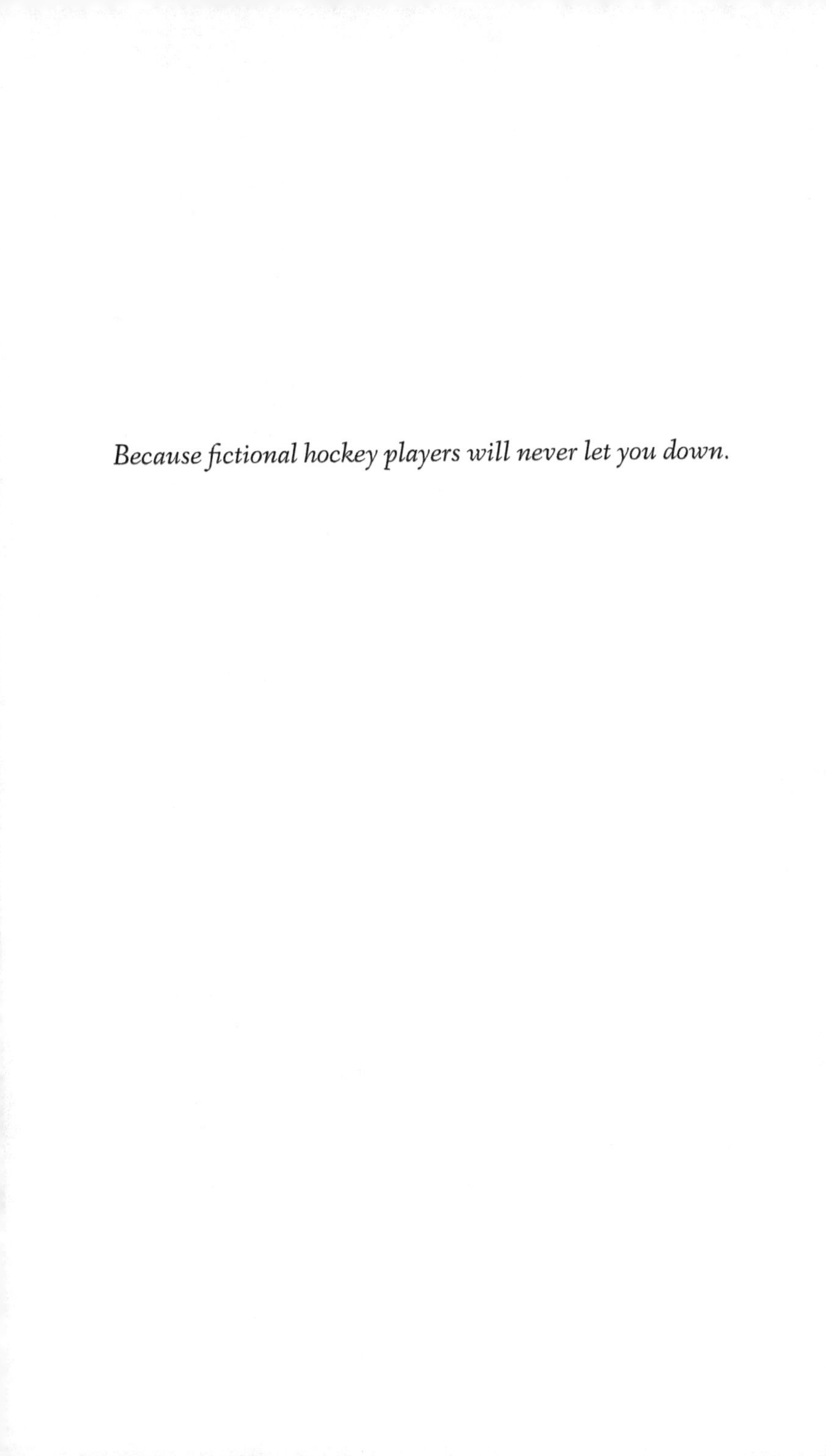

Because fictional hockey players will never let you down.

10,000 Emerald Pools- BØRNS
Can't Take My Eyes Off You- Frankie Valli
Centuries- Fall Out Boy
dorothea- Taylor Swift
Everything Changes- Jessie Mueller, Keala Settle, Kimiko Glenn
Fever Dream- Alex Warren
I Choose You- Sara Bareilles
I Do Believe In Fairies- James Newton Howard
It's You- Peter Peter
Our Song- Matchbox Twenty
Ruin The Friendship- Taylor Swift
So Easy (To Fall in Love)- Olivia Dean
That's How Strong My Love Is- Otis Redding
When Did You Get Hot?- Sabrina Carpenter
Wi$h Li$t- Taylor Swift

To listen to whole playlist, scan the QR Code!

TEAM ROSTER

FORWARDS

FLETCHER GRAFF (#48): LEFT WINGER, CAPTAIN
CALVIN MILLER (#24): CENTER, ASSISTANT CAPTAIN
ADAM DAVISON "DAVEY" (#13): RIGHT WINGER
JAKE ANDREWS (#38): RIGHT WINGER
OTTO HOFFMANN (#17): LEFT WINGER
LINUS AHLIN (#18): CENTER
GIOVANNI MARINO "GIO" (#97): RIGHT WINGER

DEFENSEMAN

SHEPHERD WAFFORD "WAFFLES, SHEP" (#7): DEFENSE
JAMIE LEVINE (#25): DEFENSE
LAKEN MONROE, "LAKEY" (#46): DEFENSE
NIKOLAI ILYIN, "NIKO" (#22): DEFENSE
DRAKE THAYER (#41): DEFENSE

GOALIES

TRYGVE AADLAND "TRIGG, ADDY" (#32): GOALIE
ANDREI FILIMONOV (#30): BACKUP GOALIE

CONTENT WARNING

Dear Reader,

Ruin The Friendship contains subjects that may be triggering to some. This content includes on page scenes of narcissistic parents, pregnancy, consideration of abortion, signing away of parental rights, labor and delivery with no complications, vomit, and fighting in the context of a hockey game.

This book includes explicit language and graphic sexual scenes. Reader discretion is advised.

Take care of yourself. Your mental health matters more than a book.

DRUG STORE VIBRATORS

LYDIA

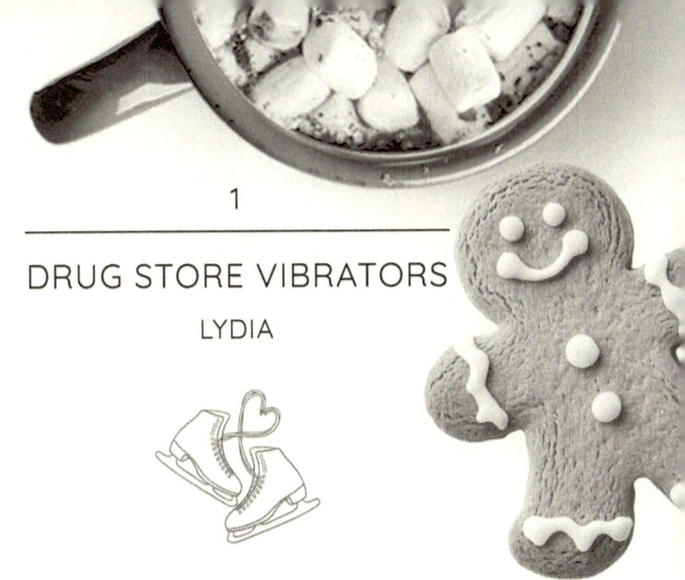

"There's no way," I mumble to myself.

The pregnancy test boxes stare me down in the middle of this small drugstore. I was only here to grab my prescriptions when something pulled me into this aisle.

It hasn't been more than a few weeks since my last period. Right? I've never been good at tracking it, but I've never needed to. My cycle has always been regular, and I take my birth control at the same time every day.

Only... the more I think about it, the more my stomach drops, and a sick feeling burns through my bloodstream. I count out the many weeks since that third date with Jude, and now, my lack of period.

No, no, no.

I cover my face with my hands, taking a deep breath.

Think, Lydia.

He wore a condom, right? And he pulled out. That has to be at least ninety-nine percent effective, doesn't it? Really, what are the chances I'm pregnant?

Glancing around the aisle, I throw three different tests into my basket and rush to the self-checkout. I ring them up and pay, tossing them into a plastic bag. Damn it. I always bring reusable bags to the store, but of course, this is the one day I didn't.

I hope Fletcher left for the arena before I get there. I can't have my best friend and roommate of over six years seeing me with pregnancy tests. Normally, I tell him everything, but I didn't tell him about Jude.

Dating has sucked lately, so when I saw Jude for a second date and then a third, I didn't want to jinx it by telling Fletcher. Every time I get excited about a person, I get ghosted or used for sex. I thought Jude was different, but when my texts went unanswered after the night we slept together, I found out the hard way that he was only looking for a hook-up. Even though he said he wasn't. He was just playing the long game.

I rush to my car, taking deep breaths as I climb in and turn it on, trying to beat the October chill. I rest my hands on the wheel as my phone rings through the stereo system.

Fletcher's name flashes on the screen, and I take one last deep breath.

"Hey, Fletch."

"Lydi, where are you? We have to leave soon for the arena."

Fletcher always gets antsy before a game, never mind that tonight is the season opener. He's a forward for the Minnesota Blue Herons, the professional hockey team. Straight out of college, he was drafted by the MBH, and he's been there ever since. It's worked out well for me; I get to keep my best friend close by, and my rent is cheap since he lets me live with him in his luxurious apartment.

"I'm at the pharmacy," I say. "I'll be home soon."

"Okay, great. We can't be late."

"You know you could go without me, right?" I start the short drive home. "I can take the bus."

"I hate when you take the bus to games." His voice is filled with unnecessary concern.

"I know, but it's fine. Then we won't have two cars at the arena."

Fletcher groans. "Just come right home, and then we won't have two cars, and you don't have to take the bus. Problem solved."

I chuckle. "Lucky for you, I'm pulling into the parking garage now. I'll be up in a few."

I park next to Fletcher's fancy SUV, grabbing the plastic bag out of my passenger seat. The tests are easily visible through the thin plastic; there's no way Fletcher won't see what's inside. I frantically dig through the random sweatshirts, blankets, and things in my backseat for a reusable grocery bag. Nothing. Shit. I'm going to have to hide it from him, I guess.

Taking the elevator up to the eighth floor, I do my best to roll up the bag and tuck it under my arm.

I open our apartment door, not announcing my arrival the way I normally would. Instead, I rush through the living room down the hall toward my bathroom, but I don't make it far.

"Lydia?" Fletcher's low voice calls. "That you?"

"Fuck," I mumble, turning and shifting the bag so it's behind my back. "Yep, it's me!"

Even my voice sounds guilty. He opens his bedroom door just across the hall, stepping out and holding a tie in the air. The sight of Fletcher Graff in a suit always does something to me. Tonight, he's in a navy blue suit with a white button-up underneath, the top two buttons undone.

Our relationship has been entirely platonic since day

one, but I can admit my best friend is objectively hot. I mean, the man is a hockey player, for heaven's sake. His body is sculpted from straight marble, all hard and muscular, with a sharp jawline. His hair is in loose dark waves that he coifs into a perfect swoop before every game. Every little detail of his features is burned into my memory after years of studying him. The tiny scar in his eyebrow from the time he got hit in the face with a stick, the slight bend in his nose from a fist fight on the ice that resulted in a break, and the way his pupils dilate when he gets excited.

Not the time to be admiring your best friend's pupils, Lydia.

I clear my throat, backing up against the wall with my arms behind me.

"What's up?" I question, hoping I sound nonchalant.

"Tie, or no tie?" He waffles his hands up and down with a tie that matches his sage-green eyes.

I glance at the outfit, and then at the fabric. "Tie. I like this one. It makes your eyes pop."

"Help me?" Fletcher holds out the tie, and I take it with one hand only to remember the bag behind my back in the other.

"Um, one second." I try to sidestep into my open bedroom door so I can chuck the pregnancy tests into my room, but, like always, Fletcher is too observant.

"What's in your hand?"

"Nothing," I squeak, trying again to step into my room.

"Lydia Elaine Ward, you're hiding something!" Fletcher's eyes glint with delight as he reaches for the bag.

"Fletcher, no!" I nearly launch into my room.

I have to think of something, fast.

One, I'm not ready for him to know I need to take a pregnancy test. Two, I'm not about to distract him on his big night. The season opener always puts him a bit on edge, and he worries about me too much. I can't distract him, not tonight.

Throwing the box into the corner of my room and slamming the door, I breathe heavily, telling him the first thing that comes to my mind. "It's a new vibrator, okay?"

The grimace that instantly flashes on his face is almost comical. "You..." His voice cracks, and he clears his throat, tugging at the already loose neckline of his shirt. His cheeks are flaming red. "You can get vibrators at the drugstore?"

I swallow my embarrassment, reminding myself this is better than the alternative. "Mhm. It's a new thing."

I take the tie from his still outstretched hand and change the subject. "Are you ready for tonight?"

Fletcher buttons up his shirt, hiding the wisps of dark chest hair. "I think so. Our new goalie, Trigg, is a machine. If anyone can help us get to the playoffs, it's him."

"Where is he from again? Denmark?" I wrap the tie around his neck, draping the fabric over and pulling it through methodically. I've helped him with his ties for years, and I genuinely don't think he knows how to put one on himself.

"Norway. He's great. I can't wait for you to meet him. You're coming to the bar after, right?" He quirks his dark eyebrows. "You can either help us celebrate or drown in our sorrows."

"Hopefully, we will be celebrating, but yes. I wouldn't miss it."

I just might not be drinking.

Once his tie is perfectly done, I pat his chest. "You're good."

"Awesome." He grins. "Thanks, Lydi. How much time do you need to get ready?"

I glance down at myself. "Fifteen minutes?"

Pretty much all I have to do is change out of my work clothes, throw on my jersey, and make sure my hair and makeup still look decent after work.

Oh, and take a pregnancy test that may completely alter the course of my life.

"Deal," Fletcher says, heading into the living room.

I swallow harshly, pointing a thumb to my room. "I'll be out in a bit."

Rushing inside, I dig in my closet for my jersey and a pair of distressed jeans. Once I've found them, I rip open the bag of pregnancy tests and grab two. I take one stick from each and wrap them in the jersey along with the instructions.

I dash across the hall into the bathroom and shut the door behind me, thankful Fletcher didn't stop me this time.

I read the instructions, and within a minute, I'm peeing on the sticks and putting the caps on. My hands shake as I set the timer on my phone. One of them is digital, so at least that will give me a sure answer.

While I wait, I change into my jersey and jeans, fluffing my just-above-shoulder-length curly hair and throwing it into a half-up bun.

My mind is racing. Can I afford a baby? The only reason I can live in this apartment is thanks to Fletcher. When we moved in together, he told me I wouldn't have to pay rent, but I insisted. I don't need a handout, even if my best friend is a millionaire.

Fletcher isn't going to want a baby living here, that's for sure. He needs peace and quiet to make sure he's ready for games, physically and mentally. I can't be interrupting his sleep with a screaming baby at three in the morning.

I suppose I could move out, but can I afford an apartment on my own? I make enough to live with my job as an office administrator for a local non-profit, but it's not enough to support an infant and me. I could ask for a raise or a promotion. I've been offered one before but turned it down. I'm happy with where I'm at. Now, I might need to reconsider it. And the cost of childcare? How can I even think of affording that?

If I'm pregnant, will Jude want to be a part of it? Do I *want* him to? He was nice enough, but you can't tell if you are ready to parent with someone for eighteen years based on three dates and a sub-par hookup you didn't even get an orgasm out of.

"Lydia, are you ready? We gotta go if we want to beat traffic!"

"Shit, shit, shit," I mutter, grabbing my makeup bag and phone off the counter. There's still a minute and a half left on the timer, and I don't think Fletcher will be patient enough to wait for me to have an existential crisis if it's positive.

That's not true, though. If I told him what's going on, he'd have all the patience in the world, and he'd even help me come up with a plan. Only, I can't lean on him right now. This is something I have to do on my own.

"Coming!" I call, shoving the flipped over tests into the top drawer and leaving the bathroom.

2

____

GOOD LUCK CHARM

FLETCHER

"Let's go, boys," I shout as I stride into the locker room. Everyone cheers, pumping my adrenaline even higher. We've got a good group of guys this year, and based on how practices have been going, it could be a great year for us.

Trigg Aadland sits at his locker in his full gear, headphones in, as he stares at the floor. At the first practice, he explained one of his superstitions to us. He has a playlist he listens to before each game, and he can't be interrupted; if he is, his focus will be off.

I get it. We all have our superstitions, myself included. Some of the guys have to use a certain type of tape or put their gear on in a certain order.

For me, I have to talk to Lydia before a game. It started in college, and I realized that on the game days when I talked to her, I played ten times better and usually scored.

Then, I started theorizing. I'd talk to her and not say goodbye, and we'd win. The days I talked to her and said goodbye, we'd lose. And so it began. I have to talk to her, whether in person or over the phone, for no less than three minutes, and I can't say goodbye. I can say 'see you later' or 'talk after,' but if I slip up and say goodbye, we lose.

Of course, there are games we still lose even if I stick to my superstition, but then I at least know it's not my fault.

Lydia Ward is my good luck charm, and I don't think she knows it.

"Feeling ready?" Calvin Miller, our center on the team and my other best friend, approaches, still dressed in his suit and tie.

"Think so." I clap him on the shoulder before taking off my suit jacket and hanging it in my locker. "I'm always optimistic for the first game of the season, you know that."

Cal and I were drafted to the Blue Herons the same year. We had a killer rookie year, and since then, we've been steady, but I want this to be the year we make it past the finish line. I'm gunning for that championship.

"You've always been quite the optimist." He winks.

"And you're not?"

He shrugs, pulling off his jacket. "I'm hopeful, but it's game one of eighty-two, hopefully more. Lots of room for improvement, and lots of room for error."

"Time will tell."

Twenty minutes later, we're heading onto the ice for warm-ups. Music blares over the speakers, and people are beginning to fill the seats. Kids line the plexiglass with signs asking for pucks in exchange for candy. Everyone is happy. Getting to interact with the fans has always been one of my favorite parts of my job.

I do my warm-ups, then look up to the suite to find my family. My parents are in town for the weekend, and it's been months since I've seen them. I grew up in Missouri and came to Minnesota for college ten years ago. Now, it's home. I try to visit them during the off-season and whenever I get the chance, but it's hard with my busy schedule.

Lydia sits right beside my parents, with an easy smile on her face. She has on the jersey I got her with my name on it. I made sure to get her one as soon as I could, because there was no freaking way I was going to let her wear one of my teammates' names.

I catch her eye and wave. She's so beautiful. She entrances me every day, and I don't mind one bit.

But something was off about her this afternoon. I'm not sure whether it was me almost seeing her with a vibrator or what. We've lived together for a long time, and I know women have needs. Just like I do. Only she's probably not thinking of me when she comes, probably not biting her tongue to stop herself from calling out my name.

But I do.

I think of her all the time. I've wanted her for years, but after she friend-zoned me, I've been forced to watch her from the sidelines as she goes on failed date after failed date. I've always been the one to dry her tears. For years, I've been scared to ruin our friendship, but I'm about done waiting. I have no idea how Lydia will react, but if I know her—and I do—I think this could be the best thing that ever happens to us.

Lydia beams, standing and waving back to me. My parents do the same, and a familiar giddy sensation rolls through me.

This is where I'm meant to be. With this team, with my family here, and with the woman I'm going to make mine, cheering me on.

DOTTIE ALWAYS KNOWS

LYDIA

"Tell me, honey," Dottie coos, adjusting in her seat. "How are you?"

The second period has just ended, and the Blue Herons are up by two with Fletcher getting one assist.

"Good." I smile. "Of course, it's always busy when the season starts, but things have been good."

I don't tell her about the nausea burning a hole in my stomach, or the constant knowledge that there is a positive or negative pregnancy test waiting in my bathroom drawer right now.

"Are you sure?" Her brow furrows, her eyes narrowing. "Something is off with you."

I swallow the lump forming in my throat. "I'm okay, really."

Ron sits back down next to Dottie with armfuls of food. One arm holds two beers, and the other is stacked with hot dogs and a bucket of popcorn.

"I grabbed you ladies some snacks," he says, passing down one of the beers.

I take it from him, lifting it to my mouth and rethinking

my choice as soon as the bubbly liquid touches my lips. If I'm pregnant, I can't drink. Awkwardly, I set the full cup into my cup holder and sink back into my chair.

"What's wrong, Lydia?" Ron asks curiously. "Not the right kind?"

"No, it's fine." I lean forward, smiling at him.

Fletcher shares so many characteristics with his dad. They have the same eyes and jawline. Sometimes, Ron will say something, and it catches me off guard how much they're alike.

"Are you sure?" Dottie says. "You're really pale."

"I'm fine, I promise." I swallow the extra saliva in my mouth and try to push down the surge of nausea.

There are three minutes left before the third period starts. I don't want to miss a second that Fletcher is on the ice, but I really think I'm going to be sick. The smell of the beer was enough to make the nausea that's been simmering in my stomach all night ramp to a new level. I wrote it off as anxiety, but now, I'm not so sure.

"Actually, I'll be right back." I rush out of the aisle toward the suite's bathroom, but I barely make it in before I'm gagging and heaving into the sink. Nothing comes up but bile.

A knock on the door sends more dread racing through my body.

"Lydia, honey?" Dottie yells.

I look into the mirror, and god, I look horrible. My eyes are watering and bloodshot, and my face is pale. "Yeah?"

"Can I come in?"

My heart drops into my already empty stomach. The sudden and aggressive nausea has passed, leaving me exhausted. Wiping the saliva from my lips with a paper towel, I unlock and open the door.

Dottie steps into the small bathroom and pulls me into a hug. Tears burn my eyes as she holds me tightly.

"What's going on? Do you need to go home?"

I shake my head into her shoulder. "I'm fine. It's been a long day."

"Are you sick? Or is it something you ate? I can bring you home if you need."

I shake my head without thinking. "No, I'm not sick."

"Lydia, honey, are you pregnant?" Dottie murmurs into my ear, quiet enough that I can barely hear, but I know what she's saying.

I take a deep breath and pull back, wiping the tears streaming down my cheeks. Shrugging, I say, "I think so. I tried taking a test today, but I had to leave before I saw the results."

Dottie wipes the tears from my cheeks. "Do you... know who the father is?"

I nod, swallowing my embarrassment. "We aren't together. We went on a few dates, and then he ghosted me. I don't know what to do, Dottie."

My voice shakes as the weight of it all grows heavy on my shoulders.

Dottie cups my cheeks, holding my gaze. "Well, you know that whatever you decide, you have our support. We are here for you, and we love you, whether you're blood or not. And you know Fletcher will be there for you no matter what. We're your family."

"Thank you," I blubber.

"Does Fletcher know?"

I shake my head. "Not yet. Please don't tell him. I'm still —I don't know what to do."

She nods, and I drop my head onto her shoulder and wrap my arms around her. She holds me for another minute while I cry, and when I'm done, she helps me fix my mascara, and we head back out to our seats. The period is already a minute in, but Fletcher isn't on the ice, so I don't think I've missed too much.

If Ron notices something is amiss with me, he doesn't say anything, and for that, I'm grateful. I'm already going to have to try to hide this from Fletcher for who knows how long, and I'm dreading that. Fletcher knows me so well. I'm sure he already suspects something after this afternoon.

The rest of the game passes quickly until we reach the final minute of play. I'm nauseous the whole time, but thankful I can watch the game as a distraction to the whirring thoughts in my brain. It's still two to zero, and it's looking like we are going to win with a shutout.

Fletcher hops over the boards, skating briskly across the ice toward the other team's goal. He rocks into an opposing player, takes him to the ground, and passes the puck to his teammate, Calvin Miller.

The play is so fast that if I were to blink, I would miss it. Calvin passes to Shepherd Wafford, one of the new rookies, and Shepherd shoots. The puck flies into the net above the goalie's right shoulder. The horn sounds, the cherry lights, and the crowd erupts.

The boys rush the ice, hugging and screaming as they celebrate their win. The other team leaves the ice immediately, ignoring the cheers of excitement from our fans.

I'm sure Fletcher will have to do press tonight, so we are in for a long wait before we get to see him. That's fine with me. I'm always happy to chat with Ron and Dottie.

4

NEVER SAY NEVER

FLETCHER

"Graff, Miller, you're on press tonight," Coach says.

"Got it." I shuck my jersey over my head.

"*Fuck*, it feels good to be back," Calvin says, shaking the sweat from his red hair.

I chuckle. "Couldn't agree more. What a way to start the season."

"Just gotta keep at it and hope for the best, my man." He ruffles my sweaty hair.

I take the rest of my gear off, shower, and head to the press room with Calvin. The thought of doing press right now irritates me more than anything. I want to say fuck it and get to Lydia, to be with her as much as possible, but I have to remember that at the end of the day, this is part of my responsibility as a player and captain.

Calvin goes to one group of reporters while I go to the other, and they congratulate me on our win. A few people speak at once, asking me questions about plays or missed opportunities for goals. I answer everything with a non-answer, turning it around into excitement for the new season and the team.

"And how is Trigg Aadland settling in?" one reporter asks.

I run a hand through my damp hair. "Great. He's fitting in really well. Of course, when you add a new person to a team, it can take time to get comfortable, but so far, it's fantastic."

"What about Crowley? Do you miss having him in the net?"

Crowley was our previous goalie who retired early to focus on his wife and kids.

"Of course," I reply honestly. "He was a great player and teammate."

How many more questions do I have to answer?

"He was two years older than you are now. Do you foresee yourself retiring early to start a family?"

What kind of questions are these? What do they have to do with anything?

I put on a fake smile and offer a laugh. "I don't foresee myself settling down or having kids."

Is that true? There's one person I would want it all with, someone with bright blue eyes I always get lost in and rich brown curls I'd love to wrap my fingers around. I'd give up everything for her.

"At least not anytime soon," I add quickly. "But never say never."

With that, I offer them a tip of my head and wave, walking away as they continue to volley questions my way.

Back in the locker room, I heave a sigh. Press is all part of the job, but man, is it exhausting. I just want to play hockey.

There are only a few guys in here now; most of them have already left, probably heading to the bar or home.

Wafford sits on the bench in front of his locker, staring at the puck in his hand.

"First NHL goal! Congrats, kid," I say, sitting next to him and shoving his shoulder. "How does it feel?"

"A little surreal," he says breathlessly, his gaze still locked on the piece of rubber.

"The feeling never gets old." I can remember my first NHL goal like it was yesterday, and I still have the puck on my shelf at home. "You coming out to celebrate?"

His eyes grow wide. "Really? I'm invited?"

I chuckle. "Absolutely. You're part of the team, kid."

Calvin flops down on the opposite side of Shepherd. "You coming out, baby boy?"

Shepherd groans. "Yes, but only if you stop calling me kid or baby boy."

"No chance," Calvin says. "You're our little baby."

"What about Levine?" Shepherd asks pointedly, staring at the other rookie across the room. "He's the same age as I am!"

"He is also baby boy," Calvin confirms, standing up and waving him to follow.

"Tell Lydia I'll be out in a few?" I ask as he walks away.

"No problem."

5

___

POT, MEET KETTLE

LYDIA

Dottie, Ron, and I leave the suite and head down to the tunnel where Fletcher will come out. Calvin appears first, stopping to give me a quick hug.

"Good game," I tell him.

"Thanks. You coming out tonight?"

"I'll be there."

"Great. Fletch wanted me to tell you he'd be out soon. See you there!" he calls as he walks toward his family.

His parents and sister are here, as well as Zoey, his friend's sister. Adam, his best friend, plays for another team.

I chat absentmindedly for a few minutes with Ron and Dottie, ignoring the nagging in the back of my mind that knows what's waiting for me at home.

"Lydia!" Fletch calls and wraps his arms around my waist from behind, lifting me and spinning me in a circle.

"You were amazing!" I squeal as he sets me down on solid ground. A wave of dizziness and nausea overtakes me, but I shake it off. Thankfully, Fletcher doesn't seem to notice.

"God, it feels good to get back on that ice." He pulls me

18

back in for another hug, and his familiar scent soothes the sickness in my stomach. Fletcher rests his cheek on top of my head, breathing me in.

"I bet it did."

Exhaling, he pulls away from our hug, reaching out for his parents. I step to the side, letting them embrace and catch up for a moment.

"Are you guys coming out tonight?" Fletcher asks.

Ron laughs. "You can't be serious. We aren't going to party it up with a bunch of you hooligans. No way. A bed is calling my name."

"Alright, alright," Fletcher replies with a low laugh. "Are we still on for lunch tomorrow?"

"Absolutely," Dottie says. "Lydia, are you coming to lunch?"

I shake my head. "I work a half-day tomorrow. I took the morning off since I knew we'd be out late tonight."

We talk for a few more minutes until Calvin yells that it's time to head to the bar down the street. After we say goodbye to Dottie and Ron, Fletcher takes my arm, leading me down the hall.

"I can DD tonight." Even if I wasn't sure I was pregnant, I'd offer to drive. After a game like tonight, Fletcher deserves to let loose and have fun with his teammates.

"You sure?" Fletcher opens the door for me.

The October air has a chill to it, but it's not bad yet.

"Positive."

Fletch wraps an arm around me as we pass a group of people, and I reflexively lean into him. He's always been my rock, always there for me when I need him most, no matter what.

Part of me wants to spill everything to him. I know he'd support me either way, but I hold back. I need to find out for myself first, and then I can tell him. I already told Dottie, and I probably shouldn't have.

The crowded bar fills with cheers as the players arrive. It's like this after every game. People know and expect the players to come here and party, so they'll stay late to party with them.

Fletcher leads me to the back corner, where they have reserved a few booths and tables for us. I sit across from Calvin's younger sister, Grace.

"What do you want to drink, Lydia?" Fletcher asks.

"Water is fine." I pour a glass from the pitcher in the middle of the table.

"You can have one drink, Lydi."

I scoff. "I know, but I already had one at the game, so I'm good. Water is fine." I take a drink to reiterate my point.

Fletcher raises one of his eyebrows. I'm sure he suspects my lie about having a drink at the game.

"Are you feeling okay?" He sits beside me, resting his hand on my forehead. "We can go home if you need to."

"I'm fine." I shrug his hand off and laugh awkwardly. "I don't need a drink every time we go out."

"I know," Fletcher replies defensively. "You love the seltzers here, so it's weird for you not to at least have one." He holds my gaze.

It's annoying how easily he can see right through me, and his sincerity makes me want to cry. He's such a good friend.

"I promise I'm good, Fletch."

"Alright. If you change your mind, just give me a shout."

"I will."

He gets up and heads to the bar, leaving Grace and me alone.

"He's right, you know," Grace says with a laugh. "You love their seltzer."

Groaning, I take another drink of water. It feels good against the sudden dryness in my throat. "I do."

"So, why not have a drink?"

"It's a long story."

Grace nods. She may be one of the sweetest people I've ever met. She knows when to push and when to hold back. Tonight is definitely a night to hold back, and she's taken the hint with ease.

"Thank you," I breathe, wiping my curls from my face.

"You know where to find me if you ever need to talk, but I'm not going to force it out of you."

"I appreciate you," I say just as Calvin drops into the seat next to her.

"Where's Zoey?" he asks, glancing around.

"Vincent works in the morning, so they went home." Grace sips her drink.

I've been around Calvin and his family and friends long enough to know that none of them like Zoey's fiancé, Vincent. As long as Zoey is happy, they've promised not to intervene.

Calvin hums something under his breath.

Grace shoves him. "She's an adult. She can make her own decisions."

"I know that," he replies, pinching the bridge of his nose.

She huffs. "Sometimes I think you forget that we aren't kids anymore."

Before they can continue the conversation, Fletcher drops into the seat beside me, setting his large beer onto the table.

"Levine has already found his conquest for the night," he says, gesturing to him.

Jamie Levine, one of the rookies, is leaning into a young girl's personal space, one hand on her hip, and she looks like she's loving it. She's leaning right back, her eyes locked on him as she hooks one hand around the back of his neck.

"It appears he has," Calvin says. "Are you on the lookout tonight?"

I know it shouldn't bother me, but I hate it when Fletcher talks about women with the guys. We aren't together. We've never been together and never will be. I have no right to get upset, but I do. Fletcher has never been one to flaunt his dates or hookups, though. I can't remember the last time he went on a date.

Not that I can talk. I'm likely pregnant with another man's baby. Talk about being a hypocrite, Lydia. Pot, meet kettle.

Fletcher immediately shakes his head. "Nope. Are you?"

Calvin shrugs, glancing around the room. "Nope."

He changes the subject, and an hour and a half later, both Fletcher and Calvin have a good buzz. Fletcher is three drinks in, and Grace and I have been chatting off and on about life, but I'm exhausted. It's nearing midnight, but knowing these guys, they could be out till bar close and not be tired.

Fletcher wraps his arm around my shoulder, leaning in close. "Lydi-bug, you okay?" His eyes are hazy, and his breath smells of beer.

"I'm good. Are you having fun?"

"Sooo much fun," he slurs. "I wish you were drinking with me."

"Next time." I pat his firm chest.

Fletcher rests his forehead on mine. "Wanna dance? Then we can go home."

"Sure." I'm not going to say no to going home. We stand, and Calvin glances up at us.

"We're going to dance, then head out," I say. "Do you or Grace need a ride?"

Calvin shakes his head. "Nope. Grace is my ride. I'll see you at practice tomorrow."

"You got it." Fletcher gives him two finger guns, and he gives Grace a high five.

"Okay, big guy," I say, pulling him from the table, "let's get your dance on."

"You know..." He hooks his arm with mine.

"What?"

"You know I love you, right?"

We step onto the small dance floor, where a few people are dancing to a slow country song.

"I love you, too," I say as he spins me into his arms, swaying.

Fletcher groans, and maybe he's more drunk than I thought. "No, Lydi, like, I *love* you. You're my best friend."

"You're my best friend, too," I answer, my heart pounding. "I think you're a bit drunk."

I laugh. He's joking. He doesn't know what he's saying. *God, he's so drunk.*

Fletcher nods, resting his head on my shoulder. "Yeah. I still love you, though."

"I still love you, too, Fletch."

My heart skips a beat. He's my family, my person. We sway back and forth to the beat of the song. The way he's holding me sends a flutter through my system. I always feel so safe when I'm with him. No one looks out for me the way he does.

This proximity to him and the way his hands are trailing up and down my back sends a wracking shiver through my body. This feels different than normal, but I can't figure out why. Maybe it's because he's drunk. That has to be it.

The song ends, and Fletcher squeezes me tightly.

"Home?" I ask, squeezing him back.

"Home," he answers, the slur even more prominent.

6

PANCAKES, POSITIVE TESTS, AND HAPPY TRAILS

LYDIA

EIGHT WEEKS PREGNANT

Getting a six foot three, two hundred and twenty pound man into bed on your own is hard work. Fletcher passed out on the drive home, and I practically had to drag him into the elevator and our apartment.

When he's sprawled across his bed, I carefully take off his suit jacket and tie, and when I unbutton his crisp button-up, I expect to find an undershirt beneath it. Instead, I'm greeted by the bare expanse of his muscled chest.

I swallow thickly, ignoring the sudden swooping low in my belly. What's with me? He's just Fletcher. My best friend. I have never thought of him as anything else, so why are my eyes trailing down his stomach to the V-line of his hips and *his happy trail*? Oh god.

Heat burns in my veins, and I focus on the task at hand, rolling him so he's out of his shirt, leaving him in just his pants. As I'm covering him with the blankets, he murmurs something that I don't catch.

"What?" I push his mussed hair out of his face.

"Lydia," he breathes, a small smile tugging on his lips.

I freeze. My heart thrums like a hummingbird in my chest in anticipation.

"What?" I ask again, hoping he says something else.

He doesn't. Instead, he rolls onto his stomach, pulling the blankets over his head and diminishing any hope of ever finding out what he was about to say.

I plug in his phone and slide out of his room, still trying to catch my breath. Anyone else probably would have left him, but I can't help it. I want him to sleep well.

With that taken care of, I shift gears. I have important things to look at.

I head into my bathroom, shut the door, and open the top drawer where I threw the tests. The two pieces of plastic stare up at me, the answer on them glaringly obvious. One has a bright pink plus sign, while the other has a single word.

YES.

Grabbing the tests out of the drawer, I slump back against the wall, blood rushing through my ears. What if these are defective because they were sitting for so long? That has to be a thing, right? Maybe it's a false positive.

I run into my room, grab the remaining tests from the floor, and return to the bathroom.

Three minutes later, I flip the tests over and swallow the giant lump of fear that's settling in my throat.

I'm pregnant.

Do I want this? Do I want to be a mom? I could get an abortion, but when I think about it, I know that isn't what I want. I watched my mom practically raise me on her own since my dad worked and traveled so much. He was never around, and it was hard on her, so I took years of subtle dig after dig from her. I know how much she resented me. She never wanted kids, but my dad did. She could have been a stay-at-home wife, but I foiled all her plans.

I want this baby.

I want to prove I can be a better mom than my mother was, that I can love my child regardless of who or what they become.

Jude and I aren't together, and I don't want us to be. Do I want to co-parent with a man I barely know? Would he reply to a message if I text him? He ghosted me, after all.

I sink onto the bathroom floor. My head falls into my hands as I take deep, calming breaths.

I need sleep. I can't do anything right now. It's nearly one in the morning.

After getting ready to sleep, a weary sense of exhaustion settles through my body as I climb into my bed. The bed Fletcher bought me after college.

Everything that I have, I owe to him. He gave me a place to live, and he's charging me way less than he should. He furnished this place, but he let me pick out things I liked, too, so we could make it *our* place.

My parents wanted me to move back to my hometown after college, but I wasn't ready to leave Minnesota. Fletcher is the closest friend I've ever had, and sure, people always assume we're together, but it's never been like that between us. He's my person. Relationships come and go, but he's always there for me, through good times and bad.

Will he be here for me now as I take on the next challenge in my life? I don't doubt it for a second. He'll be the cool uncle, the one to teach them how to skate, shout their name at hockey games, and be there to support me, too. I can't ask more than that.

He needs to focus on his career, on his own life. I need

to focus on mine, however that life may look in the near future.

MY ALARM BLARES, waking me from a deep and heavy sleep. I groan and rub my eyes, rolling over to shut it off. Why didn't I take the whole day off again? Oh, right, probably because I didn't think I'd get life-changing news the night before and have to rot in bed to process it all.

Work is the last thing I want to do right now, but at least it's only a half day. I can make it through that. I sit on the edge of my bed, swallowing thickly as a bout of nausea hits me.

I take a few deep breaths until the sick feeling in my stomach passes. The clanging sound of pots and pans in the kitchen lets me know Fletcher is awake. They have an afternoon practice today, so he will be up and out the door shortly, and then off to Vegas tonight for his game tomorrow.

I head into the kitchen, where Fletcher has his headphones in, bobbing his head to the music. Sitting down on one of the stools at the countertop, I watch him. He's always been so calm and collected. So confident in everything he does. It's something I love about him.

Fletcher flips a pancake, drinks from the giant glass of milk on the countertop, and uses the spatula in his hand as a microphone. He mouths the words to whatever song is playing, swaying his hips to the beat. When he spins around and sees me watching him, his eyes bug out, and the highest-pitched screech I've heard from him pierces my eardrums.

"Lydia!" He rips out his headphones and takes deep, calming breaths. "What the *fuck* are you doing?"

I laugh, striding over to him. Music still blares from his headphones. "Just wanted to make sure you were awake. You know, it's bad for your ears to listen to music that loud."

"Yes, because my headphones are what will cause damage to my ears, not the extremely loud horn or cheering crowds every night for eight months of the year." He narrows his eyes, pinching my arm.

"Hey," I shriek, swatting him away. "Stop that!"

Fletcher reaches for me, spatula in hand.

"Don't you dare." I hold out my finger, pointing at him as I skirt away.

"Or what?" he taunts, taking another step toward me.

"Fletcher..."

"Lydi..." He launches toward me, but I dart out of his grasp.

"No!" I laugh, racing into the living room, laughing hysterically as he chases me. Out of the corner of my eye, I catch a glimpse of the black plastic spatula as it flies past me and hits the living room wall.

I rest my hands on my knees to catch my breath. "You know, it's a good thing you don't play baseball with a throw like that."

"Oh, you've done it now." Fletcher's voice grows low and dark as he continues to saunter toward me.

I try to flee around him, but he catches me, wrapping his arms around my waist and lifting me.

We both laugh as Fletcher spins us in a circle until a clammy feeling breaks out on my brow, and a sick feeling rises in my gut. The dizziness is way too much, too fast.

"Put me down," I yelp.

He sets me on my feet, resting his hands on my shoulders as I catch my breath. I cup my mouth, and the nausea intensifies.

"Are you okay?" Fletcher asks in a high-pitched voice.

I tip my head down in a nod, keeping my hand firmly over my mouth.

"What's going on? Are you sick?"

I shake my head, taking slow, deep breaths. Once the worst of it has passed, I drop my hand. "I'm fine. The spinning made me dizzy, that's all."

He quirks his eyebrow. "Since when does spinning in a circle twice make you so dizzy you nearly puke?"

"I don't know. Maybe I'm getting too old to spin."

"You're a figure skating coach. Pretty sure you have to spin a lot. What are you going to do, barf all over the kids?"

The mental image is enough to make me heave.

"Okay, now I know something is up." Fletcher holds my wrist, his eyes brimming with concern.

"I don't know what you're talking about." I swallow the pooling saliva in my mouth and step away from him.

By some miracle of fate, the fire alarm goes off, saving me from him prying the information out of me.

"My pancakes!" Fletcher gasps, running back into the kitchen, pulling the smoking pan off the burner. He flips the burnt pancake into the sink and runs water over it.

With him distracted, I run to my bathroom to get ready for the day, avoiding any further questions.

7

FRIEND-ZONED

FLETCHER

Something was up with Lydia today, but of course, she left for work before I could get more information out of her. She was acting weird last night, too. Maybe she is getting sick or something. I wish we weren't about to leave for the next week, or I'd press the subject more. She's never been one to keep a secret from me. Usually, we tell each other everything; her hiding something sets off alarm bells in my head.

"May I sit?" Trigg asks as I sit in the plane's window seat.

"Sure thing." I pat the seat beside me. On a flight like this, Calvin would normally sit next to me, but I'm all about team bonding. I am the captain for a reason.

"Takk," Trigg says in Norwegian, then shakes his head. "I mean, thanks, Graff."

He sits, settling in as Calvin reaches us. He gives me a look, but I shrug and smile. Calvin does the same, sitting down in the aisle across from us.

The flight attendants make their rounds. We'll be taking off soon, so I pull my phone out of my pocket to text Lydia.

ME

About to take off. Are you feeling okay?

She replies instantly.

LYDIA

I was fine earlier. Just a dizzy bout,
that's all.

ME

Right.

LYDIA

Are you ready for the game tomorrow?

ME

Yep. Feeling good about it.

What I'm not feeling good about is my best
friend lying to me.

LYDIA

I'm fine, Fletcher.

ME

My parents are in town until tomorrow if
you need anything.

LYDIA

Yeah, I'm getting dinner with them tonight.

ME

Clutching pearls gif.

Without me? The audacity.

LYDIA

Pretty sure they like me more than you

ME

Can't say I blame them

LYDIA

I'm their favorite bonus child

ME

Not wrong.

I turn off my phone, resting my head back on the head-rest. I can't shake the feeling that something's wrong. Maybe she's been working too hard lately? Or maybe her parents are coming to town. She always gets weird when that happens.

I'll figure it out sooner or later. For now, I'll get to know my new teammate better.

"So, Aadland, how are you settling in?" I ask.

"Fine." His Norwegian accent is thick as he navigates the English words. "America is different."

"I can't even imagine. Did they set you up in the apartments near the arena?"

"Yes, but I would like to buy a house here if I am offered a longer contract. I like it here."

"I'm glad." I clap him on the shoulder. "Do you have a wife? Kids?"

"No. Only me." He shakes his head, his light blonde hair falling into his eyes.

"Well, you've got a team at your back, so if you ever need anything, we are just a text or call away."

Trigg offers me a fond smile. "Thanks."

I spend the rest of the flight getting to know Trigg, with Calvin chiming in from across the aisle. Bonding with new teammates can be hard, especially when trades happen mid-season, but in the long run, it's worth the extra effort. It makes a stronger team.

"Are you going out tonight?" Calvin asks as we board the bus. His red curls are sticking out under the stocking cap on his head.

Trigg sits beside me again, his eyebrows lifted.

I shake my head. "Nope. I'm going to call Lydia, then get to bed early."

"Come on, man. You're not even going to go to one casino with me?"

"You know I hate gambling, Miller. I never win."

"But you're such a good cheerleader." Calvin's blue eyes lock on mine. "Please?"

I groan. "One hour. Then I need to call Lydia. She's been weird lately."

He tilts his head. "How so?"

I don't want to tell him how much it's worrying me, but he won't let me get away with keeping secrets. "This morning, I spun her in a circle, and she got so dizzy she almost puked. And she's avoiding me, I think."

"You live together. How can she possibly avoid you?"

Trigg interrupts. "Is Lydia your partner?"

I shake my head. "No, she's my best friend."

His blonde brows raise. "And she lives with you?"

"Yeah. But we've only ever been friends. Nothing more."

"Not for lack of trying on your part." Calvin chuckles.

"You want to be more?" Trigg questions.

I groan, resting my head in my hands. I don't want to get into this right now—or ever, for that matter. "When we were in college, we were assigned lab partners in our anatomy class. When the class was done, I invited her out on what I intended to be a date. The whole time she was talking about how great a friend I was, and how lucky we were to get paired together. Needless to say, she friend-zoned me. Hard."

"Ouch." Trigg grimaces.

"Yeah. But I take what I can get with her. She's my best friend, and I love her. If she never wants more, then I guess it is what it is. Maybe someday it will happen for us, but if not, I have to accept that. She's the only person I could ever see myself wanting *more* with."

Calvin scoffs. "Who says you can't pursue her now?"

I shrug. "Maybe someday. Either way, I'm going to call her tonight. Something is up with her."

"You're a good friend," Trigg says, resting a hand on my shoulder.

"Thanks, man."

When the bus arrives at our hotel, we unload and head up to our rooms. Not even thirty minutes later, Calvin is knocking at my door.

"Do we have to?" I groan as I walk toward the knocking. Travel days are exhausting.

When I open the door, instead of Calvin dressed in his typical going-out attire, he's in sweats and a practice tee, with Trigg standing beside him in similar clothes. "Figured maybe we could watch the Lynx hockey game instead?"

I nod gratefully, opening the door wider to let them in.

They make themselves at home in my hotel room, with Calvin taking the free bed and Trigg taking the chair. Calvin turns on the game, which is already in the second period.

I flop onto my bed, grabbing my phone from the charger. I'll text Lydia, then my mom, to see if she noticed anything weird about her tonight.

ME

How was dinner with my parents?

LYDIA

It was good, we went to The Black Rooster

ME

You're kidding me, right?

LYDIA

Nope, your dad said he wanted to try it

ME

You went to my favorite place without me?????

I'm hurt

LYDIA

It's not my fault! Your dad wanted to go, and he said every time he comes here, you end up going somewhere else!

ME

We're going as soon as I get back. I've been craving it for weeks, but when I suggest it, you always say, "No, Fletch, I'm not really in the mood for The Black Rooster"

How. Dare. You.

LYDIA

Calm down. You're fine.

ME

There's a crack in my heart now, and it's all your fault, Lydi-bug.

LYDIA

Jeez, you're dramatic.

ME

How would you feel if I went to your favorite place without you? And with your parents?

LYDIA

Well, first off, you'd never be caught dead alone with my parents. Second, you hate Thai.

ME

Again, I'm hurt.

But you're also not wrong.

LYDIA

My point stands.

I'll make it up to you

ME

Thank you. I appreciate it.

Are you feeling better?

LYDIA

I told you I was fine, Fletch

ME

And I don't believe you, Lydia

LYDIA

I'm fine. I'm going to bed, though

ME

It's not even ten!

LYDIA

So? We were up late last night!

ME

Something is up with you

LYDIA

I'm fine.

Goodnight, I'll talk to you tomorrow

ME

Goodnight, Lydi-bug

I toss my phone to the side, ignoring the incessant tug in my brain.

"Lydia?" Calvin questions, pulling my attention back to the world around me.

I nod. "I can't shake this feeling that something's wrong. She's a night owl. It's not even ten at home, and she's going to bed."

"Maybe she is ill," Trigg says.

"Maybe." But something about it doesn't seem quite right.

I'm going to text my mom to be sure.

ME

How did Lydia seem tonight?

MOM

Fine, why? We had a very nice dinner at The Black Rooster.

ME

Yeah, about that, I'm mad at you all. I leave town and you go to my fave restaurant without me? What the heck is that?

MOM

Lydia was craving it.

ME

Lydia never craves it, I have to practically beg her to go.

MOM

I'm not sure, but she suggested it, so we went

ME

She got dizzy this morning and almost puked when I spun her around. I think she's getting sick or something else is up, but she won't tell me.

MOM

Whatever it is, I'm sure she will tell you in time.

Well, that's encouraging. It makes me think my mom knows something but is hiding it.

ME

So there is something?

MOM

I never said that

ME

Liar

MOM

She's stressed at work, that's all I know.

ME

What's going on?

MOM

She didn't elaborate, only said work has been stressful.

Stressful enough to make her physically ill?
I don't buy it.

8

HEY JUDE

LYDIA

My phone on the coffee table taunts me. I have to reach out to Jude, I know that, but something inside me is holding me back. He probably won't want to be a part of this, but I have to give him the option. If I had a child roaming around the world, I'd want to know.

I groan, grab my phone, and look at the last messages I sent Jude.

ME

Hey, I had a great time last night. Would you like to get together again tomorrow?

Doing my best not to look at the pitiful message I sent, I type out a new one.

ME

Hey, Jude, it's Lydia. Can we get coffee soon? There's something important I need to talk to you about.

There. Easy enough.

Now, I just have to hit send.

Nausea roils in my gut, and it's not from the baby. I have to put on my big girl panties and do this.

I click the little blue button, and the message goes off with a *whoosh*. There. I did it. I set my phone back on the coffee table upside down as I take a few deep breaths.

Now, the inevitable waiting period. If he doesn't reply, I can say I tried, right? It's not like I'm going to creepily find his address and show up at his doorstep. That'd be way too much.

My phone vibrates against the table, only it's a call. I flip it over, expecting to see Jude's name, but surprise—my mom's contact is on the screen. I rub my temples, a headache already forming from the thought of talking to her. But if I don't answer, she'll keep calling.

"Hi, Mom," I answer with a tight smile.

"Lydia, how are you?" I must wait a second too long to answer, since she continues. "Wonderful. Your father and I are coming to town the weekend of the twenty-fifth, and we'd like to get lunch with you. Tell me when you'd like to meet."

"Um." I swallow the continued nausea. "I'm not sure. I'll have to look at my schedule. I think Fletcher has a game that Saturday afternoon. Would you want to go?"

"You know your father hates loud crowds." She sounds almost accusatory.

"Right." I glare at the phone, willing this conversation to come to a swift end. "Sunday might work better then."

She sniffs. "You don't have to go to *every* game."

"I know I don't, but I already have plans with a few friends, which is why I thought you'd like to go, since we have the suite." The one and only time I took them to a game of Fletcher's, they were in a mood the entire time, and they left between the second and third period, stating hockey had no decorum.

It was a pretty physical game, but clearly, they don't get the same thrill out of watching fights. Calvin is more of a fighter than Fletcher, but every so often, he gets into one, and even though I'm always worried about him getting hurt, it makes things extra exciting. Losing a few teeth comes with the territory when you play hockey.

"Fine," she says in a clipped tone. "Sunday it is. We'll make reservations for eleven. I will text you with the location."

"How long are you in town?"

I suppose if I have to tell them I'm pregnant with their first grandchild, there could be worse ways to do it.

"Friday evening through Sunday afternoon. We decided to detour and pay you a visit before our trip to Spain."

"Oh, Spain?"

Considering my mother's love of travel and her expensive taste, the trip doesn't surprise me. Spain is one of her favorite places to be.

"Yes, Spain. Your father gifted me a month-long trip there for our anniversary."

"That was nice of him."

It would have been nice to know sooner, but oh well. My parents have never been fond of communicating—or rather, they don't seem to care about communicating with me. Usually, I get around thirty-six hours' notice before they arrive in town. This much time is pretty good for them.

"It was." She hums. "We'll see you then, darling. Wear something flattering."

Without waiting for me to say 'I love you,' or even goodbye, she hangs up. No shock there. She's been like this since

I was a kid. Mom shows me what would be considered the appropriate amount of attention before leaving me alone again.

As little as I want to see them, it really is good timing. Part of me knows my parents will have less-than-enthusiastic reactions to the news that I'm having a baby when I'm not married, but there's also a small part that hopes they'll be happy and supportive. I want them to be excited to be grandparents, but I can't say I'd be surprised if the lunch turns into a mess.

When I set my phone back down, a new message pops up.

JUDE

Lydia, nice to hear from you. I'm in town, want to grab lunch today?

Nice to hear from me? Did he forget that I messaged him after our date, asking if he'd want to get together again soon?

Might as well get it over with.

ME

That works. Did you have a place in mind?

JUDE

The Forester at noon?

ME

Okay.

Today is my day off, which is lucky. This wouldn't have worked otherwise. I inhale a deep breath and exhale slowly.

I can do this.

An hour later, I'm standing outside The Forester. The restaurant is much nicer than my usual, which is another reason why Jude and I would never work. As much as my parents love their fancy restaurants, I'm more of a bar and grill type of person.

I walk up to the hostess station, smiling gently. The hostess is tall, and she doesn't hide the way she looks up and down my body in displeasure. I withhold my irritation because I know I don't look like I belong in a place like this, but I'm here for a reason.

"Hi, I'm meeting Jude Freeman. He said he placed a reservation."

She looks down at her tablet, her brows raising. "Oh, yes. He's already been seated. I can take you to him."

"Thank you," I mutter under my breath.

She leads me through the restaurant to the back, where Jude sits in his work suit and tie at a table for two. He's focused solely on his phone as we walk up to the table.

The hostess extends her arm and says, "Mr. Freeman, your friend has arrived."

Jude looks up from his phone, looking me up and down.

"Lydia, hi." He gestures for me to sit.

"Your waitress will be with you in a moment," the hostess says as she leaves.

Jude leans back in his chair, taking a sip of brown liquor out of the crystal glass he has in front of him. He smiles coyly. "I was surprised to hear from you."

"Right," I say slowly.

Before I can say more, the waitress steps up to the table.

"Hi, can I get you something to drink?" she asks, pulling out her pad and paper.

Jude cuts in before I can even ask for a glass of water. "I'm ready to order. I'll have the steak, medium with grilled mushrooms on top. As for the sides, I'll do the grilled prosciutto asparagus and tropical quinoa salad. Lydia?"

Panicked, I glance at the menu, which has way too many options in a font way too small. "Uh, what soups do you have?"

"Today we have split pea and clam chowder."

Ew.

Never mind then. I swallow the gag in the back of my throat.

"Um. Okay." I know there's no way Jude will want to pay for my meal after he learns that instead of asking for a quick hookup, I am, in fact, here to tell him some life-changing news. "Can I have a Caesar salad?"

"Absolutely. And to drink?"

"Water, please."

She promises to bring the water right away and steps aside, leaving me alone with Jude. Hopefully, she comes quickly. My mouth is as dry as cotton.

"So, how have you been?" Jude asks, taking another sip of his drink.

"Fine," I croak. I clear my throat. "Um, fine."

Mercifully, the waitress comes back with a tall glass of water with lemon for me.

"Thank you." I take a long sip, wetting my dry throat.

"What made you reach out?" Jude questions, his eyes narrowing on mine. "I didn't think you were interested after our last date."

Is he serious? *He* ghosted *me.*

"What are you talking about? I texted you the next day, and you never replied."

"You weren't exactly an enthusiastic fuck." Jude shrugs. "Like I said, I didn't think you were interested."

"Oh, my god." I rest my head in my palms. Mind you, the man didn't even make me orgasm. "Whatever. It doesn't matter now."

Jude narrows his eyes. "I'm confused."

"Jude, I'm pregnant," I blurt.

Might as well get it all out there in the open.

The hand holding his drink stops halfway to his mouth. "I'm sorry?"

"I'm pregnant. It's yours."

"I think you must be mistaken," he says in an eerily firm tone.

"I'm not. You are the only person I've slept with in the last six months, and I'm nine weeks pregnant. Do the math."

If he wants to pretend he ghosted me because I wasn't enthusiastic enough, fine, but I will *not* sugarcoat this for him.

Jude's face shifts to a deep shade of red. "Do you think you're going to get some hush money out of me? Because that's the last thing that'll happen. I'll prove that fucking bastard inside of you isn't mine. You're a lying, gold-digging bitch."

His words slice through my skin like blades.

"You know, not everything is about money. I'm here because I wanted to give you a chance to be in your child's life, but I can see that's the last thing you want, so I'll go." I move to stand.

"Sit down," Jude replies sternly.

I freeze in my seat, my mind whirring.

"Are you keeping it?"

"Yes, I'm keeping it. I know you might not want it, but I do. I want this baby."

"No. Let me rephrase that. It's not a question. You're not keeping it."

I flinch, narrowing my eyes at his cold expression. "*I am keeping it.* I'll sign whatever you want, saying I won't come after you for money, child support, or anything. I won't even put your fucking name on the birth certificate, but I thought I was doing the nice thing by giving you the chance to know your child. This child is mine, and mine alone." This time, I stand successfully.

"I want it in writing."

"Fine," I reply through gritted teeth.

"Right now." He points at the chair.

He's seriously about to make me do this here?

"Are you kidding me?"

"Sit."

I scoff, narrowing my eyes. Who does he think he is, ordering me around like this?

He wasn't this big an asshole on those three dates. Apparently, news like this changes a person, and not always for the better. I never expected him to want anything to do with me, but I thought maybe he might have some interest in being a father. Apparently not.

I sit, throwing my hands up. "I need paper if you want it in writing."

Jude whistles for the waitress. "I need a pen and paper now."

Fucking rude asshole.

The waitress's eyes widen, and she scurries off.

"I don't want your money," I say. "I didn't even know you had money."

Why can't I stop talking? Maybe I'm trying to make it better. Who knows?

He rolls his eyes and taps his fingers against the table. "Right. As if you didn't look me up."

"I didn't!"

I'd look him up now, but it doesn't matter. He's not worth any more time than necessary. The waitress rushes back to the table with a pen and a blank sheet of white paper.

Jude snatches it from her, scrambling to write. I apologize to her, and before she can dart away, I stop her. "Can you get me my check and put my food in a to-go box, please?"

"Of course," she sweetly replies.

Jude doesn't acknowledge me for the next few minutes. When he's finished, he thrusts the paper and pen across the table. "Sign it."

I take my time reading through his terms, making sure there's no hidden bullshit. He really just wants nothing to do with the baby or me. I guess it is what it is.

I sign my name and date it. "I need a copy."

That's the responsible thing to do, but I'll ensure my child never sees it. They'll never know the lengths their sperm donor went to in the hopes of erasing them from existence.

Jude waves, and when none of the servers acknowledge him, he leaves the table. Five minutes later, he comes back with a copy for me. The waitress is back with my food and bill, and I pay her in cash, leaving a decent tip since she has to deal with this asshole for the rest of his meal.

I face him one last time. "Have the life you deserve."

And I walk away, taking a deep breath and feeling a weight lift off my shoulders. Some part of me knew Jude wouldn't want this baby, but I never guessed he would have reacted like this.

It's for the better. I can do this. I can be an amazing single mom all on my own. My mom practically raised me alone, and I turned out okay-ish. But I'll be much better to my baby than my parents ever were to me.

I walk out of the restaurant and into the cool late fall air, more determined than ever. I'm making the right choice.

9

UNANSWERED QUESTIONS

LYDIA

NINE WEEKS PREGNANT

The boys are heading home today, and I won't be able to keep this a secret from Fletcher for much longer. With Jude officially out of the picture, I have a clearer idea of what my future will be, and I know I'm ready for the challenge of being a single mom.

Based on the pregnancy tracking app I downloaded, I'm about nine weeks along—not that I needed an app to tell me how long it's been since I slept with Jude. I still have a bit before I'll start to show, but based on Fletcher's texts, he already suspects something is up. Dottie and I briefly talked about things over dinner, and she's texted me more than once to check in. It's been nice having her as someone I can lean on.

I'd be lying if I said I wasn't nervous about my parents' reaction, though.

They've always expected greatness from me, and according to them, working as an office administrator and event coordinator for a community ice rink and non-profit for youth sports is not it. My dad wanted me to become a CPA or something like that, something he could boast to his friends. My mother expected me to marry rich, like she did, but that was never for me. I like working. I like the routine it gives me, even though having a baby will throw that out of whack.

I don't want the life they lived. I barely have a relationship with my father. He was always traveling when I was a kid, and he's so closed off that it's impossible to get to know him. My parents barely interact with me, and when they do, it's about how disappointed they are in me.

But they'd love for Fletcher and me to be together. He's rich, has status, and is attractive. To them, he's the whole package, but he's just my best friend.

Could I see myself falling in love with him? Sure, that'd be easy. I already love him. But we've never had that type of relationship, and I'm not going to be the one to cross that boundary, even if some small part of me is curious about what it might be like.

Fletcher and I have run the learn-to-skate event for a few years now, and the first of the season is tonight. While I'm there every week, Fletcher comes anytime he doesn't have a game or practice. His presence has helped with attendance and encouraged more kids to get on the ice. Perhaps I should be ashamed of exploiting my best friend's status as a professional hockey player, but I don't care. It works, the kids love it, and so does Fletcher. He's always asking when the next event is.

Seeing him with the kids is always fun. If he ever gets married and starts a family, he'll be an amazing parent; not only that, but he'll be an amazing partner.

I also coach figure skating on weeknights, which has brought me a lot of joy. I used to compete in high school, but after I graduated, I decided I would much rather do it for fun. Skating has always been an escape for me, so to be able to still have it is amazing. I love seeing the joy on the kids' faces when they nail a new skill or land a jump they thought was impossible. It's fulfilling work.

Fletcher will probably be home soon, so I should start getting ready. I head into my room and pull on my favorite fleece-lined leggings, long-sleeve shirt, and thick socks. I'll grab my hat, gloves, and light blue puffer vest from the front hall closet on our way out.

I head into the bathroom to fix my hair. It's too short to pull into a pony, but a half bun or braid will be enough to keep it out of my face while skating. For a second, I let myself wonder... What will my baby look like? Will it have my curls and blue eyes? Or will it look like Jude? He also has dark hair, but he has brown eyes. Will it be a boy or a girl?

There are so many unanswered questions.

I glance up and down my body, wondering what will happen to that, too. I run my hands down my soft stomach, turning to the side to admire it from a new angle. My stomach isn't perfectly flat. Never has been, never will be. I like my body the way it is, the rolls and curves and softness. Ten years ago, I wouldn't have been able to imagine it, but I love my thick thighs and apron belly. It took a lot of time and experience to get to this point, but I'm not ashamed of my fat body anymore.

I never had the typical slim, athletic build most figure skaters have, and my mother certainly didn't let me forget it. Still, that didn't hold me back from the sport I love. There were sidelong glances and whispers in the changing rooms, but my determination led me to the top of the podium time and time again.

I'm excited to see what changes my body will make to accommodate the baby. Change isn't always a bad thing, especially in this case.

I finish my hair and head into the living room to wait for Fletcher. He should be home any minute, but maybe I can get a few rows of work done on my newest crochet project. I tend to find new hobbies every so often and hyper-fixate on them. Crocheting is my current interest. I've made a few little stuffed animals and donated them to some shelters, and I'm trying to make some blankets for them as well.

Fletcher foils my plan before I get started when he walks through the door with his bags. He smiles warmly. "Hey, Lydi."

"How was the flight?"

"Good. Miller snored the whole time, but otherwise, it was quick." He kicks off his shoes and heads down the hall.

"Why does that not surprise me?"

"Nothing surprises me when it comes to Cal. I got to know Trigg a bit more on this trip, so that was fun." Fletcher re-enters the living room without his bags and flops next to me on the couch. He rests his head on my shoulder. "Missed you."

I ruffle his soft hair. "Missed you, too."

"Are you feeling okay?"

I groan, shoving him off. "How many times do I have to tell you, I'm fine!"

"You really worried me! Can you blame me for being concerned?" He sits up and widens his eyes; they're filled with emotion and concern.

Do I tell him now? No, I can't. I'm not ready. I have to see the doctor and make sure everything is okay, and then I can tell Fletcher. I have a plan.

"I'm sorry." I open my arms to him. "I didn't mean to

worry you. I promise I'm okay. It was just a weird thing, nothing to be worried about."

Fletcher leans into my embrace, holding me tightly. "I'm always going to worry about you, Lydi. You're my closest friend."

"I know. I appreciate you more than you know." His familiar embrace soothes me, and his spicy-scented cologne tickles my nose more than usual.

"Right back at you. I'm glad you're okay." He holds me for another moment before pulling back. "What time do we have to leave?"

I glance at the time on my phone. "Probably within twenty minutes or so. Are you still coming?"

"Wouldn't miss it for the world. Let me change and grab my stuff, and we can go. Can we grab a smoothie or something for the road?"

"Yeah, that sounds great."

Fletcher heads to his room. "I still can't believe you went to The Black Rooster without me. Can we get it for dinner, please?"

"Fine." It sounds like the least appetizing thing in the world, even though just two nights ago, it was the best food I'd ever tasted.

10

FALLING FORWARD
FLETCHER

Seeing Lydia in person eased my concerns. She seems fine today, and watching her out on the ice with the kids has always been one of my favorite things.

One half of the ice is for the figure skaters, the other for hockey, so Lydia and I are always on opposite ends during these events. It never stops me from keeping an eye on her.

She takes off her mitten and uses her hand to demonstrate to the young girl how to lift her arms higher before she goes into a skill. When the girl does it right this time, Lydia cheers and offers her a high five. I can't help but smile as I watch her. She's always been so good at coaching. It's not my favorite thing. Nothing against the kids, I'm just not a great teacher. I can't verbalize how they should change a minor detail to get the puck in the net. Lydia, however, sees the little things.

I notice that instead of putting her mitten back on, she shoves it into her vest pocket. Her hands are going to get cold. I tilt my chin in the direction of another coach, letting him know I'm stepping away, and skate over to Lydia.

I stop in front of her, making sure I don't spray her with any snow.

"Hey!" She greets me with a smile. Her cheeks are rosy red, and her hat is askew on her head. "What's up?"

I reach up to fix her hat. "You need to put your mittens back on."

She furrows her brow, glancing at her hands. "They're fine, Fletcher. I'm demonstrating. I need my hands."

"Use your hands *with* your mittens on." I pull the mittens from her pocket. "You're going to freeze."

Lydia huffs, holding out her hands for me to put her mittens on. "There, is that better, you weirdo?"

"Much." I boop her nose before skating away.

A voice pulls my attention. "Mr. Graff."

It's Luke. He's one of the boys I've been working with for a few years, and he skates over to me when I'm back on the hockey side of the ice.

"Hey, buddy. What's up?"

He's only seven or eight years old, but the kid is good at hockey. If he keeps up, he could be phenomenal. The next Adam Davison, but I'd never tell Adam I said that. Can't let his head get too big.

"Can you help me?" his voice is small, hesitant.

"Of course. What do you need?" I crouch down to his level, taking in the sadness in his eyes.

"I can't get my shot straight anymore, and my dad said if I don't get better, he's going to stop bringing me." A lone tear streaks down his red cheek.

"Oh, buddy, no." I pat his shoulder. "I won't let that happen. We'll keep you coming to hockey, and I'll help you work on your shot, don't worry."

"Thank you." He sniffles. "I want to keep playing. I can be better, I know I can."

I help Luke with his shot, coaching him on getting the angles right and strengthening the power behind it until he feels more confident.

An hour later, there's an announcement over the PA system that there are five minutes left in today's practice. The hockey kids scoop up pucks and throw them in buckets, while the kids on the figure skating side continue working on their skills.

Out of the corner of my eye, I see Lydia, her cheeks flushed as she crouches down to help another child, much like I crouched down earlier to get on Luke's level. They're smiling widely.

She's so amazing with kids.

Another girl practices a jump, lands it, and skates backward, not paying attention to where she's going. I'm too far away to stop her, but a few other people and I see it coming and shout as Lydia stands.

The girl skates right into her, knocking her hard onto the ice. I skate as fast as I can. The girl who hit Lydia is kneeling beside her, crying.

"Lydia," I grit out as I drop to my knees beside her. Anxiety pounds through my body.

She's prone on the ice, and I reach for her, but she's already moving to sit up, her brows furrowed as she cradles her wrist to her chest.

"I'm fine," she says to me, but I can see in her eyes that she isn't. She turns to the kid. "Polly. You need to remember to watch where you're going, especially when there are other people on the ice."

"I'm so sorry," Polly cries, her regret seeping through her words.

"I'm okay. But now you know for next time, right?"

Leave it to Lydia to use an injury as a lesson.

Polly nods, her eyes leaking tears faster than a faucet. The kids are moved away as I bend into Lydia's space, taking her hand in mine to examine it.

"What hurts?" I ask, tenderly taking off her mitten and moving her palm so it's facing up.

"I'm not sure. It's not bad. I don't think it's broken, but I landed pretty hard on it. It's probably sprained."

"We'll see."

She fell hard, and landing on an outstretched hand like that puts the wrist at a higher chance to break. Lydia hisses as I twist her wrist to check mobility.

"It doesn't hurt that bad," Lydia says, pulling her hand from me. I'm not sure whether she's trying to convince herself or me. Her wrist is already swelling.

"You're lying. We should go to the ER."

"Now you're being ridiculous." She cradles her hand back against her chest and holds her good hand out. "Help me stand?"

I rise to my feet, taking hers and pulling her up. "We're going to the ER."

"No, we're not. I'm fine, see?" She holds her arm out and flexes her fingers, but when she moves to twist her wrist, she gasps, swallowing a soft shriek.

"Yeah, that's what I thought. Come on. They can handle the teardown without us tonight." I wrap my arm around her waist, guiding her off the ice. Everyone claps and taps their sticks to the ice, lauding her as if she's a player who was injured.

Lydia waves with her good hand as we leave. I help her get out of her skates and into her boots, then rush to get my own gear off. It's a good thing we rode together; at least now we don't have to worry about getting her car home later.

I start my car, so hopefully it's at least a little warm by

the time we get to it in the parking lot. I grab her jacket and wrap it around her shoulders, pulling her into my body. Stopping at the locker room, I make an ice pack and pass it to her before we head outside.

"It feels better with the ice," Lydia says as I open the car door for her. "I really don't need to go in."

"I'd rather be safe than sorry. It was swelling before we even left the ice."

She climbs in, and I help her get buckled in, being careful of her arm.

"I know, but really, I don't need to go."

"You need X-rays."

"No, I don't."

"Stop fighting me on this," I say, a bit harshly, as I shut her door.

I take a deep breath, trying to slow my rapidly pounding heart. She's okay, it's just her wrist. It's not like she hit her head or anything.

Shit, I didn't even ask her if she hit her head.

I race to my side of my car, climbing in and shutting the door behind me.

"Did you hit your head?" I ask in a panic.

She leans forward to adjust her heated seat. "What? No, I didn't."

"Are you sure? Let me see your pupils." I turn on the center light and take her chin between my thumb and fore-finger, turning her head to face me.

Her eyes are wide as she takes in my worried expression, but her pupils look okay. I let my gaze linger on those beautiful blue orbs of hers. They're the first thing I see when I close my eyes every night. I could spend hours finding each and every speck of navy in them, watching them widen when she gets excited about her newest project or fixation. Her breath catches as I stare at her for longer than necessary, but I allow myself one more moment.

"Does your head hurt at all?"

With an irritated huff, she rips her eyes from mine and says no. At least I'm confident that she doesn't have a concussion.

"What hospital should we go to?"

"Please. I'm fine. There's no need to go to the hospital."

"We're going. If it's broken, you need a cast, and if it's not, well, at least we got it checked." I put the car in drive and head out of the parking lot. "Put your hospital into the GPS. I want to make sure it's at least in-network for you."

"Fine," she grumbles. "But when nothing is wrong with me, you're paying my hospital bill. I can't afford an ER bill for nothing right now."

"Deal." I was already planning on footing the bill regardless, but she doesn't need to know that.

Money is tight for her, especially since she insists on paying rent. She doesn't have to. I bought the place outright with my signing bonus six years ago, but she insisted.

What she doesn't know is that I've saved every single penny of rent she's paid me in a high-interest savings account for the day she eventually moves out. She deserves the world, and I'm going to do my best to give it to her.

11

———

LITTLE BEAN

LYDIA

We linger in the waiting room for nearly two hours before getting taken back to a room. My wrist aches, but I really don't think it's broken. If it were a weekday or if any urgent care were open, I'd suggest we go there, but we're out of luck because it's a Sunday night.

My plan of waiting to tell Fletcher I'm pregnant is about to be blown out of the water. They're going to want to do X-rays, and I'll have to drop the news. Only now, I'm worried about the baby.

Could my fall have hurt them? Would an ultrasound be able to see anything this early? My uninjured hand shakes as I climb onto the hospital bed, cradling the now-melted bag of ice to my wrist. The nurse asks me a few questions, and I debate whether now would be an appropriate time to tell her, but she finishes her questions and leaves, saying the doctor will be in shortly.

Fletcher scrolls aimlessly on his phone while I build up the courage to reveal my secret. I have to tell him now; it's the right thing to do. What will his reaction be? Will he be disappointed in me? I mean, why wouldn't he? My life is a mess, and I have no idea how to fix it.

My parents never hesitate to tell me anytime I do something wrong, and no, Fletcher has never been like that, but this is life-altering news, and it's going to change everything.

What I need to do is stop overthinking this.

"I have to tell you something," I blurt.

He drops his phone into his lap, staring at me with those insightful sage-green eyes. He's always so in tune with me that I'm not surprised how worried he's been over me for the last few days.

His eyes narrow. "You can tell me anything. What is it?"

"Fletcher, I'm—"

There's a knock on the door, and a young doctor strolls in. I drop my head back onto the pillow behind me.

Of course.

"Hi, I'm Dr. Evenson. I heard we have a possible broken wrist?" She strides over to me, snapping gloves onto her dainty hands.

"I'm pretty sure it's sprained." I offer my wrist to her.

She asks me a few questions about my fall and how it happened. When she prods it and turns it a bit, I wince, prompting her to apologize under her breath.

"I think you're right, but to be safe, we should probably do some X-rays."

I don't stop the furrow from forming on my brow. "Do we... have to?"

"I would highly suggest it. It's the easiest way to diagnose accurately."

"She'll do it," Fletcher says sternly from across the room.

Irritation with him burns in my chest. I don't need him

telling me what to do, not right now. It only makes me worry what he'll say when he finds out.

"Fletcher," I grit out.

I'm not a child. I'm a twenty-eight-year-old woman.

"The doctor says you need it."

I put my good hand to my face, taking a deep breath. "Can you get X-rays if you're pregnant?"

The room goes still.

"Ah," Dr. Evenson says, finally breaking the silence. "How far along are you?"

"I think nine weeks," I whisper. "I found out last week."

"In that case, we can forgo the X-rays. But I would still like to get an ultrasound to check on Baby. Is that something you're okay with?"

I nod, my mouth dry.

"I'll place the order, and someone will be in shortly. Would you be comfortable if we did some labs, too?"

I nod again, still unable to speak.

"As for your wrist, why don't we do a brace for a few weeks, and if it is not getting better, you can follow up with an orthopedic provider."

I shake my head, finding my voice. "Okay, that sounds good to me."

"I'll be back in a while."

I look up and thank Dr. Evenson as she exits the small room. Only then do I look at Fletcher. He's staring off into the distance, looking totally lost. His eyes have lost all their light, his face a blank mask of confusion.

I clear my throat, swallowing thickly. He's not saying anything. Why isn't he saying anything? I take a deep breath as I prepare for his disappointment. It seems like I'm always the disappointment in my parents' lives, so why wouldn't I be one for him, too? It was only a matter of time until the person who matters most to me realizes how much of a mess I am.

"Say something."

Fletcher grunts, shifting in his seat. "You're pregnant? Why didn't you tell me?"

"I found out the day of your home opener, and I didn't want to stress you out." My voice is small.

"You can tell me anything. I knew something was up. I *knew* it." He runs a hand down his face as he breathes heavily. His eyes widen. "The bag you threw in your room. It wasn't vibrators, was it? It was a pregnancy test?"

"Yeah." I swipe a tear from my eye. My emotions are all over the place. One minute, I'm frustrated with him. The next, I'm crying. "I'm sorry I didn't tell you. I've been processing, trying to talk to—"

"Is the father—" Fletcher starts to speak, but he's interrupted by a nurse striding in.

I shake my head, and his face falters for only a moment before he maintains a passive look.

She greets us with a smile. "Ready? I can take you down the hall to radiology, and if everything looks good, you'll be out of here before you know it."

"Great." I climb out of the bed and into the wheelchair she brought.

"Dad, are you coming?" The nurse directs her question to Fletcher, who blanches, leaning back in his chair and looking at me, a silent question in his eyes.

Neither of us corrects her. He's not the dad, but he *is* my person.

I can't make him come back with me. If I'm going to be a single mom, I need to get used to doing things on my own.

Before I can say anything, Fletcher stands, coming to my side as we leave the small room. His silent support sends a wave of gratitude through me, and I close my eyes as we make our way through the quiet halls. I know everything is going to change in the next few minutes. It's all about to become real, not just a line on a plastic stick.

An uneasy feeling eats at me. I thought I wanted this. I thought I was ready for a baby, for this major life change, but as it comes to a head, maybe I'm not. I can barely take care of myself. How can I care for a baby?

"Alright, Lydia, you can undress from the waist down and get on the bed. There's a blanket to cover you." The nurse gestures to the thin white blanket. "The tech will come in just a moment."

I swallow the lump in my throat. "Thank you."

She exits, leaving Fletcher and me alone.

"I'll—uh—" he stutters. "I'll step out while you change."

Things have never been awkward between us, and I hate that this is changing things. A change in our friendship is the last thing I need right now. He's been my constant for years now, and I don't think I can do this without him or his support.

"Okay," I murmur.

He leaves, quickly shutting the door behind him.

I strip down and fold my leggings, putting them and my underwear on a chair next to the wall, being sure to shove my underwear into my leggings so they're out of sight. Getting out of my clothes one-handed is a bit of a struggle, but I do it. I climb onto the bed, avoiding using my injured hand.

Just as I'm covering up with the blanket, there's a soft knock on the door. "Lydia, are you ready?"

"Yep." My voice cracks as I rest my head on the thin pillow.

Fletcher follows the tech back inside, the dazed look

still on his face. He sits in one of the plastic chairs against the wall, resting his head in his hands again. The physical distance between us feels like a chasm with jagged rocks waiting at the bottom, and I fear that soon, it will morph into him pulling away from me completely.

The tech introduces herself, explaining how she'll perform the ultrasound and what to expect, but I'm only half listening. I know I gave her consent to do the ultrasound, but outside of that, there's not much I'm comprehending. My heart pounds furiously in my chest, panic thrumming through my veins as she lifts the blanket and slides the ultrasound wand inside me.

Discomfort rages through me, and I squeeze my eyes shut. She moves it around a bit until she finds a spot.

"There it is," she says. "Want to see?"

I tentatively open my eyes, turning my head to the screen.

She's pointing at a little bean-sized black and white blob, and just like that, everything changes. That's my little bean. *I made that.*

I gasp, and the tech softly laughs. "Want to hear the heartbeat?"

I'm nodding before she finishes her sentence. A fast, steady whooshing fills the room, and my heart flutters. I'm so focused on the tiny bean on the screen that I don't notice I'm reaching out a hand, needing something to ground me.

Warmth wraps around me as Fletcher senses my needs, his hand squeezing mine. His eyes are wide and moist as he takes in the screen.

"That's your baby," he says, his voice cracking.

I can't speak, so I rest my head on his shoulder as tears stream down my face. I know with absolute certainty that I'm making the right choice.

12

AND I'M A HOCKEY PLAYER!

FLETCHER

Holy shit, Lydia's having a baby.

So many questions and ideas race through my brain, the most prevalent being excitement. Excitement for Lydia, for this baby. I get to watch my best friend, the person I love most in the world, become a mom. There's bound to be challenges, of course, but right now, I'm basking in the glow of this moment, in the beauty of it all. Watching her baby's heartbeat on the screen hits me right in the heart.

I'll be there for her every step of the way, no questions asked. If she wants me to go to every appointment, to every birthing or parenting class, I will. I never considered kids, never thought of anything past Lydia, but now that the future is staring me in the face, I have to admit it's bright.

The rest of the ER visit goes quickly once we're back in our room after the ultrasound. Lydia is silent, but she no longer has an anxious crease between her brows. Now, there's a soft glow in her eyes, a half-smile at the corner of her lips every time she looks at the ultrasound photo. I've caught her tracing her fingers over the shape of the baby a few times, and it's the cutest thing I've ever seen.

I take my phone out, capturing a photo of her. I want to remember this moment, the excitement I can so clearly see.

She catches me taking the photo, and that small frown line forms back on her brow again as she stares at me.

Dr. Evenson knocks on the door, entering the room with a smile. "Everything looked great on the ultrasound, and your labs look fantastic. We'll wrap your wrist for now, but get a stable brace in the next day or two, and you will be good to go. Follow up with orthopedics in a week or so if it's still giving you trouble."

The nurse comes in, shows her how to wrap her wrist, and gives Lydia her discharge paperwork.

"Thank you," Lydia says.

I rush to her side to help her from the bed, careful of her wrapped wrist.

"Ready to go home?" I ask, helping her with her jacket.

"Yeah, I'm exhausted." She stifles a yawn.

"Let's go." I lead her out of the room, wrapping my arm around her. I've always been protective of Lydia, but for some reason now I feel this urge to cradle her in bubble wrap, to watch her every move to make sure she's okay. Is it instinctual?

Something shifts as we walk. Lydia tries to pull away from me, but I hold her close until she huffs out an irritated sigh, unraveling herself. What's happening?

Despite wanting to keep her safe, I have so many questions she has to answer. Who's the father? Are they secretly together? Does he know? Why didn't she tell me about him?

My burning questions will have to wait until we get home. I don't want to upset her in the middle of an ER parking lot.

I help her into the car, then climb in myself, and we exit the parking ramp in silence. The drive home only intensifies Lydia's mood shift. She won't look at me, focusing on the road in front of us and fidgeting the entire way. Her body is coiled, like she's ready to run for her life.

"I'm having a baby," she finally mumbles.

I'm not really sure what I should say.

I don't want to upset her, so I reply a quick, "Yep."

Which apparently was the wrong choice, since Lydia lets out an irritated noise, going back to looking out the window.

No more words are said on the short drive to our building, and as we take the elevator to our floor, the tension between us increases with each ding of the elevator.

Once we are in the confines of our apartment, I'll ask my questions. I just have to hold out a few more moments. I unlock the door and let her in.

"Will you please say something?" Lydia chokes out as soon as I shut the door.

I freeze, stunned that she's so upset. But if she wants to get this over with, so be it.

"Fine, how did you get pregnant?" I ask, my tone bordering on accusatory, though I don't mean it to be.

What the hell am I doing? Why are we fighting right now?

"Well, when a man and a woman..." she replies with a snarky edge, though it feels half-hearted. Her shoulders sag, and pure exhaustion washes over her face.

I wish I could hold her in my arms and eliminate all her fears. I know right now that's her driving force. Fear. This is a big life change. She has to be scared.

I interrupt her. "Stop it, Lydia. You know what I mean.

You live with me. How did you find the time to get pregnant?"

"I have a life outside of you, you know." Her cheeks burning red with each word.

I was gone visiting my parents for a week this summer. Was he in our apartment?

A clawing jealousy steamrolls through me as I gasp, clutching my chest dramatically. "Did you bring him here when I was away this summer?"

"That is *so not* the point right now!" She mutters something under her breath.

I need to fix this. The last thing I want is to fight with her. I reacted when she did, and I shouldn't have. She's obviously had to keep things to herself for a while and is stressed. What I should do is relieve her stress, not add to it.

"You're right. I'm sorry." I reach for her, but she steps away, breaking off a piece of my heart with it.

"Just say it." Her voice is timid as she stares at the floor.

"Say what?"

"Say you're disappointed in me," she screeches. Her wrapped hand is still against her chest, the ultrasound photo held tightly in her good hand.

"What? Disappointed?" I growl, stepping closer to her. This time, she lets me. "How could I *ever* be disappointed in you?"

"I'm pregnant!"

"And I'm a hockey player!" I lift my hands in exasperation.

"What the fuck are you talking about?" Her eyes narrow, burning with the fire I know and love.

"I'm just stating facts. I thought that's what we were doing!"

"Oh, my god." Lydia groans, walking to the coffee table

and setting down the photo before sitting on the couch, rubbing her face with her good hand. "I'm spinning in circles at this point. It's making me dizzy."

I sit beside her. "Come here."

I open my arms for her. Thankfully, she scoots into my embrace, and I hold her close, breathing in her familiar warm vanilla scent.

"I'm not mad or disappointed in you. *Never*. I have questions, but those can wait if you aren't up for it."

She shakes her head into my chest. "No, I need to get it all out. Hiding this from you was brutal, even if it was only for a short time. I was scared because when I told you, I knew that would make it real."

I take a deep breath. "Alright. I'm going to start with the big one, then."

The small seed of information I got from her in that shake of her head at the hospital makes it seem like maybe the father isn't around, but I still have to ask.

"Okay..."

"Who's the father?"

Lydia closes her eyes and takes a deep breath. "His name is Jude. We went on three dates at the end of summer, right when you went back to training camp. I didn't tell you about him because I didn't want to jinx anything. I really liked him. He told me he wanted more than a hookup, but after we slept together on the third date, he ghosted me. I was on birth control, and I thought he wore a condom, but somehow, here we are."

"Asshole," I mutter through gritted teeth.

I can't believe any man would give this woman up. If I had it my way, I'd never let her go. To hear that he hurt her this way sends a jealous rage through my body. What I'd give to find out where he lives and give him a bit of a lesson.

Maybe Calvin would be interested in joining me. He's always down to throw a few punches.

"And to get ahead of your next question, no, he doesn't want to be involved. I met with him last week, and to say it didn't go well would be putting it lightly. He made me sign a contract saying I wouldn't go after him for money or list him on the birth certificate."

Okay, now I really need to get a few punches in on this guy. Selfishly, I'm glad he's out of the picture. It sounds like he doesn't deserve anything from Lydia, but knowing he hurt her is enough to piss me off.

More than anything, I wish I were there for her during all of this. I *hate* knowing that she had to do this alone.

"Fuck, Lydi." I squeeze her a little tighter, smoothing my hands over her hair. "I'm sorry he was an asshole. You and your baby deserve better."

"Yeah, well, it is what it is. No one else knows yet—well, besides your mom."

"My mom knew before me?"

I shouldn't be surprised. My mom can sense things, and she and Lydia have a close relationship.

"Your dad gave me a beer at the game, and I couldn't drink it. Then I puked in the suite's bathroom, so yeah, she knows. I don't know if she's told your dad yet, but you can't be mad at her. I told her not to tell you." Lydia rushes to get that last part out.

"I'm not mad at her. Or you, for that matter." I squeeze her, running my hand up and down the length of her arm. "What do you need from me?"

A shuddered laugh falls from her lips. "I don't know. I'm scared. I want this baby, and I know I won't regret keeping it, but so much is going to change. I'm going to have to move out and find my own place."

"Hey, hey." I tilt back so I can see her face and swipe some of the tears from her cheeks. "I know how scary this is, but you can always count on me. I'll be here for you every step of the way. You're not losing me, and I don't know why you're talking about moving out, because that's *not* happening."

If anything, this is making me more determined to take the step I've always held back from, the one that would change everything for us. It's all I can think about now, and I might not be willing to wait any longer.

Lydia lets out a watery chuckle. "Oh, so you're going to be totally fine with a baby screaming in the middle of the night, keeping you up and messing up your sleep schedule right around playoffs?"

"Yep. And I'll be right there with you, helping with nightly feeds and diaper changes." I hope she can hear how sincere I am.

She waves me off. "I'd never ask you to do that."

"I'm still going to do it. I'm here for you. You're my best friend, the person I trust most in this world. I'm not going to leave you high and dry."

Lydia nods, the tears falling harder as she burrows into my chest. "Thank you."

"There's nothing to thank me for." I press a kiss to the top of her head.

Everything I am is because of her, and I'm going to prove to her I'm not going anywhere. Maybe if I'm lucky, she'll see that I want something more, that I've wanted more for a long time.

13

CURLY GIRL ROUTINE

LYDIA

I glance at the kitchen sink, letting out an irritated groan. This is going to be an absolute pain in the ass, but I have to do it. My left hand twinges at the thought, but if I don't wash my hair or do my curly routine now, my hair will be a frizzy mess for work tomorrow.

Heading over to the sink, I turn the faucet on. While I wait for it to warm up, I take my old ratty tee off, leaving me in my comfortable bralette. This thing has been a lifesaver in the last week, since my boobs have started getting super sore, along with a myriad of other pregnancy symptoms.

Throwing a towel over the side of the sink, I bend over the edge of the counter. I douse my hair with water and pump a few squirts of shampoo into my hand. It's definitely uncomfortable trying to lather up the suds in my hair, and I can't seem to get the left side scrubbed as well as I'd like with how sore my wrist is. This is not going to end well.

Grabbing the retractable faucet, I direct it over my hair, hoping my head is at least a little clean. I try to get the back of my head, but instead of it actually rinsing my hair, it sprays all down my back, making me shriek, and I proceed to smack my head on the metal faucet.

"Fuck!" I grip the top of my head with my good hand.

A familiar voice distracts me from the throbbing in my head. "Lydi?"

"Fletch?" I question, my dripping wet head still hanging over the sink. "What are you doing? You weren't supposed to be home for like an hour."

"Practice got done early." His voice lilts at the end, like he's trying his best to hold back his laughter.

Of fucking course, it did.

"Do you need help?" His footsteps grow closer until I can sense him standing right beside me.

God, I'm so embarrassed. I'm in only a bralette and cotton shorts, bent over the kitchen sink. I'm sure this was not the sight he expected to come home to.

"No, I'm good," I say, hoping he doesn't see through me.

"Whatever you say, Lydi-bug." He sets something down on the kitchen table while I continue to attempt to rinse my hair.

I reach for the conditioner and can't even open it because of my wrist, spewing out a few choice words as the bottle flies into the metal sink.

Fletcher steps beside me once more, this time, pushing back a piece of my wet hair. His fingers tilt my chin so my eyes lock with his. "Let me help. Please."

The words are so soft as they leave his lips but said with so much sincerity that it makes my heart melt a little.

"Okay," I whisper.

Fletcher steps back. My head is still at an angle with water dripping down my face, but I see it clear as day when he crosses his hands over his torso, gripping his white MBH shirt and lifting it over his head.

I have to do my best to attempt to swallow a gasp when his bare skin comes into view.

Oh.

The happy trail I saw when I put him to bed last week flashes into my line of sight again, and this time, the heat runs straight to my clit. Where did this attraction come from? I never used to react to him like this.

Fletcher returns to my side, and my cheeks burn as I turn my head back to face the silver metal of the sink bowl. I grab the tipped-over bottle of conditioner and hold it up for him.

He opens the bottle with ease, squirting the liquid into his palm and running his long fingers through my hair. His touch sends an unexpected shiver down my spine, making goose bumps erupt on my arms.

"You have to kinda squish it into my hair." I use my good hand to demonstrate.

He hums an acknowledgment before continuing the motion all around my head. His warm body is pressed up against mine, our bare skin meeting, and my skin grows sensitive to his touch. The sensation spreads throughout my body until my already sensitive nipples are hard.

After he's squished the conditioner in my hair, Fletcher grabs the faucet, running it over my head and rinsing.

"Perfect," he says, voice low and rumbly. "What's next?"

"How did you know there was more?"

"You've got no less than four bottles of product lined up in the sink, Lydia."

Right.

"I'll squeeze a bit of the extra water out, but can you grab the curl cream? It's the orange bottle. Put a good amount in your hands and rub them together."

He does as directed, then stands. I demonstrate how to do praying hands and how to get the cream all over the curls. He does the next step with ease, and when I tell him to, he scrunches the curls again.

When he's done, I grab the T-shirt that I use specifically for this and plop my hair. I stand back straight, glancing around at the absolute mess we made. The countertops are covered in water, and there's even some on the floor. I have a feeling most of it was my fault when I was doing it on my own, but still.

"Oops." I grimace, glancing down at myself. I'm still only wearing a bralette and my high-waisted sleep shorts. "Oh god." I cross my arms over my chest, wincing at the pain from the pressure on my breasts.

My tits better not hurt like this the whole pregnancy.

Fletcher clears his throat and smiles at me with so much endearment, I want to cry. There's a crinkle in the corner of his eyes. It's so sweet. *He's* so sweet. He didn't have to take time out of his day to help me wash my hair, but he did.

Whoever he ends up with will be so lucky to have him. He would be such a great partner. So willing to jump in and help, no matter what.

But why does the thought of him with someone else sting? I shake it off. Why am I thinking about Fletcher like that? Why am I reacting to him like this?

"I'm going to finish this—" I gesture dramatically to my head. "I'll be back."

I rush down the hall to my bathroom, starting up my blow dryer to diffuse my hair. When it's done and actually looks fairly good, I cross over to my room to put on a dry bra and shirt.

I head back into the living room, finding Fletcher sitting

on the couch. He looks up at me when I enter, and a giddy smile crosses his face.

"I did pretty good," he says.

"You really did." I fluff my hair with my hand as I flop down onto the couch. "What are you up to the rest of the day?"

"Nothing." He pulls my feet into his lap and rubs them.

"That feels amazing," I moan, my head dropping to the couch cushion.

Fletcher adjusts in his seat, digging his thumb into the arch of my foot. "Can I help you with anything?"

"What do you mean?"

"With the pregnancy. I mean, I hate that I couldn't be there to support you when you told Jude, but I want to be here for you, every step of the way. I'm here for you."

I can hear just how much he means it in every word he says.

"Oh," I whisper, my heart pounding. "I don't know. I mean, I should get used to doing this on my own. Right?" I chuckle awkwardly.

"You're not alone, though."

"I know. But I am, I mean, I'm going to be a single mom."

His brows knit together, and he slowly nods. "I guess."

"I won't say no to your help." I rest my palm on his forearm, and when my hand connects with his skin, that sensation I had earlier rushes back to life, and it throws me off. I pull my hand away. "But I'm okay. Really."

Fletcher nods, the conversation dies, and I can't help but feel some sort of tension in the air.

I don't know what these feelings are, but I'm not sure I can brush them off as pregnancy hormones.

14

LONG STORY SHORT

FLETCHER

W e play in Boston tonight, Seattle on Thursday, then fly home Friday for our home game on Saturday. It's going to be rough not seeing Lydia until then. I miss her already. I miss her easy laugh and our chats about her current fixation project on my nights off. I haven't even been gone a day, and she's all I can think about, this need for more with her. I won't even get to hang out with her before the game on Saturday since we have a press event at the Mall of America.

I haven't told anyone Lydia is pregnant—well, outside of having a conversation with my mom—and I'm practically bursting at the seams. I have to get my thoughts out. Right now, there's a lot going on in my head, which is not ideal before a game.

"What's the deal, Fletchy baby?" Calvin drops onto the bench next to me.

I groan, looking around the locker room. It's fairly empty as of now, with only Trigg, Levine, and a few of the other guys milling around.

"I have to tell you something," I whisper, leaning back. "But not here."

I trust Trigg not to tell a soul even if he could hear me with his headphones in, but I don't trust Levine farther than I can throw him.

"What?" Calvin's eyes grow wide as he leans in.

"*Not. Here.*" I stand, taking my phone with me since I'll need to call Lydia shortly, anyway. I lead him into the hall and peek into the athletic trainer's office, finding it empty. "Here."

I gesture for him to enter, and he raises his brows. "Is it that serious?"

"Yes." I run a hand through my hair. I put some gel in it, but that's not lasting long at all.

"Alright, chill." Calvin holds up his hands and enters the small room, leaning against the table as I shut the door behind us. "Well?"

I let out a long exhale. "Lydia's pregnant."

His eyes go wide. "You're kidding."

"No. It's a long story, but no."

"*You got Lydia pregnant?* Graff, what the hell! When did you sleep together? I don't know whether to fist-bump you or smack you upside the head. I can't believe you didn't tell me."

"*What?*" I whisper-shout, not wanting to draw attention to us. "No! We haven't slept together. It's not mine."

"Why do you sound so disappointed?"

I shrug. I don't think I'm ready to elaborate on that.

"Who's the dad if it isn't you?"

"Some guy she went on a few dates with this summer. He ghosted her after they slept together."

The irritation I have for the guy burns in my core again.

"Asshole," Calvin mutters.

"Right?" I shake my head. "Not the point. I'm worried about her. I haven't seen her since we left last night, and she hurt her wrist, and I'm stressed."

"You're also in love with her."

I don't confirm or deny because I've realized that I don't want to be stuck in the friend zone with her. Not anymore.

"What are you going to do about it, then?" Calvin asks.

"I don't know. I need to think about it."

"You want more with her?"

I press the heel of my palm into my eyes as I nod. "You of all people know I do. I have for a long time. But I took what I could with her and always hoped maybe someday she'd want me back. What if she doesn't want me back, man?"

"She will. You two would be perfect together."

"But this is a crazy time in her life. I mean, she's having a baby. What if she thinks I'm doing this because I feel bad for her?"

So many thoughts are swirling in my mind, but most of all, I can't stop thinking about how badly I want this, how badly I want her. I want to be a part of the baby's life. Any piece of her is something I want.

I want to be there for her, now more than ever, and in a completely different way than before. I want to be her partner, her lover, the father to her baby. I want to be the man Jude wouldn't step up to be.

"She won't. And if she does, prove her wrong." Calvin rubs my shoulder. "For now, do your pre-game ritual. Call her. She'll ground you. Then, get your head on straight, 'cause we've got a game to play."

"Right." I stand up straighter, pushing my hair out of my eyes. "You're right."

"There's my captain," Calvin says with a shit-eating grin. "I'll see you in the locker room."

Once alone, I take a deep breath, pulling my phone out and calling Lydia.

On almost the last ring, she answers, her voice full of sleep. "Hello?"

Some of the tension instantly leaves my body at the sound of her voice.

"Hey Lydi-bug, what's up?"

She groans loudly. "Tired."

"I bet. Your body is working overtime lately."

"Yeah," she mumbles.

"How's your wrist? Did you go to the doctor today?"

Lydia's always off on Mondays, so I assume maybe she'd go in today.

"Yeah. They want me to keep the brace for another week, but he's not worried about it. Enough about me. You're in Boston, right? Ready for the game?"

My shoulders slump, and relief washes through me. Her wrist is okay. She's okay.

"Ready as ever," I respond. "Boston is always a fun team to play against. They play hard, but we can play harder."

"You've got this. Hey, what are you doing on Sunday?" Lydia asks unexpectedly.

"Umm, not sure. Probably practice since there isn't a game."

"Ugh, my parents are coming to town. My mom called me last week. Apparently, they're going to Spain for a month and decided to grace me with their presence for lunch. I'll probably tell them about the baby, but I might need backup."

Lydia's parents can be hard to deal with on a good day,

so I'm sure it will be interesting when she tells them she's pregnant. Honestly, I have no idea how they might react.

"I'm there," I reply without hesitation.

"Ugh, thank you. I owe you."

"No, you don't."

"Yes, I do. You do more for me than you know," she says, her voice growing softer at the end.

"I feel the same about you, so we're even." I need her to understand that simply by existing, she changes me daily. "Hey, I gotta go, but I'll text you after, okay?"

"No problem. I'll be watching!" I can hear the smile in her voice.

She's always been my biggest supporter besides my parents. It's rare that I even hear from my siblings with encouragement or excitement about my career, but I can't blame them. They have busy lives of their own, with kids.

"Talk later." I end the call the same way I always do, without an official goodbye.

A renewed sense of energy takes over my body. I can make this work with Lydia. I know I can. Things are already so easy between us. Taking that next step is only natural.

I just have to figure out how to get us there, and the rest will fall into place.

15

BUTTERY SALTY GOODNESS

LYDIA

TEN WEEKS PREGNANT

I slide the stiff brace onto my left wrist, thankful it's been getting better every day. I got lucky that it wasn't my dominant hand, or this week would have been a bit rougher than it already is.

I've been so exhausted all week. If I'm not at work or eating, I'm asleep.

Fletcher was out late last night, and I was already asleep by the time he got home, so I won't get to see him until after the game today. I miss him. Like always, we talk every day. Nothing has changed there, but the adjustment back to the season after the summer's off is always rough.

I'm meeting Grace and Zoey at the arena, and we have the suite again today, which will be nice. While there's not much privacy, there is still a little more than if we were in the lower bowl. I'm planning to tell them my news. They'll figure it out anyway when I don't have a drink.

We play Colorado today, which is the team Zoey's brother, Adam, plays for. It's always a fun time watching

Calvin and Adam play against each other. They played together for their entire childhood and college years until Adam was drafted to the Colorado Lynx and Calvin to the Blue Herons.

Once I'm finished getting ready in my standard game outfit—Fletcher's jersey, a stocking cap, and jeans—I head to the arena. All I can think about is how badly I need popcorn. Something about the buttery, salty goodness is calling to me today.

I love these afternoon games because once the game is over, there's still plenty of the day left to hang out with friends and not be out until one a.m. Which will work in my favor tonight since I'm already looking forward to the moment I can climb back into my cozy bed.

The suite is still empty, but they've already set up all the food and beverages for us. I grab a box and fill it with popcorn from the warm machine, snacking on a few pieces as I do.

The door opens, and Grace and Calvin's parents enter. Stan and Mabel Miller might be the sweetest people I've met—well, besides Fletcher's parents. They're the epitome of Minnesota Nice. I chew quickly, swallowing the lump of popcorn in my mouth.

"Hey, guys," I say.

"Lydia, how are you?" Mabel opens her arms.

"I'm good." I smile softly, returning her hug carefully so as not to smush my popcorn or bad wrist.

Her eyes widen. "What happened to your hand?"

I wave my hand. "Nothing bad. A kid ran into me at the community skate event on Sunday, and I landed on my wrist."

"Is it broken?"

I shake my head. "I think it's a sprain."

"You think? Did you go to the doctor?"

I wish I could swallow my tongue.

"Yeah."

"And they didn't do X-rays?" Her voice rises in pitch. "What if it's fractured, and you don't know?"

Stan comes up behind Mabel, resting a hand on her shoulder.

"I'm sure they did, sweetie." Stan offers me a smile. "Hi, kiddo."

I frantically nod. "Yep. Sorry, I said that weirdly. No break! I should be fine in a week or two."

"Oh, good." Mabel sighs. "How have you been otherwise?"

"Good!" I reply quickly, thankful to change the subject.

The door opens again, and this time, Zoey and Grace stride through, looking adorable in their jerseys. Usually, Zoey wears one with Miller on the back to support Calvin, but tonight she's wearing a Colorado Lynx one with Davison on it.

We all exchange hugs, and Mabel and Stan take their seats as Zoey, Grace, and I grab more snacks and sit at a table.

"How are you?" Zoey asks as she adjusts her black-rimmed glasses. "I feel like I haven't seen you in ages."

"I know, it's been a weird few weeks." I laugh, and my eyes burn with tears—stupid hormones.

"Hey, what's going on?" Grace coos, resting her hand on my shoulder.

I take a deep breath, glancing over to Stan and Mabel, who are lost in their own world. Warm-ups haven't even started yet, and I'm already losing it. It's going to be a long afternoon.

"I'm pregnant."

"Holy shit," Zoey blurts, slapping a hand over her mouth.

"What?" Grace gasps, squeezing my arm.

I panic, not knowing what to say, so I shove a handful of buttery popcorn into my mouth. The flavor bursts on my tongue, helping with some of the emotion flooding through my body.

"You're pregnant?" Zoey questions. "Who's the father?"

Grace's eyes widen. "Is it Fletcher?"

"Oh my god!"

The only downside to all the popcorn in my mouth is that I can't deny them and tell them he's not the father.

"I knew it," Grace shrieks. "I knew you two were together."

I shake my head aggressively, muttering through my mouthful, "No, no!" I really didn't think that through. I swallow the popcorn, choking on a hull. "Fletcher isn't the father."

Grace's face falls. "Dang. Who is, if it's not him?"

I groan. "His name is Jude, and he's decided not to be involved. We went on a few dates, slept together once, and I'm still not quite sure how it happened, but here we are."

"And you're keeping it?" Zoey asks.

"I am."

"We are here to support you in any way that we can." Grace runs her hand over my arm.

"Thanks." I sniffle as a tear streaks down my cheek. "I'm scared, but this is what I want."

"You're going to be an amazing mom," Zoey says.

Oh, great, more tears.

"Stop it. I need to quit crying."

They hug me, and I soak in the comfort.

"What does Fletcher have to say?" Grace asks.

I look over to the ice, where the players are running through their warm-ups. A memory of Fletcher shirtless, leaning over the kitchen sink to help me with my hair, flashes in my mind, and those traitorous goose bumps prickle my skin again.

"We haven't really had much time to talk about it, but he knows and is going to be there for me. I tried to tell him I'll move out, but he said no."

"Wait, when are you due?" Zoey questions as we stand to head to the seats to watch warm-ups.

"May twenty-seventh," I mutter under my breath, my cheeks heating. "They told us the due date during the ultrasound in the ER, but they want the OB to confirm it at my first appointment."

"Oh, shit," Grace murmurs.

"Yeah. Right in the middle of the playoffs." I wince. Because of course it is. "Which is why I offered to move out. If we make it past the first round, Fletcher isn't going to want his sleep interrupted by an infant."

"If he says it's fine," Zoey says, albeit unconvincingly. "I would believe him. I think he's the type of guy to know what he's okay with."

"Yeah, except he's never been around an infant for more than a few hours. To have one dumped into your normally quiet apartment during one of the most intense times of the season? How is that going to work?"

"Who knows? We might not even make it to the playoffs this year," Grace says with a wave of her hand. "This might not be a problem."

"Don't you dare speak like that," Zoey says curtly, pushing her glasses up her nose and wagging her finger in Grace's face.

We sit in the comfortable seats as we watch the guys take the ice.

"It's true, though," Grace says in defense. "We've all been around hockey players enough to know things change in the blink of an eye. They could win the cup, or they might not make it to the playoffs."

Zoey huffs and swats Grace's arm. "You're right, but still. Don't speak such things into existence."

"Would you guys mind keeping this to yourselves?" I ask. "Not that I think you'd tell anyone, but I'm not ready for my business to be out in the world yet."

"Absolutely." Zoey takes my hand and rubs it soothingly. "This is a big deal, and you should be able to tell who you want to tell, without fear. You have nothing to worry about."

Grace agrees, and I relax a bit. It's nice to know I have them at my back and that they understand my want for privacy. Fletcher already lives a fairly high-profile life, and I'm not one to enjoy the spotlight. I never have been.

Zoey and Grace continue chatting, but my focus shifts to the men on the ice. I love watching warm-ups, mainly because typically Fletcher is at ease, and you get to see some of his familiar personality bubble through. Watching him interact with the fans is my favorite, but as soon as the puck drops, he's a different person. Focused, hard-wired, and set on the game.

Watching him play the game he loves has always made me proud, but for some reason, tonight, there's an extra special burst of pride in my chest. Maybe it's because of his endless support for me and his ability to help me through even the toughest of times. I'll never take him for granted.

He skates around the ice and slows to a stop as he

reaches the length where we are sitting in the suite. Fletcher looks up, and through his visor, there's a gleam in his eyes.

He waves his gloved hand, a giant smile crossing his face, and it's like a weight is lifted off my chest. Just being in his presence helps ease some of the fear simmering in my body since I walked out of that meeting with Jude. I mean, really. Who am I to think I can raise a child on my own? But I want this baby, and knowing I have Fletcher in my corner helps more than I can express.

I wave back, an easy smile on my cheeks. I missed him so much the last few days.

He skates off, joining Calvin and Trigg, who both skate to the red line to greet Adam. They exchange handshakes and hugs before going their separate ways to continue their warm-ups.

We chat for a while longer as we wait for the game to start, and both of them are already planning a baby shower for me. I'm sure my mom won't be in a rush to host one, so it's sweet that they're willing to.

The game starts, and as it always does, my heart pounds the second Fletcher's skates hit the ice. He morphs into a different person.

The puck is dropped, and my focus on the game vanishes, replaced by thoughts of my future, of the baby I'm carrying inside me. I don't doubt that being a single mom will be hard, but I'm ready for it.

For some reason, my mind strays to thoughts of Fletcher. What would he be like as a father? Not to my baby, no. Things aren't like that between us, but I'm imagining him holding a small bundle, with my curly hair and blue eyes. The image is far too real, and it makes my heart clench.

I'm so distracted that the game flies by in a whir. After

three hard-fought periods, the Blue Herons win three to one. It was sad to watch Adam and his team leave the ice dejected, but it's part of the game, I suppose. Hopefully, the guys don't give him too much of a hard time when we go out to dinner.

As we walk out of the suite to make our way to the tunnels to meet the guys, I stare longingly at the popcorn. It's fine, I'll just get more at the next game.

16

WHATEVER IT TAKES

FLETCHER

"Way to go, boys," I shout as I enter the locker room. I'm met with cheers and hoots of excitement. We've been on a bit of a winning streak this week, which is always a good way to start the season.

Calvin says a few encouraging words and sends us off. I head to do my post-game cool-down routine, massaging a foam roller over my muscles. I don't take as much time as I normally do, knowing everyone is waiting for us. After a quick shower, I throw some fresh clothes on and meet Calvin back at his locker.

Trigg is waiting, too, his headphones in as he goes through his post-game routine.

I tap him on the shoulder. "Ready, Addy?"

He takes his headphones out, and a song I can't place plays loudly for a moment before he shuts it off.

"Yes," he replies, pocketing his phone and headphones.

If I had to guess, I would say he's nervous to go out with us, but I've taken him under my wing this week. As I've gotten to know our new Norwegian goalie a bit more, I have to say, I'm excited to call him my friend. He's so laid back, but at the same time, you can tell he's working hard to make a good impression.

We head out of the locker room, saying goodbye to some staff as we do, and find our friends and family in the hall waiting for us.

The sight of Lydia smiling as she talks with Grace sends a thrill down my spine. She looks as gorgeous as always, with her curls popping out of the bottom of her hat, and in the jersey with my name on it. A zing of excitement hits me as I realize that soon I'll be buying baby clothes with my name on it for the little ladybug inside of her. I can't stop picturing a sweet little girl who looks just like her mom, or a little boy with brown curls that fall into his face.

Without hesitation, I stride to her, opening my arms and enveloping her in a hug. The way my body melts into hers should be studied. Everything about her is home to me.

"Missed you," I whisper.

"You too."

I don't get a chance to say anything more as Adam marches over. Mabel opens her arms, and he sinks into them, letting her hold him for a moment. It's cool how close Adam and his twin, Zoey, are to the Miller family. From what I understand, the Millers practically took Zoey and Adam in when they were in high school.

Zoey sneaks in beside them, and when it's finally her turn to hold her brother, they both hold tight and don't let go. I suppose maybe they haven't seen each other for a long time, since Adam lives in Colorado full-time.

Grace and Calvin hug, and we chat for a few minutes before we head across the street to one of the bars we frequent after games.

There are cheers when we walk in, and a few boos once they spot Adam among us, but mostly, everyone is excited to see us. My arm is wrapped around Lydia's shoulders, holding her close to me as we head back to find a table big enough for all of us.

I'm still wrapping my mind around Lydia being pregnant. It changes things, sure, but not in a bad way. I want to see where we can go. I just need to figure out how to bring it up to her authentically.

Lydia sits across the table from me, next to Zoey and Adam, and I fight the urge to sit beside her. I mean, of course, she doesn't have to be by me all the time, but we haven't seen each other all week. I want to spend time with her.

Trigg is on my right, while Grace and Calvin are on my left. Zoey and Lydia are all smiles as they talk about something, but I'm only focused on her. This urge for *more* continues to take over every fiber of my being. Our friendship has always been incredible, but there's the underlying question of 'what if?'

There's no doubt in my mind that we could be amazing together. When she friend-zoned me all those years ago, I was content to keep her any way I could. I spent years watching from afar, cataloging every detail about her: the way her nose crinkles when she's trying to lie, or the way she falls asleep every time we try to have a Star Wars marathon, then complains that I didn't wake her up. I couldn't, though, not if I wanted to risk the wrath of a grumpy Lydia.

A nudge in my side pulls me from my thoughts. I glance to my left, where Grace is, a sly grin on her face.

"What?" I lift my eyebrows.

Grace glances across the table, her gray eyes narrowing on Lydia. She subtly jerks her chin to her. I repeat my question, knowing she can see right through me. If she's talked to her brother, she knows.

She leans in close, whispering, "So, how are we going to get you your girl?"

Yeah, Calvin totally told her.

Those two are the worst at keeping secrets from each other, I've learned. One time, Calvin wanted my help planning a surprise party for Grace's twenty-fifth birthday. We planned it at their parents' lake place, and everything was going off without a hitch until Calvin got too excited and spilled the beans a week before the party. Grace didn't care. She was more excited to have a party with everyone, but it just goes to show that the man cannot keep a secret. Honestly, I'm impressed he kept my feelings for Lydia to himself for as long as he has.

I run my hands down my face and take a drink of my pop. "I don't know. Do you have any ideas?"

"Well, you're in this for the long haul, right? She has a baby on the way."

"Of course, I am. The baby is as much a part of my life now as it is hers. I'm going to be there for both of them, no matter what."

I glance at Lydia again. She's talking animatedly with Zoey and Adam, her eyes bright. She is the light in my life, more so than I think she knows.

Grace nods, pushing her blonde hair out of her face. "Good. I'd dick punch you if you weren't on board."

I grimace, scooting an extra inch away from her, holding myself back from covering my dick with my hand to protect it. As scary as it is, I appreciate that Lydia has people looking out for her.

"Noted." I confirm with a nod, and a realization hits me. "Wait, when did you find out?"

"Today. She told us during warm-ups. Sounds like the father is a real piece of work."

I scoff. "Yeah, you could say that."

"Which is why if you're in this, you need to be *in this*." Grace narrows her eyes once more.

"I'm in this. I'll do whatever it takes. I just don't know how to cross this bridge into something more."

She ponders for a moment. "I'll help you. We can set up a meeting or something and come up with a plan. How does that sound?"

Trigg and Calvin lean over at the same time.

"What are we talking about?" Calvin asks, his brows raising curiously.

Trigg echoes the question.

Grace offers the guys a sly smile. "Operation Ruin The Friendship."

17

MOMMY ISSUES

LYDIA

I smooth my hands over my black skirt, hoping it's nice enough for my mother. My rust-orange sweater is tucked into the skirt. It's not extremely fancy, but it'll do. I have tights under the skirt because I couldn't be bothered to shave my legs, and it's chilly this morning. I'll find a pair of nice shoes to help the outfit pop.

My hands shake as I run my hands over my shirt, and I pull the sleeve down in an attempt to cover the brace still on my left wrist. I've been nauseous all morning, and at this point, who knows if it's from the baby, or the fear of meeting with my parents. Of course, my mother will have questions about what happened, and I don't want to share my news until I'm ready.

My phone rings with an incoming FaceTime call from Fletcher. His face is dripping with sweat as he bends over, taking off his skates. He should already be on his way.

"Hey, are you leaving soon?"

He groans. "Nope. Practice went long, and now Coach called an emergency team meeting for some reason. I don't think it'll take long, but you should drive separately in case I don't make it home on time."

A speck of fear digs into my chest. "You're still coming, right?"

"I'll be there as soon as I can, I promise," he says, determination strong in his voice. He glances up at the screen, looking at me for the first time. There's a long silence.

"What?" I ask, my voice growing higher. Is my outfit horrible, or is my hair wrong? "Oh god, I look awful, don't I?"

I prop my phone against the wall, trying to fix my curls. I can't look like this. My mom will freak.

"Wait, no!" he blurts, halting my motions. "You look incredible. That's all. I couldn't form words."

I let out an awkward chuckle, trying to play off the swirling butterflies in my stomach. "Oh, you mean the sheen of sweat from nausea?"

Fletcher shakes his head, and he shifts on the bench. "You're beautiful, Lydi. Absolutely stunning. But to answer your question, yes. I'll be there as soon as I can."

Thank god. I really don't want to do this alone. I absolutely can, but Fletcher is my biggest support, and my parents won't be as harsh on me if someone else is present. At least I don't think they will.

"Okay," I say. "Thanks. I appreciate you."

"Right back at you. I gotta go, but I'll text you when I'm on my way, okay?"

I agree, and we hang up, leaving me alone with my thoughts. Maybe I shouldn't tell them today. I mean, I'm still early on in this pregnancy. You never know what could happen.

No, I have to tell them. They're going to be gone for a month, and I should tell them this in person.

I sigh and check the time on my phone. I have to leave in fifteen minutes to make it to the restaurant on time. After finishing my hair and makeup, I slip into my shoes and pull on my favorite wool peacoat before leaving.

Traffic isn't too bad right now, which is good. I don't need more time to sit and overthink this brunch. When I pull into the parking lot, I scan the area in search of Fletcher's car. When I come up empty, I check my phone, but there's nothing there either.

He's going to be late.

It's not his fault, but it means I have to do this on my own.

I take a deep breath and head into the restaurant. My parents are always prompt, and I'm still five minutes early, but I'm certain they're here. Sure enough, they're standing at the hostess station, waiting to be seated. My mother is dressed nicely in black slacks and a deep mauve shawl. Her brunette curls match mine, but she keeps hers longer and pulled back into a tight, smooth bun at the nape of her neck. Her designer purse is slung over her elbow.

My father is in a button-down white shirt and black pants, with a striped tie. They both look nice, and my heart aches. I miss the relationship I could have had with them. Not because of distance, but in a way, I wish they were different. I wish they cared more. Maybe their first grandchild will change things.

"Hi," I say.

They both turn. My mother gives my outfit a look, and my stomach sinks. I immediately regret my choice. I thought it was nice, but maybe it's not nice enough.

"Lydia," my father says, opening his arms for a quick side hug. I breathe in the familiar, clean scent of his cologne, and it triggers memories of my childhood. Of the same one-armed hug he'd give after coming home from travel.

"Hey, Dad."

I hug my mother, who's as tense as always. The softness she had when I was a young child had faded away when I entered high school. It seemed like she thought I was old enough to fend for myself. As soon as I got my driver's license, my parents stopped showing up for my competitions since I could get there myself. I'd come home from events, and they'd ask if I made the podium, disappointed when I came in less than first, despite my best efforts. Most nights, I would have to make my own meals, eating alone at the dining room table while my dad was at work and my mom was out with her country club friends.

The hostess leads us to the table. When we sit, she pours water and leaves us with menus. I quickly decide what I'm having, and my parents peruse the menu in silence. Some might find it awkward, but my parents have never been the type of people to fill the silence with meaningless small talk. Our waitress returns, and we order.

"Fletcher should be here soon," I state. "I ordered for him."

"I didn't realize he'd be joining us," Dad says.

"Yeah, he thought he'd say hi. It's been a while."

Mom hums under her breath.

"He's had a good season so far." Dad's voice changes to a more curious tone. He's always willing to talk about Fletcher's stats. He doesn't watch the games, but he keeps up with the analytical side of his career.

"Yeah, they had a great game yesterday. I wish you guys could have come."

Mom sighs, sipping on her lemon water. "You know we don't like crowds."

The little girl in me is still yearning for their approval, for their attention.

"I know, but I would have liked to spend time with you."

"We're spending time with you now," Dad says, a hint of irritation seeping through.

"Right." I smile half-heartedly, taking a sip of my water. "So, Spain?"

My mother grins widely, starting on a tangent about all the things they are going to be doing while on vacation. It sounds like it's going to be an incredible trip, and I'm excited for them, but at the same time, I'm jealous. We never went on trips when I was a kid, even though my dad got discounted or free airline tickets through work, and as a pilot, he made a lot of money.

When the food arrives, Fletcher still isn't here, and I get nervous that he isn't going to make it. I check my phone again, and there's still nothing. What kind of team meeting goes on this long? Usually, when things run late, it's never more than thirty minutes.

I take a few bites of my food, but it's sitting in my stomach like a rock. I don't want to do this without Fletcher here to support me.

It doesn't matter. I think I have to.

I clear my throat. "I have news."

My mom lights up. "Did you get a promotion? A new job?"

I shake my head. "No, um—"

"You know you should really find a different job," Dad says. "You could be doing so much more."

"It's not work-related," I blurt. "I'm pregnant."

My parents are stunned silent for a long moment. The blood drains from my father's face as he stares at me.

"You're pregnant?" he finally says through gritted teeth.

I nod slowly, giving them another moment to take it in.

"You're having a baby?" Mom gasps. "And who is the father? Lydia Elaine, I cannot believe how careless you are."

"I'm not careless." I look around the room, desperately wishing for Fletcher to appear. I need my rock. "Sometimes things happen that you don't expect. I thought maybe you'd be excited. I mean, it's your first grandchild!" I dig through my purse for the ultrasound photo, ignoring the twinge in my wrist when I twist it just right.

I sit up, holding out the photo for them to see. "It's still early, so I don't know if it's a boy or a girl, but I'm excited."

Neither of my parents takes the photo, staring at it in disbelief.

"You're keeping it?" Dad asks incredulously.

"I mean, yeah. I thought through all my options, but I want to keep it. I'm ready to be a mom." I rest my hands in my lap, clutching the photo of my baby as waves of sadness take over my heart.

My mother scoffs. "No, you aren't."

"I watched you practically be a single mom. Dad was never around. I can do this on my own."

Dad makes an irritated noise, running his hands down his face.

"And Fletcher is the father?" Mom asks, gesturing at the empty seat. "Is that why he was supposed to be here?"

I shake my head rapidly. "No, no. He's not the father. The father and I aren't together. He was someone I saw for a few dates, but he decided not to continue things."

A bustling behind me pulls my attention, and Fletcher drags his hand along my shoulder, flopping into the seat beside me. He's out of breath, his cheeks flushed as he pushes his still-damp hair out of his face. "Sorry, I'm late. How are you, Mr. and Mrs. Ward?"

"Did you know Lydia is pregnant?" Mom asks, her tone sharp.

Fletcher glances over to me, his brows furrowed like he's not sure how I want him to respond. They don't give him a second to try, though.

"She can't do this on her own," Dad snaps. "And the father isn't involved, we're learning."

My frustration bubbles to the surface. I should have known they wouldn't even be happy for a second. They can't be.

"I can and *will* do this on my own," I state.

"She's not doing this on her own," Fletcher responds.

My head whips in his direction, my eyes widening. What is he talking about?

"What, you're going to pretend to be the baby's father? And what will you get out of this, Fletcher?" Mom snarks. "You two are going to play a game of a happy little family?"

"It won't be pretend. If Lydia wants me to step up and be the father, I will, but for now, I will be there for her in any way I can. And what do you two know about happy families anyway?" Fletcher reaches over to where my palm is resting on my thigh, taking it and squeezing hard.

I look up into his familiar gaze, seeing the sincerity there.

For a moment, all I can do is look at him, bask in his support and strength. Something in his eye looks different, but I can't quite place it. There's a determination, sure, but something about this almost reminds me of the moments right before he steps onto the ice. He always appears eerily calm and ready to take on anything the game throws at him.

The waitress appears.

"Can we get some boxes, please?" I ask.

For the second time in a week, I'm leaving a restaurant before fully eating my meal, but I can't stay a minute longer. I don't know what I expected.

My mother lets out an irritated sound. "Oh, you're leaving now?"

"Yes. I won't sit here and be berated by two people who are supposed to love and support me. You know, I thought you would be at least a little excited for me. I'm having a baby—your first grandchild. This is going to be a huge change in my life, so forgive me for wanting my parents to support me, even if it's unexpected and scary. I thought my mom would have some advice for me as I become a mother."

I stand from the table as the waitress brings by some boxes for Fletcher and me. I grab my purse to dig out some cash, but a hand on my wrist stops me. Fletcher pulls his wallet from his pocket, fishing out a hundred-dollar bill and two twenties. He tosses them in the middle of the table with a tilt of his chin.

"Enjoy the rest of your meal," Fletcher says in a tone unlike anything I've ever heard from him. It's a mix of disappointment and contempt, and I never wish to hear it again. "Come on, Lydi."

I give my parents one parting glance, noting that neither of them has moved or made any effort to stop me, or say anything worth my time.

Fletcher holds out his hand, and I lace our fingers together as he pulls me in close, leading me out of the restaurant. The familiar scent of his body wash helps keep me grounded. Instead of wanting to scream and cry, I'm weirdly calm, like a weight has been lifted off my chest. I don't know if I'll ever be good enough for them, but I'm no longer seeking their approval.

Fletcher leads me to his vehicle, opens the passenger door, and ushers me in. I climb in before I realize my car is here.

"I drove here," I say once he's inside. I point to my car a few rows down.

"I know." He exhales heavily. "I figured you maybe needed a few minutes before driving. I know I do."

"I'm alright." I shrug despite the dull ache in my chest. "You know my parents. It was naïve of me to think that they'd be excited for me."

Fletcher's eyes widen. "They should be excited for you. You're going to be an incredible mom, and I'm so excited that I get to be by your side."

My eyes prick. "Thanks, Fletch. They've never been proud of me or excited about anything in my life, so I'm not sure why I thought they would be now. I mean, I'm single, pregnant, and work an entry-level job. How is that accomplished?"

"Stop that." Fletcher rests a hand on my arm. A tear streaks down my cheek, and he swipes it away, his hand lingering. "Your parents aren't good judges of what accomplishment is, clearly. Just because you don't make millions of dollars a year, or aren't a manager at your job, doesn't mean you aren't incredible."

"You're one to talk. You have a three-million-a-year contract. I make forty thousand a year. We are not the same."

He groans, taking his hand away from my cheek to rub up and down his face. "Again, not the point. You don't have to be rich to be amazing. If your parents don't see that, it's their fault."

I nod slowly, taking a deep breath. "Thank you."

"You have me, every step of the way."

"You're going to be the best uncle."

The pull in my chest says the title feels *wrong*. When I found out I was pregnant, it fit, but something has shifted. Fletcher is so much more to me than an uncle to my child, but there isn't an accurate term.

I think back to something he said at the table. Would he really want to be my baby's father if I asked? Why would he want that? We aren't together. It wouldn't make sense, yet something inside of me yearns for it.

Fletcher winces, taking his palm away from my arm. "Uncle Fletcher reporting for duty," he says with a self-deprecating laugh, but there's no familiar joy in his words.

"Fletcher..."

"*No*, actually, I don't want to be the fun uncle. I meant what I said." Heat burns in his green eyes. "I will be this baby's father. I love them so much already. I will prove to you that I can step up if you need me to."

Words catch in my throat but don't come out.

I nod, grabbing my to-go box of food and opening the door. "I'll see you at home, okay?"

The urge to stay is strong. Guilt swarms through me. I hurt him, but I don't know what to say. I rest my hand on his muscled forearm.

After a moment, I pull away and step halfway out the door.

"I—never mind." I shake my head.

What was I going to say? I don't know, but I'm being pulled in a million different directions.

Fletcher rests both of his hands on the wheel, his hair falling in his face as he looks down. "See you at home."

I rush to my own car, climb in, and take deep, steadying breaths. Something has shifted in our friendship, and I'm not sure if I'm ready for what comes next.

18

OPERATION RUIN THE FRIENDSHIP

CALVIN

When's our first meeting? I think it's time we get this show on the road, don't you? Fletchy baby won't shut up about Lydia and the baby.

GRACE

I'm free next week, there's no school on Friday

TRIGG

We have morning practice but could do after

FLETCHER

Works for me

Also I have not been complaining!

GRACE

We can meet at my place since it's kinda in the middle

CALVIN

Dude, yes you have. Every day you talk about how much you love her, and can't wait to see her be a mom. If it weren't cute, it'd be gross

TRIGG

I think it's adorable

We all need more love in our lives

GRACE

We'll get you your girl, don't worry Fletcher

19

TEN DATES TO FALL IN LOVE

FLETCHER

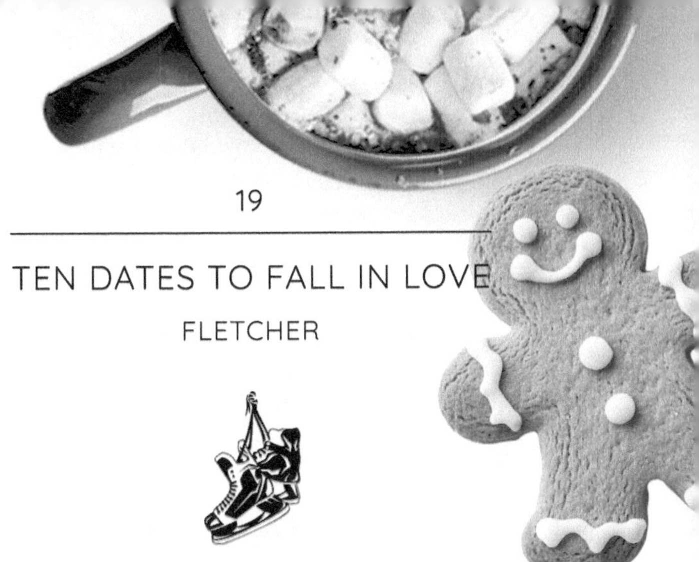

THIRTEEN WEEKS PREGNANT

"Alright." Grace taps her can of pop on the table. "Operation RTF's first meeting has begun."

A few weeks have passed since the meal with Lydia's parents, and things have been awkward. It's like the walls I erected all those years ago have crumbled, and all I can think about is how badly I need her. She's my every waking thought. I can't focus on anything but her.

It doesn't help that we've lost the last three games, and we're about to leave for a two-week away trip tomorrow. Things feel so off-kilter between us that even my regular pre-game call with her hasn't worked. I'm playing like crap, and I can't get my head on straight. Which is why it's so important to make a plan I can start implementing as soon as we get home.

"So, what's the plan?" Calvin sits, holding his seltzer water.

Lydia is at work, and the guys and I are off today, only having a morning practice.

I groan. "Isn't that why we're here? To make a plan?"

"It's been a few weeks, so I dunno. I figured you at least had the bones of a plan."

I glare at Calvin, the irritation seeping through my veins. "No, Miller. I don't. You've seen how off my game I am. Do you think I've been capable of getting a plan together to ruin my friendship and hope my best friend could fall in love with me?"

He shrugs, a shit-eating grin on his face. "You never know."

"Stop it, Cal." Grace hits him on the shoulder. "Lucky for you, I've been thinking."

Trigg interjects. "I have, too."

"You have?" I ask.

Trigg smiles. "Of course. We are a team, yes? I want to help you get your girl."

"Thanks, man."

"What are your ideas?" Grace questions, pulling out a notebook and pen from her bag.

"Have you ever seen the movie *How to Lose a Guy in 10 Days*?" Trigg asks.

"I don't think you understand that movie, Addy." Calvin chuckles and raises an eyebrow.

Trigg shakes his head. "No, but I do. They fall in love at the end, yes? What if instead, you have Ten Dates To Fall In Love?"

"Oh my god, yes. I love that! That's way better than anything I had." Grace jots that down on a blank page, then writes the numbers one through ten down the sheet.

"I do like that," I say as I watch Grace.

"Aadland, you're a bit of a romantic, aren't you?" Calvin teases.

Trigg shrugs. "I watch a lot of movies."

"What dates could you go on?" Grace bites the top of her pen. "What are some of Lydia's favorite activities?"

"Figure skating, baking, crocheting, musicals, hockey—*obviously*—Christmas." I continue listing various things.

"Hmm... What about a Christmas festival? I saw on Facebook that there's one opening up down by Cinder Valley. That could be fun."

"She'd love that. Write that down." I point to the pad of paper, but Grace is already writing.

"What if you took her to one of those baby stores?" Calvin asks. "That could show her you're not just there for her, but for the baby, too."

Grace points her pen at him. "*Yes*. Genius."

We spend the next hour plotting out elaborate date ideas, comparing schedules, and even calling the GM of the Minnesota Blue Herons to see if I can borrow the arena for one evening. Once we have them all listed out and a few days on the calendar, I'm much more confident in this plan.

All that's left to do is ruin the friendship.

20

THE SIZE OF A LEMON

Hey Lydi-bug, did you know that the baby is the size of a lemon right now?

I did. How did you know that?

I downloaded one of those week-by-week apps. It asked me a bunch of questions about my menstrual cycle, which… I don't have one, but I got it figured out when I entered your due date.

Why did you download a pregnancy app?

Curious. Wanted to learn a few things

Um, okay then

Tell the little lemon I say hi

LYDIA

I will

FLETCHER

Miss you, Lydi

LYDIA

Miss you, too

LYDIA

Tough game last night. How's your cheek?

FLETCHER

I've got a nice bruise, but I'll survive.
Thankfully, my good looks are still intact.

LYDIA

FLETCHER

You can admit it, you know. I'm good
looking.

LYDIA

Sure, Fletcher.

FLETCHER

So you agree?

FLETCHER

Pleaasseee tell me you saw that goal
tonight.

LYDIA

Wow, it only took you thirty seconds after you walked off the ice to boast about it. I think that's a new record.

FLETCHER

Thirty five seconds. You have a delay, remember?

LYDIA

How could I forget.

It was a beautiful goal. Sorry you guys couldn't pull the win.

FLETCHER

Oh well. We'll get the next one.

Miss you

FLETCHER

You're going to watch the game tonight, right?

LYDIA

Of course, I always do unless I'm coaching, you know that.

FLETCHER

I'm going to score a goal for you tonight.

LYDIA

For me? Why?

FLETCHER

I'm going to show you that I'm in it to win it. Make sure you're watching.

I'll call you before the game.

21

MORE THAN FRIENDS

LYDIA

FIFTEEN WEEKS PREGNANT

Something has changed with Fletcher since that lunch with my parents. It's been so hard having him out of town for the last two weeks, only available for scattered text conversations and quick calls before games. He was off for the first half of the road trip, but in the second half, it was like he turned into a brand-new player.

Even his messages had a different tone. Dare I say, almost flirtatious? I shake my head. No. I'm overthinking this.

When he gets home, I'm going to talk to him. I can't stop thinking about his offer to be the father to my baby. But that had to have been a spur-of-the-moment thing. I mean, there's no way he was serious.

It's past eleven at night, and I'm sitting on the couch working on my latest crochet project. My wrist is finally feeling better, so I haven't been wearing the brace at all this week. The front door opens, and Fletcher walks in, looking absolutely exhausted. His bag is slung over his shoulder, and he drops it to the floor, kicking off his boots.

"Hey, you," I say.

Fletcher gasps, his eyes growing wide. "What are you doing awake? I thought you'd be asleep."

Some of the familiar puppy dog excitement he gets when he sees me seeps into his face, a grin tugging at his lips.

"I wanted to see you." I shrug. "Missed you."

Fletcher rushes over to the sectional where I'm bundled up on the chaise. He sits, scooting close. He wraps his arms around my shoulders, and his whole body relaxes. I put my project on the side table to my left. Relief floods through me. Maybe things are okay between us, and I'm overreacting. The comfort he brings me sinks in like a warm blanket.

"How are you?" I ask.

"Been better." His jaw visibly ticks. "Rough few weeks."

"Same," I say, hoping this is my opening to talk to him.

Fletcher stiffens. "What happened? Is the baby okay?"

I can't help but laugh. "The baby is fine. But I can't shake this feeling that something is off with us." I gesture between us.

Fletcher nods, looking down.

"I know you mentioned stepping up to be the baby's father, and if you're having regrets, that's fine, we can forget you ever said—"

He slips a hand over my mouth.

"Don't even think about finishing that sentence. I meant what I said, and I'll say it over and over again until you hear me." His tone leaves no room for argument, so I nod. "When I said that, I wasn't saying it because I want to play a part. Not only will I be the baby's dad, but more than that. I want to be your partner. In all of the ways I can be."

My breath catches in my throat. What does he mean? He wants to be my partner?

"My—What?" I can't get a full sentence out.

My brain is whirring, unable to compute the words that came from his lips. Is this a new pregnancy symptom? Hallucinating things? There's no way this is real.

"I want more. Have for a long time. I've been ready to take a step and prove to you that we could be more, that we could be amazing together. I'll be the first to admit I'm scared, but there is nothing I want more."

One look at his face and I know he's telling the truth. There's no way he isn't. I've known this man for a long time, and he's never been one to lie. Well, other than when he tells me he didn't drink the last of the milk, even though he definitely did.

"You—you want more?" I ask in a shaky voice.

"I do. And I know this is a lot, so if you need time to think, I get it." He takes my hand in his, running his thumb over the top of it. His knuckles are bruised and cut open from a fight he got into on the ice last night, and I wrestle with the urge to rush him to the bathroom and clean the wounds.

I don't know what I want. I need time to think. Is he doing this because of the baby, or does he truly want me? Has he felt this shift between us the same way I have? I can't deny I want this, but now that he's handing it to me on a silver platter, I feel like I need to look at this from a logistical end.

"What do you say to a date Tuesday night?" he asks, opening my palm and drawing swirling circles on the skin. "No strings attached, no expectations. Just something I have planned for the two of us."

"You already have a date planned?"

How long has he been planning this?

"Sure do. And I think you're going to love it." A contagious smile crosses his face as he looks up at me.

"What are we doing?"

"You'll see. I'll pick your outfit, so don't stress about that."

"You'll pick my outfit?" I question, raising my brows.

"I have impeccable style, Lydi. Trust me. You're going to love this."

I look at his handsome face and those sage green eyes I love, taking in the grown-out length of his beard. "Are you going to shave?"

He smirks. "Tomorrow ends the no-shave donation challenge we were doing, so yeah."

"Are you going for a clean shave or a mustache this time?"

"Depends." Fletcher winks. "What do you prefer?"

I shrug. "Surprise me."

Easy, carefree moments like this have always been my favorite, but now I'm looking at them through a different lens. Could we be more than friends? Am I ready to take that step?

"Will do." Fletcher wraps his arm around me, pulling me so my head rests on his shoulder.

"Is it weird that I'm still processing this? I'm having a baby. It doesn't feel real."

Fletcher hesitates, biting his lower lip. "It doesn't for me, either. But I know that it's going to be amazing. *You're* going to be amazing."

I squeeze my eyes shut as the world becomes blurry.

"Thanks." My voice wavers. "I don't think I could do this without you."

Fletcher scoffs. "Yes, you could. I don't know how to

take care of babies, so I'll probably hurt more than help, but there's nowhere I would rather be."

The soft press of his lips to the top of my head makes me shiver. It's not something I'm used to, but it feels nice, like a bridge into this new chapter of our friendship. Or maybe something more.

"CAN YOU TELL ME NOW?" I ask for the tenth time since we got into Fletcher's car.

Fletcher laughs under his breath. "No. Like I said before, you'll see when we get there."

He drapes his hand over my thick thigh, only instead of a simple tap like usual, he rests it there, his large palm spread, giving it a gentle squeeze. Those traitorous goose bumps spread down my arms, a regular occurrence now when he touches me.

I must admit, he did a good job picking my outfit. He chose my favorite pastel pink sweater dress and tall boots. The only thing I added was a pair of sheer tights. He even picked a matching hat and my wool peacoat.

As for him, I nearly melted when he stepped out into the living room. He shaved his beard, leaving a nice trim on his cheeks, but above his lip sits a dark mustache. On anyone else, I would hate it, but on him? It's so handsome.

He is wearing a pair of dark brown slacks, a tan turtle-neck sweater, and his tan wool peacoat over it all. He looks like he stepped straight out of a magazine.

Giddiness thrums through my body as we drive outside of the city and into a small town. I've been in this area a few times, but not recently.

Fletcher keeps his hand on my thigh for the remainder of the drive until we reach our destination. When we pull into a parking lot, and the only thing I can see is Christmas lights, my heart skips a beat.

"A Christmas festival?" I wonder aloud, smiling to myself.

I don't get an answer out of Fletcher before he's climbing out of the car and around to my side, opening the door, and holding a hand out to me.

"Ready?" he asks.

I can barely see the hint of redness in his cheeks. Is he nervous?

"Yes," I whisper, taking his hand.

Instead of dropping it when I'm on my own two feet, he laces our fingers together, swinging our arms as we walk toward the entrance.

TWINKLING LIGHTS
& HOT CHOCOLATE

FLETCHER

This was a perfect idea. I'll have to thank Grace tomorrow when I send an update in the Operation Ruin The Friendship group chat. Seeing her eyes light up with the realization of where we were was like a shot of joy straight to my heart. And now, our hands are entwined. I never want to let her go.

I show our tickets at the entrance, and once we are through the gate, it's like stepping into a completely different world. Lights are strung up on trees, with giant ornaments hanging from branches. A photo op is set to our right, complete with a large red sleigh and a Santa performer sitting inside, taking photos with kids and families.

I glance down at Lydia, taking in the look of childlike wonder on her face. Her mouth is slightly agape, her blue eyes brimming with delight. I know this was the right choice.

"Where to?" I gesture to the food trucks to our left. "We could get some snacks and hot cocoa, or we could go through the light trail and get snacks after."

"After," Lydia responds without hesitation, her excitement palpable as she tugs me toward the lights.

"Perfect." I turn us to the right, following a small group.

One of the perks of having a bizarre schedule is that there aren't as many people here on a Tuesday night as there would be on a Friday or Saturday. Lydia works a later morning shift tomorrow, so it worked well that she was willing to be out a little later than normal on a weeknight.

She and I meander down the trail, taking everything in. We don't speak much outside of pointing out a specific ornament or decoration, but there's no need for words right now.

There's a tunnel ahead, illuminating the world in sparkling white light. We stop at the same time, looking up at the display, and I wrap my arm around her waist, pulling her close. She rests her palm on my chest. Her hand is cool through my sweater, and I realize I should have brought her mittens. How could I forget?

"Are you cold?" I ask when a light wind sends a chill down my spine. I look down at her pink cheeks.

Lydia doesn't answer my question as she's so enthralled by the beauty surrounding us.

I only see her.

The lights shimmer all around us, people talk nearby, but my focus resides solely on her. She's enchanted me. The light she brings to my life is something I could never survive without.

"Isn't it beautiful?" she asks as she stares up at the lights, her voice breathy and in awe.

"Yeah." But my gaze never leaves her.

When she breaks away from the lights to look up at me, I nearly drop to my knees to beg her to never leave. If this plan doesn't work, I don't know what I'll do. But with the way she's looking at me, I think I have a shot.

We stare at each other for a long moment, only breaking apart when someone walks by us and nearly trips over a hard chunk of snow on the path.

I clear my throat and kick at some of the snow at my feet. Once the person is gone, we're left in a weird silence.

Chuckling awkwardly, I say the first thing that comes to my mind. "This would be a great place for a first kiss. The lights are so pretty."

I don't mean anything by it, but color me surprised when Lydia perks up on her tiptoes and presses her cold lips to my cheek.

She smirks. "I agree."

I can't stop the smile that breaks out on my lips or the heat flaring in my cheeks as I bend down to kiss her cheek in return. Only she turns slightly, so my lips catch the corner of hers.

I pull away, the heat burning my cheeks even hotter now.

Lydia's breath catches, her pupils dilating, and she touches the corner of her mouth where my lips were.

I'm not ready for our first official kiss yet. I have something special planned for that.

"Are you cold?" I ask again, staring at her fingers caressing her lips.

"No." She shakes her head and drops her hand to her side. "I'm fine."

"Where are your mittens?" I cup my hands around hers and lift them to my lips, blowing hot air into the space.

Our eyes lock. Lydia's breath catches. My heart pounds in my chest, threatening to burst from the perfection that is her. Her eyes widen ever so slightly, brows raising.

After she composes herself, she says, "I think they're in my pocket." She pulls her hands free, digging in her pockets. When she comes up empty, she shrugs. "I must have forgotten them on the coffee table. It's no biggie. I'm not cold."

"The icicles you call fingers beg to differ." I take her cold hands again. In her defense, I also forgot mittens, but I'm always more focused on her. Besides, I practically live on ice. Cold runs through my blood.

I rub our hands together to create friction. "We can't have you cold."

She laughs softly. "I promise, I'm fine. I want to keep exploring, and we can't do that with my hands held captive. I'll put them in my pockets."

"At least give me one of your hands." I let go of both of hers to offer one of mine.

She takes my left hand in her right, tucking her left hand into the pocket of her jacket. I rub my thumb over her skin, using the friction to keep her warm.

Before we continue, I fix her hat so it covers her ears again. "There. Now we can go."

I don't miss the twinkle in her eyes as we turn and continue our journey through the winter wonderland.

Once we've made our way through every trail and light show, we head back to the main area, and I sit Lydia down in front of the bonfire to warm up. No matter how many times she's told me she's not cold, I saw her shiver more than once.

I grab us hot chocolates with whipped cream and some warm chocolate chip cookies. When I sit next to her and pass her the hot cup, she smiles as if I've just given her the world. "This smells amazing."

Her comment reminds me of something I keep forgetting to ask her. "Have you had any weird cravings? I remember when my sister was pregnant, she would eat the weirdest things. Once, her husband caught her eating a pickle covered in chives, sour cream, and mustard. It was gross."

Lydia laughs. "No, nothing outlandish yet."

"But you have had cravings?"

She nods as she takes a sip of the hot chocolate. I wish she'd told me, so I could have provided them. The whipped cream sticks to her top lip, and I don't hold myself back from swiping it off her skin and licking it from my thumb.

Her pupils dilate.

I probably shouldn't have done that.

"Sorry," I mutter with a laugh.

She shakes her head, a soft smile twitching on her lips. "No reason to be sorry."

"What have you been craving?"

"Popcorn. But not just any popcorn. The popcorn from the arena. It's the best. The perfect mix of salty and buttery." Her words drift off into a sigh. "I'm going to have to start coming to every single game so I can get some."

I laugh and take a sip of my hot drink. The chocolate flavor is rich and definitely homemade, and not from a powder. It's amazing. I withhold the groan rising in my chest.

"This might be my next craving, though," Lydia says as she takes another drink. She practically melts. "So good."

"I'll go see if I can get the recipe." I stand, ignoring her protests as I head back to the food truck.

The teen at the register has a brief look of panic on his face as I stride up to him, probably scared that something is wrong with the drink and I'm about to ream him a new one.

"Hey man," I say. "What are the chances I can get the recipe for this hot chocolate?"

His eyes go round as he gets a second look at me. "You're Fletcher Graff," he says with a shaky voice.

"In the flesh." I chuckle.

This may work in my favor.

His name tag reads Dylan.

"You a hockey fan?"

He nods rapidly. "Yeah. I watch every game I can."

"Do you play, Dylan?"

He nods again, eyes growing even wider at my use of his first name. "Yeah. I work here at my grandpa's booth so I can put money toward my gear and stuff."

"Hard worker, love to hear it," I answer wholeheartedly. "What position?"

"Goalie." He grimaces. "My aunt works two jobs so I can play and join the private leagues."

Yeah, no wonder. Being a goalie is expensive as heck.

An idea pops into my mind. "What would you say to a deal? If you give me the hot chocolate recipe, I'll see what I can do to get you a private lesson at the arena with Aadland and me."

The kid is at a complete loss for words, his jaw on the floor until an older man steps up behind him, resting a hand on his shoulder.

"Everything alright here?" he asks.

"Perfect," I respond. "My—uh—"

How do I refer to Lydia? She's my best friend, of course, but things are starting to blur, and I'm not about to reveal that she's pregnant to strangers. Who knows what kind of weird headline might come from that?

"My friend. She really, *really* loves the hot chocolate

here, and I was wondering if I could get the recipe. I offered Dylan a deal."

"A deal?" the old man asks warily.

"It's *Fletcher Graff*, Grandpa." Dylan gestures to me, still in shock. When his grandpa doesn't connect the dots, Dylan groans. "From the Minnesota Blue Herons. The captain!"

His grandpa's eyes widen, and his eyebrows lift, so I offer an awkward wave.

"We'd be happy to give you the recipe. You don't need to do a lesson," he says, waving a hand.

Dylan groans in disdain. "A *private* lesson, Grandpa!"

The older man is already searching for a pad and pen to write down the recipe while I pull out my phone. "Give me your aunt's phone number, and I'll see what I can do, okay?"

The smile reappears on Dylan's face as he pulls his own cell phone from his pocket. We craft a message to send to his aunt, while his grandpa also texts her, so she doesn't think it's a prank. There's something special about Dylan, I can already tell. I want to help him achieve his dreams.

I know that Lydia and I are still testing the waters, but I already think of the baby growing inside of her as mine. The realization that I could someday have a son like Dylan makes my heart clench. I would move heaven and Earth to make my son or daughter's dreams come true, and I can't wait to help with Dylan's.

Five minutes later, I'm walking back to Lydia with another cup of hot chocolate, a recipe, and a heart full of joy.

23

A PACKAGE DEAL

LYDIA

Fletcher takes my hand as we head into our apartment. It was a magical night, complete with everything I could ever want on a first date. It's wild to think that I just went on a first date with *Fletcher*. We've officially shifted into the new territory, and honestly, it felt easy and oh so real.

"I had a great time tonight," I say.

Fletcher drops my hand so I can bend over to unzip my boots and kick them off.

"Me too." He's quiet for a long moment, running his hands through his hair. He glances up at me, those green eyes burning with heat and a hint of trepidation. "Is it too soon to ask if you want to go on a second date?"

I can't stop smiling at the boyish expression on his face. "No, not at all."

"What do you say to next Thursday night?" He steps up close and holds me tight, his thumb rubbing small circles on my back.

I lean into the simple touch. "I'd have to check my calendar."

Fletcher coughs out a laugh, squinting at the fridge. Of course, my insistence on keeping our schedules up to date is coming in handy. "The calendar doesn't have anything on it for you besides work, so I think your schedule is clear."

"Hmm. I think I'll say yes, then."

Fletcher's eyes gleam, and he gives me an even more endearing smile. "Great. I'll add it to the calendar."

"Can't wait."

He pulls me in for another hug and kisses the top of my head. I rest my cheek against his chest, listening to his heart thump rapidly.

"When's your next baby appointment?" he asks, surprising me.

"Not for a few weeks." My first real appointment was a few weeks ago, and I go once a month for now until later in my pregnancy.

"Would you..." He clears his throat. "Could I maybe come to the next one?"

I pull back so I can look into his eyes. "You'd want to come?"

He nods slowly. "Only if you want me there. I'm all in, Lydia. And I know you're a package deal with the baby, so I'll do whatever you need to show you that."

He has such a kind and genuine heart, I know I could trust him with it. If I let myself, I could easily fall for him. He'd be right there to catch me, and my baby, too.

"Yeah. I want you there. We may have to rearrange our schedules, but we can make it work." I rest my hand over his pounding heart and follow my gut, standing on my tiptoes to kiss his cheek for the second time tonight.

The warmth of his cheek and the stubble from his beard sends a tingle through my body and a swoop through my belly. The moment reminds me of earlier, when I accidentally turned at the right moment, and our lips just barely touched. It was shocking in the best way. I couldn't help but reach up and touch my lips to make sure what I'd felt was real. If the soft half-kiss felt that good and surprised me so much, I have no idea what I'll do when we actually kiss for the first time.

I pull back and brush some of the tousled hair from his face.

"Thank you." Hopefully, the simple words convey how much I feel. I can't stop the yawn that falls from my mouth.

"Alrighty, time for bed, Lydi-bug." He takes my hand, squeezing gently and leading me down the hall to my bedroom.

We stop outside my closed door, and I realize I don't want this night to end. It's been perfect from start to finish. I want more.

I turn and rest my back against the door in the dark hall. When I look up at him, there's a new expression on his face, one I'm unfamiliar with. Fletcher tucks a hair behind my ear and drags his thumb across my cheekbone.

"Good night, Lydia," he says, breathless.

I reach up to rest my palm flat on his chest. "I don't think I'm ready for this night to be over."

The corner of his mouth twitches. "Me neither, but we're going to take this slow."

I want to pout. I'm desperate for his lips on mine, even for a quick kiss.

"Don't give me that look."

"What look?"

Fletcher groans, resting his forehead on mine. "I have a plan."

His breath is hot against my skin, and a shiver wracks through my body as my heart pounds.

"What is your plan?"

"That's for me to know, and for you to find out." Fletcher pulls away for only a moment before pressing his lips to my forehead in a long kiss. "Good night."

He steps backward into his bedroom.

"Good night, Fletcher," I say, even though it's the last thing I want.

I stay here for a moment after he closes his door, then go into my room, sitting down on the edge of my bed to process this night. I knew I would have a great time. It's Fletcher, after all. He knows me better than anyone. But I never expected the immediate shift in our friendship, or the way sparks would fly between us at the slightest contact.

I have to talk to someone about this. Get all my excitement and nerves out. Usually, I'd talk to Fletcher about this type of thing, but for obvious reasons, I can't. I pull my phone out and open the thread with Zoey and Grace. It's late, past ten, but maybe they're still up.

ME

Is anyone awake?

ZOEY

Yep, what's up?

GRACE

Seconded.

I glance at my closed bedroom door. It would be easier to call them, but there is no way Fletcher would have fallen asleep that fast. I groan a little, then start typing.

ME

Fletcher and I went on a date tonight. And not just like a "oh, we're just hanging out as friends" kind of date. No. It was a full-fledged date. I didn't tell you guys before because I wasn't exactly sure how it would go, but oh my god. It was amazing. He took me to a little Christmas festival in a small town, and it was perfect.

I send the message, then continue typing.

ME

He was so sweet. We held hands the whole time, and when he went to kiss my cheek, I turned a little on accident and he caught the corner of my lips with his, and you guys. I've never felt a spark like that before from an accidental kiss. It wasn't even a full kiss! Am I going to die when we actually kiss?

And he didn't kiss me good night because he has a "plan that is for him to know and me to find out." Did I step into an alternate reality? What is happening? Is this my life? HELP.

ZOEY

Yayy! Oh, I was hoping this would happen eventually. You two would be perfect together.

GRACE

I love this!

What are you freaking out about? It sounds like it was an amazing night!

ME

It was! I'm not really freaking out, more so… unsure of what to do with myself. I didn't want the night to end. I wanted more.

ZOEY

I think it's admirable that he wants to take it slow. I think it shows you that he's in it to stay. This isn't a one-night-only thing for him.

GRACE

Agreed.

ME

No, I also agree. He's said that so many times, but I just don't know how to process this. I never expected this sudden rush of feelings for him after one date. Sure, I always found him attractive, but I assumed he was never interested.

GRACE

I love you to death, Lydia. I do.

ME

Okay?

GRACE

But anyone with two eyes can see that Fletcher has been in love with you for a long time. He says I love you all the time.

ZOEY

Yep.

ME

Now you're being ridiculous. He's not in love with me.

GRACE

Okay.

ME

He's not! Maybe he has a really really strong crush, or his feelings are developing fast like mine are, but no. There's no way he's already in love with me. And again, we say I love you all the time, that doesn't mean he's in love with me.

ZOEY

Okay.

GRACE

When's your next date?

ME

Ugh. Fine, change the subject.

GRACE

You're in denial. It's fine. But you'll see.

ME

Next week. Thursday night.

Oh, and he offered to come with me to my next baby appointment.

ZOEY

That's adorable.

GRACE

CUTTEEE. Okay. This is going to be amazing, Lydia, I can already tell.

ME

Whatever you say. I need to get to bed, but we should get coffee this weekend. Are you guys going to a game soon?

GRACE

Not until Christmas break.

ZOEY

Ugh, I wish. Vincent has a ton of work commitments and Christmas parties, so I'm out until the New Year.

GRACE

Ugh. Ditch him.

ME

Agreed.

ZOEY

Can't. But let's plan a coffee date!

ME

I'm crashing. Talk tomorrow!

GRACE

Love you bitches.

ME

Love you!

ZOEY

Love youuuuu

24

SHARE WITH THE CLASS
FLETCHER

"So?" Calvin slaps my back as we skate off the practice rink.

"So, what?" I wipe some of the sweat from my face.

"How'd it go?"

I can't help but smile.

"Oh, I know what that look means," Calvin teases.

"Fuck off, Miller." I shove him.

"Not *that*. Are you ready to admit that you're in love yet?" he asks seriously.

Trigg skates over to us, taking off his helmet and revealing his sweat-drenched, long blonde hair. "Was date one a success?"

Again, I smile. "Yeah. It was."

"Fletchy baby is in loooveee," Calvin croons.

"Aw, look at you with the red cheeks." Trigg takes off his blocker to pinch my cheek.

"Stop that." I swat at his hand. "It went really well. We have a tentative date planned on Thursday next week."

"Come on. We need details!" Calvin groans.

"I'm not sure what kind of details you want. It was

amazing." A memory pops into my mind of Dylan. "Oh, by the way. Addy, do you think I can enlist you to do a private lesson for a kid? I owe him."

Trigg shrugs. "Sure. Sounds fun."

"Wait, what about me?" Calvin pouts.

"You're not a goalie," I say.

"Why do you owe a kid?" Trigg questions, stopping Calvin from speaking further.

I take a deep breath. "On our date, Lydia mentioned that the hot chocolate we were drinking was going to be a new craving for her. So, I went over to the food stand and asked for the recipe. Turns out the boy working, Dylan, is like sixteen and a goalie. He works when he can, and his aunt works two jobs just to afford his gear and everything he needs. His grandpa wanted to give me the recipe for free, but I don't know. I feel like he could use some encouragement."

Trigg nods slowly. "I am happy to help. I like to give lessons."

Calvin sighs. "Of course, he's a goalie. All the cool kids are."

"Yes, they are," Trigg says with a smile. "Text me the details. We will make something work."

"Great." I pat his large, padded shoulder and nod in thanks.

"So, what's next with Lydia?" Calvin asks.

"We are going out next Thursday after she gets off work. It's an afternoon practice day. What date do you think we should do then?"

"Baking date, obviously," Calvin says without hesitation. "Get in the Christmas spirit, man. Make some cookies. It will be perfect timing."

"That's actually perfect." I can't believe I didn't think of that. "I'll have to grab all the supplies when we get home from our away game, but that should work perfectly. I'll have everything ready when she gets home from work."

"Can you make me some krumkake?" Trigg's eyes shine with delight.

"Crumb-what?" Calvin furrows his brows as he stares at Trigg.

"Addy, I don't even know what that is, man," I admit.

"Do you not have it here?" Trigg frowns. "I thought everyone had krumkake."

"I have never heard of it."

"Hmm. I will make some. I will also bring lefse."

"You do that," Calvin says with a chuckle. "I'm always down for a Christmas treat."

"Have you kissed her yet?" Trigg questions, bringing the subject back around.

"Yes and no." I shrug.

"How on earth is that an answer?" Calvin's voice is filled with laughter.

"She kissed me on the cheek, and when I went to kiss her back, I caught the edge of her lips. It wasn't a full kiss, but it also was sort of a kiss."

"And you didn't kiss her good night?"

I shake my head. "No. I have a plan for how I want our first kiss to go."

They stare at me, like they're waiting for me to elaborate.

To no one's surprise, Calvin breaks first. "Would you care to share with the class?"

"Nope," I say, popping the P. "Like I said, I have a plan. I don't want to jinx it, so I'm keeping it to myself for now."

"You're no fun." Calvin taps the top of my skate with his stick.

"This whole thing has awoken the romantic in me, what can I say?"

"I love romance," Trigg says with a dreamy smile.

Calvin kicks at the ice, and I wonder what that might be about, but I don't get a chance to ask as Coach blows his whistle, signaling the end of our brief break.

25

PRACTICE MAKES PERFECT

LYDIA

SIXTEEN WEEKS PREGNANT

"**G**ood!"

My student, Anna, lands perfectly on the outside edge of her blade, gliding backward with her arms outstretched and a wide smile on her face. She's been trying to nail the axel for nearly an hour, and she finally did it.

"That was perfect. Now, do it again, exactly like that."

She nods, a mask of raw determination on her face as she skates around in a circle, gaining speed to perform the jump. When she does it perfectly for a second time, I squeal, clapping my hands.

She skates over to where I'm standing at the bench, and I wrap my arms around her.

"That was amazing! You've got it down."

Anna breathes heavily. "I want to keep practicing."

"Go for it," I say, waving to the ice.

Her determination reminds me of a younger me, before I lost the love I had for competing and learning new skills. As much as I love skating, I reached a point where I didn't love it the way I used to, and I decided to cut ties with competitions and training before I lost the joy the sport brings me. Now, I get to share the love I have for it with kids and teach them new skills, watching them grow into amazing athletes.

When she does it perfectly three more times, I call it for the day.

"Great job. Next week, we'll add another element. But you're doing amazing, Anna."

"Thank you." She hugs me again and steps off the ice to where her mom is waiting.

"How did it go today?" Anna's mom, Kali, asks.

Kali and I used to skate together as kids, throughout high school. We always got along well, encouraging and supporting each other's successes rather than seeing the other as competition.

"Great. She's a fast learner, a lot like you were," I say pointedly. "She's determined and focused. She'll be ready for regionals in no time, if she wants to compete."

"Really?" Anna chimes in, a hopeful expression on her face.

"Absolutely." We talk for a few more minutes about a possible program for her to work toward competing in.

Watching my students gain their skills and grow as skaters is my favorite part of my job. I only coach one to two nights a week, but it's one of the best parts of my week.

When I wave goodbye to Anna and her mom, I head down the hall to the admin hall of the rink, unlocking the door to my office. It's a small room, nothing fancy, but I love the little touches I've added to it. Pictures hang on the wall and sit on my desk of me with my friends, with Fletcher, and even with my parents.

The photo of my parents and me stings a bit, but I

haven't had the heart to take it down. I still have hope they'll come around. I want our relationship to be better, and for my child to have their grandparents, too.

They should be back from Spain by now. I can't help but wonder if maybe they will call me.

I sit at my desk to finish a few things I didn't complete earlier, getting lost in the event graphic I'm making.

At the end of the day, when I'm leaving, my phone rings. For a brief moment, a flicker of hope burns within me, but it's not my mom or dad. It's Dottie. Which, to be honest, might be better.

"Hey! How are you?" I haven't talked to her in a while.

To be honest, I'm not sure if Fletcher has told her about the shift in our relationship, and that we're giving dating a try.

"I'm great. I just wanted to check in and see how you were feeling."

"Pretty good. I'm not nearly as nauseous or tired anymore, which is definitely a perk."

"And how have your appointments gone?"

"Good. I really like my doctor. She's so nice."

"How are you feeling about everything?" Dottie asks cautiously.

"What do you mean?"

Maybe Fletcher has told her?

"Becoming a mom. It's a big life change. When I had our oldest, it was a lot. My mom had died the year before, so I was doing a lot of it on my own. Ron was working, and I was a stay-at-home mom. I also struggled with postpartum depression, so it was, overall, a hard time."

Her words strike me, and a sadness for a young Dottie makes my eyes burn with tears. "I'm so sorry."

"It's in the past. We made it through. Talking about

these things was taboo back then, but you shouldn't be afraid to ask for help. There are people around you who will drop everything for you."

As she speaks, I know exactly what I need. "I've been worried about what happens when the baby is born. I don't know how to take care of a baby. My mom"—I swallow the lump in my throat—"My mom was never the loving type, and I'm scared I'm going to mess up."

"Oh, honey. You *will* mess up. That's just part of being a parent. But you'll learn so much as you go."

"Fletcher told me I can stay in the apartment, so that's helpful, but I can't rely on him for everything. What if he resents me?"

The worry tumbles out of my lips before I can stop it.

"He won't. Never."

"The baby is going to be born in the middle of playoffs. How could he not?" Everything I've been thinking bubbles to the surface. "I don't think I can do this alone."

The line goes quiet before Dottie replies. "Now, you can tell me if I'm overstepping, but would you like me to come spend some time up there once you have the baby?"

A sense of relief washes over my body, bathing me in peace. "Please? I'll check with Fletcher, but I need you. I need all the help I can get. I don't know what I'm doing."

"You check with Fletcher, and I'll stay as long as you need, sweetie."

"Thank you," I breathe, my muscles relaxing.

"Absolutely. Now, tell me about your latest project at work."

I appreciate the change in subject, since I was about three seconds from bursting into tears. I tell her all about the new grant I was approved for today, and she lets me talk her ear off about it for the next thirty minutes while I pick up my food and get home.

We hang up the phone just as Fletcher's game is set to start, since we both will be distracted soon anyway.

At the game, Calvin got into a fight pretty much right away and spent five minutes in the penalty box. Thankfully, the boys were able to keep the other team from scoring on the power play, and Calvin hasn't picked any more fights.

Yet.

26

CHRISTMAS COOKIES
FLETCHER

SEVENTEEN WEEKS PREGNANT

I check the recipe for the third time, making sure I have all the necessary ingredients. Lydia is due home any minute, and I'm ready with our surprise date. Once again, I was purposefully secretive with the plans. Perhaps I'm being a bit too elaborate, but when you're on a mission to get your girl, you do what you have to do.

The front door opens, and in walks Lydia, looking absolutely adorable. Her loose curls frame her face, and she's wearing another cute sweater—this time deep maroon—with black pants. I can't help but notice how the color brings out the brightness in her eyes.

"Hey, Lydi-bug." I stride to the entryway and take her bag from her shoulder, placing it on the bench. "How was your day?"

"Great." Her cheeks are flushed, and there's excitement in her eyes.

"Yeah?"

"Yeah. We got more funding approved today, so we're going to set up another free skate camp for kids."

"Awesome!" I pull her in for a hug, holding her tightly and smoothing my hands up and down her back. "Proud of you."

"I didn't do anything," she responds quickly.

"Yes, you did. You've been working hard. The events are a success because of you, so your hard work makes a difference."

"Thank you." Her voice cracks a little.

"Now go change. I have a fun date planned for us." I spin her and lead her down the hall, blocking her view of the kitchen.

"Do I get a hint?"

"Nope. Wear something you won't mind getting dirty, though."

She quirks an eyebrow.

"Go." I push her playfully toward her room. Once she enters her doorway, I spin and head back to the kitchen, doing another look over.

A moment later, Lydia calls from her room. "Hey, what is your schedule like next week?"

"Um, I'm not sure. Why?"

"The doctor's office called today to schedule my anatomy scan. I told them I'd call them back once I had a better idea of what might work." Her voice grows louder, and her footsteps carry her down the hall into the kitchen.

In the few minutes she was gone, she changed into a baggy T-shirt and leggings, and she pulled her hair back into a clip. This just might be my favorite version of Lydia. Casual and comfortable.

"What days are they thinking? I can look at my calendar."

Lydia rattles off a few days and times they offered her. Thankfully, we find one that works on a Thursday afternoon. I'll have to leave right after the appointment to get on a plane to Nashville, but I'll be able to go, and that's the important part. After the game in Nashville, we'll come home for Christmas. I already have a few things planned for that.

She sets a reminder on her phone to call the office in the morning, then turns to the kitchen.

"Oh, my god." Her voice is filled with awe. "What is all of this?"

"Christmas cookie baking and decorating!" I chirp, holding out my arms to showcase all the ingredients on the counter.

"This is amazing." Her lips curve into a smile, and she covers her mouth; her eyes grow glassy. The smile drops, and a tear streams down her cheeks before I know what's happening.

"Hey, what's wrong?" I reach for her, rubbing her shoulders and tilting her chin to look at me. I run my thumb over the apple of her cheek, hoping to soothe her. "We don't have to do this. We can do something else."

"No, no," she blubbers. "It's perfect. I've cried three times today. My emotions are all over the place. This is just *so sweet*. I didn't expect it."

I swipe the tears from under her eyes before they have a chance to hit her cheekbones. "You're adorable."

"I am not."

"Yes, you are. Also, you're glowing this week." I gesture to her. "That's a thing during pregnancy, right? Gorgeous."

She is. Maybe I'm biased, but there's a literal glow emanating from her.

"Now, do you want to make some cookies?" I ask.

Lydia sniffles, giving me a gracious smile. Her voice is watery as she whispers, "Yes."

"Perfect." I grab the paper recipe I got from my mom, and together, we make the sugar cookies. It's a quick process, and soon, the dough is in the fridge to cool for a bit before we cut and bake them. I even got Christmas cookie cutters for this occasion.

We clean up the mess we made, but the entire time, we talk about everything and nothing, all while I keep stealing longing glances at her. Her curvy hips sway to the Christmas music playing softly in the background. I have to fight to keep my cool when her ass brushes against my groin as she moves to put a cookie sheet in the oven. When she gets a dusting of flour on her cheek, I use my thumb to wipe it off, but I let my touch linger as my thumb drags down her face. Her plump lips taunt me. God, how I can't wait to feel them on mine.

We're still us, but with a new layer to it.

"Have you heard from your parents recently?" I ask Lydia as we roll out the dough.

She shakes her head, and I pick up on a hint of sadness in her expression.

"No." Her voice grows sad. "I should have known they wouldn't be happy for me."

My hands are full of dough, so I can't reach out and offer her the comfort I want. "I'm sorry, Lydia. I shouldn't have brought it up."

She shrugs. "It is what it is. I've been talking with your mom a lot the last few days, and that's helped. She's going to drive up for the baby shower, whenever that will be. Grace and Zoey are planning one. She wanted to plan one, but I told her not to worry about it, since it would be hard to plan from a few states away."

If I know my mom, and I do, she'll do whatever she can to make this special for Lydia. She loves her like one of her own.

"Yeah, that makes sense. I'm sure she would love to help however she can, though. You should pass her number on to Zoey and Grace."

"Oh, don't worry, I already did," Lydia says with a soft laugh. She presses a tree-shaped cut into the dough. "Speaking of your mom..."

I wait for Lydia to say more, but it takes her a moment to build up the courage.

"I was wondering if you would be okay with her coming to stay for a few weeks after the baby is born. You'll hopefully be in the middle of playoffs, and I don't have anyone else besides you to help me. It's not like my mom would be willing to help. I think it might be nice to have another person here, and it would be helpful when you're out of town."

I hold up a hand to stop her. "Whoa, whoa, slow down. Of course, my mom can stay with you for a few weeks. I'm sure she'd love to."

"Really?" she asks hesitantly as she looks up at me with wide eyes.

"Absolutely. I want you to be comfortable, and if I can't be here, I want you to have someone who can help you. If that's my mom, then absolutely." I go to push some loose pieces of hair out of her eyes, but I think twice, silently cursing my messy hands. Maybe I didn't think this through enough.

"Thank you. It's starting to sort of become real now," Lydia says with a soft smile. "I passed by a baby store downtown the other day, and it all kinda hit me. I know I'm not really showing yet, but maybe soon it will feel even more real."

Her eyes drop to her slightly rounded stomach, and I want to touch her. To cradle her soft belly and the little ladybug that's growing inside her. The baby I already love as if it's my own.

"I can't wait," I say honestly. I was planning to keep all of our dates a surprise, but I think maybe I'll tell her about one. "What would you say to a baby shopping and registry date?"

Her eyes light up. "Really? You'd want to go with me?"

"Duh. I want to do everything," I reply with a smile as I line the cut-out cookies onto the baking sheet and pop them into the oven.

"That sounds like a fun time."

"Then it's a date. It might have to wait until the new year, though."

"That works."

We finish putting the cookies into the oven and clean up the rest of the baking supplies. After the cookies finish baking, we put them on cooling racks and gather the supplies for the icing. We might have to cut this night short, since it's already nearing eight, and Lydia looks exhausted.

"Do you want to do the decorating another day?" I ask when she lets out a long yawn.

"What?" She gasps. "No! It's not even eight. Besides, when will we get time to finish them? You have a game tomorrow night, and I have an event this weekend. We have to finish tonight!"

"Alright, alright. I just wanted to be sure." I pull her in for a hug, making up for all of the touches I couldn't have earlier when my hands were dirty. We hold each other for a long moment.

"I didn't expect this," Lydia mumbles into my chest.

"Didn't expect what?" My heart pounds heavily as I breathe in her intoxicating perfume.

A shudder runs through her body, and as I run my hands down her arms, I feel the goose bumps spreading across her skin.

"For it to feel like this with you." She leans farther into my touch, nuzzling her nose against my shirt.

I sit with that for a moment, letting myself hold her as long as physically possible. "Is it bad?"

She shakes her head ."No. Not at all. Unexpected, sure, but maybe it was inevitable."

I nod, resting my cheek atop her head. "I think you may be right. It feels good, doesn't it?"

Lydia bobs her head in agreement, tightening her arms around my torso. "Yeah. It really does."

27

PLANS CHANGE

LYDIA

My fingers are covered in sticky red icing, and I can't remember the last time I felt so happy. Well, except maybe the Christmas Festival date.

Fletcher is more of a romantic than I realized. He's been so attentive to me, making sure I have everything I need even when he's out of town. These dates are so thought out. I can't wait to see what's next. All his focus has been on me tonight; I don't think he's looked at his phone once.

"What on earth are you doing?" I ask Fletcher as I look at the catastrophe in front of him.

He's holding a tube of icing to a gingerbread man-shaped cookie. The cookie is covered in blue icing, but all the lines he was trying to draw on it are seeping together, creating a mess.

"I'm trying to make myself." His focus is so intense. His brow is furrowed, his eyes locked on the little cookie.

"Yourself?" I question, before I can finally visualize what he's doing. "Oh my god, you really are trying to make yourself into a cookie."

The gingerbread man is covered in a teal icing, and on

the sleeves is a little "forty-eight" in black, but it's slowly merging into a black dot. Little black skates are on its feet, and Fletcher is trying to draw the Minnesota Blue Herons logo on the front of the jersey.

"You have to wait until it dries before you add more to the top. That's why it looks like that." I point to the blob of black icing.

"I know, but I got too impatient. We can pretend this one is Calvin. I'll make myself into a different cookie."

I laugh loudly. Of course, he'd turn his failed cookie of himself into his other best friend.

Fletcher grabs the red icing and puts some on the cookie's head to make Calvin's hair. "There, it's perfect."

Grabbing my phone from my pocket, not even caring about it getting covered in icing, I open the camera and snap a photo, sending it to Grace and Zoey without context. They'll love it.

Fletcher moves on to the next two cookies, this time doing a better job outlining and waiting until the first layers of icing are dry before adding the details. It's still a bit of a mess, and not perfect by any means, but fifteen minutes later, he's holding the three hockey players side by side. One has dark hair to match his, the other has yellow for Trigg, and the messy one has red for Calvin.

"Take a picture. The guys are going to love this."

I dutifully take a photo and send it to him right away. When he puts down one of the cookies, one of them must still be a little wet, as he gets some of the blue icing all over his pointer finger.

"Oops," he mutters, staring at his finger. "Hmm."

"Oh no, you messed up Trigg's sleeve." I point at the arm.

Fletcher shrugs. "Oh, well."

A devious glint appears in his gaze, and before I know it, he brushes his finger onto the tip of my nose. He doesn't even try to stop the smile on his face as he glances down at his handiwork.

"If this were red, I'd call you Rudolph," Fletcher teases.

"You have to clean it off. I can't walk around forever with a blue nose."

I can see the shift in his gaze as the workings of a plan take over his features. He hums and holds out his still-covered finger, staring at it for a long moment before sucking it into his mouth.

He slowly licks it clean, and my mouth literally waters.

I've never thought that the act of sucking another person's finger was erotic until now, but I would give anything to have his finger in my mouth. My knees wobble, and I clutch the edge of the counter for stability.

Fletcher holds my gaze the whole time, and when he pops his finger out of his mouth, it glistens in the kitchen light.

I can't even stop the harsh exhale from my lungs. "Oh."

Fletcher takes a step toward me, wrapping his large hand around my waist. I try to step backward for some reason, but he stops me, leaning in close.

Is this finally happening? Are we really about to *actually* kiss? My eyelids flutter, but I hold back from closing them fully. I want to see him until the last second.

Fletcher's lips twitch as he leans in more, only instead of kissing me like I so desperately want, he presses his lips to the tip of my nose, where the icing is hardening. He swipes his tongue, cleaning off my nose. He rests his forehead against mine for a moment before completely pulling away.

What. A. Fucking. Tease.

"Fletcher," I whine.

Yes, I'm whining. I'm not above pleading at this point. I don't want to wait any longer to feel his lips on mine. The smirk that crosses his face gives me an idea. Fine. If he wants to play, so can I.

I swipe a dollop of white icing from the bowl. Without thinking too much, I spread it across my lips and stare up at him with a silent dare. He kissed my nose to get rid of the icing, after all. Two can play at this game, Fletcher Graff.

He raises his eyebrows, tilting his head to the side while his shoulders shake in a silent laugh.

This time, he uses his thumb to tilt my head back, and I let my eyes fall shut as he leans in, the voice in my mind chanting *finally*!

There's a graze against my lips, but... it's not right. My eyes open, and Fletcher is dragging his thumb across my lips, cleaning off the icing before popping his thumb into his mouth.

My jaw drops. While yes, he looks sexy licking off the icing again, I'm irritated. What do you mean I laid out a perfect way to get him to kiss me, and he denied me?

"What the fuck?" I groan.

I try to pull back from him completely, but his grip tightens on my waist. Fletcher pulls me close, so I'm pressed against his chest, his lips level with my ear. "You're messing with my plans, Lydia Ward."

My breath hitches. "Plans change," I state coolly.

"Not mine." He nuzzles his stubbled jaw against mine before pulling away, breaking the tension and leaving me waiting, wanting, panting, pussy pulsing.

I want to yell at him. How dare he leave me like this? I should be humiliated, but at the same time, I'm not. I'm *curious*. What does he have planned? Is he really going to work me up like this every time? I don't know if I can handle being worked up this much. I might die from antic-ipation.

"Don't worry. I've got it all figured out." Fletcher gives my hip one last squeeze before breaking contact and turning back to the cookies. "I think we should go on the *Great British Baking Show*, don't you?"

How he can so nonchalantly switch from whatever that was to talking about a baking show surprises the heck out of me. He really is calm, cool, and collected under pressure. I, however, am not.

What I want to do is stomp my foot like a bratty toddler. Instead, I shake out my hands and point to a bell-shaped cookie I decorated beautifully. "This one would win."

Fletcher laughs. "Yeah, it totally would."

As time passes, the heat between my thighs does too. Once everything is cleaned and the cookies are put away in containers, Fletcher holds out his hand.

"I think we had a very successful second date," he muses as I take his palm in mine.

I hum, still a little peeved about the fact that he didn't kiss me.

"Think I can ask you for a third one?" he asks, his voice hesitant.

"Depends. Will you kiss me if I say yes?" I tilt my head in question as I stare at him.

He breaks out into raucous laughter. "Nope. You aren't going to break me. I've got a plan."

"Fine. Yes, you can ask me for a third one, but only if you promise not to fuck me and ghost me after."

His green eyes flare with heat, and his thumb and pointer finger tilt my chin. God, is this what he looks like when he's about to fuck you? My knees tremble, my core bursting into flames with the intensity of his gaze.

Fletcher's voice drops low. "Don't make jokes about him."

"Okay," I mumble, my mouth dry.

The heat slowly fades as Fletcher straightens, the half-smile I love coming back onto his lips.

"Would you like to go on a third date, Lydia?" he asks earnestly.

"Yes, I very much would," I blurt, doing my best to shake off the heated moment.

The smile he gives me makes my panties wet. "Thank you."

He squeezes my hand and walks me down the hall to my bedroom. When we stand outside my bedroom door again, I'm not wishing for a kiss anymore; now, I'm simply waiting for whatever perfect moment he has planned.

"Good night, Lydia." Fletcher lifts my wrist to his lips, kissing my rapidly thrumming pulse point. He drops my wrist, leaving me yearning for more, and pulls me in for a long, tight hug before letting me go and stepping to his own door.

"Good night, Fletcher."

My knees are weak as I go into my room, my stomach swooping, and my mind spiraling. Holy mother of god.

28

OPERATION RUIN THE FRIENDSHIP

FLETCHER

Sends photo of gingerbread men

CALVIN

What the heck are those?

GRACE

Aww did you guys have your baking date tonight?

FLETCHER

Yep. It was great.

CALVIN

WAIT IS THAT SUPPOSED TO BE US?

WHY DOES MY GINGERBREAD MAN LOOK LIKE THAT

TRIGG'S LOOKS LIKE IT COULD BE ON THE COVER OF A BAKING MAGAZINE

I'm hurt

TRIGG

Wow, I look good!

FLETCHER

Sorry, Cal, that was attempt number one

CALVIN

You can't even see my number. It's a blob.

GRACE

I love this so much it's not even funny

But the date went well?

FLETCHER

It was amazing. It's getting harder not to kiss her, though.

TRIGG

Stay strong man.

CALVIN

Kiss her!!!

FLETCHER

No! I have a plan, dude.

CALVIN

Plans change.

FLETCHER

She said that, too. But I need to hold out. It's going to be an amazing first kiss, and I don't want to mess it up.

GRACE

I'm sure whatever you have planned is super romantic.

You're still planning on going to the cabin for New Year's, right?

FLETCHER

Yep, as long as your parents are cool with it.

GRACE

Totally

29

BETTING ON LOVE

FLETCHER

"You've had a lot going on, it seems." There's a hint of humor in my mom's voice.

The last few weeks have been so crazy, but I've been meaning to call her, so I'm excited to talk to her now.

"You could say that. I hear you're coming up to stay here once the baby is born?"

I'm more than fine with her coming to stay. Anything that helps Lydia is fine by me.

"Yes, if that's fine with you?" Something in her voice tells me she'd do it whether I agreed or not.

"Of course. With the potential of playoffs, I might not be around as much as I'd like, and she's going to need someone around. Her mom is..."

"Oh, I know," Mom replies, her tone scathing. "Lydia told me about her, and I just cannot believe it."

"She wants her parents to be happy for her. I understand why, but I hate watching them hurt her time and time again." I run a hand through my hair, still so frustrated over the lunch when she told them she was pregnant. I never liked her parents, but I gave them the benefit of the doubt for years, thinking maybe they'd change. They haven't. If anything, it's gotten worse. "Part of me wants her to cut them off, but I know how badly she wants their approval."

"Can I offer you some advice?" Mom asks tentatively.

"You know I'm always open to advice from you."

And it's true. My mom is often someone I turn to for guidance, though when it came to figuring out how to ask Lydia on a date, I held back. I didn't want her to get too excited.

"She may not know what she wants to do about her parents yet, but she'll need you through it all. You're her rock, and this is a time in her life when she needs you most. Be there for her in any way she needs."

"I will." Now is as good a time as any to tell her about the developments in our relationship. "Are you with Dad?"

"No," she replies, a small chuckle coming through the phone. "He's out in the barn doing some chores, probably trying to wrangle Dave."

"Well, you'll just have to tell him later then."

"Tell him what?"

"Lydia and I—"

I don't get the rest of my sentence out before she squeals. "Oh, finally! I've been waiting years for this, you know. Your dad and I have had a bet going, but he didn't think you'd ever make a move."

"Wait—" I sputter. "You have a *bet*?"

"Absolutely. Anyone with a set of eyes could see how much you love her."

I chuckle. "Well, she's a special person."

"She is. What about the baby?"

"I'm stepping up," I state, not leaving any room for doubt. "I'll do whatever it takes to prove I can be a good partner and father."

"You're a good one. I'm proud of you." Mom's voice wobbles, and I wish I could hug her. She always gives the best hugs.

"I wouldn't be who I am without the people who raised me." The sentiment sinks home because it's so true. My parents taught me to be a good man, and I'm proud to be their son, proud of who I am.

"I love you. I'm so happy for you two."

"Thanks, Mom. I love you, too. It's still pretty new, and it's not even official yet, but I thought you should know."

"Well, I can't wait to see where it goes," she whispers, her voice full of emotion.

"Me too."

30

DOING THINGS BACKWARD

FLETCHER

EIGHTEEN WEEKS PREGNANT

"Alright, are you ready to see your baby?" the tech asks, holding the wand over Lydia's stomach.

I glance down at her with a smile. Her brows are knit together, showing her nerves, but her eyes are round and bright.

"Ready," Lydia replies confidently.

The tech smiles and starts the ultrasound, moving the wand a bit before positioning it to find the baby's heartbeat. When the whooshing sound plays over the monitor, I swear my own heart stops. It's such a beautiful sound. I wish I could bottle this feeling of pure contentment and keep it forever. The baby wiggles on the screen as the tech moves and shows us the baby's brain and other parts of its body.

"And we aren't finding out the sex today, right?" she asks.

Lydia and I shake our heads, and I reply, "No, I'm taking the envelope home with it, though."

"Perfect."

Lydia watches closely as the tech takes her time taking pictures of the baby for the doctor to review, but everything seems fine. Lydia's beauty is incredible. Her eyes are glassy, but the soft look in her expression and the smile gracing her lips are adorable. I secretly take a photo of her, knowing I'll want to remember this moment for so many reasons. Once the ultrasound is done, the tech prints off several pictures for us, and I snap a few photos for my phone, even taking some of Lydia beaming at the strip of photos.

Smiling lazily, I change my background from a photo of Lydia and me from this summer to the photo of her holding the ultrasound photos.

We head upstairs to her appointment, and once the doctor does her exam and confirms the ultrasound looks great, we're on our way home. The envelope with the baby's sex is heavy in my back pocket, but I have to wait until I get home from the trip before I open it. There's no way I can play a game with that knowledge hanging over me and not accidentally tell her when I call her tomorrow before the game.

I got something at the store and made sure to get one for a boy and one for a girl. The rest of my plan will be a surprise to her, one of many. I'm not worried about it.

I have to get over to the airport soon, so instead of taking Lydia out for more shopping, we head back to her work.

"Thanks for coming today," Lydia says when we're a few minutes away.

"I wouldn't have missed it for the world."

"It means a lot to me." She rests her hand on my thigh, and the unexpected contact sends a zing through my body.

I never want to let this feeling go.

"Do you think I should reach out to my parents?" Lydia blurts.

I rest my palm over hers, hesitating. "Do you *want* to reach out to them?"

She sighs heavily. "I'm not sure. After seeing the baby today, I wonder if I should at least send a photo of the ultrasound. It's their grandchild. I don't want to leave any room for them to say I shut them out when it was the other way around."

I want to tell her to reach out, to hope that her parents have changed, but, in all honesty, I'm not sure they have. "I think that's up to you, Lydi-bug. I have no idea what you're going through. Pregnancy is a big journey, so I feel like it's only natural to want the support of your mother."

Lydia nods and says nothing for several moments.

"Hey," I murmur, tilting her chin to look at me. "Whatever you decide to do, I'm here for you. I'll be there no matter what."

There's a quick quiver of her lip before she composes her expression. "Okay. Thank you."

I run my thumb over her cheekbone and give her an affirmative nod when she takes a deep breath and pulls away from me, running her hands over her thighs.

"Can I ask you something?" Lydia questions, her shoulders tense.

I nod warily. "Anything."

"What are we doing here? Are we officially dating?" Her voice is timid, and I want to eliminate the hesitation with a single word.

"Yes. We're together. There is no doubt in my mind that I want this to be long-term, Lydia." I cup her cheek, my large palm practically engulfing her face, but I need this contact with her.

She melts into my touch, and I smooth my thumb back and forth across her skin.

"I thought so, but I wanted to make sure. Can I ask one more thing?"

"Absolutely." I press a kiss to the tip of her nose.

Perhaps we're doing things backward. I mean, we haven't even kissed on the lips yet, but I know where I want this relationship to go, and I'm confident we'll get there.

"I know with your job, it's hard sometimes to keep things private, but can we try to keep our personal lives as private as we can? We don't need to announce to anyone that we're dating or having a baby. I don't want people to be in our business any more than necessary."

Her request is so easy to say yes to, even though I want to tell the world she's mine. I want to have her on my arm, boasting to everyone that she belongs to me, but I want her to be comfortable, and if that means not being in the spotlight the way my life is, I'm more than happy to oblige.

"Yes. Whatever you need, Lydi-bug."

"Thank you," she breathes, her shoulders relaxing. "I mean, we'll still go to your games and everything, but social media is just such a messy place. I don't want to fuel any drama."

"I get it, and I agree." The press can be invasive, and I'll do my best to protect Lydia and our baby from it. I'm only on social media the bare minimum, and the only people I want to know about our relationship and life together already know, so I have no problem with this.

I get out of the car before she can and open the door for her, helping her out. Before she can step away, I'm pulling her into a tight hug.

"I'm going to miss you," I whisper in her ear.

"Same. But it's only two days," Lydia says into my neck. "Two days is nothing."

It feels different. Leaving is so much harder now.

"Two days. Then it's Christmas. Just us."

"Just us."

We've been doing Christmas Day on our own for years now. Since my schedule is all over the place, it's hard for my family to come up or for me to go down there.

The day after Christmas, we'll get together with Calvin and Grace's family for a little Christmas brunch, but the day of is our thing. We exchange presents and stay in our pajamas all day watching Christmas movies and eating our weight in Christmas cookies. Lydia will usually crochet me a hat or some mittens as one of my presents, but she makes them that day.

Lydia's parents have never come to visit, and whenever she asked about celebrating the holiday together, they always said they had other plans or conveniently planned a trip on Christmas.

It's our little tradition, and officially our last year as just the two of us. Next year, there will be a baby to love on. I can't wait.

"Text me when you land," Lydia says as she pulls free from my embrace.

"Always." I kiss her cheek, feeling grateful that in just nine days, I'll be able to kiss her for real.

31

ICE CREAM MAKES EVERYTHING BETTER

LYDIA

My phone rings as I finish writing Fletcher's name on the gift tag. I glance down, expecting it to be one of the girls or Dottie, since we've been talking about baby shower ideas all morning, but my mom's name lights up the screen.

I take a deep breath and debate my options. I could answer it, wish her a Merry Christmas, and listen to her talk for however long about the next trip she's planning, or what drama her friends at the dinner club are getting into lately.

Or I could ignore it, like I told myself a few weeks ago that I should. Part of me is curious to see what she has to say, still yearning for the attention my inner child needs.

I sent my parents the ultrasound photo the other day, giving them a quick update and letting them know all is well with the baby and me, but I haven't heard back. I've been talking Dottie's ear off, texting her with random questions, and basically pretending she's my mom.

Without thinking more, I swipe my thumb across the screen, answering the call.

"Merry Christmas," I say, resting a hand on my not-quite-there baby bump.

"How are you?" Her voice is the familiar cool tone it always is.

"I'm doing well." It's surprising that she asks how I am. I keep speaking so she doesn't try to take over the conversation. "I had my ultrasound the other day. Did you see the photos I sent?"

"I did, yes." Her voice is even, not betraying any sort of emotion—joy or otherwise.

"What do you think?" I cautiously ask.

"It's an ultrasound photo. It's not like I can see what it looks like."

The small amount of hope I had deflates like a balloon. "Right," I murmur, picking at a loose string on the hem of my shirt. Hanging up would end badly, so I change the subject. "What are you and Dad doing for Christmas?"

"Your dad's co-pilot invited us to the dinner club with his wife."

"Oh, that's nice of them," I say, trying to hold back my tears.

"Yes, very nice. Now, are you going to be having a baby shower?"

Her words are such a shock that I nearly choke on air.

Why is she asking about a baby shower when a minute ago she couldn't care less about the ultrasound of her grandchild? I haven't heard from her in months.

"I am," I tentatively say. "My friends and Fletcher's mom are hosting it."

"And you didn't think to include your mother?" she asks, more quietly. "That's just cruel."

"I..." What does she want me to say? "I didn't think you'd be interested in coming."

Mom scoffs. "My daughter is having a baby. I should be the one hosting your baby shower. It would make the most sense to have it at the dinner club, so all the ladies can come."

What is happening? The dinner club? *Hosting?* "What? *No*, Mom—"

She interrupts me. "We will have to plan it for some time before you can no longer fly. When are you due?"

"May twenty-seventh," I say, my mind running on overdrive. "Wait, Mom, no."

She finally stops her rambling.

"I'm having my baby shower here," I state firmly. "I don't want to fly for my baby shower. Besides, if we had it there, none of my friends would be able to come."

"Well, you can't expect me to host it when I'm across the country." The subtle irritation I've heard in her voice anytime something doesn't go her way is slowly appearing. "Mothers typically host their daughter's baby showers if there are no aunts on her mother's side. I can't believe you would take this opportunity away from me. You know I love hosting parties."

I try not to let the guilt take over, but it's there, sinking its claws into my chest and digging deep.

"I already have someone to host it." I press a palm to my forehead. This conversation took a turn, and I am still trying to catch up. "Remember?"

This is the last chance I have for her to try to be a part of my pregnancy, of this part of my life, hits me. I know it's futile, but I want to try anyway.

"I know it would be hard to host it here, but I want you to be a part of this. Will you please come here? I can give you Grace and Zoey's numbers. I'm sure they'd be happy to have you help."

There's a long beat of silence, then a heavy sigh. "Yes. Give me their numbers."

A breath of relief escapes my lungs. "I will. Thank you. I'm excited for you to be a part of this."

Really, I am. I want my mom to be happy for me, to be happy for me, and to be part of my child's life. If this is the first step, I'm ready to take it.

"Yes, well, we'll see," she says hesitantly. "I should go. Send me their numbers so we can coordinate."

"I will, I love you," I say, hoping that she says it back.

"Mmm, yes. You too. Goodbye." She hangs up the phone before I can speak another word.

After the call ends, I'm left feeling conflicted, confused, nervous, and honestly a little steamrolled.

Was I guilted into that? The last five minutes are a blur. I set down my phone, slumping back into the couch. Thankfully, Fletcher will be home soon.

I didn't even get the opportunity to tell my mom we're dating.

A SHAKING on my shoulder pulls me out of a deep sleep.

"Lydi," a familiar voice says.

My eyes flutter open to meet the green ones that take up residence in all my dreams.

"Hey," I mumble, my voice scratchy from sleep.

"I brought you ice cream." Fletcher looks a little anxious for some reason. His brow is furrowed, deep lines marring his forehead.

"What's wrong?" I sit up on the couch.

Must have fallen asleep after the phone call with my

mother. I was a bit overwhelmed, and resting on the couch felt like one of the only options to keep me from going overboard.

"Nothing," he rushes to say. "I didn't want to wake you up. I've heard to never wake a pregnant person, but I didn't want your ice cream to melt."

I quirk my eyebrow, stifling a giggle. "I think the saying is to never wake a sleeping baby, not a pregnant person, but thank you." I scoot back, pulling my blanket over my lap. I hold out my hand, making a grabbing motion with my finger. "Gimme."

Fletcher laughs, then hands me the pint of double brownie chocolate ice cream. He passes me the spoon and sits on the couch next to me.

"Santa came early," I say, gesturing to the ice cream. "Thank you, Santa."

"You're welcome, Mrs. Claus." He laughs again, leaning over and kissing my temple.

I scoop a hearty spoonful out and shovel it into my mouth. When the burst of chocolate lands on my tongue, I groan. "So good. How did you know I needed this?"

"Hunch. Gimme a bite." Fletcher opens his mouth.

I offer him a spoonful of the ice cream. "My mom called me today."

I take another bite, so my mouth is full.

Fletcher doesn't say anything at first, just rubs my shoulder. "What did she say?"

"The whole conversation was a bit of a blur."

I tell him about the call, leaving no details out, and explain that she wanted to take over the baby shower.

"Do you want her at your baby shower? I mean, she hasn't exactly been supportive during your pregnancy this far."

"I do," I say carefully. "I mean, she's my mom."

"That doesn't mean she has to be there," he replies, eyeing me slowly. "She upset you. If you want her there, that's your choice, but I don't want you to get hurt again."

"I know. I'm still a little raw after everything, and the call happened so fast, but I do want her there. I want a relationship with her."

Fletcher pushes my hair from my eyes, wiping a tear I didn't realize had fallen. "Okay, beautiful."

I can tell he wants to say more, maybe to protect me or stand up for me, but he doesn't, and I'm grateful. I may have made the wrong choice, but I can't help hoping she changes for the better. That she asked about the shower gives me faith that the time apart has changed things, and maybe she'll be more excited. She'll want to be a part of this chapter of my life.

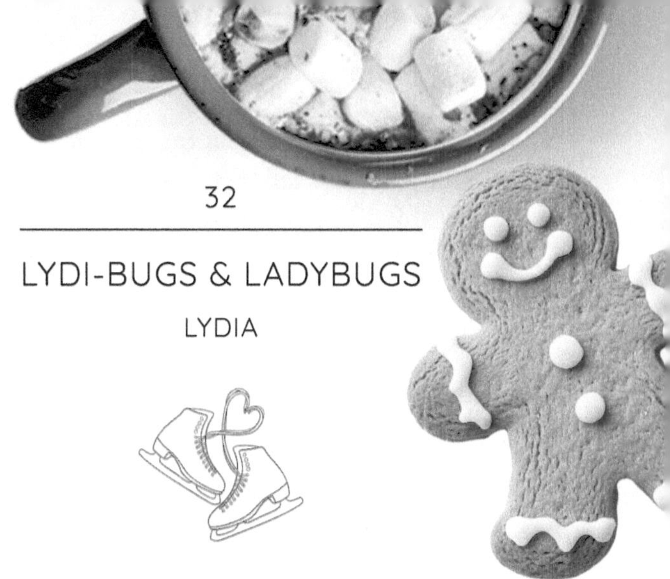

32

LYDI-BUGS & LADYBUGS

LYDIA

"I'm glad we don't have to go anywhere today." I peer out the balcony window at the heavy snow falling. It's absolutely beautiful, like something straight out of a movie.

"Me too." Fletcher comes up behind me and wraps his arms around my waist. "The hot chocolate is almost done."

"I can't believe you got that recipe from them." I chuckle. "I didn't need it that badly."

"Yes, you did. It worked out well. I promise." Fletcher nuzzles his head into my neck, inhaling deeply.

"Whatever you say." I lean into him, breathing in the sharp zing of his body wash. It's so familiar now, so him.

"Sit down and get comfy." Fletcher pulls away, and I miss the heat of his body immediately. "I'll grab the hot chocolate."

I do as he says as he makes his way into the kitchen. The sound of clinking mugs and spoons makes my mouth water in anticipation.

"When do you want to open presents?" I call, tucking a blanket around me. We don't do many presents for each other. This year, there are only three for each of us under the small tree in the corner, but the random seventh present sitting in the middle is calling to me.

I didn't think I cared much about finding out the baby's gender. It truly doesn't matter; I'll love them no matter what, but after Fletcher mentioned it, I can't stop thinking about it. I'm excited. I want to know, now.

"Whenever you want." He strides back into the living room with two mugs of hot chocolate.

He's constantly asking how I'm feeling, doing little things for me, and providing for me in different ways. The other day, I mentioned that my feet were sore after a long day of coaching, and he rubbed them for an hour. He didn't have to do that, but he didn't even question it. He just did it.

He came with me to help me set up my registry, picking out all the things I'll need, but that doesn't even compare to the way he listened to the store associate as she explained the different types of car seats. She helped decide which one would be best, and he made sure to get a second car seat for his vehicle as well. He's been to every doctor's appointment, asking about what to expect in the coming weeks of my pregnancy, and more.

I can't help but think about how our future might look, what our life together might be, and what he'll be like as a father. Surely, he'll be incredible if he's already an amazing partner to me in the short time we've been doing this.

He's always been attractive, of course, but now that we're dating, I've really given myself permission to ogle him.

He's in a pair of low-hanging red-and-green flannel pajama pants, showing his impressive V-line and muscles. He's shirtless, and my eyes roam over his bare chest. His chest hair is trimmed, and his muscles are prominent. The difference between then and now is that before, I found him attractive, but I wasn't turned on by him. Now, he can give me one simple look, wink, or flex his muscles, and I'm a puddle. Seriously, I don't think I've been so turned on in my life, let alone my best friend.

Fletcher winks at me—*because of course he does*—and I promptly let out a squeak.

"Sorry," I mutter, taking the mug from him.

The heat from the ceramic warms my cold hands as I take a sip of the creamy liquid, distracting me from my embarrassment.

"Nothing to be sorry for. You can look anytime you want. I'm yours for the viewing." He sits, sipping his hot chocolate. "As for presents, we can do it anytime."

I nod, trying to hide my eagerness.

"You don't care about any of the presents but one, do you?" Fletcher says, his voice filled with humor.

I groan. "I didn't think I cared, but now, it's all I can think about! Especially knowing that you know. It's killing me."

Fletcher laughs softly and stands from the couch. He sets his mug on the coffee table and strides over to the tree, collecting all the presents. When he picks up the seventh present, my heart pounds.

He arranges the presents on the coffee table and takes my mug, replacing it with the small, square-shaped present. Butterflies swirl in my belly, and I place a hand there. Holy shit, this is really happening.

Fletcher sits beside me, tucking himself under my blanket. He wraps his arm around my shoulder, pulling me in as close as possible. "Go for it."

My heart thumps. Those sage green eyes of his are glassy. Oh god, I'm not ready.

"Open it." He tips his chin at the box.

My fingers find the edge of the paper, and I rip it slowly.

Once the wrapping paper is off, I'm left with a white cardboard box. I stare at it for a long moment, trying to bring myself to open it. It's not that big of a deal, but I'm so nervous and excited that I can't help but pause. Fletcher squeezes my shoulder, kissing my cheek. I take a deep breath and lift the lid.

Inside is a pastel pink onesie. On the front of it is a red and black ladybug with the words Little Lady in a cursive font.

"Oh my god," I blurt, tears of excitement streaming down my cheeks. "It's a girl?"

"It's a girl." Fletcher's voice is tight, and I look over at him to see matching tears running down his cheeks, too.

He pulls me into a tight hug where we're both crying, clinging to each other in the pure happiness of this moment.

When we finally break apart, I swipe at the stray tears from my cheeks. "I'm so excited. I would have been excited either way, but I can't wait to watch you be a girl dad."

Fletcher smiles. "This little ladybug is going to be so loved."

"Ladybug?" I question, glancing back down at the onesie. "Why ladybug?"

"It's what I've been calling her in my head, before I even knew it was a girl. You're my Lydi-bug, and the baby is my ladybug. It made sense, I guess."

I want to kiss him so bad. I don't, though. If he has a plan, I'll let him take the lead. Instead, I throw myself back into his arms for another hug, where I tuck myself into his neck, breathing him in.

He kisses my cheeks, my forehead, the top of my head, anywhere he can, but the one place I know we both want. For now, this is enough. Being in his arms is perfect.

"Thank you," I say into his neck. "I'm so glad we found out like this."

"Me too. It was hard to keep it from you, but it was so special to be the first one to know."

"I can't imagine it any other way."

FLETCHER BRINGS me another cup of hot chocolate a few hours later, once all of our presents are unwrapped and we're snuggled up on the couch watching *Elf*.

"Do you have New Year's off?" Fletcher asks.

"Yeah. The offices and rinks are all closed."

"Great. Don't make any plans." He brushes a curl off my cheek. "I have a morning practice on New Year's Eve, but I'll pick you up after."

"Where are we going? Or is it another surprise?" I ask, though I get the feeling I already know the answer.

"Another surprise. But it will be fun, I promise."

"I never doubted that." I squeeze his hand. "I always have fun with you."

"Me too."

The sun has set now, leaving us alone in the glow of the Christmas tree. It really has been the perfect day. I never thought something like this—a relationship— would happen between us, but I can't imagine going back. I never even gave myself space to hope for more with him.

I'm determined to give my daughter a better childhood than I had, and Fletcher is willing to step up and be there for me and for her. But he has a busier schedule than even my dad did. He has at least ten years left in his professional career, probably more. That's ten years of a childhood he might be missing out on. Am I willing to put my daughter through what I went through?

No. I know better than letting my thoughts run wild.

Fletcher is a better man than my father ever was. He's more present, more dedicated, and more freely giving with his love. Sure, he might have a demanding career, but I have a feeling he will do whatever it takes to be present for my—*our*—daughter.

It feels weird to reference the baby as *our* daughter, but that's what she is. She's his, too, and I know he will prove to us every day that blood or not, it doesn't matter. Family is who you choose. I think it's at this moment that I fully accept Fletcher is going to be my child's father. He's told me time and time again he's in it for the long haul, but it fully sinks in. It's not just going to be me as her parent.

33

HOCKEY SHRINES AND FROZEN WAFFLES

FLETCHER

The air is expelled from my lungs on a groan as I slam the player from Winnipeg into the boards.

"Fuck you, Graff," the young player spits as we chase after the puck.

I get it before he does, handling it with my stick as I skate out of our zone toward the red line.

"Graff!" Shepherd Wafford calls my name, tapping his stick on the ice twice to signal that he's ready for the pass.

I shoot the puck toward him as he races for the goal.

Calvin calls out to Shepherd and passes the puck to him. He passes it back to me, and I angle my stick just right, shooting the puck straight into the net before the goalie even has a chance to block it. It's a beautiful goal. The horn sounds, and our goal song, "Centuries" by Fall Out Boy, plays.

I skate over to Shepherd, wrapping him in a giant hug with Calvin and Levine.

"Here we go, boys," I shout. "Only one more. We got this."

They shout in agreement, and we skate to the bench,

fist-bumping the rest of the team. My shift is done, so I climb over the bench and sit. I drink my water and shift my gaze up to the stands.

Lydia is in the third row of the lower bowl with Zoey and her fiancé, Vincent, at her side. I wave to the three of them, and Lydia and Zoey wave back excitedly. Lydia has a big bucket of popcorn in her lap, making me smile. I'll have to figure out a way to get popcorn from here at home for her to snack on.

The puck drops, and we win the face-off.

I play three more shifts, and somehow we pull the win when I score again with only two minutes left, bringing us up three-two.

"Way to go, boys!" I say as we storm the ice after the horn blares, our goal song playing once more as the crowd erupts in cheers.

Getting a win is always good for team morale. We have a couple of days off this week with the New Year's holiday, and an optional practice on New Year's Day that I will definitely be opting out of. I've got better plans.

When I check my phone in the locker room, there's a text from Grace in the Ruin The Friendship group chat.

GRACE

You guys are good to go! The heat is on, and I put out some firewood for you, if you want to start a fire!

ME

Thank you! You're the best, Grace

CALVIN

It's my parent's cabin too, y'know.

ME

Thank you, Miller.

CALVIN

You are so welcome.

You better not have sex in my room.

ME

Whatever you say

CALVIN

I'm serious, man. Don't defile it. It's innocent.

GRACE

It's his hockey shrine. He's got trophies from pre-k in there.

TRIGG

I want to see this shrine.

GRACE

We'll get everyone down to the cabin this summer! It's so much fun. Then you can see the bar I work at in the summers!

TRIGG

Sounds fun!

CALVIN

No one is allowed in my room.

I turn to my right to look at Calvin. "Couldn't let Grace take the credit, huh, Miller?"

"I helped." He frowns. "I asked my parents if we could use the cabin."

"Thank you," I tell him sincerely. "I do appreciate everyone's help with this."

He sets a hand on my shoulder. "No problem. Happy to do it."

Calvin, for all his goofing off and antics, really is a great guy and friend.

"Well, when the time comes, and you need help with a girl, I'll be there." I tip my head in gratitude.

A pained look crosses his face as he looks at his feet. "Hah, right."

"What?" I watch him closely.

"Nothing." Calvin shakes his head. He looks like he's about to say something, but he shakes his head again. "Nothing."

If his mood hadn't soured so quickly, maybe I would press the subject more, but I don't.

"Well, the offer stands," I say. "What are you up to tonight?"

A familiar smile crosses his face. "Trigg and I are going out with some of the young kids." He glances across the locker room to where Levine and Wafford are taking their gear off. "Gotta make sure they don't get into too much trouble."

"Have you taken it upon yourself to keep an eye on them?"

As the captain, perhaps this should be my job, but Calvin's always been a great alternate captain.

"Sure have. You've got more important things going on." He shoves my shoulder again. "I've got them."

I let out a sigh. I have been slacking as a captain. I should be better about it, but this thing with Lydia has taken priority over hockey. "I'm sorry, man. I haven't been as present this season."

"Nothing to be sorry about. You're a great captain, and you're going to be a daddy now. This is my own personal side quest."

"You sure?" I ask just to check.

"Positive. Have a fun night, and New Year's. Keep us updated if you need anything." Calvin turns to the rookies. "If you two want a ride, the car leaves in twenty, children."

"Do I have time to eat something?" Shepherd asks.

"Dude, we're going to a bar," Jamie says. "They have food there."

"I want a frozen waffle, though. I put some in the athletic trainer's freezer. She said I could use the toaster in her office if I wanted to."

"Oh my god," I mutter under my breath. "Shepherd, your new nickname is Waffles."

"Fuckin' genius, Fletch." Calvin laughs. "Waffles, you seriously want frozen waffles over bar food?"

"They're protein waffles," he whispers, trying to defend himself.

Now, I can't contain my laughter. "Oh, my god. Go eat your fucking waffles, Waffle."

Calvin shoos him out of the locker room, and I head down the hall to do a quick cool-down workout, my body still tense and worked up after the game.

Twenty minutes later, I'm showered and heading out to meet Lydia. As soon as I open the door, my eyes hunt for her. When I finally find her, I rush to her side, pulling her into a tight hug. Having her in my embrace soothes me. My body relaxes, tension leeching from it from her touch.

"Good game," Lydia whispers in my ear.

"What's wrong?" I pull back, furrowing my brows.

She shakes her head. "Nothing, I'm just exhausted."

"You're sure?"

"I promise. I'm good." Lydia smiles, and I squeeze her to me.

"Let's go home then. You need your rest."

"You don't want to go out with the guys?" Her eyebrows knit together.

"Not tonight. I have someone else I'd rather be with."

A pink flush creeps up her neck and cheeks, and I can't help but cup her warm cheek in my large palm.

"We can pick up dinner on the way home and have a movie night," I say.

Lydia sinks into my chest. "That sounds like exactly what I need. This pregnancy exhaustion is hitting me hard this week."

I lead her down to the parking lot and get her into the car, making sure she's buckled before I get in and pull the car onto the busy street. "You still have New Year's off, right?"

I rest my palm atop her thick thigh, reveling in the warmth of her.

"Yep. Are you going to tell me what we're doing yet?"

"Nope." I smirk, turning and giving her a sly wink. "You'll just have to wait a few more days."

"I'm getting impatient." Lydia tilts her head to look at me.

Taking her hand in mine, I lift it to my lips, pressing a long kiss to the back of her hand and ignoring the way my cock twitches in my pants from such a simple touch. It's getting so hard to resist touching her the way I want to, but I know it will be worth the wait.

"I promise, you're going to love it."

34

PATIENCE IS A VIRTUE

LYDIA

TWENTY WEEKS PREGNANT

My stomach swoops as Fletcher drives us down the long, snow-covered driveway. We got a dusting of snow last night, and it made the hour-long drive out of the Twin Cities look like a winter wonderland.

He didn't tell me what we were doing until this morning, but something about today feels extra special. What he's doing means the world to me. Taking time out of his busy schedule to plan dates—and not only just a date, but elaborate, thoughtful ones—is so special. He's really trying to prove he means what he's saying.

It's so sweet.

"I can't believe I've never been here," I say as we pull up to the cabin. It's nothing fancy, but it looks so homey.

"Same. I told Cal we're going to have to do a long weekend up here this summer, maybe over the Fourth of July."

"That would be so fun! And the baby will be here by

then," I say, automatically placing a hand on my lower stomach.

My soft stomach now has a small bump that isn't too visible to others yet, but I can see it. I can't wait to get bigger and really be able to see my bump in all my clothes, not just when I'm naked and looking for it. You can't even tell in the oversized, comfy sweater I'm wearing today, and you especially can't tell with my jacket over it.

"Holy shit, you're right." Fletcher puts the vehicle in park and shifts to look at me. "We're going to have so much fun."

A scene plays out in my mind before I can stop it. Fletcher, holding a baby girl in a ladybug hat in his arms on the boat. It's a beautiful scene, and I can't wait to have it become a reality.

"Let's go inside." He rounds the car and opens my door, holding his hand for me. "It's a little slippery."

He holds my hand as I get out and doesn't let go, protesting when I try to pull away to grab my bags from the backseat. "I'll grab them in a minute. I want to get you inside, and a fire started first."

I gasp. "There's a fireplace?"

"Yep. Grace got some wood for us, so it's ready to go."

"This is amazing." Stopping in my tracks, I admire the wooded area surrounding us. I pull Fletcher's hand and step onto my tiptoes, wrapping my arms around his neck. "I can't say thank you enough."

The urge to kiss him is strong, but he doesn't make a move, even though I can see in his gaze that he wants to. So, I do the next best thing and press my lips to his cheek. My body lights up with desire at the simple touch. Fletcher's arms tighten around my waist, and he groans, his hips pressing into mine. A hardness presses against my core, and

I nearly groan in delight. My fingers twist in the hair at the nape of his neck. I have a feeling I won't be waiting much longer to have his lips on mine.

"Come on. I need to get you inside before I do something." The words come out sounding tight.

A breathy sigh falls from my lips as he releases me, and I slide back down to flat feet. "What if I want you to do something?"

Fletcher groans again, this time pinching the bridge of his nose. "You're testing my patience."

I laugh. "Haven't I always done that?"

"This is a different type of patience." Fletcher bends to get the key from under a rock, and he not-so-subtly adjusts his pants as he stands.

Oh.

I guess maybe he's right. Heat burns in my core, and I'm not sure how much longer I can take this. The image of a half-naked Fletcher runs through my mind, particularly the trail of hair that directs a path to the thing I want most. His tempting touches have been driving me wild. I want him so bad that images of him between my thighs, his lips glossy with my release as he lifts his head to gaze at me with those intense eyes, have infiltrated my dreams. I've been so horny lately. When I wake up soaking wet after a dream of him, I can't help but get myself off to the thought. I need him.

A shiver runs through my body at the fantasy, and Fletcher looks at me with concern. "Cold?"

I shake my head and hold his eyes, hoping I can convey what's going on in my mind to him with only a look. "Opposite, actually."

"Oh." His voice cracks on the single syllable.

"Mhm."

Fletcher opens the creaking door, taking my hand again

and leading me into the warmth of the cabin. The smile I give him is immediate.

You can tell this place is decorated as a summer house, with wood-paneled walls and log furniture and decor. At the same time, it's perfect for tonight. Small, with an open plan, displaying the kitchen and living room, and a hall to the right where the bedrooms must be. Grace also must have taken the time to decorate for the holiday season for us. A small artificial tree sits in the corner with silver bulbs, just waiting to be plugged in. White string lights are hung from the mantle and the low ceiling. I can't wait to see it lit up tonight.

"I guess Calvin and Grace's parents have had this place since they were kids. Calvin offered to upgrade or update it for them when he was signed, but they all decided to keep this one for its nostalgia."

"I don't blame them." It's like the memories are practically seeping out of the walls. I can't begin to imagine all the fun they've had here.

Fletcher releases my hand to grab some wood by the fireplace. He starts arranging it, grabbing some paper and the lighter from the stand next to it. I sit on the deep green couch, letting my body sink into the plush cushion.

My hips and lower back have ached more as this pregnancy goes on, and my doctor says it's normal but mentioned I could see a chiropractor or something if I need it. I don't think I'm there yet. This pregnancy so far has been a dream; I didn't even have much morning sickness. The only thing that's been getting me is the exhaustion and pregnancy brain.

Fletcher gets the fire started a minute later, and the heat immediately seeps into my bones.

"That feels great," I comment as he stands from the floor.

"I'll go grab our bags, okay?"

He heads outside while I stand from the couch, taking a more thorough look around. There are sliding glass doors on the front wall, with a small deck that has stairs down to the beach. On the lake, there are multiple ice houses, and even a few people out and about.

I bet it's a gorgeous view in the summer. I glance around, taking in photos of Grace and Calvin on the walls, as toddlers and throughout high school, with cheesy grins on their faces. Adam and Zoey are in a bunch of them, too. It's so sweet how close the four of them are.

I head down the hall to the bedrooms. There are four of them, one that's obviously Grace's, with posters of boy bands and other artists on the walls. Calvin's is also pretty obvious. He has a bunch of hockey posters on the walls. There's a room that must be their parents', and one guest room.

When I enter the guest room, my heart pounds.

Fletcher and I have never shared a bed. Anticipation blooms as I realize what this means. I don't want to sleep away from him tonight. Sure, there are plenty of beds but only one guest room. And I'm not about to share a bed with him in Grace's old room with pictures of One Direction staring me down all night.

No way.

I hear Fletcher before I see him. His footsteps carry him down the hall until he finds me staring at the bed in the guest room.

"Hey," he says, setting our bags on the floor. "Are you—"

"Yes."

"You don't even know what I was going to say." He chuckles, taking both of my hands in his cold ones.

"What were you going to say?" I squeeze his hands.

"Are you comfortable sharing a bed?" Fletcher glances toward the bed, his eyes narrowing at the plaid quilt. This night could either be awkward or amazing, but my bet is on amazing.

"Yes. I would rather stay in here than in Grace's One Direction shrine, or Cal's pre-teen hockey room."

"Fair." Fletcher smirks.

There's almost an expectation now that we're here, and what may occur between those sheets starts to sink in.

"Though it may be fun to defile Calvin's room and tease him about it," I say, hoping to break some of the tension.

It works, Fletcher chokes on a laugh, his face turning red.

"He *specifically* asked me not to defile anything," he says.

"All the more reason to defile it." I put one of my hands on his chest, smoothing his shirt and giving me any excuse to touch him. His heart thrums rapidly under my palm, mirroring my own. "Relax."

"I'm relaxed."

His voice is anything but relaxed.

I raise my eyebrows. "Sure, and I'm the Virgin Mary."

That gets a laugh out of him. "I want tonight to be perfect."

"It will be. We're here, together. That's all I need."

"Me too."

35

SPARKS FLY

FLETCHER

"You're cheating!" I say as Lydia moves her piece further on the game board.

"How can you cheat at Chutes and Ladders?" she yells back, her body shaking with laughter.

It's been the perfect day. Shortly after we got here, we bundled up in our snow gear and went for a walk out on the lake, then we came inside and warmed up by the fire. I made a frozen pizza for dinner, and now we are playing board games while we watch the New Year's shows on TV. We are nearing midnight, and with each tick of the clock, my heart pounds harder.

I've probably been putting way too much pressure on our first kiss, but I want it to be perfect. This felt like the way to do it.

"I don't know, but you are." I laugh. "You can't seriously be about to beat me at this."

"Suck it up, buttercup." She points to the turn spinner. "Your turn."

I chuckle under my breath but spin the wheel.

Of course, she wins the game, but I couldn't care less. All I care about is time with her.

"Want to go again?" Lydia asks.

I shake my head. "Nah. I have a few things I want to talk to you about."

"You do?"

I nod, gesturing to the couch. "Come on."

I help her stand, then settle her on the couch, wrapping her in a fluffy blanket. Then, I turn off the few lamps, leaving us in the glow of the string lights, the small Christmas tree, and the fireplace. It's the perfect vibe for tonight.

I take one more look at the clock. Ten minutes till midnight. Perfect. "Be right back."

I head over to the small kitchen, grab the champagne flutes Grace made sure were available, and get the sparkling juice from the fridge. No champagne for us tonight.

I pour two glasses and bring them over to Lydia.

Her face lights up. "Bubbly?"

"Bubbly *juice*." I hand her a flute. "White grape."

"Yum." She takes a small sip and shimmies.

I sit next to her, scooting her close to me and wrapping my arm around her shoulder to hold her as close as possible. With a deep breath, I take one more look at the clock. Eleven fifty-seven.

"I really like you," I say, clearing my throat as my voice catches.

Lydia nuzzles her head into my chest. "I like you, too."

"I probably sound like a broken record at this point, but something about today feels special, and that's why I wanted to bring you here, just us two."

"I'm glad it's just us."

"You're special to me, Lydia Ward. I hope you know I

didn't start pursuing you because you were pregnant. Truth is, I've had feelings for you for a very long time."

Saying that feels like a weight lifted from my shoulders.

Lydia's eyes soften, and she offers me a smile when her cheeks flush. "How long?"

There's a burning in my veins. "Remember the day I asked you to hang out after anatomy lab?"

"Since then?"

I glance down, and her beautiful blue eyes are wide as saucers, tears brimming in them.

"Fletcher..."

"I know. But I valued our friendship, and I always figured our time would come eventually. When I say I didn't do this on a whim, I mean that. I want you to be mine, and I want you and your baby to be a part of my family." I swallow the lump forming in my throat. I just have to get through these next few words, then I can kiss her.

In the low light, her eyes shimmer with tears.

"I wanted to start the New Year as a new chapter in our relationship. A partnership, as well as our friendship."

A smile tugs on the corner of Lydia's lips. "I want that too."

On the screen, the countdown has started, and there are only fifteen seconds until the New Year. I set my glass on the coffee table and take hers, doing the same. I haven't even had a sip.

I adjust myself so I can fully see her, and I hold her face in my hands. "I'm not going to wait or hold myself back from you anymore. Are you ready for that?"

"So ready," she breathes.

In the background, I hear the sounds of midnight, but I don't pay attention. I have more important things to do. Our lips meet in the middle, and fireworks explode inside my chest. All the years of wanting, imagining, never could have prepared me for the first taste of her.

She clutches at my chest, her fingers finding purchase in my shirt, gripping me tightly.

I move gently at first, tugging her bottom lip with my teeth before sliding my tongue into her mouth. She tastes like the bubbly juice I gave her. Somehow, the kiss is already familiar, like we've been doing this forever instead of it being the first time.

Lydia gently sucks on my lip, sending a burst of pleasure through my veins, straight to my cock.

I groan into her mouth.

A loud boom makes us both gasp and break apart.

"Oh my god," Lydia shrieks.

Bright, bursting color seeps through the windows as more explosions occur in rapid succession.

"Fireworks," I say.

We rest our foreheads against each other as we breathe heavily.

"Oh," she whispers, breaking apart for a moment.

I press another soft kiss to her lips.

"Let's watch them." I stand and offer my hand to her, entwining our fingers. We stand in front of the large sliding glass doors, offering a perfect view of the icy lake and the fireworks bursting over it. I grab a blanket and wrap it around Lydia's shoulders before standing behind her, holding her back to my chest. My arms are around her torso, and I rest my head on her shoulder, not even caring that I have to bend uncomfortably.

We watch the fireworks for a few moments before Lydia whispers something.

"Hmm?"

"Thank you," Lydia repeats, resting her head on my chest.

I kiss her cheek, and she turns her head, seeking me out. My fingers move up her body, tracing between her breasts, over her collarbone to her jaw. I turn her head so our lips can meet again.

She drops the blanket in a puddle at our feet, and my hands fall to her waist, gripping her soft curves. Dragging my hands up her side, I kiss her, the earlier, gentle kiss gone, turning into a heated one that will forever live in my mind.

"Lydi—" I breathe, my voice hoarse as I touch her everywhere. My hands skate over her body, her soft stomach, the curve of her breasts, without going too far.

Lydia breaks us apart, breathing heavily. "Touch me, Fletcher."

"Really?" I ask, words not fully computing.

"I need you." She nods furiously, her hands dragging down my chest to finger the hem of my T-shirt.

"Fuck," I groan as she lifts my shirt. I help her take it off, leaving me shirtless and aching to feel her skin on mine.

Lydia traces her dainty fingers over my muscles, leaving goose bumps in their wake.

"I've always wanted to touch you like this," she mumbles absentmindedly, her eyes wide as she traces my skin.

"I'm yours." I hook my thumb under her chin and take her lips again, stepping forward and pressing her up against the door. I hold her face in one hand while the other rests palm flat on the cool glass. She steps back, but her hand never leaves my chest, still drawing delicate circles and patterns on my skin.

"Where else can I touch you?" she whispers against my mouth.

A shiver wracks down my spine. "Wherever you want. Where can I touch you?"

Her eyes blaze. She reaches for my arm that's on the door, pulling it down and sliding it under her chunky knit sweater.

"Can I take this off?" I ask.

She nods.

I kiss her gently, lifting her sweater off. The moonlight glows on her skin, making her appear ethereal. I can't help it, I lean forward, pressing my lips to her shoulders, her neck, while my hands explore her body.

Lydia gasps as I cup her breasts through her thinly padded bra.

"Too much?" I whisper with a chuckle.

She rapidly shakes her head. "They're really sensitive."

"Ah." A wicked grin takes over my face as I duck my head to the breasts in question. Her sharp inhale spurs me on. A glance at her face and she's nodding, allowing me to palm them in my hand, finding her hard nipple through the fabric. I pinch them gently, reveling in the moan that falls from her lips.

"Take it off," she whispers.

Like a good boy, I follow her directions. I slide my finger under the straps, pushing them down and unhooking the clasp.

Once free, she slides the bra down her arms, letting it fall to the floor next to her sweater. A groan slips free from my own mouth this time. She's fucking incredible. Her teardrop-shaped breasts are better than I could have ever imagined, with dusky rose nipples that are practically begging to be marked with my mouth. I squeeze my eyes shut, hoping like hell this isn't a dream.

When I open my eyes, Lydia is pushing down her

leggings and underwear, kicking them aside without a second thought. My dick pulses, and I make quick work of unbuttoning and shoving my pants down. Before I can shuck my boxers off, Lydia surprises me, dropping to her knees.

"I want to do that," she says with a sly grin and a twinkle in her eye.

"Oh fuck."

I'm not sure how long I'm going to last with her mouth on me, but I'm going to try, because this is my biggest fantasy come true. Her hand palms my erection through my boxers, and she leans forward, kissing the hard length through the fabric.

"Lydia—"

But I don't get the next word out, as she takes my boxers off and palms my cock, squeezing and jacking me in slow strokes. I don't even get a moment to process because her lips are around my cock.

My brain malfunctions. No thoughts, pure heat and pleasure. Her mouth is sinful, sucking me deep in her throat as she bobs her head. One of my hands threads into her short hair, tugging softly to get her to slow down. She's going to make me embarrass myself.

"Slow," I breathe, leaning forward and resting my palm on the glass again.

I'm going to have to wash these windows. Otherwise, the Millers will definitely know what happened.

Lydia's eyes give me the saddest pout, but she does as I say.

"There's my girl."

She slows her ministrations, using her hand on the base of my cock to give it a squeeze. I jerk, the sensation zipping the base of my spine. I grip her hair a little harder, pulling her from my length. "You gotta stop, beautiful. I'm going to come, and I am nowhere near ready for that."

"But—"

I cover her mouth with my hand, using the other to pull her back to standing. Face to face again, I drop my hand from her mouth, kissing her again. This all feels so surreal. I take a step back to look at her.

She turns her body slightly as I trace my gaze over her, and as she does, her stomach catches in the moonlight.

"Holy shit, is that..." I rest my palm against the bump.

Lydia's smile softens. "Yeah, it made an appearance this week."

I drop to my knees, cradling her stomach in both hands and pressing a kiss there. "Hi, little ladybug. I love you so much."

Her fingers thread through my hair, and I glance up, my eyes locking with hers.

"I'm so glad we have you." Lydia bends down, kissing me deeply. Her tongue slips between my lips, and the heat that had turned into a sweet moment ramps back up.

My hands glide down her stomach to her thick thighs. I break apart from our kiss, and she straightens. I hold her gaze as I kiss down her stomach, to the outside of her thighs, slowly trailing inward with each kiss.

"Please, Fletch." Lydia gasps.

I chuckle gruffly and press the sweetest of kisses to her pussy.

"Fletcher," she whines.

"Be patient, beautiful girl."

"I can't. I've needed this for weeks. You've been teasing me."

"Oh, have I?" I press my nose to her cunt. "How rude of me."

"So rude," she squeaks, slapping the glass behind her. "I didn't make you wait."

"Mmm, you're right. I suppose I should rectify this." I slide my tongue through her absolutely soaked pussy, drowning in the taste of her. When I find her clit, I moan, circling it with my tongue and sucking gently. She opens her legs wider, and I lift one up and over my shoulder.

"Oh, god," Lydia wails as my fingers glide and press into her. Her fingers tighten around my hair, tugging as I bring her closer to orgasm.

I flick at her clit with my tongue, enjoying the way her pussy tightens around my fingers as I slowly thrust in and out of her. My free hand grips my dick after it twitches, aching to be inside of her, aching to come. I can't do that yet, though.

"Fletcher, I'm—" She gasps, attempting to grip the slippery glass.

A late burst of fireworks explodes into the sky over the lake, bathing our world in shimmers of gold, blue, and red. Lydia screams as her orgasm hits her, her body clenching tight around me, her hips jerking. I don't stop my motions as she squeezes my fingers so tight. I'm dreaming of the moment she comes around my cock.

When she pushes my head away, I slide her leg from my shoulder and fall back onto my ass, breathing heavily. Her slick wetness is coating my lips and chin, and fuck if I'm going to clean myself off. I'll wear her release like a brand.

Lydia drops to her knees and mauls my mouth. She clearly doesn't care about her own cum on my face either.

I break us apart, cupping her cheeks in my hands. "Do you—"

She stops me with another kiss.

"Yes," she whispers. "Please."

NEVER LETTING GO

LYDIA

Fletcher frantically jumps to his feet, running down the hall bare ass naked.

"Where are you going?" I shout through peals of laughter.

"Stay there," he yells from down the hall.

I stand, so I'm at least not kneeling on the hardwood floor, and the need to pee is suddenly all I can think about. I hurry to the bathroom.

"What are you doing?" Fletcher asks.

"Bathroom!"

"Okay, fine. But stay there until I tell you."

"Fine."

I take care of things and wash my hands, staring at myself in the mirror as I take a deep breath. Fletcher just ate me out as literal fireworks shot off behind us. I wasn't sure what the start of the New Year would bring, but I'm not mad about it.

Internally, I squeal. This all feels too good to be true. My pussy is still aching for more, desperate to feel him inside me.

And holy shit, Fletcher is stunning. I mean, I have eyes, but something about seeing him naked for the first time broke my brain. His body is insane. Feeling his skin under mine, the way his muscles flexed and tensed with each movement was wild. Not only that, but he continued to make me feel safe in that familiar way he does. I was able to lose myself in the moment because it was with him. No one else has ever made me feel like this.

After another minute, I hear him say my name.

I stride down the hall, fully embracing my nudity. When I walk back into the small living room, it's transformed. Fluffy blankets are laid out on the floor in front of the fireplace, and the coffee table has been moved into the kitchen. Pillows are piled on the blankets too, and Fletcher stands there, awkwardly holding a pillow over his junk.

"Drop it," I say with a smile.

His own smile grows as he drops the pillow, showing me his still very hard, very impressive length. "Like what you see, beautiful?"

I bite my lip, striding toward him. "You know I do."

His hand grips my hip, and he pulls me into him, crashing our lips together.

"Fuck, you're gorgeous." Fletcher groans as his hands roam all over my body, my hips, my rolls.

"So are you," I say through breathless gasps as we lower to the blanket-covered floor.

"Lydi, you're going to make me blush."

I lie back, resting my head on a pillow.

The air between us changes, no longer playful and teasing but drenched in seriousness. Fletcher settles between my spread thighs, his fingers going to my still-soaked core. "Are you ready for me, beautiful?"

"Please."

He reaches behind one of the pillows, fingers coming out with a square foil packet. I stare at the condom, almost dreading using it.

"Wait."

Fletcher stops in his tracks, leaning away from me.

"I was..." I swallow thickly. "I mean, I can't get pregnant again." I gesture to my bump. "And I was tested at my first appointment. Everything was negative."

Fletcher rocks on his heels and drops the condom onto the floor. "I got tested a few weeks ago."

I sit up. "You were planning on this?"

He shrugs sheepishly. "No. But I hoped."

My heart skips a beat. "Come here, please."

Fletcher leans in close, kissing me deeply, heating my body from the inside out. A horrifying thought snakes its way into my brain. What if he feels the same as Jude? What if I'm not enthusiastic enough, or don't satisfy him the way we've both been craving? This will change us forever. And if our relationship doesn't work, I'll lose him. I wouldn't survive that broken heart. Losing him would break me.

"Look at me, Lydia," Fletcher breathes, his gaze locking with mine. The connection grounds me. "Whatever you're thinking, don't. It's you and me, and I'm never letting you go. I can never go back to the way we were before."

"Please don't break my heart," I whisper, a tear springing to my eye.

"I'll protect it. I'll protect *you*. Both of you." He rests his forehead against mine, and my hands twine around the nape of his neck. Fletcher lays me back down against the soft blankets and pillows.

He reaches between us, guiding his cock to my core and pressing gently. Our eyes lock, those familiar green eyes filled with so much care and tenderness.

Fletcher watches me carefully, and I nod. When he thrusts into me, the moan that falls from my lips is completely involuntary. He's so deep, but my body accepts him like it's second nature. I breathe out his name as he begins to move, pacing himself as he thrusts in and out.

"Fuck. I never thought it would be like this, this good." His head drops into the crook of my neck as he groans.

My legs wrap around his waist, his muscled thighs slapping against mine with each movement, my body aching for him even though it's physically impossible for him to get any closer to me.

I scrape my fingers down his back, holding his hips. "Fuck." I groan when he hits that perfect spot inside.

"Are you okay?" he asks, slowing his pace. "Am I squishing the baby?"

"No," I rush to say, gripping his ass, making sure he doesn't stop. "Don't stop, please."

"Never," he grunts. He gets back to the pace he was at before, kissing me and touching me everywhere, branding me with every touch. Reaching between us, he finds my clit and deftly strokes it, matching the pace of his thrusts. "You still good?"

"Yes, I'm close," I say, my body tightening in anticipation.

"Fuck, Lydia." He whimpers into my neck.

My pussy clenches around him, my orgasm detonating unexpectedly as he rocks into me a few more times, groaning as he fills me with his own climax.

He stays inside me for a few minutes as we catch our breath. I don't have words or even brain power to describe this moment. Lying here, with my best friend hovering over me, still inside me, I feel whole.

We catch our breath together, and when we lock eyes, we both burst into a fit of giddy laughter.

"That was amazing," I say through my giggles.

Fletcher agrees, pressing kisses up and down my cheeks, my jaw, and chest as he pulls out of me, his cum dripping down my thigh. His laughter ceases as he watches the cum slide out of my used pussy. His jaw twitches, his gaze roaming over our combined releases.

"Why is that so hot?" he murmurs. "All I can think about is keeping you full of my cum."

My cunt flutters at the thought of him filling me up with every drop of his release.

"Oh god," I breathe. "Yes."

"You like the thought of me filling you up, baby?" Fletcher tears his gaze from my center to my face.

"So much." I nod.

He drags his fingers through the mess between my legs, circling my clit with the pad of his thumb.

"Fletcher," I gasp, my back arching as my still sensitive clit tingles back to life, sending a burst of unbridled pleasure through my body.

He continues to strum my clit, and my body is thrust into yet another hard and fast orgasm.

As I come back down, Fletcher stands, heading down the hall and starting the water. He brings out a warm, wet washcloth and cleans between my thighs. "As much as I don't want to clean this off, I know it probably wouldn't feel comfortable to sleep in."

I shake my head and sit up. Fletcher helps me to my feet, but instead of letting me walk down the hall toward the bedroom, he sweeps me off my feet into his arms.

I nuzzle my head into his neck, wrapping my arms around him. "Thank you."

The connection between us is stronger than ever. When he sets me back on my feet, I take care of myself in the bathroom and find him waiting for me in bed. I snuggle up to his side, our naked skin pressed against each other. I can't get close enough. He's awoken this burning heat within me, and now that he lit the flame, it will take a lot to extinguish it. I'll never have enough of him.

37

OPERATION RUIN THE FRIENDSHIP

CALVIN

So, how did it go?

FLETCHER

Amazing.

CALVIN

That's it? We need the deets, dude!

GRACE

Ignore him.

We don't need details.

TRIGG

I mean, I would not be opposed to details.

Did you kiss her at midnight?

CALVIN

I think they did more than kiss.

GRACE

Leave him alone!

FLETCHER

Yes, we kissed at Midnight, and yes, it was amazing.

Cal, we knocked one of your trophies off the wall. I'll pay for a replacement.

CALVIN

I SPECIFICALLY ASKED YOU NOT TO DEFILE MY ROOM, GRAFF

Which trophy was it? It better not be my pee-wees one that Adam and I won!

FLETCHER

Chill. I'm joking, we didn't defile your room lol

CALVIN

Good. You and I were going to have words if you did.

TRIGG

I'm proud of you, Graff. You did it

FLETCHER

Thanks, man. It was a good night.

GRACE

When's the next date?

FLETCHER

I'm not sure. I have to look at the list again.

Figure skating at the arena. I have to talk to the GM about that one. If not, I'll talk to her boss, and we can do it at the community rink I bet.

CALVIN

Good plan. I bet they let you use the arena. They trust you. Me on the other hand? Yeah, no way would they trust me to be in the arena alone after hours.

TRIGG

No chance.

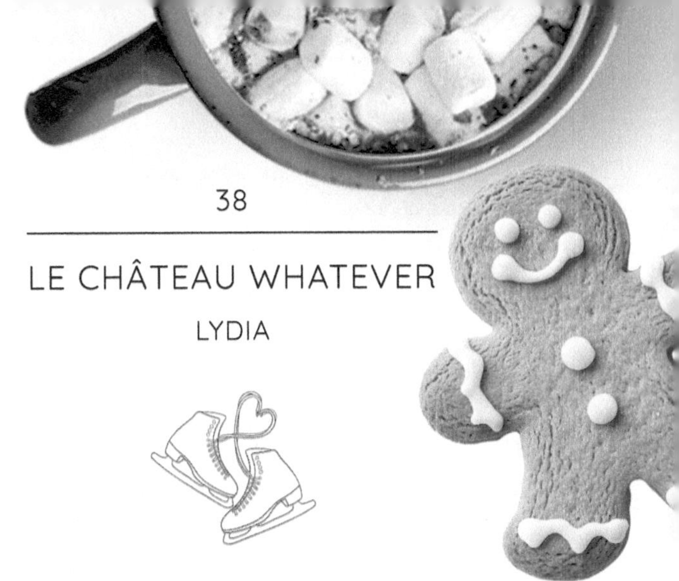

38

LE CHÂTEAU WHATEVER

LYDIA

TWENTY-ONE WEEKS PREGNANT

"**D**o you want to have a theme for the shower?" Grace asks, scribbling in her crinkled notebook.

We're at Grace's small apartment this morning to plan the baby shower. We have a FaceTime meeting with my mom and Dottie soon, but Grace wanted to get a few things decided before we got started.

I shake my head. "Nope. I'm not picky." An idea pops into my head as soon as I finish, though. "Actually, what about ladybugs?"

"Ladybugs?" Zoey questions.

"Yeah," I reply sheepishly. "Fletcher has always called me Lydi-bug for some reason, and when he found out I was pregnant, he started calling the baby ladybug. He told me the baby was a girl with a 'Little Lady' ladybug onesie."

"Oh, that's adorable. We have to do a ladybug theme," Zoey squeals, clapping her hands together.

"Should we start the call?" I glance down at the time on my phone, noticing a text from Fletcher.

FLETCHER

> Have fun today, beautiful. I'll be missing you all day.

> Can't wait to taste you again as soon as possible.

I can't stop the heat creeping up my cheeks, or the goofy smile that appears on my face.

"Oh, I know that look," Grace teases.

I snap my attention back to her. "Sorry."

"Fletcher said something flirty, didn't he?" Zoey slides into the chair beside me, handing me a mug of tea.

"No." I shake my head, hoping I don't look guilty, and I wrap my hands around the warm mug, bringing it to my lips.

"Sure." Grace laughs. "Whatever you say."

"He didn't!"

A third message appears from him.

FLETCHER

> Might have to reenact the dream I had last night. God, it was so hot, and now I'm thinking about

I slam it back onto the table face down, my cheeks burning as I do.

"He totally did," Zoey screeches, squeezing my shoulders. "We are so happy for you."

"Thanks," I mumble, pressing my hands to my cheeks to quell the heat. "It still feels a little surreal, but I'm getting used to it."

"And he's all in? With the baby and everything?"

I nod, my smile growing. "Yeah, he definitely is."

My phone rings, drawing us away from the conversation. I smile when I see Ron's name. "It's Ron. I bet Dottie is having trouble with her phone."

"Hey, Ron," I answer, "Is she having some trouble?"

Ron sighs heavily. "Yep. She wants to do it on the fancy computer Fletcher got us, but we can't get it to work."

"I'll talk her through it." I laugh as he passes the phone to Dottie. I walk her through pulling up FaceTime on her computer, and then I hang up the phone and call her back from my phone.

"We did it!" Dottie cheers as she answers the call, her face lighting up my screen.

I chuckle, and we all say our hellos before I try to add my mom to the call. It's just a minute or so past the time we said we'd call, so she should be ready. The line rings, and she doesn't pick up. I give it another minute, and yet again, no answer.

I press my lips together, trying to hide my disappointment. I should have known she would do this.

"She probably forgot," I say, embarrassment creeping through my veins.

I thought I confirmed with her again this morning, but did I? I can't check my texts since we are using my phone for the call. Grace takes my hand, squeezing. I've talked with both Grace and Zoey in depth about how things have been with my mom lately, so they know what's going on.

"We can fill her in later," Grace says. "No worries."

Zoey starts listing off ideas for venues and dates, possible budget, and more, but I'm not paying attention. Not anymore. Mom wanted to be involved in this, or did I misunderstand? I pick at my fingernails while they chat, offering yeses or nos when needed, and twenty minutes later, they finish up.

I shouldn't let this get to me, but she hurt my feelings. I

want her in my life, but how long can I keep doing this to myself? The anger that's been simmering inside me bubbles up, and I shut down, my frustrations getting the best of me.

We hang up with Dottie, who blows me a kiss and promises to call me later, and I can only offer a nod.

"Sorry," I mutter as the call ends, pushing my hair back behind my ears. "She said she would be ready. I don't know why she didn't pick up."

I reach for my phone, swiping to my messages to the thread with her.

ME

Our call is at ten this morning, we will FaceTime from my phone! Does that still work?

MOM

Yes, that's fine

I scoff and set my phone on the table, pushing it away. "She knew, so either something happened that she suddenly couldn't make it, or... Or I don't even know."

"Moms can suck sometimes." Zoey rubs my back as I try not to cry. "I know you want her there, but even if she doesn't help us plan, we're going to give you an amazing baby shower."

I lean into her side. "Thanks."

"That's what friends are for." Grace wraps her arms around both Zoey and me.

After letting them comfort me for a few moments, I pull away from them. "I know we had plans to get lunch, but would you mind if I take a rain check? I kinda want to try to call my mom, and I think I need a nap."

"Absolutely." Zoey smooths my curls down.

"Thanks." I slowly stand from the chair, resting my

hand on my lower stomach when Baby Girl kicks me softly. My heart clenches. I'm still getting used to feeling her flutter inside me. It's like she's reminding me that she's here, a small comfort amidst my inner turmoil. "I appreciate you guys. I can't wait to plan more."

"Oh no, your part is done," Grace says quickly. "We just needed you here today to get some basic ideas of what you want. The rest is up to us. I'll be in charge of your mom."

"She can be a lot." I grimace.

Grace waves her hand. "And I can handle it. It will all work out. We will confirm the final date and venue with you, but all you have to do now is show up."

"Really?" I breathe, feeling a little better.

"Yep," Zoey confirms. "Now go. Stop and get some popcorn on your way home, then take a warm bath and a nap."

"I love you guys." I hug them before they send me on my way.

Thirty minutes later, I'm strolling through the sliding doors at the grocery store a block from home. I walk through the aisles on a mission to find some popcorn. Obviously, I can't get popcorn from the arena, which is a tragedy, but this will work. It's the only food that sounds good right now. I grab a few different bags, toss them into my basket, then grab a twelve-pack of pop on my way to the register.

While I pay, my phone starts buzzing in my purse. I pull it out, a pool of dread swirling in my stomach when I see my mom's name.

I silence the call before sending her a message.

ME

Can I call you back in five minutes? I'm checking out at the store.

She answers right away.

MOM
Yes.

I shove my phone back into my bag and finish checking out. Once I'm back in my car, I connect my phone to the stereo and call her. She answers on the second ring. I'm not sure what I expected, maybe hurried apologies or a reason for missing the call earlier, but what I got is not that.

"Lydia, wonderful," she says, her voice chipper, as if she didn't miss the meeting.

"Where were you?" I ask, not bothering to hide my frustration.

"Well, I figured I could make better use of my time. I just got off the phone with Mr. Harmon, who is the event coordinator at Le Château Arnaud. He would love to host the baby shower."

"I'm sorry—what?" Again, I'm lost in the direction of this call.

"I was talking it over with your father, and we agreed that since Fletcher is so high profile, it would be best to have the shower as more of a networking event for both of you. Even if he's not the father, your connection to him is huge. Think of the opportunities!"

"We don't need any opportunities. I just want to celebrate my baby with my friends and family. I don't want some big thing."

"No, you need this. What are you going to do after your maternity leave? Go back to that job that's going to get you nowhere?" She scoffs. "No. We're going to get you out there. It's the perfect opportunity. Think of how far his status can carry you!"

Nausea roils in my gut. My palms are clammy as I brace

them on the steering wheel and take a few deep breaths. I haven't even told her Fletcher, and I are dating, or whatever it is we're doing. It feels like way more than dating. "No. We aren't having it at Le Château *Whatever*." I wave my hand in a dismissive motion. "We called you today to discuss venue options, but you didn't answer. We can't afford that venue, even if I wanted to have it there."

"Fletcher can afford it," she says nonchalantly. "I'll get in touch with Grace. She's the one who's planning, right?"

"Yes, but—"

"Perfect! I'll give her a call."

I swallow down all the curse words that want to fly out of my mouth. "I want you to help plan this, really, I do."

"Great, so you agree—"

I'm the one to interrupt her this time. "No, I don't. I want this to be a low-key event where I can wear a sundress and slippers. I don't want it to be at a fancy hotel and use my boyfriend as bait or for networking. We have decided to keep our relationship and family private. I don't want this to turn into a press event. We don't want anything to do with the press." I realize, after the words fall from my mouth, that I've referred to Fletcher as my boyfriend, but I don't have time to take it back or explain it to my mom.

"You make it sound so derogatory—"

"Please. I want you to be involved, but I'm putting my foot down. This is a hard no."

Mom sighs heavily. "Fine. I suppose I can see about canceling the venue."

"Do it. I don't want this to be a whole thing, Mom. I want my mom at my baby shower. But not like this. Please."

"Okay."

"Thank you."

We end the call after another minute of her talking

about nonsensical things, never asking about how the baby or I are doing, only about how her 'friend' got lip filler and it's migrating. Irritation bubbles over by the time we end the call, and angry tears stream down my face.

I drive home, tears never ceasing. When I make it into our apartment, I curl up under my favorite blanket and rip open a bag of popcorn, turning on my comfort movie, the 2003 version of *Peter Pan*.

As the opening plays, I burrow in, shoving handfuls of popcorn into my mouth. It's definitely not good popcorn, at least not compared to the popcorn at the arena, so I push that bag to the side and open the next one.

I'm not sure if it's pregnancy hormones, if I'm being dramatic, or if I'm reacting appropriately, but I'm so frustrated. It hurts that she blatantly missed today's meeting to do something I would never want. It hurts even more knowing she treated Fletcher like a pawn in a game of chess, using his name and status to get ahead.

I take a handful of popcorn from the new bag and throw it into my mouth, chewing and testing the flavor. It's not the same. Frustrated tears fall as I shove the bag aside, moving to the next one, then the last bag, after nothing tastes as good as the popcorn from the arena.

An irritated groan bursts from my lips as the front door opens.

39

THE B WORD

FLETCHER

I fumble for my keys in my pocket, digging them out and unlocking the front door. I adjust the giant bag in my right arm, so it's hidden in my jacket as I open the door. The sight that greets me stops me in my tracks. I nearly drop the popcorn as I break out into a sprint to get over to her side.

Fat tears roll down Lydia's round cheeks as she sits on the couch, huddled under her thick blanket with open bags of popcorn surrounding her. Music blares from the TV, and Lydia flicks her gaze to me for only a moment before throwing her head back with a groan.

"Go away." She wipes her tears.

"No chance of that." I have to push like four bags of popcorn out of the way, but I get closer, sitting beside her and holding her and rubbing her arms. "What's going on?"

Lydia lets out a frustrated groan. "My mom."

"What happened?" I don't want to upset her more, but I can't help unless I know what's going on.

She sniffles, taking a deep breath. "She missed the scheduled call this morning because she decided we need to use my baby shower as a networking event for me. Well, us, I suppose."

"A *networking* event?" I frown. "Why on Earth would we do that?"

"Because my job 'isn't going to get me far,' and I should be using you to 'take my career further.'" Lydia looks over at me, her eyes shining.

My anger at her mother burns. I should be upset that she wants to use me, but right now, I'm only focused on Lydia.

"Then, I was so upset, and all I wanted was popcorn, but none of it is as good as the popcorn they have at the arena. So now I'm crying because of the four bags of popcorn I got, they all taste horrible."

I laugh softly, reaching into my jacket. "Well, I can solve one of your problems right now."

"Oh, really?" Lydia replies with a hint of sass, waving her hands flippantly. I love it when she gets a little feisty. "Pretty sure you can't get the concession stand at the arena to open just to make the pregnant woman in your life a bucket of popcorn."

She pinches the bridge of her nose. "Even I realize how ridiculous I sound. I'm crying over popcorn."

"Beautiful, look at me." I use my other hand to grip her chin between my fingers.

Lydia squeezes her eyes shut for a moment before opening and locking her gaze with mine.

"There's my girl." I kiss the tip of her nose. "I got you something."

Pulling the large—*but definitely not big enough*—bag from under my jacket, I hold it out to Lydia like a present. "Maybe this will make you feel better."

Pure shock breaks out on her face. "How did you get that? Fletcher! Did you break into the arena?"

I laugh, passing her the bag. "No, I didn't. Don't worry about it. But when you run out of this bag, I'll get you more. You only have to ask."

"Really?" More tears well in her eyes.

"Absolutely. That's my job, isn't it? To take care of you and our little ladybug." I reach out, resting my hand over her bump.

I haven't felt the baby kick yet. Hopefully soon. I can't wait.

Lydia's watery grin sends sparks of lightning through my body. My life's purpose is her. She's my reason for breathing, for living. And now, we get to bring a baby girl into the mix, and I couldn't be happier. An image of Lydia teaching a little girl with curly brown hair and bright blue eyes flashes in my head, and it makes me so irrationally happy. I know that I'm doing exactly what I'm meant to do. They're my people, the ones I want to make my family.

"Thank you." She cups my cheek with one hand, kissing me quickly. The popcorn is in her other hand, and when she pulls away from the kiss, I know she's trying her hardest not to rip it open and devour it.

"Dig in, beautiful." I open the bag for her.

To my surprise, she yanks it from my reach, her eyes wide. She lets out a heavy sigh when she sees the smile on my face.

"I thought you were going to take it from me," she admits. "Apparently, I'm a little territorial of my popcorn."

I laugh. "I can tell."

She opens the bag, sniffing in the buttery smell and taking a handful of popcorn, shoving it into her mouth. The instant look of relief on her face is almost comical.

"Good?" I ask, not daring to grab some, even though I desperately want to.

She only nods, scooping more into her mouth.

It's funny to see how instantly she relaxes. I know we still need to discuss things more with her mom because it clearly upset her, and I can't have that, but for now, she needs the comfort. I adjust myself on the couch so I'm comfortable beside her. Lydia scoots in and rests her head on my chest. Right where she should be.

"DO you want to talk about it more?" I ask Lydia a while later, when the popcorn is gone, and the movie is over.

We adjusted a bit during the movie, so I'm lying flat, and she's tucked between me and the couch on her side, her head on my chest, knee hooked up over my legs, almost like I'm her own personal pregnancy pillow.

She nuzzles her head into my chest. "Probably. I'm more hurt than anything. She wanted to be involved in planning the baby shower, practically demanded it. But when the time came, she ditched the meeting to plan something totally outside of any realm I would ever want."

I smooth my hand over her messy curls, twisting one around my finger mindlessly. "What exactly did she plan?"

"She made a reservation at a fancy hotel in downtown Minneapolis called Le Château Arnaud. Told me that since you're so high profile, they'd love to host the shower." Lydia frowns, her eyes growing glassy. "She used you."

I wrap my arm around her, squeezing her gently. "I'm sorry."

She shrugs. "I guess I should have known. She didn't

even congratulate me on our relationship when I dropped the B-word."

"The B-word?" I question, a smirk toying on my lips. "Lydia Ward, did you call me your *boyfriend* to your mom?"

She tucks her head into my chest, surely hiding red cheeks. "To be fair, she already kinda assumed it. At least, I think she did. I'm sorry."

"You don't have anything to be sorry for." I kiss the top of her head, reveling in the familiar scent of her, with a hint of buttered popcorn. "I think it's fair to say that I'm your boyfriend, Lydia."

"Yeah?" she asks, leaning up on her elbow.

"Yeah." My heart pounds wildly at the simple word, one that alters everything.

She cups my cheek and rubs her thumb over my stubbled beard that definitely could use a cleanup. "I really like you, Fletcher. You stepping up and taking care of me means more than you will ever know. I can't lie and say I'm not scared of this, of how big my feelings are, and the potential of losing you, of my baby losing you, but it feels right."

"It does. You mean more to me than anyone in this world. I know this baby will be all the best parts of you, and I already love her more than I can even explain." I rest my hand over my thumping heart. "You've been etched into my heart for a long time. Now, there's a spot that's been carved right next to you, and it's for her."

A single tear falls down her cheek. "Thank you."

Leaning forward, she kisses me, and it's not long before the kiss deepens, our mouths melding as our hands explore.

My hands trail down her body, caressing over her growing bump. I slide my fingers under her top, and she adjusts so she can pull it up and over her head. Her breasts fall free, brushing on my chest as she rests against me, her hips rocking against my hip.

My cock grows impossibly hard in my sweats, and I can already feel a drop of pre-cum leaking from the tip. Lydia kisses her way up my neck to my jaw, then to my mouth, where she captures my lips in a bruising kiss. I love these moments when she takes over.

One of her hands slides down my chest, and I yank my shirt over my head, while her small hand cups my hard length through the fabric of my pants.

"Fuck," I groan.

"I need you," she begs.

I work to get my pants and boxers off quickly. Lydia pulls her leggings off, and we're both naked in a matter of moments. I pull her back to me so she's resting on my chest, her leg hiked up over my hips. Her pussy is hot against my skin as I trail my fingers over her hip.

"You need me, beautiful?" My fingers knead into her skin.

She nods, her head dropping to my chest, while her fingers grip my pec. I move my hand lower, sliding two fingers deep inside her in a smooth thrust. Lydia gasps, her fingernails digging into my skin.

I pump into her, my fingers hooking to find her G-spot as she rocks into my movements, her gasps hot on my chest.

"Fletch—"

I find a spot deep inside her, and she grips me even tighter, and her mouth comes down on my pec, her teeth sinking into my flesh. Not enough to break skin, but enough to send a zing through my body, making my dick twitch against my thigh.

"Holy hell, did you just bite me?" I ask through a

clenched jaw. I'm not upset. If anything, I'm more turned on than ever.

She lets go, her head falling back on a cry as her orgasm rocks through her. My fingers thrust in a steady pace, her wetness completely soaking my hand. When she comes down from the full body climax, she breathes heavily, and I slow my movements, sliding out and using the wetness that remains to cover my cock.

I shift us so we're on our sides, fixing a pillow underneath her head.

"Good?" I question, and she nods.

She adjusts her leg so it's higher on my hip, opening herself up to me. Reaching between us, I grip my length so I can slip inside her.

That first thrust is like pure bliss. Cupping her cheek, I slant my lips over hers, soaking up the now familiar flavor of her. I have so much adoration for this woman. I can't believe this is my life, that I actually have her the way I always dreamed of.

Her tight cunt flutters around me as I pump inside of her. God, she's so perfect.

"Fuck, Lydi," I moan, kissing her again.

I can't stop touching her everywhere with my lips and hands, until finally my hand cups the back of her thigh, lifting it higher to give me deeper access to her.

"You feel so good," Lydia breathes. "Please don't stop."

"I won't. Not until you come again."

I chase my release, my balls tightening as I coast higher and higher, bringing Lydia with me. She clenches her pussy around me, and it sets me off. Her body tightens, brows furrowing as she comes for the second time.

The fluttering of her pussy makes my release shoot from me in waves as I fill her with my cum. When I've emptied every single drop inside of her, I stay still for a moment while we catch our breath, but when I move to pull out, Lydia presses a hand against my chest.

"Wait," she whimpers.

"What is it?"

She shakes her head. "I just want to feel close to you for a little longer."

I nod, pressing gentle kisses all over her cheeks, jaw, neck, down her chest, anywhere I can reach.

We stay like that, with my cock still inside her, for a long time. Having this connection with her is something I didn't realize I needed, but I can't deny it feels amazing.

Lydia's eyes slowly close, until finally, she's fast asleep. I cradle her against my chest, reveling in the closeness.

40

BUNNY HOPS &
FORBIDDEN FANTASIES

CALVIN

Ready for tonight?

ME

More than ready.

GRACE

Do you need anything?

ME

Nope. I triple-checked with Coach and the GM. We're good to go.

GRACE

Awesome. Have fun!

CALVIN

I can't believe they are actually letting you do this

ME

Me either, honestly, but I'm stoked.

TRIGG

Wait, what is this?

GRACE

Skating at the arena!!

TRIGG

Oh yes! So fun.

Wait. Is this the private lesson? Should I be there?

ME

Nope, that's not for a few more weeks, you're good, Trigg. This is a date night for Lydia and me.

TRIGG

Yes. Now I remember. Have fun!

ME

Thanks! I'll let y'all know how it goes.

The front door opens, and Lydia enters, dressed in her work clothes. Her bump is fully on display now, especially when she wears a tight dress or skirt. It's the most beautiful thing I've ever seen.

"Hey, beautiful." I stride over and take her lips in a kiss.

I just got back from a long weekend road trip, so it's been a few days since I've been able to hold her. I sway back and forth with her in my arms, reluctant to let go. It's getting harder to be apart from her, even for a night.

"Hey, you." She squeezes my torso.

"Missed you." I kiss her again. Ever since our first kiss on New Year's a few weeks ago, I take every opportunity to kiss her. Her lips are addicting. "Ready for a date night?"

"Yeah. What should I wear?" She sets down her bag and kicks off her shoes.

"It's all ready for you." I gesture to her room.

Her face pinkens, a deep blush spreading across her round cheeks. God, she's cute. I palm her hip, walking her backward until her back hits the wall, then I plant my elbow above her head and lean in close.

"What are you hiding in there, Lydi?"

"N-nothing."

"Mm. More of those drug store vibrators?"

"I don't know what you mean." She turns away, her gaze darting to the floor.

I run my nose down the side of her cheek. "I just want to know what kind of teammates I'm working with here, not that I need them."

Lydia pushes me away gently and staggers backward, jerking her thumb over her shoulder. "I'll get changed. When are we leaving?"

Flustering her is one of my new favorite activities.

"Whenever you're ready."

Fifteen minutes later, we are heading out of our apartment hand in hand.

"Should I ask where we are going? I'm assuming it has something to do with skating." She gestures to her outfit.

She's dressed in a deep navy frilly skirt that I've seen her wear to skating events a few times, with tights underneath and an athletic long-sleeve top. The tights and top are fleece-lined. Her bump is hidden under the ruffles of her skirt, and I'm a little bummed I can't see it.

"Yes, it has to do with skating," I concede. "I've got all your skating gear in the car."

Lydia lets out a small squeal, and I squeeze her hand. We get into my car, and I start the drive to the arena. Her eyes widen as we pull into the garage and park.

"Fletcher..." she says, her voice full of trepidation. "What are we doing here? Are we breaking and entering?"

Shaking my head, I laugh under my breath. "We aren't breaking and entering. You'll see."

I grab the bag with her skates from the trunk, hauling it over my shoulder and wrapping my free arm around her. I lead her through the arena and into the locker room, where I sit her down on the bench in my locker.

"Alright, let's get those skates on." I bend down to pull her banged-up figure skates from the bag.

"I can do it myself," she says, trying to pull her feet away and reach for her skates.

"Nope." I hold out my hand for her foot, glancing up at her with raised brows. "Gimme."

She groans. "I've been putting my own skates on for over twenty years, Fletch. I can do it on my own."

"Yes, you can. But you don't have to, and besides, I want to."

Once both her skates are on, I take off the light purple blade covers and shove them into the bag, grabbing her hat and mittens, which I help her put on. Then, I get my skates from my locker and put them on.

I stand and take her hand again, leading her out of the locker room and down the tunnel.

"What are you doing?" She asks warily, pulling my hand. "We're going to get into trouble."

"No, we aren't. I got permission. I just have to text them when we're done so they can clean up the ice and turn off the lights."

"We're not about to skate in the arena, right? There's no way."

"Yes, we are." I laugh, taking in the scared look on her face. "It's just ice."

"I know it's just ice." She huffs. "You seriously got permission for this?"

"Yep. You're going to teach me some tricks, Coach."

She scoffs. "You're kidding."

"Nope. Figured it was about time I learn some fancy shit. Maybe it can be my new celly. I'll do a triple axel."

Her mouth drops. "I can't even do a triple axel."

"Really?"

"That's Olympic level, Fletcher."

"I bet I could nail it."

"Whatever you say. I won't be doing any jumps." She gestures at her stomach, and I stop before we step onto the ice.

"Of course, gotta protect the little ladybug. You'll teach me some tricks, though?"

"Sure, we can start with a loop, or a waltz."

"Fancy."

"I'm only doing this if you promise to do one for your next goal celly." She pokes her finger into my chest.

"Pinky promise." I steal her finger, interlocking our pinkies and lifting her hand to my lips.

Lydia inhales sharply, her gaze softening.

After I drop her hand, I open the door to the ice and step on, reveling in the familiar glide as I take my first strides.

Being on the ice feels like home to me. It's the same feeling I get when I have Lydia in my arms. I look around the empty, dark arena that's only lit up with a few of the spotlights above us. Having Lydia here with me feels even better than I could have imagined. With my two worlds colliding into one, a sense of rightness seeps into my bones.

"You coming?" I ask, skating back to the bench and holding out my palm for her.

She takes my hand and glides onto the ice like an angel. I pull her into me, turning us in a small spin.

Her eyes widen as she looks up at the arena. "Wow, so this is what it looks like from your perspective."

"Mhm," I mumble, but again, my eyes are locked on her. I take her hand. "Let me show you my favorite spot on the ice."

We skate until we're in perfect view of the suite she usually sits in when she comes to games, unless she chooses to sit in the lower bowl. Even then, she's in this area, in the third row. I pull her against my chest, wrapping my arms around her, and pointing up to the suite. "Perfect view."

Lydia looks up. "I like it up there, too. I love seeing you on the bench. You're always so focused. It's hot watching you play."

I choke on air and clear my throat. My dick throbs in my pants, and I have to subtly adjust myself before saying, "Ready to teach me some tricks?"

"Absolutely." She giggles, clearly seeing my reaction.

We skate back to center ice, and Lydia explains how to do a loop jump. She's such a good coach. It sounds like another language, the things she's saying, but when she puts it all together, it makes perfect sense.

"I'm not going to do a full demonstration," she says. "I don't trust my center of gravity anymore."

"Yeah, I wasn't really thinking when I came up with this idea."

She shakes her head. "I love this idea, but I'd rather err on the side of caution."

"Same."

She adds a few more notes, showing me with her body how to take off and land, and showing me what to do with my arms. I stand next to her, mirroring each movement, then she sends me out to give it a try.

I can totally nail this, no problem. I'm a professional, and six-year-olds do these tricks all the time. I got this.

I replay her instructions in my mind, skating backward,

gaining speed, ready to propel myself. Holding my arms out, I turn and lift off the ground, only to promptly land on my ass with a loud grunt.

Laughter fills the air as I sit up, finding Lydia clutching her stomach, her phone in her hand.

"Did you record that?" I stand and wipe off my ass.

"Yes," she says through her laughter. "Maybe we should start with a bunny hop instead."

"A bunny hop? I can do a bunny hop. I jump all the time!"

"Show me."

She demonstrates a bunny hop, and I do it, no problem.

"Told you," I grumble. "I'm going to try again."

"Try not to dip your right shoulder and stay straight during takeoff."

I repeat the movements, and this time, I land it, only to look up and see Lydia. I get lost in her beaming smile and proud eyes. Which promptly sends me backward on my ass again.

"What the fuck!" I groan as I stand.

"Practice makes perfect." Lydia leans against the boards.

I do it again, this time paying more attention to my shoulders and posture. When I land, I wobble a bit but hold steady.

"You did it," Lydia shouts. "It was a bit sloppy, but we'll work on it."

For the next hour, I practice until I'm consistently landing them, only falling every once in a while when Lydia distracts me with her smile. Then, I hold out my hand, looping our fingers together as we skate slow laps around the rink. We spend a long time talking, making plans for the future, and I dream of the day we can bring our little girl along with us to an evening like this.

"I think that's probably enough for the day," I say when my body aches in unexpected ways.

Lydia wraps her arms around my neck.

"Thank you," she says, pulling my head down for a long kiss. Her lips and cheeks are cold.

We kiss at center ice, and for a moment, I'm in a dream. My girl in my arms, in my favorite place. I couldn't ask for anything more.

Well, maybe a championship win, but that's not the point right now.

I reluctantly pull away, my heart pounding.

"What are we doing the rest of the night?" Lydia questions with a dazed look in her eyes. A look I now recognize after New Year's.

She wants more, and so do I.

"Whatever you want, beautiful." I take her hand and pull her off the ice, leading us back into the locker room where I shut and lock the door behind me.

Lydia drops down in my spot, bending to unlace her skates.

"I've got them." I rush over, dropping to my knees to do it for her. I pull them off her feet, but don't put her boots back on.

I take my own skates off and hang them on my locker, kneeling back down and resting my hands on her thighs, slowly gliding up and down her tights-covered skin.

"What are you doing?" Lydia asks with a humorous glint in her eyes. She glances around the empty room.

I shrug, letting a smirk cross my lips. "I've always dreamed of having you in here."

Lydia's lips contort into a frown. "Like... having me in here? Or *having* me in here."

I wink.

The frown stays on her face. "*Ew*. It smells gross in here."

My jaw drops. "What? No, it doesn't. It's so clean in here."

"The sweaty foot smell almost made me puke when we first walked in. I don't even think I could blame it on my pregnancy. It's nasty. I am all for ticking off lists and fantasies, but I think this one might need to stay a fantasy."

"Ugh." I groan and stand. "Fine. But you owe me." I peck her on the lips.

"Gladly." She closes her eyes and kisses me deeply. Her hands roam my chest, and my pulse ramps up in delight. I love it when she lets her body take the lead.

41

YOURS FOR THE TAKING

LYDIA

I cuddle up next to Fletcher on the couch, resting my head on his chest. This all feels too good, and I'm waiting for the other shoe to drop.

"What are you thinking about?" Fletcher asks, always knowing me so well.

"It feels too perfect. I mean, this shouldn't be so easy."

He shrugs. "Why not? We've known each other for a long time. It makes sense that this is coming to us naturally."

I nuzzle deeper into his chest. "I guess that's true." I can't help but still feel a bit off. "When do you leave for your next road trip?"

"Monday." His fingers twist a curl of my hair. He's always playing with my hair.

"How long are you gone for this time?"

"A week."

"I hate away games." Even more so since I've been pregnant and we've been exploring this. I hate having him away from me.

Fletcher kisses the top of my head, squeezing me. "I know. I do, too. I wish I could be here all the time. I hate leaving you. I imagine it's going to be even harder once she's here."

The thought is painful. My daughter will be going through what I did as a kid. Except Fletcher is going to be a better dad than mine ever was. Even when he's not physically here, he will be attentive and care about us. And there's always FaceTime.

Fletcher adjusts so he can rest a hand over my stomach. "I can't wait to feel her kick."

"Same." I rest my hand over his.

"You haven't felt it yet? I was looking it up, and it looks like it could be anytime now."

"A little, but nothing more than fluttering inside. I'm excited for when I can feel it on the outside."

"Do you have any name ideas?"

"Nope. Nothing feels right on any of the names I've looked at."

"What about Freida?" he teases, rubbing his hand soothingly over my stomach.

I laugh. "She's not an eighty-year-old meddling grandma, Fletch."

"Eh, we've got time. We'll think of something. Did you guys set a date for a baby shower?"

I swallow harshly. After a lot of back-and-forth between my mom, Grace, Dottie, and Zoey, we have finally picked a date. Of course, the real holdup was my mom choosing when she had to forfeit her weekend dinner plans with her friends. It was rough, but Grace—with my approval—put her foot down, picked a date, and told Mom that if she wanted to be present for the shower, that was the weekend it was happening. I haven't been involved with any other planning besides approving the invitation designs and a few random things from Grace.

I, of course, got a mouthful from my mom.

"Why couldn't we do it on a Friday evening so she could fly back Saturday morning in time for her plans?"

No matter what we do, it's always going to be a fight.

"Yeah," I say. "March fourteenth. Your mom will be here that weekend, and then we will go to your game on Sunday."

At least that part was easy. Knowing I get to spend the weekend with Dottie afterward and go to a game with her makes things easier.

"Sounds perfect."

I let out a long yawn, stretching my arms over my head. The exhaustion is hitting hard tonight, and my body is starting to ache more and more every day.

"Bedtime?" Fletcher asks with a laugh.

"Yeah, I think so."

He helps me off the couch and leads me down the hallway.

"Thanks for another great date," I say as we stop in front of my door. I want to invite him in. "I still can't believe you were able to get access to the arena for us."

"I'm glad you had fun. I had a great time, too."

Fletcher leans forward, cupping my cheeks in his massive palms and kissing me gently. "Good night, Lydia."

I don't want to say good night, but I do. Maybe he needs rest. I mean, he does have a game tomorrow, after all. I shouldn't assume he wants me in his room because we're dating. Space is okay, right?

I watch him close the door behind him and head into my room, changing and getting ready for bed. But I can't sleep. All previous exhaustion is gone, leaving me wired and my brain running. I toss and turn for an hour, watching each tick of the clock in irritation.

Fletcher wants me; he's proven that without question, but this is going to be a huge change. I can't deny that I'm worried. What if it's all too much? He has a career to think about.

The thoughts in my head are getting worse with each passing second, and I know that only one thing will stop them. I throw my sheets off and roll out of bed. Crossing the hall, I hesitate for only a moment before I knock gently on his door.

"Fletch?" I whisper. There's rustling behind the door.

"Come in."

I open the door, stepping into his space. It smells familiar, like him.

"Are you okay?" Fletcher sits up in bed, rubbing his eyes.

He's shirtless, and the soft light from outside illuminates his bare chest. How is he this attractive?

"I couldn't sleep." I shrug, still standing in his doorway.

"Come here, beautiful." He reaches out an arm to me and opens the sheets next to him.

I rush to the other side of the bed, crawling under the sheets and cuddling up next to him.

"Sorry I woke you," I say, curling into his warmth. His bare skin against me feels like heaven.

"You didn't." He wraps an arm around my shoulders, squeezing me.

"Liar. You were rubbing your eyes."

"You didn't. I was lying here with my eyes closed. I had to make sure it wasn't a dream that you were in my room."

"It's not a dream." I press a kiss to his collarbone. "I'm here."

"Right where I wanted you." His voice is soft. "I should have brought you in here right away."

"Why didn't you?"

"I wasn't sure if you wanted it."

"I do," I say quickly.

"I'm glad you came in here. I probably would have snuck into your room if you hadn't. I was five seconds away from getting up."

My heart is pounding. "Maybe we should be better about telling each other what we want, then."

"I think you're right." His head dips closer to mine, and he tilts my chin to look at him in the dark room. "Tell me, what do you want right now?"

"You." My voice is pitchy and breathless.

"You have me. What else?" I can't see his eyes clearly in the dark, but I can imagine that they're filled with the same heat that's burning in mine.

"I want you inside me." The words spill from me before I can stop them, but I need the comfort only he can provide me. I need the connection I felt when he was inside me that night.

Fletcher doesn't say anything, only rolls us, so I'm on my back. He kisses down my body through my shirt and sleep shorts, settling between my spread thighs. I shift my hips upward, taking off my shorts and flinging them to the floor.

Without hesitation, Fletcher dives forward, sucking my clit hard. I'm soaking wet, and he easily slides two fingers inside of me, pumping and hooking them. The pleasure starts in my core as he flicks his tongue on my clit in a staccato rhythm, making my hips buck.

"Fletcher," I gasp, the sensations growing stronger with each passing second.

My climax builds, burning hot and spreading through my body like wildfire as he twists his fingers, finding that spot deep inside my cunt that triggers my orgasm. My hips rock into his face as he carries me through the waves of pleasure. I cry out his name as I come back down to Earth.

My fingers thread into the dark strands of his hair, yanking to get him to stop his delicious torture on my clit. Fletcher chuckles as his green eyes lock with mine, the evidence of my release glistening on his chin.

"Take control, Lydi," he mumbles, a sly grin crossing his face.

I sit up, and he follows my movements, his eyes raking over my body as I lift my shirt over my head, tossing it to the floor.

I tip my chin at him. "Shorts off."

"You got it." He pushes his shorts off his legs and frees his cock. It bobs before resting across his belly.

"Fuck," I breathe, taking in his naked form.

"I'm yours for the taking." He leans against the headboard, crossing his ankles and lifting his arms to rest behind his head.

"Oh, are you?" I crawl up the bed to kiss him. Just as he tries to deepen the kiss, I pull back. "I'm in charge now."

Those sage-green eyes flare with desire, and it heightens my already thrumming pulse. Fletcher licks his lips as he watches me, and he makes me feel like the sexiest woman alive. I settle between his legs, resting one of my palms across his thick thigh, as I wrap my fingers around his shaft with the other.

I let spit roll off my tongue to drip onto the head of his cock, my mouth watering as I bend down, taking him into my mouth. Sucking him in deep, I twirl my tongue around the head each time I slide up, and Fletcher's groans are like music to my ears.

He tries to tangle his fingers in my hair, but I smack

them away. I have plans, and they don't include him finishing in my mouth. His eyes close as I take him deeper in my throat, my gag reflex kicking in, but I push past it, swallowing around him.

"Fucking Christ, Lydia." Fletcher's voice comes out strangled.

I lift off his twitching cock, hiding my smile. I wipe at some of the spit on my lips, using it to lube up his dick as I pump him slowly. An idea pops into my mind, and before I can stop myself, I'm spitting on the tip and leaning forward. Gathering my heavy breasts in my hands, I wrap them around his hard length, moving them up and down.

Fletcher groans, dropping his head to the headboard.

"You're trying to kill me, aren't you?" he whimpers, eyes snapping back open.

"Nope, just trying to make you feel good."

He pinches one of my nipples between his fingers, eliciting a cry from me as pleasure zings to my core. The pulsing feeling between my thighs grows, and I can't do this much longer. I need him inside me.

I fuck him with my tits as he continues to beg for me, his hips bucking up into me with each movement. It's hot as hell, but I can tell we both need more.

My boobs bounce as I rock back on my heels. I move up his body, straddling his thighs. My wetness soaks his skin, and I can't wait to get him inside me. I reach between us and give him a few more pumps. Grinding my hips against him, I groan when it hits just the right spot. I can't wait any longer.

I angle him at my entrance, sinking, letting him fill me at an agonizing pace. When he's fully seated inside me, I rock my pelvis, getting used to this angle. It's so deep and full. I rest one hand on his shoulder, the other on his chest as he lies down.

Fletcher lets out a long, growling curse under his breath, gripping my hips. His fingers dig into my skin, but the bite of pain only spurs me on. I lift myself a few inches before dropping back down with a gasp as he fills me again.

"Ah," I cry as I fuck him, finding a pace that feels absolutely incredible. My thighs burn, and I fall forward into his chest, nipping and biting his sweat-slicked skin, needing contact with him anywhere I can get it.

Fletcher's grip on my hips tightens as he fucks up into me, taking control and increasing the pace. My pussy throbs as he fucks me, bringing me higher and higher.

A sharp, stinging sensation hits my ass, and I realize he's spanked me.

"Fletcher! More."

The skin of my right ass cheek stings, but morphs into pleasure as he kneads the skin, swatting my ass once more.

"Oh, god," I say.

I'm no longer in control, but I'm fine with that. I had my fun, but now it's his turn. He alternates spanks between my ass cheeks as he thrusts, and the burning tingles deep in my core, heightening my pleasure. I strum my clit fast and rough as Fletcher nears his climax. My orgasm flares to life in my core as I tremble, my body heavy as Fletcher holds me through it, pounding into me with relentless thrusts.

He comes with a ragged moan, loud in my ear, and his cum fills me. The warmth spreads inside me as he slides out. His cum drips out of me as I catch my breath, resting on his chest. Fletcher brushes his fingers up and down my spine as he kisses my forehead.

"You're amazing," he breathes.

"Right back at you." I chuckle. Slowly, I roll off him, my

legs like jelly. "That was a lot of work. I need to start doing some squats or something."

We lie side by side for a long moment as Fletcher traces my features, his calloused fingers sliding down the bridge of my nose, to the corners of my eyes, then down the line of my jaw. When he hits a ticklish spot on my neck, I shriek, pulling away from him.

Fletcher laughs, leaning over and kissing my cheek. He climbs out of the bed, and the water runs for a moment before he comes back into his room.

"It's a shame to clean this up," he whispers, gently opening my thighs, cleaning the cum from between them.

"Thank you." I cup his cheek and pull him down to kiss him deeply.

Our mouths tangle together, and we kiss for a long minute. I pull away from him, excusing myself to use the restroom. When I come back, Fletcher is under the covers again, but pulls the sheets back, patting the space beside him.

I climb in next to him, letting him tug my naked body against his. There's nothing like being held by him. When I roll onto my side, Fletcher wraps his arms around me, my back to his front. He rests his large palm across my lower belly, and butterflies flutter in my stomach.

The baby picks that moment to swirl in my stomach, and I rest, knowing Fletcher is holding us.

42

MILLIONAIRE SUGAR DADDY
LYDIA

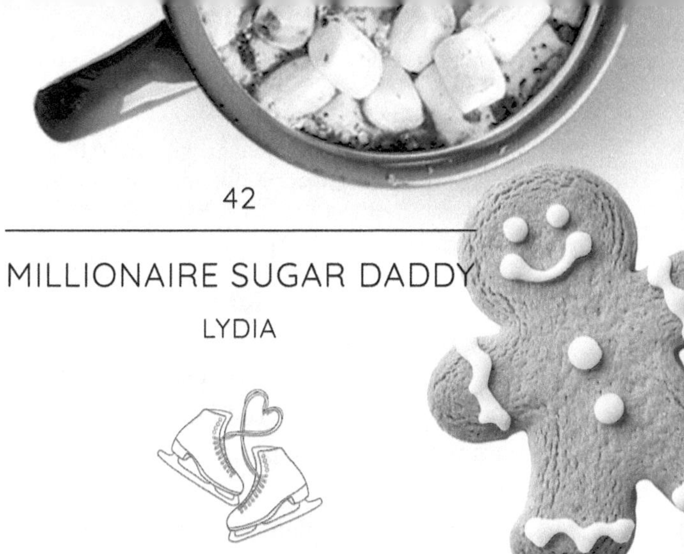

TWENTY-FOUR WEEKS PREGNANT

FLETCHER

Where are you?

ME

I had a meeting with a daycare near work. I'll be home soon

FLETCHER

Where?

ME

Like two blocks from work, it's a nice place, but I'm not sure. I can't get a vibe on how I feel yet.

FLETCHER

What's it called?

ME

Helping Hands

Everyone's really nice, but something about it isn't clicking.

> Maybe it's because I'm scared to leave her with someone else and she's not even born yet.

> I'm ridiculous. Ignore me. I'll be home soon.

The daycare owner, Tina, who has been giving me a tour, says something, but I don't catch it.

I put my phone in my pocket and offer her a smile. "I'm sorry. What was that?"

"We have a slot available starting in August." Her voice is firm but informative as she directs me down the hall toward the infant area. "Drop-off starts at seven, and pickup is at five-thirty. Any later and you incur a late fee."

There are still quite a few kids here, and the place is full of laughter and joy. I can't quite place what feels off. I don't think it has anything to do with the people or the way they run things. It's a me problem.

The thought of leaving my daughter with near strangers every day is enough to give me hives. She's not even here yet. What am I going to do when she's born, and I have to go back to work? I can't afford to be a stay-at-home mom, though it sounds more appealing now than it did when I first found out I was pregnant. I love my job, I do, but maybe I could look into going part-time, at least for a while. But then would I lose my health insurance? Ugh.

I'm barely listening to Tina as she talks about how each room is separated by age, and they have a certain number of caregivers per room. My phone buzzes in my pocket, surely Fletcher.

We continue the tour, and with each passing minute, my skin grows clammy and my heart pounds harder. Why did I do this alone? Fletcher surely would have come with me if I'd asked.

I press my hand to my stomach, where the soft flutter of my baby girl kicking helps calm me momentarily. She's been doing that more often. The first few times freaked me out, but now, I'm constantly hoping she will flutter to remind me of the life inside me, and of my future.

"Sorry, what was that?" Tina says into her walkie-talkie. "Oh, really?"

I turn my attention to her, realizing again that I wasn't listening.

"Your partner is here." Tina looks at me with a look of confusion.

"My partner?" *Holy crap, did Fletcher drive over here?* "Fletcher?"

"That's what he says his name is. He's at the front desk. Said he was sorry for being late."

I pull something out of thin air. "Oh, he must have gotten off work early. I'm sorry, I didn't realize he was going to make it."

If she sees through me, she doesn't say anything, although I do sense a hint of irritation from her.

"We don't have to start the tour over. We can just continue with him."

"Perfect. We have pickups starting soon," Tina says abruptly, turning on her heel to head down the hall toward the lobby.

When we enter the lobby, all the tightness in my chest eases as soon as he's in view. He's wearing a Minnesota Blue Herons ball cap, his branded sweatshirt with his number on it, and a pair of running pants. He must have come straight from practice because the ends of his hair are wet.

"Fletcher," I say.

He strides over, holding his hand out for me. I take it gratefully, already feeling better with him here.

He squeezes my hand tightly and shakes Tina's hand with his free one. "Nice to meet you. I'm Fletcher Graff, Lydia's partner."

Tina looks him up and down, nodding carefully. I do my best to ignore the little thrill I get from him calling me his partner.

"Yes, well, we only have a few minutes, so let's continue." She waves us down the hall, walking fast.

"What are you doing here?" I mutter under my breath so only Fletcher hears.

"You needed me. You were spiraling." Fletcher looks around the room we've just entered.

We're back in the infant room, where two young women are feeding the babies their bottles. When they see Fletcher, their eyes immediately widen. One of them is slack-jawed.

He waves. "Hi."

"You're Fletcher Graff," one of the women says.

"Yep. Nice to meet you."

I withhold my irritation. It's not his fault he gets so much attention in random places. He's a pro-hockey player and the captain of his team. Of course, people are going to recognize him.

Tina narrows her eyes at the girl and turns back to us. "Sorry about that. Now, down the hall here, we have our group play area."

We follow her, and Fletcher subtly leans down to whisper in my ear. "Are you alright?"

I shrug. I'm definitely better now that he's here, but I can't stop the itchy feeling just below my skin. "I'll tell you later."

Fletcher accepts my answer, squeezing my hand as we listen to what Tina has to say about their facility.

All the kids look happy, so why can't I shake this feeling?

Ten minutes later, we finish the tour, and Tina waves goodbye as we walk out the door. She gave me some paperwork and information, with lots of reminders to call as soon as possible if I want to lock in the August opening.

Fletcher drags me out to his car, which he thankfully left running. I walked here from my work, and the thought of walking the two blocks back to my car right now seems like too much to handle.

I get into the passenger seat, pull my seatbelt on, and rest my head against the headrest.

"I didn't like it there," Fletcher says immediately after he starts driving away.

A long sigh escapes my lips as my eyes burn with tears. "I didn't either. I couldn't place it, but something was off."

"I'm glad it wasn't just me."

"It wasn't." I take a wobbly breath as I try to stop the tears from falling down my cheeks. "I don't know what else to do, though. Nothing else has any availability, and I can't afford to go part-time at work. Plus, I'd lose my health insurance."

My lip trembles as Fletcher pulls up next to my car in my work parking lot.

"Hey," Fletcher croons, leaning over and swiping a tear from my cheek. "If you didn't feel comfortable there, you wouldn't feel comfortable leaving our baby there. No one is going to fault you for that. It makes you a good mom, with great instincts."

I turn away, embarrassed to be crying over this. "That doesn't solve the problem."

"No, but what if I had a solution?"

My head shifts over to look back at him. "What solution?"

"There's a daycare at the arena. You'll be off for most of the summer, right?"

"Depending on when she's born, yeah. I'd be off until probably the beginning of August. I have some extra PTO I could use to be off another week or two, maybe." I furrow my brows. "What are you suggesting?"

"Well, what if we look into the daycare the team provides? A ton of the guys use it. I could reach out to some of them, or we could get a hold of some of the WAGs to see if they like it. I could drop her off when I have practices, and if I'm not working, I can stay with her."

"What about when you have games?"

"The daycare is still available. It's year-round, all day, every weekday."

"I didn't know that."

"I've been looking into our benefits a bit more in the last few weeks." Fletcher shrugs like it's no big deal.

"You have?"

"Yeah. We can put the baby on my insurance, too. I know you like working, but you don't have to if you don't want to. You have options."

I shake my head. "I want to work. I like my job."

I know I waffled a bit on that inside the daycare, but knowing what I do now, I'm already warming up to the idea. "Can we tour the daycare?"

"I'm sure we can. I'll talk to our HR lady tomorrow and get all the info." Fletcher cups my cheeks, kissing me gently. "We'll get it figured out. And if we don't, I bet my mom would love to stay with us longer until we do."

"We can't ask her to do that," I say quickly. "We can't

ask her to leave her life, longer than we already are, just to watch the baby, so I can work."

"She'd do anything for you, and you know it. You wouldn't even have to ask, Lydia."

The contrast between my mother and Fletcher's mother will always shock me. I adore Dottie and Ron, but I'm still getting used to having supportive parental figures in my life. My mom has barely spoken more than a few words to me since talking about the baby shower, and she still rarely asks how the baby or I are doing. My dad hasn't reached out once, besides sending a thumbs up to a picture I sent last weekend of my bump.

"I don't know what I'd do without you," I whisper, leaning forward to kiss him quickly.

Fletcher smiles into the kiss. "You'd be just fine, but we're in this together." He pulls back after pressing another kiss to the tip of my nose. "Now, let's get home. I have some chicken defrosting, and then I want to watch a movie."

"Okay. I'll see you at home."

I get out of his car and into my own, feeling a lot better than I did an hour ago. Everything will fall into place, and knowing I have Fletcher by my side will help.

FLETCHER COVERS me with a blanket while I pull the baby mittens I'm crocheting out of the basket next to the couch.

"What are we going to watch?" I ask as he flops down next to me, pulling my legs into his lap.

"Whatever you want."

We had a nice dinner, and after, Fletcher reached out to

some of the guys on the team who have kids. Everyone was super helpful, and it was nice to learn that none of them have any complaints about the daycare.

"I'm fine with anything," I say, adjusting my hips a bit. My bump has started to pop this week, so everything is slowly getting more uncomfortable.

"*The Princess Bride?*"

"Perfect." I settle in and start a few rows of my project while Fletcher pulls up the movie.

Once it's started, we both get sucked in, and Fletcher mindlessly massages my ankles, legs, and thighs before moving up to my bump, resting a hand there.

"She's been kicking more," I say with a smile.

"Really?" His eyes light up, and a boyish grin takes over his face. He puts his other hand on the other side of my bump.

"Yeah. I can't really feel much on the outside yet. Only a little bit of a thump. Try to feel. She's pretty active right now." I lay a hand over his, applying some pressure to show him he can press a little harder.

The baby moves a little inside of me, and I gaze up at him. "Did you feel it?"

He shakes his head. I move his fingers a little lower. She kicks again, and this time, Fletcher gasps.

"Oh my god, was that her?"

A huge smile breaks out on my lips. "Yes!"

"This is incredible," Fletcher breathes, awe lighting up his face. When he looks up at me, his green eyes are glassy. "That's our baby in there."

I nod, my own eyes stinging with tears. "Yeah, it is."

Fletcher leans forward, keeping his hands on my bump and pressing a kiss to my lips. "I can't wait to meet her, and for this part of our lives to start. I hope she's just like you."

I swallow the lump in my throat. "Me too."

The baby stops fluttering inside me, and reluctantly, Fletcher removes his hands.

"What else do you need before she comes?" Fletcher asks a while later. "It's going to go by quickly."

I sigh heavily. "Everything, pretty much. I registered for a bunch when we went shopping, but people aren't going to buy the big stuff, and that's going to be the most costly."

"What if..."

"What if what?" I ask, my curiosity piqued.

"What if money wasn't an issue?" The way he's not looking at me has me worried.

"You can't pay for everything. I know you can afford it, but it would take me forever to pay you back."

"You wouldn't have to pay me back. I wouldn't be paying for it."

"Then who?" I furrow my eyebrows.

What is he talking about?

"Hypothetically," Fletcher says, sitting up and taking my hands in his, giving them a gentle, reassuring squeeze. "What if there was a savings account that was set up for you roughly six years ago with monthly deposits for you to use toward whatever you want or need? Hypothetically, of course."

He didn't. He couldn't have.

My jaw drops, and my mind races. "You... You never used my rent money, did you?"

I can't believe this.

He shakes his head, wincing, his gaze apologetic. "Sorry, but also, I'm not. Not even a little."

I don't have words.

"How much?" I ask, but I honestly couldn't care less about the amount.

"Roughly sixty thousand. Give or take."

"Fletcher! That money was supposed to be for you."

"I didn't need it. I told you I didn't, and you insisted on paying, so I figured I would put it aside for you. I wanted you to have something if you ever moved out or had an emergency or something."

I know I can't be mad at him. He's always taken care of me, even when I didn't need him to.

"I don't know what to say," I admit.

"You don't have to say anything. Even if you want to keep that money for something else, it's there if you need it." Fletcher presses a kiss to my forehead and swipes tears from my cheeks, tears I didn't realize I'd shed.

"Thank you," I whisper, curling into his chest.

"That went easier than I thought." He pushes a curl away from my face. "With how stubborn you can be, I totally thought I'd have to beg on my knees for forgiveness."

I let out a watery laugh, tears streaming down my cheeks freely. "I should probably yell at you."

"You could." He shrugs. "Doesn't change anything. I'd give you a credit card with your name on it tomorrow if I thought you'd let me."

"Don't push it," I say sternly, trying not to laugh.

"That's what I thought." He squeezes me. "Now, for the topic of rent. Unless you want to keep paying it and putting it into the savings account, you don't have to pay me anymore."

I should have expected this. "What if we put it into a college or savings account for the baby?"

That has to be a good compromise. Except Fletcher doesn't say anything. I glance up, and he cringes.

"You already started a savings account for her, didn't you?"

"Maybe. But there's only five thousand in it."

"Only five thousand." I scoff. "I should have known better when I started dating a millionaire."

"You really should have." Fletcher laughs. "I can't be held accountable for this. I'm doing what I do best, taking care of my girls."

"Thank you," I say again. "I really don't know what to say. You do more than take care of me financially, though. I'm not with you because of your money. You're here for me all the time. I don't trust anyone the way I trust you."

He kisses my nose. "I know. I never thought you were only with me for the money. I trust you, Lydi. More than I've ever trusted anyone."

"So, you won't be my sugar daddy then?"

"Baby, I'll be whatever you want me to be," Fletcher says, dropping his voice an octave and tickling my side.

We both burst into hearty laughter, and I sink into his embrace, trying to get as close as possible.

"Can I bring up one more thing?" he asks.

"Depends."

"What do you think about turning your room into a nursery?" He pushes some of my hair from my face, tilting my chin to catch my reaction.

"Where would I sleep?" I ask, then stupidly realize. "Oh."

Fletcher narrows his eyes. "I want you with me always. When I'm away, I want to know you're in my bed waiting for me."

I suppose we have been sharing a bed ever since that night a few weeks ago, and sometimes I've been sneaking into his room when he's gone. It smells like him, and if I hold his pillow, I can pretend I'm in his arms.

"Yes. Okay. I want that, too."

"Thank god," he breathes. "I can't bear the thought of another night without you in my arms."

Fletcher places a kiss on the top of my head. "I'm glad you're not mad at me."

"Why would I be mad at you?"

"I lied to you for six years about rent."

"I think I can forgive you. Just don't do it again."

43

ZAMBRONIES

FLETCHER

Trigg, does Feb. 19th work for you to do that private lesson at the arena?

TRIGG

Of course. I will be there.

CALVIN

Can I please come?

FLETCHER

He's a goalie, we don't need a center, there, Cal

CALVIN

You still need people to try to score on him, Graff.

FLETCHER

Fine, whatever, you can come

CALVIN

YESSSSSS

FLETCHER

Lydia wants to come so she can meet Dylan's aunt. I'll text Grace and see if she and Zoey want to come too.

CALVIN

Family fun day!!!!

TRIGG

How old is his aunt?

FLETCHER

Our age. She got custody of Dylan a few years ago, I think.

TRIGG

Wow. That's tough.

FLETCHER

Yep. He's a good kid, though. I've talked to him a few times through Hattie. He's a hard worker. Lots of potential. I went to one of his games the other night.

TRIGG

I will go to his next one.

44

THE GANG'S ALL HERE

FLETCHER

TWENTY-SEVEN WEEKS PREGNANT

"Fletchy baby," Calvin calls from down the tunnel.

"And this is Calvin Miller," I say to Dylan as we stand in the hall, waiting to head onto the ice. "He's notoriously late when it's not a game day."

His eyes widen. "Calvin Miller is coming too?"

"Sure is. The gang's all here." I clap Dylan on the shoulder. He's tall, probably six foot one, and bulky.

Calvin rushes up to us, offering Dylan a hand. The kid stares at him with those wide eyes as he takes off his glove to shake his hand.

"Nice to meet you, kid," Calvin says.

"You too," Dylan replies, voice cracking. He clears his throat. "Sorry. Nice to meet you."

"Ready to get a lesson from the best group of guys in the league?" Calvin asks.

"Absolutely," Dylan says, squaring his shoulders and nodding. "This is... this is the coolest thing that's ever happened to me."

"Just wait," I say. "You haven't even met Addy yet."

I swear he audibly gulps.

"Come on. Let's get you on the ice." I chuckle, turning and heading out toward the arena.

Lydia, Zoey, and Grace are all sitting on the bench with Hattie, Dylan's aunt. If I had to guess, this won't be the last we see of Hattie or Dylan. I think the girls found a new friend, and I love it.

I step onto the ice, looking backward to see Dylan standing at the edge of the boards. He stops and looks around the empty arena, his eyes wide with awe.

"This is so surreal," he says.

"Have you been to a game here?" I ask.

He shakes his head. "Games are expensive, and my team has never made it to state. All my junior league games are played at college arenas. This is wild."

Well, we're getting him to a game immediately.

"Come on, kid." I wave him onto the ice.

He steps on, gliding onto the blue line, the look of amazement never leaving his face. I lead him over to the net, where Trigg is standing. When I introduce them, Dylan has no words. Literally, the boy is speechless.

Trigg chuckles. "Nice to meet you, Dylan. Why don't we do some warm-ups, then we'll get started."

Dylan nods, and they start their stretches, while I do a few laps and shots on the opposite end of the ice.

I do my stretches, and when Calvin finally gets on the ice, he skates over to me with a puck. "What's Dylan's aunt's name?"

"Hattie."

"I think Addy has a crush," he says, pointing his gaze back and forth between the two.

I look over to Trigg, who is on the ice doing his hip

stretches. Every few seconds, he lifts his head to look at Hattie, who is in an in-depth conversation with the girls.

"Hm. I think you may be right." I'll have to talk to him about it later.

"That would be one heck of a meet-cute," Calvin says.

"Yeah, it would."

Calvin passes me a puck, and we start doing some easy passes to each other.

"So, you told Coach your girl is pregnant, yet?"

I sigh. "Yeah, I told him right away. He was surprised, and I think I saw him clutch his chest a few times when I told him her due date. I thought he was going into cardiac arrest."

"Can't say I blame him. What's your plan? I mean, chances are high that we'll make the playoffs. First round ends in early May. If we go into the second round, it's going to be cutting it real close, dude. And that's just the first two rounds. If we go all the way?"

"I know." I shoot the puck to him, a little harder than necessary. "It's a lot. My mom is planning to come up for the birth, but I don't want to be gone for most of her first month of life."

"It's not like you can take time off, Fletch," Calvin says.

"I know that, Miller." My irritation grows. In all honesty, I've been avoiding thinking about this.

Lydia can't help when she's due, but it sucks that she's more than likely going to have the baby during the play-offs. What if I'm out of town when she goes into labor? The thought has my heart pounding and sweat beading on my brow. I don't want to miss the birth of our daughter.

Because that's what she is. Blood or not, she is my daughter. And Lydia is my partner.

Trigg cuts off my train of thought, calling over to us to start running a few drills with Dylan.

45

GIRLHOOD

LYDIA

"How long have you been together?" Hattie asks after I explain that Fletcher isn't technically my baby's father.

I pause to think. "December second was our first date, but we've been friends for years."

"Wow. He seems like a great guy." She tucks a piece of her reddish-blonde hair behind her ear.

"He really is. Do you have a partner?" I ask. "Or if that's too invasive—"

Hattie cuts me off with a wave of her hand. "Girl, I just asked if Fletcher was your baby's father. Clearly, I have no boundaries... Oh god, I was so rude asking you about that, wasn't I? I'm the worst."

"Stop it," I laugh, wrapping an arm around her shoulder. "You're fine. I would have told you, anyway. It's not a secret."

Hattie sighs. "Okay, good. To answer your question, no. I haven't had time for dating. Not since I got custody of Dylan."

"How long ago was that?"

"Four years. He was twelve. I was twenty-four. We've done a lot of growing up together, if I'm being honest. It's been a rough few years, but I think he's turned into a great kid." Hattie looks at her nephew fondly. "I work two jobs, and even that's not enough, but I'll be damned if he doesn't get to play hockey. There's no way I'm taking that away from him, even if it would make my life ten times easier. It helps that he has his driver's license now and can use my dad's car."

"Does your dad help out?" Zoey asks.

Hattie shakes her head. "Yes, and no. He's in his seventies, and the only thing he cares about is his food truck that's open for two months a year. I was an 'oops baby,' and my mom died when I was young. He has a lot of health problems. The list goes on. He shows up to games for Dyl and lets us live in the apartment above his garage, but that's about all he can do with his age and health issues."

"Well, now you have us." Grace squeezes Hattie. "I can pick him up from practice or whatever you need."

"Do you know of any places hiring?" Hattie whispers. "The place I'm working at now is... not great. The cooks are all assholes, and my boss is a prick."

"Actually, yeah. The bar I work at in the summer. But it's in Wisconsin, on Willow Lake."

"That's only like thirty minutes from me. I could make that drive if the pay is good, and you get treated well."

"We get treated amazingly. The summers are the best because all the rich folks are at their huge mansions, and they tip so well. I'll put in a good word for you, if you're interested."

"Yes, please." Hattie relaxes. "I need out of that job. It's my part-time gig, and my full-time one isn't much better."

A bell goes off in my mind. "What's your full-time job?"

"I'm a bank teller. It was all I could find when I needed to land something quick, and I'm scared to try to find something else now. I've always loved planning big events like that. I wanted to be an event planner, but well..." She gestures to the ice where Fletcher is taking shots at Dylan, who is surprisingly holding his own against a top professional hockey player.

I can see from here that all three of the men look impressed.

"We have an opening at my job," I say quickly. "I'm the office admin for a non-profit organization, Frozen Fundamentals. We're based in the community rink in Lino Lakes, but we host skating and hockey events throughout the Twin Cities. They've been considering hiring an event planner, expanding a bit, and doing more high-end fundraisers and galas. My expertise starts and ends with free skate camp days, so they decided to hire someone."

"Really?" Hattie asks, her eyes brightening.

"Really. Give me your number. I'll drop a hint to my boss that I have someone in mind and give her your info. She's amazing."

"I can't believe this." Hattie swipes at her eyes. "Is this real life?"

"Sure is," I say, pulling her in for a hug.

"You're stuck with us now, whether you decide to take the jobs or not," Grace says, also hugging her.

"I can't offer you a job, but I can offer a friendship," Zoey chimes in.

"I'll gladly take it." Hattie gives Zoey a watery smile, looking at her engagement ring. "Are you engaged?"

Zoey smiles softly. "Yeah. My fiancé, Vincent, and I have been together for three years."

"Congratulations," Hattie shrieks, while Grace and I share a look.

Vincent is no one's favorite person, but he makes Zoey happy, so we support her. He's not inherently a bad person, or bad for Zoey, he's just... stiff. He doesn't know how to let loose. "When's the wedding?"

Now, Zoey looks uncomfortable. "We haven't set a date yet. Vincent says he wants a long engagement, so we're waiting another year before we decide."

"That's fair," Hattie replies. "Think of all the fun you'll have when you start planning."

"I can't wait," Zoey says, her cheeks heating. "I already know what dress I want. As soon as I can, we're going dress shopping."

"Yes!" Grace cheers.

"I'm there," I respond.

All three of us turn our gaze to the ice, where Fletcher fakes a shot at Dylan, and Dylan still makes the save over his right shoulder. It's an impressive save. Trigg hoots, rounding the net from behind to slap Dylan on the shoulder and tap their helmets together. Fletcher and Calvin both do the same, hugging Dylan and tapping foreheads. It's adorable.

"I'm lucky I get to be his aunt." Hattie sniffles. "I'm so proud of him."

46

SOMEONE SPECIAL

LYDIA

TWENTY-NINE WEEKS PREGNANT

"Hey, beautiful," Fletcher says as I answer the incoming FaceTime call.

I try not to blush as he stares at me through the screen, but I can't help it. Every time he calls me that, I swoon, even if I look gross right now.

I'm lying on my side in bed with my giant pregnancy pillow stuffed between my thighs and under my ever-growing belly. Since I wasn't in his arms last night, I barely slept, and I'm exhausted.

"Hey," I say. "How are you?"

"Alright. Missing you, but I'll be back tomorrow morning." He scoots against the headboard of his hotel bed.

"Thank goodness."

"Why? You miss me, too?" His eyes glisten with humor.

"Nope." I bite my lip to try to stop myself from smiling.

"You liar." He laughs, his smile giving me an extra boost of serotonin. "Whose bed are you in right now?"

I shift the phone closer to my face. "None of your business, Mister."

"Sure. If you tilted that phone three inches, I bet I'd see my wood headboard."

"I don't know what you're talking about," I squeak. Lying isn't my strong suit.

In reality, I'm in here because I miss him. And his bed is more comfortable than mine. Maybe it's the way his pillow smells like him, or the memories that accompany this space. It's all him.

I haven't fully moved into his room yet, or rather, our room, but for all intents and purposes, this is my room now, too.

"Whatever you say. But you miss me too."

"Fine," I say. "I do."

"I'll be home before you know it."

"You're in Colorado tonight, right?" I change the subject, fully knowing I'm about to get weepy if he keeps talking about how much we miss each other. He's been gone less than twenty-four hours.

"Yep. Calvin and Trigg are out getting lunch with Adam now."

"Why aren't you with them?"

He shrugs. "I'd rather talk to you."

"You only see Adam a few times a year. You should be hanging out with him," I say, but the conviction isn't there. I don't really want to hang up on him.

He shakes his head. "I'm right where I want to be. How's my little ladybug?"

"She's good," I breathe, running my other hand over my bump. "Kicking like crazy today, but she's sleeping now."

"Let me talk to her."

I giggle, a hit of warmth worming its way into my heart.

He's been talking to her any chance he gets, and it's adorable every time. I shift so I'm sitting up and put him a little lower so he can see my bump.

Fletcher's smile widens when he sees me in full, and then he starts talking. There's nothing special about what he's saying; he's mainly talking about hockey or some stupid thing Calvin did on the team plane today, but it doesn't matter. He's talking to her, letting her get to know his voice. I talk to her all the time, too, but it feels special when he does it.

The tone of Fletcher's voice changes when he switches back to talking to me. "Are you excited for the baby shower next week?"

"Yes and no. I'm so excited to see your mom, but nervous to see mine. I keep pressing Grace to see if she's causing trouble, but you know how stubborn Grace is. She won't give me a peep of information."

"I'm glad. If your mom is making things difficult, we don't want to stress you out," he says, and something about his tone has me wondering....

I knew it.

"Has Grace talked to you about her? Is she causing issues?" I blurt, sitting up straight.

"Relax, beautiful. It's fine. She's just being dramatic about some of the decorations. You know how your mom is. She has a vision, and ladybugs aren't it."

I groan, rubbing my face. "I'm sorry."

"You have nothing to be sorry about. It's handled."

"Thank you. You're lucky your mom is so chill."

"She's excited to see you," Fletcher says with a smile.

A realization hits me. "Have you told your parents?"

His brow furrows on the screen. "Told them what? They knew you were pregnant before I did."

"No, no, not that," I say, waving my hand. "About... us. Y'know, that we're *together*."

"Oh." He chuckles. "Yes. They know. I'm surprised my mom hasn't said anything to you. She's ecstatic."

I laugh. "I'm surprised she hasn't either, though I'm sure we'll talk about it in person next week."

I can't believe I never brought it up. We talk often, and I've told her about some of the things we've been up to, but I guess, since things have felt so normal between us, it's felt like a natural shift in our relationship. I didn't even think to mention it directly.

"I think Hattie is going to come to the shower as well," I state

"Great," Fletcher says. "That will be fun."

"My boss reached out to Hattie earlier this week, so hopefully we can get her working for us. I think she'd be a great fit."

I want to do all that I can to help her. She deserves it.

"I'm so glad you guys are taking her under your wing. We'll take care of Dyl if you take care of Hattie." Fletcher pushes his hair back with a yawn. "I'm getting them tickets to a game soon. Can you go with them?"

"Absolutely. You know I'll go to any game. You don't even have to ask. Though my jersey doesn't really fit anymore." I gesture at my bump. "I need a new sweatshirt or something."

"I'll pick something up this week," Fletcher says.

"Thank you."

He yawns again.

"I'll let you go. It looks like you need a nap before the game."

He nods. "Yeah. I didn't sleep well last night. I was missing someone special."

Again, a blush creeps up my cheeks. "I miss you, too."

"I'll call you before the game, okay?"

"Okay," I reply, and we say our goodbyes.

I rub at my stomach, where the baby starts kicking at my bladder.

"Thanks for waiting until I was off the phone," I tell her, chuckling.

47

EMOTIONAL SUPPORT GROUP CHAT

CALVIN

Holy shit, did you guys see the news?

FLETCHER

What news?

ZOEY

Yes!!! I just got off the phone with Adam!!!

CALVIN

Adam got traded!!

TRIGG

Where to???

CALVIN

HERE! MY BOY IS COMING HOME YA'LL

FLETCHER

Holy smokes! This is HUGE

ZOEY

I'm so excited!!!

HATTIE

I have no idea who Adam is, but Dylan is practically running circles around the house.

LYDIA

Ahhhh this is so exciting!!

GRACE

Wait, really? Is this a prank?

CALVIN

NO!!! His flight leaves in an hour!!!

FLETCHER

This is wild.

CALVIN

He'll be at morning practice tomorrow and suit up for the game tomorrow night!

TRIGG

A deadline trade?? We are definitely going to the playoffs! Buckle up, boys!

FLETCHER

CALVIN

I need to get my guest bedroom set up.

ZOEY

Uhhh. He's staying with me.

CALVIN

No, he's not. Don't break my heart, Zo.

ZOEY

You can call and ask him, but he asked me if he could stay with me for a few days so he didn't have to stay in a hotel.

CALVIN

I'm going to call and yell at him.

TRIGG

He can also stay with me if he needs a place. I have two extra rooms.

CALVIN

NO. He's staying with me. I'm his best friend, Addy.

ZOEY

What am I then? I'm his SISTER, Cal.

CALVIN

I just called him. He's staying with you, Zoey. I'm no longer friends with him.

CALVIN

Unless we can share custody until he finds a place.

FLETCHER

Dude, chill. He's not even here yet.

CALVIN

How can I chill? I get to have all my boys together in one place for the first time ever! I'm so excited I can hardly breathe.

GRACE

I'm still in shock. Is this really happening?

LYDIA

This is so cool!

HATTIE

Dylan just explained it all to me, so happy you guys get to have your friend here!

ZOEY

My brother is finally coming home!!!

48

WELCOME HOME

FLETCHER

"This is the best day of my life," Calvin says, hopping up and down. He's so jittery.

"Really?" I ask.

"Yes! I get to have all my favorite people in one place, and playing with Adam again will be a dream."

We're standing outside the SUV the GM sent to pick up Adam. We were adamant about getting to pick him up, even though the GM wanted it to be just him and Adam. Trigg and Grace were going to come too, but Trigg was busy, and Grace had already committed to picking up an extra shift at the bar she works at sometimes.

Zoey's here, but she's waiting in the car to stay warm. It's a balmy ten degrees. We watch the plane land and slowly start its way over to us. Zoey climbs out of the truck, adjusting her hat over her long, dark hair that matches her brother's.

Calvin wraps an arm around Zoey's shoulders to pull her in close.

"I can't believe this is happening," she murmurs.

"Believe it," Calvin replies.

Something flashes across Zoey's face, and she shrugs his arm off. Calvin's face falls for only a moment, but I catch it. He schools his expression immediately, focusing on the plane as it stops.

A minute later, they have the stairs down, and Adam is coming down them with a bag over his shoulder and a carry-on in the other hand. He's barely got two feet on the ground before he and Zoey are wrapped in a tight embrace. Even though she saw him a few months ago, I'm sure this is different. He's home for good. They signed him to a preemptive three-year contract, so he's not going anywhere for a while.

Calvin stands next to them, and when Zoey and Adam finally break apart, Calvin and Adam hug for a long moment. Zoey takes his bag, rolling it over to where I'm standing at the truck. The GM gets out, greeting Adam with a shake of his hand and welcoming him to the team.

"Good to be home," Adam says, a fleeting smile on his lips. He wraps his arm back around his twin sister, holding her close.

I smile and give him a quick hug. "Ready to get down to business? Playoffs are almost here."

"Ready as I'll ever be," Adam says. We climb into the SUV to head to the arena. The GM peppers questions throughout the drive, while I send Lydia a text to check in.

ME

Miss you.

LYDIA

Miss you too. How's Adam?

ME

Great. This will be huge for us.

LYDIA

I think it will be, too.

ME

We're all going to go to dinner tonight. You in?

LYDIA

Yeah. But I'm going to nap first. Can you call me when you pick a time?

ME

No problem. Get some rest, Lydi-bug.

"How's Lydia feeling?" Zoey asks, looking over my shoulder.

"Good. Tired, but everything I've read says that's normal at this point in pregnancy."

"Her baby shower is going to be so cute." Zoey grabs her phone and pulls up a picture. "We ordered these cute ladybug cookies from a local baker, and we also have a sign being made that says, 'A little ladybug is on the way.'"

"That's perfect." I smile as I look at the photos of the sign and the cookies. "She's going to love it."

"I agree." Zoey bites her lower lip. "Is her mom always this..."

"Bitchy?"

Zoey chokes on a laugh. "I was going to say abrasive, but I suppose bitchy works."

"Yeah, she is, but this situation has brought out a new level. I didn't know she could be this bad. Lydia's parents have always been rough and too hard on her, but this is a lot."

"Why? I mean, Lydia is so accomplished and wonderful. Why don't they treat her like the amazing person she is?"

"Her mom thinks she should marry for money and join the posh lifestyle she and Lydia's dad live. Especially now that Lydia and I are together, she thinks Lydia is on a one-way ticket there. It's hard because that's the total opposite of Lydia."

"It is. I never would have guessed Lydia came from them, knowing her as well as I do."

"Me either. Honestly, I wish she'd cut her parents off. Her mom hasn't even been excited about the pregnancy, just the networking opportunities it gives her, and it's disgusting."

"She *should* cut them off. What little I've interacted with her mom has been rough. I mean, she hasn't even offered to help besides sending a list of people to invite and trying to convince us every day to switch the venue."

I sigh heavily. "Yep. It's weighing on Lydia that her mom only cares about that, and not her daughter."

"I'm sure."

"I appreciate you, Grace, and my mom for stepping in and doing this for her. It means a lot."

"We'd do anything for her. I'm so excited for the two of you."

"Thanks, me too. It's going to be tough to have a baby in the middle of playoffs, but I know she's got a good group of people to help her."

"She does." She rubs my arm. "We'll take care of her, don't you worry."

"So, you and Lydia are officially together, then?" Adam chimes in from the row in front of us.

I flash a cheesy, uncontrollable grin. "Sure are."

He laughs. "About time."

"Yeah, yeah." My tone is sarcastic, but it's funny to me that even Adam could see how much I wanted her. He only saw us together a few times a year, if that.

We pull into the arena and exit the vehicle, heading

down to the locker room while our social media girl follows, taking pictures and videos of his arrival. Getting him on our team is going to be huge. Not to toot our own horn, but we're a good team, and having a player like Adam is going to make us even better. That Adam and Calvin have played together since they were kids is going to be amazing. In any sport, when you play with someone on the same line for that long, you sort of create a silent, secret language with them. Calvin and I have one of our own, but we've only been playing together for six years. These two grew up together and learned to play hockey together. They know each other like the back of their own hand.

None of us knew this was a potential. From the sounds of it, Adam was planning on getting re-signed since his contract was up, but the team decided to trade him instead.

The news has been buzzing, as this was a huge, unexpected trade. Lucky for us, we got him. Once Adam is shown to his locker, poses for a few more photos, and takes a quick promo video, they let him know he's good to go.

We'll have a quick practice tomorrow morning so he can get acclimated to the team, but from the sounds of it, he'll start at tomorrow night's game.

I open the text thread that includes everyone, including Hattie, and add Adam.

EMOTIONAL SUPPORT GROUP CHAT

> Me: Game tomorrow at 7. I'll get the suite reserved. Hattie, are you and Dylan in?

HATTIE

> Really? We're invited?

TRIGG

Of course you are.

Do either of you have jerseys to wear?

Me: I'll grab some.

HATTIE

Oh, no you don't have to do that, we don't need jerseys.

TRIGG

Yes you do.

CALVIN

Yes you do! You're part of the team now.

ZOEY

I hope they get me a new jersey before tomorrow.

CALVIN

You don't need a new jersey, Zo. Just keep wearing the one with my name on it.

ZOEY

Yes, I do, Calvin. I need to rep my brother now that he's on the team.

HATTIE

I actually have the day off tomorrow, so we should be able to come. Are you sure? I can pay you for the tickets.

Me: Nope. We've got it covered. It will probably be easier if you carpool with the girls though, so you guys can get that arranged.

GRACE

This is so exciting!

Me: Oh, Hattie, what are you guys doing tonight? We are all going out to dinner to celebrate.

HATTIE

Well Dylan is working tonight, but I can join! I get off at five.

TRIGG

Perfect!

ME

See everyone soon! Black Rooster at six-thirty.

An idea pops into my head as I finish sending the message. I call Lydia to let her know when and where we're going. "Does anyone know if there's someone here who could make me some popcorn?"

49

I PROTECT THE FAMILY

FLETCHER

I tap my stick on the ice, signaling to Adam to pass to me. He shoots the puck across the ice as I dodge a player from Calgary named Marquis. He's a rat, constantly making dirty plays the refs choose to ignore. Marquis chirps at me under his breath as I skate toward the goal, passing the puck between my legs to Calvin, who gets a clear shot and slaps the puck straight into the net.

It's a beautiful play, and the crowd erupts, the horn blaring as all five of us hug against the boards, celebrating the goal. We skate back to the bench, fist-bumping the rest of the team and switching shifts. I sit next to Waffles, who's still breathing heavily after the shift.

I clap Waffles on the back. "Good job."

He nods, taking in a sharp inhale. "Feels good to be playing on the same line as you three."

"Keep up the good work, and you'll go far, kid." I turn my attention back to the ice. We're only in the second period, so plenty of time for the game to turn, but we're up by one.

It's an adjustment, playing with someone new in the

middle of the season, but so far, it's gone well. Adam is meshing with the team, and watching him and Calvin work together is electric.

I turn my gaze up to the suite and lock eyes with Lydia. She's standing with the rest of the girls, a giant bucket of popcorn tucked under her arm, cheering as the puck drops at center ice, and we win the face-off. She waves to me, smiling as I tip my chin in a nod. I focus back on the ice, watching my team and preparing for my next shift.

My mind is locked on so many things all at once: the game, my teammates, and her. The beautiful woman who supports me no matter what. She'll always be here for me, and I'll do the same for her. We have so much life ahead of us, and while things are going to change even more once the baby arrives, it's going to be incredible. This time next year, Lydia's going to be standing up in that suite holding our daughter, watching me play the game I love.

The image is so stunning that my heart pounds. I can't wait.

Once my next shift starts, my focus narrows back to hockey. I hop the boards and skate toward the puck. Adam hits the opposite side of the ice, with Calvin at our center. Levine took the place of Wafford for this shift, and our other defenseman, Laken Monroe, has the puck. He passes to me, and as soon as the puck leaves his stick, Marquis checks Monroe into the boards.

Monroe collapses, holding his arms to his chest as the ref blows the whistle. Calvin, being our enforcer, drops his gloves, skating to Marquis. It was a clean hit, but Calvin doesn't care. He's a kid, and it was unnecessary.

"You motherfucker," Calvin shouts, landing a right hook to his jaw with the first punch.

The two go at it while I skate over to Monroe. One of

the refs watches the fight while the other checks in with Monroe, who's now standing.

Marquis gets a hit right in Calvin's nose, and blood drips down his face. Calvin answers the punch immediately, hitting his right eye. Marquis collapses to the ice, and the ref pulls them apart.

We tap our sticks to the ice and boards as the ref leads Cal to the penalty box with a five-minute major for fighting. He wipes at the blood streaming from his nose. He'll be fine. Marquis skates to his own penalty box, goading Calvin. Calvin laughs them off as he always does.

The rest of the game is tense, with insults thrown as Calgary ties it up. No more fights occur, but late in the third period, Adam shoots the puck and finds the back of the net, giving us the lead again.

With only thirty seconds left, I'm back on the bench, panting as I look up once more to the suite. Dylan is watching intensely, while Hattie points at Trigg, who's just made a killer save. The kid is going to go far, that's for sure. I'm excited to watch his growth, and hopefully, we can get him to the right place. I genuinely think he could go pro.

The final horn sounds, and we all rush the ice toward Trigg, giving him head taps for a job well done.

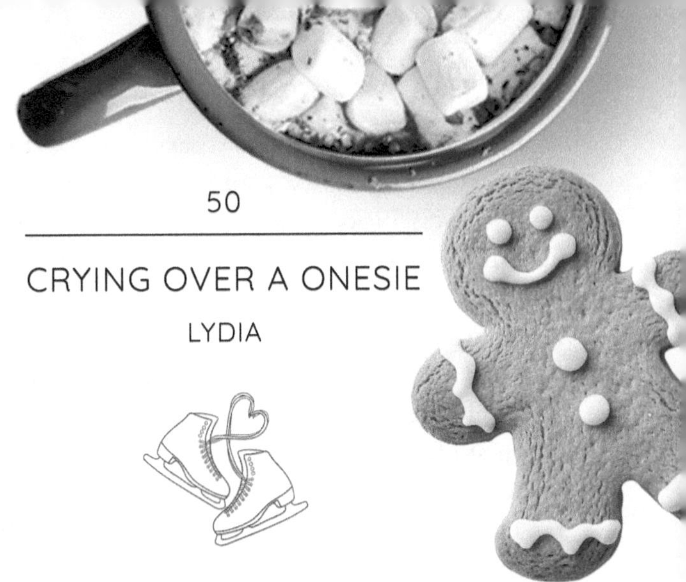

50

CRYING OVER A ONESIE

LYDIA

I fucking love hockey.

Calvin won a fight against Marquis, and Grace and Zoey are screaming their heads off as the ref leads him over to the penalty box. Calvin smirks as he spits blood from his mouth, wiping at his nose. I don't think it's broken since there's a cut on the bridge, but we'll have to see. It wouldn't be the first time I've seen him break it.

The second period ends, and I poke Grace. "Want to run down to the store with me?"

She furrows her eyebrows. "What for?"

"I want to see if there are any cute baby things. I can ask Fletch to pick them up later, but I want to get a look at them in person."

"Alright, you've convinced me. I love baby clothes." She stands and offers me a hand, so I take it.

"We're going to the store to look at baby clothes. Does anyone want to come?" I ask the others.

Hattie and Zoey shake their heads, and Dylan is too engrossed in the mascot race that's about to start to care. Grace and I head downstairs to the big store, where we both begin to browse. They don't have any Davison gear for Adam yet, but I'm sure it's only a matter of time.

Zoey was lucky Adam was able to convince them to make an extra jersey for her to wear today, so besides Adam, she's the only one in the arena to have a Davison Minnesota Blue Herons jersey.

I make a beeline to the back corner of the store where all the children's and baby items are. There are little Blue Heron stuffed animals, toys, and blankets, but I'm focused on the assortment of clothes.

There are a few different designs: some with the MBH logo, others with cheeky sayings, but one tucked behind all the others catches my eye instantly. It's a turquoise blue to match the color the boys wear at home games, and it has two hockey sticks crossed on the front.

In block letters, the shirt reads: 'My favorite hockey player is my Daddy.'

I gasp as I pull it off the rack. The fabric is soft under my fingers as I trace over the printed words.

Grace steps up behind me. "Find anything good?"

I jump, not expecting her to appear behind me, and I hold the onesie to my chest. "Yeah. I did."

"Let me see." She extends her hand.

I give her the onesie, also spotting another one out of the corner of my eye. This one is long-sleeved and looks like a jersey. It has Fletcher's number on the sleeves and the back, along with his last name. So obviously, I need that one, too.

"Aww, Lydia, this is adorable," Grace coos, running her hand over the words. "It's perfect."

I smile as I look at the items, overwhelmed with emotion. Everything locks into place. It feels right. Baby girl kicks the side of my stomach, like she's telling me I'm making the correct choice for us. I smooth a hand over the spot.

I know, baby. We've got a good one.

Grace passes the onesie back to me, and I lay it over my arm with the other one. I grab a baby-sized beanie with the Herons logo and head to the register.

"What are you doing?" Grace asks curiously. "You know you could get one of the guys to get these for you tomorrow."

"I know, but I need this now."

I can't explain it, but if I walk away from this store empty-handed, I'll feel like I'm leaving a piece of me here.

Grace rubs my shoulder. "Alright, Mama."

Tears burn behind my eyes as I check out, rolling up the onesies to hide what they say. I need to wrap these up so I can give them to Fletcher.

We head back to the suite, where I tuck the bag under my seat, then I refill my popcorn. I've eaten more popcorn than anything else in the last twenty-four hours, and my stomach may hate me later, but right now, I'm in bliss. Fletcher brought me home another massive bag of popcorn last night after they picked up Adam from the airport, and I almost cried. I was so excited. He's been bringing it home any chance he can.

Last night was a lot of fun, but I'm definitely not made for late nights anymore as this pregnancy progresses. I was ready for bed by eight o'clock. Fletcher saw how much I was yawning, and we left soon after. He always notices the little things. I was happy to stay a while longer so he could have fun with our friends, but he was insistent.

The period starts, and we all settle in for one final stretch, hoping we can snatch the win. It's been a close, tense game, but I think we can do it.

Adam scores with a few minutes left, bringing us up by one, and hopefully clinching the win. The last thirty seconds of the game fly by as Trigg makes an amazing save. Dylan cheers, throwing his fist in the air. He and Hattie both have brand new Aadland jerseys on, courtesy of Trigg. My Graff jersey doesn't fit over my bump anymore, so I have on one of my comfy MBH sweatshirts that has Fletcher's name and number on the back. Not quite the same, but it works for now. Maybe I'll get a bigger one so I can wear a jersey during the playoffs.

In the past, when we've made it to the playoffs, Grace, Zoey, and I have gone to every home game, and I'm sure this time won't be any different, depending on when I deliver. This time, we'll have to make sure Hattie and Dylan are present as well.

The game ends, and the boys all skate onto the ice, all giving goalie taps to Trigg and celebrating the win. We hang back in the suite while the boys do press, and once the arena is empty, we make our way down.

My phone rings as we show our badges to take the elevator and be let into the tunnel.

My mom.

I don't know why, but I answer the call. She's only going to sour my mood, but with the baby shower being this upcoming weekend, I'm sure she has things to discuss with me.

"Hi," I answer. "What's up?"

"Are you ready for this weekend?" she asks without preamble.

"Yeah! I'm really excited. I think it will be fun."

"What are you going to wear?" Her tone shifts slightly.

Where is this going?

"I have a long-sleeved red dress to match the theme."

Mom sighs through the phone. "I cannot believe it's a ladybug theme. You don't expect me to wear something red, do you? Red washes me out."

"No, you can do whatever you want." I pinch the bridge of my nose.

"Well, clearly I can't do whatever I want." She scoffs. "If I could have whatever I wanted, we would be having a dignified event at Le Château Arnaud. Not at a local ice rink's party room with dollar store decorations."

I withhold the groan rising in my chest. "We are doing it at the rink because my boss offered to waive the event fee, and it has the most room. Besides, it's where I wanted it to be. Doesn't what I want matter?"

"Of course it matters. I simply thought that after how I raised you, you would have more taste. Ladybugs are better for a toddler's birthday party. We should be decorating in gold and pearl luster."

"The ladybugs have meaning." I stop myself from saying more.

She probably wouldn't care that Ladybug is the nickname Fletcher has given the baby, or that he's called me Lydi-bug for years. This isn't worth the fight.

"Did you call me to shit on my baby shower?" I ask. "Because if that's the case, I'm going to hang up now."

Mom huffs. "Watch your tone, young lady. No. I will try to find something to wear. My flight lands at four on Friday, so I will see you then."

I mutter a response, hanging up the phone with a quick goodbye.

Hattie eyes me carefully as I slump against the brick wall of the tunnel.

"Everything okay?" she asks cautiously.

I shrug. "My mom. Has Grace told you about her?"

She winces. "Yeah. I hope that's okay. She gave me a heads-up about her when I came along."

"It's totally fine. I'm glad you know, honestly. Especially before the shower."

"Hopefully I'm not overstepping by saying this, but... it kind of sounds like you'd be better off without her."

I sigh, resting a hand over my bump. "Yeah, I agree. It's hard. She has such a narcissistic personality, but I keep giving her second chances because she's my mom. Now that I'm becoming a mom, I feel like I should give my parents a chance to know their granddaughter. But at the same time, I want to protect her from the pain I experienced as a kid."

"It's tough," Hattie laments, rubbing my shoulder. "Whatever happens, I already know you're going to be an amazing mom. You're already protecting her."

I nod as tears spring to my eyes. "Thanks."

"Anytime. You guys are amazing. I still can't believe I'm lucky enough that you're helping me the way you are."

"You're such a hard worker, and you deserve every bit of happiness, and so does he." I point to where Dylan is standing, waiting for the team to exit the locker room.

There's a look of pure awe written over his young face, and it's so fun to watch his dreams come true.

"He's had a hard life," Hattie says, "but he deserves the world."

A minute later, all the guys start exiting the locker room, and when Fletcher arrives, he pulls me into his tight embrace, giving me a kiss and a tight hug before resting his palm flat over my rounded stomach. "Hey, Lydi-bug."

"Hey, you. You had a great game."

"It was a blast out there. They're not all like that, but man, was it fun."

"Is Adam settling in?"

"Think so. We need more than one quick practice and game to know for sure, but the odds are good for this to be a good fit."

"Awesome."

"Want to go home?" He pushes my hair out of my face and kisses my lips once more.

"Don't you want to go out with everyone?" I look around at the rest of the group, who are all smiles and excitement.

Fletcher shakes his head. "Nope. I'm tired and want some alone time with my girl before next weekend."

"That sounds nice." I'm ready for some time, just the two of us, before the baby shower and game on Sunday.

"Home?"

"Home."

51

A LITTLE LADYBUG IS ON THE WAY

LYDIA

THIRTY WEEKS PREGNANT

"Oh my god, look at you!" Grace squeals as Fletcher and I enter the event space at the rink. "You really popped this week."

I run a hand over my even bigger bump. "Yeah, it seems that way."

"It's sexy as hell." Fletcher holds me close, rubbing a soothing hand up and down my arm.

I scoff. "I look like a beached whale, and I still have ten weeks left."

Grace frowns. "Stop that. You look beautiful. This dress is stunning. Red is definitely your color."

"Agreed," Fletcher says, looking at me adoringly.

I blush furiously, glancing around the empty hall. "Are Mom and Dottie here yet?"

Grace winces, shaking her head. "Not yet. We haven't heard from your mom, but Dottie called in a panic. Her car wouldn't start, and she hit some traffic. But it's fine. Everything is all set up."

Fletcher squeezes my arm, and I sigh heavily. Yeah, I should have expected that my mom would be slacking on communication.

"How was dinner last night?" Grace asks in an obvious attempt to change the subject.

I cringe. "She was late for that, too."

"I'm sorry. Was it okay otherwise?"

"It was awkward. She kept asking all these questions about where I plan to send the baby to school, if she's going to go to private school since Fletcher could afford the admission fees, if she's going to take Fletcher's last name... the list goes on." I wave my hand dramatically.

"It was an interesting night to say the least," Fletcher says.

"Well, we are going to make today amazing." Grace beams. "Want to come and see everything?"

"Yes!" I clap my hands together.

Grace leads us down the hall, where a red, pink, and black balloon arch is strung across the doorway. She opens the door to reveal a room decorated so beautifully that I hardly recognize it.

The tables are covered in alternating pink, red, and black tablecloths with beautiful floral arrangements in the center. There are cookies shaped like ladybugs and flowers, an assortment of cheese and crackers, and so much more. My eyes grow wide as I take every detail in, including the large, handmade banner that reads, *A Little Ladybug is On The Way,*' with '*Congratulations, Lydia,*' underneath.

Zoey stands up from the table she was arranging a few items at, beaming. "You look adorable," she shouts, running and wrapping me in her arms.

I hug her back as I continue to take in all the details in

the room around me. It's absolutely perfect, and everything I wanted.

"You guys, it's amazing," I gush.

Hattie skips over, joining our hug. "It's so cute in here, isn't it?"

"It's perfect." Out of the corner of my eye, I spot Dylan standing on a stool, hanging a little red and white speckled mushroom from the ceiling.

"Hey," he calls, turning back to the task.

Fletcher rushes over to spot him, and when he steps down, the two hug.

There won't be a ton of people here, mainly my mom and Fletcher's, a few of my co-workers, a group of the WAGs from the MBH, and some friends from college that I keep in touch with now and then. Honestly, I prefer when things are more low-key.

The door opens, and Dottie rushes in, hauling a few gift bags. "I'm so sorry I'm late! There was an accident on the freeway, so I got stuck in traffic."

"Mom, slow down." Fletcher laughs, returning to my side. "It's fine."

"Hi, honey." Dottie sets the bags down, kissing Fletcher on the cheek before stepping over to me. "Sweet girl, look at you. You're glowing!"

Her hands rub up and down my arms. I haven't seen her in person since the night I found out I was pregnant. So much has changed since then, but I've been sending her bump photos whenever I can. I send them to my mom and dad, too, but Dottie is the only one to respond.

"Thank you." I give her as tight a hug as I can with my growing bump in the way. "And thank you for coming. It means the world to me."

"I wouldn't have missed it," she replies, pulling back

and pressing a hand to my cheek. "May I?" She gestures to my bump.

I nod, and she rests her hand over my stomach, caressing.

She looks back up at me with tears in her eyes. "I'm so proud of you, Lydia."

Her words strike me in the chest, warmth swimming through my veins. I don't think anyone has ever told me they were proud of me. Certainly not either of my parents.

"Thank you," I whisper, tears filling my eyes. I blink rapidly, trying to make sure they don't ruin my makeup.

Dottie swipes under my eyes as my baby girl kicks.

"She's saying hi to her grandma," I say.

"Hi, baby girl." Her voice shakes as she speaks. Dottie keeps one hand on my stomach, reaching out to take Fletcher's hand in the other. "Oh, this is just so perfect. I'm so happy for you two."

Fletcher's flecked green eyes grow watery as he glances between his mom and me. He leans forward, pressing a kiss to my temple, and I melt into him.

"Thanks, Mom," Fletcher whispers as the door to the event space opens.

At long last, my own mother finally arrives.

"Hi, Mom." I try to sound excited, even though I'd be lying if I said I wasn't nervous. Who knows how she'll act today? I can only hope she doesn't make a big deal out of something minuscule.

"Hello." Mom glances around the room, cringing subtly before she straightens her expression. "This is... something."

I drop Fletcher's hand and stride toward her. "They did a wonderful job." I point at the table with the cookies and desserts.

"Yes," Mom mutters, still glancing around apprehensively.

"It's exactly what I wanted." I smile at Grace, Zoey, and Hattie before bringing my mom over to introduce her to Dottie.

The two shake hands awkwardly while Dottie asks a few questions to get to know my mother, but my mom shows no interest in returning the gesture. The whole thing is so awkward that I call out to Grace from across the room.

"Grace, do you need my mom or Dottie's help with anything?" I raise my eyebrows to plead with her. She's standing beside Dylan on the step stool, directing him to hook one of the hanging mushrooms to the ceiling.

"Oh," Grace squeaks. "Umm." She glances around the room, biting her lower lip. "Sandra, can you wash the rest of the fruit and cut the strawberries?"

My mother looks affronted. "You didn't hire a caterer?"

"It didn't make sense to hire one when we are only having snack foods," I say to my mother, turning to look at her with soft eyes. "Please?"

Mom sighs heavily and heads over to the attached kitchen, where Zoey is. I feel bad about sending Mom to Zoey, but at least she's out of the main area for now. Dottie exhales heavily once the door closes behind Mom, wrapping an arm around my waist.

"Well." Dottie tuts. "Someone needs to take the stick out of her ass."

"Mom!" Fletcher scolds.

But I'm laughing so hard I can barely breathe. "You are so right."

Fifteen minutes later, the first guest arrives, and Grace promptly throws a sash over my body that reads 'Mama to be.'

I greet my boss as she enters, offering her a hug and another thank you for allowing us to use the space. Guest after guest arrives, each toting a gift bag or box, and everyone cooing over my growing bump and the adorable event space.

Fletcher is by my side the entire time as I mingle with people I haven't seen in ages, and I introduce him as my boyfriend. After the first time, the term rolls off my tongue easily, but it feels like he's more to me than simply my boyfriend. Perhaps partner is the right word.

My mom pops out from the kitchen, glowering, but I choose to ignore her. This is how I'm choosing to be celebrated, and it's not my fault that our tastes don't align.

When it's time to open presents, Fletcher tries to sit in the group of people who are staring at me, but I pull him with me.

"I can't handle having that many eyes on me alone," I whisper, to which he laughs.

"I wasn't sure if you wanted it to be all about you or not." As he helps me into the chair, he pulls an extra one up beside me right as the door opens.

Three people walk in, and I can't help but smile. I wasn't expecting them to come, but I appreciate it, none-theless. Calvin, Adam, and Trigg grin and wave as they enter, finding Grace, Zoey, Hattie, and Dylan at the edge of the crowd.

My mom sits in the front with a glass of punch, while Dottie settles beside her. Fletcher hands me the first present, and I get started opening the mountain of presents.

I CAN'T KEEP track of all the adorable clothing sets, blankets, toys, and baby gadgets I've received, but thankfully, Grace is making notes for me. I've cried more than once at just how cute and small everything is. I can't handle it, especially not when Trigg passes a box forward that contains an adorable hat and a tiny hockey stick with the words 'my first hockey stick' painted on it. After that, Calvin and Adam both give me little Minnesota Blue Herons gear, including some mittens and a sweatshirt.

The gifts from his teammates and friends make me think about Fletcher teaching her how to skate and play hockey, and another round of tears starts. I'm pretty sure everyone thinks I've lost it, but I don't care. I'm so incredibly happy, it's not even funny.

To make it even better, my mother has been snapping photos the entire time, and it puts me at ease. Maybe she does actually care enough about her granddaughter and me.

With only two gifts left, I stand and stretch while Fletcher runs to get me something to drink. He comes back over with a glass of punch and a cookie for me but kisses me gently on the lips before handing them over.

"Doing okay?" he asks.

I nod, taking a kiss of my own from him before grabbing the snack and drink. Fletcher rubs a hand over my stomach as our baby girl kicks, while everyone in the room lets out an "aww." I blush furiously, turning my head to avoid everyone's eyes, but note that my mother is snapping pictures. I'll have to see if she can send me some of them.

Once I sit back down and set my half-empty cup on the table next to me, I reach for one of the final boxes. The tag on it says it's from my mom, and I offer her a smile before ripping open the pristine gold wrapping paper. I pull off the top of the box to find an envelope nestled in white tissue paper with a plaid headband with a bow underneath it.

"The real gift is in the envelope," my mother says as she holds up her phone.

I nod, lifting the envelope and opening it carefully. I don't want to think the worst, but my hands are trembling. There's no saying what this could be. When I pull the stiff paper from the envelope, I open it to read a very properly written letter.

Scanning the words twice, my heart sinks farther into my chest with each beat. She didn't.

"What is this?" My voice shakes, and I look at her.

Fletcher takes the letter from my shaking hand, reading it.

"Guaranteed admission into the top private school in the country." She beams. "And the best part is, it's only thirty miles from her grandparents."

"Right," I mutter.

Fletcher takes the box and sets the paper in it. I don't want to get into this right now, but my mom continues speaking.

"It's perfect. The admissions director was all too happy to guarantee a spot for her once she heard that Fletcher is her father—well, not *technically*, but what's a little white lie?" She chuckles, waving her hand dismissively. "Fletcher is more than able to foot the bill, and it's the perfect school for the daughter of an NHL player. I mean, just think of how much she will learn!"

I don't realize I'm pinching my skin through my dress until Fletcher places his hand over mine, stopping me.

"We'll have to discuss this later, Sandra." His voice is colder than I've ever heard. "Thank you."

My mom beams, clearly not seeing my anger, sadness,

or distress. Dottie and I lock eyes, and she offers me a sad smile.

"There's one more, sweetie," Dottie says, gesturing to the final present at my feet, wrapped in highland cow wrapping paper.

Based on the paper, I know it's from her, and my heart thumps back to life.

Fletcher hands me the gift, and I rip open the paper, a little sad to be destroying the adorable print. I open the box to see red tissue paper lining the cardboard, and underneath, a beautiful white blanket with little red and black ladybugs stitched into the fabric.

"Oh, Dottie," I breathe, pulling the blanket out and holding it to my chest. "Did you make this?"

I run my fingers over the carefully stitched design as I hold back tears.

"I did," Dottie confirms, tears streaming down her cheeks. "Each of my grandbabies have gotten one from me. It felt only right that hers be ladybugs."

Nodding, I swipe a tear from my cheek. "Thank you. It's absolutely beautiful."

I look to my right at Fletcher, who's wiping a tear. "Thanks, Mom." He stands and takes her in a long hug, where she rubs and pats his back as she whispers in his ear.

My fingers don't stop running over the fabric of the blanket, my heart soaring with the love I can feel in every single stitch. In the bottom corner, she's sewn on a small patch that has the words, '*From your grandma, with love*' stitched into it. I stand and make my way over to her, hugging her tightly when she and Fletcher finally break apart.

"Thank you." I cry into her neck, still clutching the blanket between us.

"I'm so happy you love it," Dottie replies, her voice wobbling.

"I love it so much. She'll love it, too."

Her arms tighten around me as she rubs my back. When I finally pull away, I step aside and realize I should probably hug my mother, too, even though I'm unsure of how to feel about the gift she gave us—if it could be considered that.

I step over to my mother, and she opens her arms for a hug. "Thanks."

I'm not sure I mean it, and it's not really what I want to say.

"It's going to be such a good choice for her future," Mom says.

"Hmm." I pull away, turning to the others. "Thank you so much everyone for coming, and for the amazing gifts. I can't even express how much they all mean to us."

Slowly, people filter out and say their goodbyes as we clean up the discarded wrapping paper and organize the items into boxes. The guys all start taking trips out to Fletcher's SUV, and my mom pulls me aside again.

"Well, what did you think of the gift?" she asks. "It's going to be so wonderful. Think of her future."

I swallow harshly. "I don't know. We need to talk about it—"

"What is there to talk about? There should be no question. You went to a nice school, but with Fletcher's money, your daughter could go to the best of the best."

"I don't care if she goes to the best school," I snap. "I don't want my daughter living across the country from me for nine months of the year."

"Well, she'd have us. She'd be fine."

"Right," I scoff. "I appreciate the gift, but I don't think private boarding school is the right choice for her."

"She's not even born yet. How could you know?" Mom asks in a scathing tone.

"I just know," I yell. "She's my daughter. I don't want her going to a boarding school. I want to raise her, be there when she gets off the bus every day, show me what project she made, and tell me what she learned that day. I don't want to watch my daughter be raised by teachers across the country and see her grow up through a phone."

She raises her eyebrows, and when I feel a hand wrap around my wrist, I relax.

"Maybe we should talk about this another time," Fletcher whispers.

"No need." She grabs her purse, her eyes still wide. "I see that my kindness and effort in making pathways for my granddaughter that my own daughter didn't take are unappreciated. I'll go."

I lean into Fletcher's arms as they wrap around me. I don't have the energy to stop her or make things right. I can't do it. If she doesn't understand why I don't want to raise my daughter that way now, I'm not sure she ever will.

My mother scrambles out without a second glance or another word, and I sink into Fletcher, resting my head on his chest as he rubs my back.

He kisses my hair. "I'm proud of you."

"Why?" I choke out a laugh between tears.

"You stood up to her, even if it was hard."

"It didn't feel like it. She just doesn't listen or get it."

"She doesn't. But there's only so much we can do."

Nodding into his chest, I take a deep breath. "Thanks."

"You're amazing, Lydi. I know that was hard."

Another hand joins Fletcher's on my back. "How are you doing?"

I recognize the voice as Zoey's.

Turning from Fletcher's arms, I fall into hers, accepting another long hug. "Fine, I guess. Sorry everyone had to see that."

"Hey. We don't care. We're here for you." Under her breath, she says, "It really was a shitty gift."

A laugh bursts from my lips. "It really was."

The rest of our friends make their way over, pulling us into a big group hug.

"I hate to be the one to say it," Calvin says, fully breaking the tension, "but Lydia, your mom is kind of a bitch."

We all laugh, and I'm reminded that family isn't always blood. It's the people who are there for you every step of the way, cheering you on, and picking you up when you fall, no matter how messy it gets.

52

BITING MY TONGUE

LYDIA

I groan as I shift in bed, my body aching after the long day yesterday. Fletcher is lying behind me while I cradle my pregnancy pillow, his body latched and intertwined with my limbs like an octopus.

"Wha—" he mumbles when I scoot away.

"I have to pee." I throw the pillow from my front and roll out of bed.

After the shower last night, we went to dinner with everyone and dropped Dottie off at the hotel. She could have stayed with us now that I'm pretty much living in Fletcher's room, but she chose the hotel a block away.

She's going to meet me at the arena for the game this afternoon, and I can't wait. We decided to get seats in the lower bowl rather than a suite, since it's just the two of us. The only thing I've heard from my mom is a message from my dad letting me know she made it home safely, and that they were both disappointed in my reaction to the gift.

I don't know where my relationship with my parents goes from here, but I need to figure it out.

Once I'm finished in the bathroom, I head back into the

bedroom to find Fletcher awake and waiting for me. "Come here."

I saunter over to the bed, climbing on and lying on my side so we're face to face.

Fletcher pushes a curl behind my ear, pressing a tender kiss to the tip of my nose. "Good morning, beautiful."

"Good morning." I smile softly, running a hand through his tousled hair. "How did you sleep?"

"Amazing. Though I always sleep amazingly when you're next to me." Fletcher's hands smooth down my arms and over my bump where the baby kicks. "Good morning, my little ladybug. Did you keep your mommy up all night?"

I groan because yes, she did. "She was kicking or punching my ribs the whole night. Then as soon as she'd stop, I'd have to get up to pee, and the cycle would repeat."

"That was not very nice," Fletcher says to my bump, poking it through my shirt.

I rub my hand over Fletcher's. "As much as I wish it would, I'm not sure scolding her will help."

"Hmm."

"Do you have practice this morning?"

I would love some time just the two of us before Dottie and I do some afternoon shopping for more baby things. After this weekend, we are officially going to move my mattress out and turn my room into the baby's nursery. It's time.

Fletcher shakes his head, trailing his hands up my body until they caress my neck, my cheek. When his green eyes meet mine, there's a heat in them. "Nope. I'm a free man until three."

"Whatever shall we do to pass the time?" I tease, gripping his chin and pressing a kiss to his stubbled jaw.

Even though my body aches, there's still a constant and

yearning need for Fletcher and all things sex. I genuinely cannot remember there ever being a time when I was this horny.

"I think I have a few ideas," he says, kissing me deeply.

His tongue teases between my lips until I grant him access, and his hand drags back down my body, sliding under my sleep T-shirt to cup my sensitive breasts. My nipples harden immediately, so much more sensitive now than they were even a week ago.

I gasp into his mouth, my brain faltering as my pussy grows wetter.

"Fletcher." His name falls from my lips as he tweaks my nipples and kisses down my jaw to suck on my neck.

"Yeah, beautiful?" he cockily asks.

"I need more."

He heeds my request, moving down my body eagerly, and nudging me so I'm on my back. I scoot up, pulling my shirt up and over my head while he pulls down my sleep shorts and underwear, baring my soaked core to him. I lie on a pillow in a half-seated position, since the baby loves to rest on my lungs, making it impossible to breathe.

Fletcher lies down on his stomach, a single curl falling into his eyes as they lock with my own. A devious smile lights up his face as he licks a line straight from my entrance to my clit before settling there and sucking hard.

"Oh god," I cry, gripping his hair.

His tongue flicks in circles on my clit, bringing me to a fast climax. My body shudders with the intensity of the quick release, my breath coming in quick succession.

"Fuck, Fletcher," I groan when he doesn't stop.

When he pulls back, his chin is soaked in my arousal. He doesn't move to clean himself, simply licks his lips, offering me a cheeky grin. "That was quick."

"You're efficient." I push on his shoulder. "Your turn."

He flops onto his back, giving me room to kneel beside him. I take his cock in my hand, pumping it slowly, twisting with each long tug.

"Lydia..." Fletcher moans, his voice strained.

"Let me play." I bend my head to take his cock in my mouth.

Fletcher's hips jerk as my mouth makes contact with the fat head of his cock. I flick my tongue against the slit, reveling in the salty taste of his pre-cum.

Fletcher gasps, his hands flying to the back of my head to guide me up and down as he tries to control the pace. I let him, but only for a moment before I take over control, gripping the base of his cock with my hand, squeezing.

"Oh, baby," Fletcher groans, his muscles rippling.

I try not to smile as I suck him deeper into my throat, saliva seeping out the sides of my lips as I take him as far as I can, hollowing my cheeks. Fletcher shouts, his hands flying to my face to gently pull me off him.

Pouting, I rock back on my heels and shimmy. Honestly, I'm quite proud of myself. He's never gotten that close that fast before, so it's a job well done. Fletcher's hand replaces mine at the base of his cock, his fingers gripping tightly as he tries to stave off his orgasm.

"God, I almost came," he murmurs through shuddering breaths.

"Why'd you stop me, then?" I ask, letting the fake innocence drip in my tone.

"You know why."

"I think I need you to show me." I lean forward, my breasts swaying.

He smooths a hand over my tits, plucking at my nipples.

"Hands and knees, beautiful." Fletcher sits forward and

kisses me quickly before shifting me to the middle of the bed.

I get into position on my hands and knees, eagerly waiting for him to get behind me. I shake my ass for him, and he groans, gripping my ass cheeks in his strong hands.

"You're going to finish me before we get started."

I press my hips back against him, his hard erection pressing against my bare pussy. "Please," I moan, needing him so badly it aches.

One of his hands grips tightly at my hip while the other guides his cock to my core. He slides the head through my wetness a few times before pushing into my pussy in one hard thrust.

I let out a keening shriek, my upper body sinking into the mattress as I land on my elbows. Both of his hands are on my hips as he bottoms out inside me, pulling out all the way and thrusting back in.

Our bodies move together to find the perfect momentum that sends us spiraling over the edge. His cock hits my G-spot on the next thrust, making my pussy quiver and tighten around him.

"Fuck, Lydi—" Fletcher growls, one hand threading around my short hair and pulling just enough to tilt my head back. The other hand scoops under my breasts, lifting me so I'm flush against his chest. His mouth finds my neck.

"This pussy is so fucking good," he says under his breath. "So fucking tight. Don't know how I lived without you for so long. Can't get enough of you."

I hold behind his neck, tangling in the hair at the nape of his neck as my mouth drops open. His words are like kryptonite, and the change in angle is the match to set me off, my second orgasm of the morning exploding inside me.

"Fuck, you're so pretty when you cum." His voice is hoarse. "Give it to me."

I couldn't stop the cries of pleasure from falling from my lips even if I wanted to. I twitch and writhe as he holds me up, thrusting into me. He jerks, his pace faltering for a moment, and his warm cum fills me.

"Fuck, Lydi, I lo—"

His words break off in a whimper, and warmth spreads through me. Those words, the ones he almost said, have been burning a hole inside me for weeks now, but the timing hasn't felt right. I'm glad he didn't say it yet. I'm ready, but this isn't the right moment.

Fletcher holds me tightly as our breathing slows, and he guides me back to my hands on the mattress, pulling out. His cum leaks from my pussy slowly, but Fletcher's fingers are there, pushing it back inside.

I tremble when his fingers slide inside me, pumping his cum in and out of me.

"Fletcher," I whine, my pussy so sensitive. It feels so good.

"Can't let you waste it," he says in a low, husky voice. He presses kisses up my spine as he slowly pumps his fingers.

I groan when he finally pulls out, leaving me so empty. I roll to my side, my eyelids fluttering shut. "I'm gonna need a minute."

A chuckle bursts from Fletcher's lips before I hear him leave the room. He re-enters a moment later, cleaning up before joining me back in bed.

He wraps his naked body around me tightly. "I think we have time for a quick nap before you head out with my mom, right?"

I glance at the clock on the nightstand. It's not even eight. "Yeah, another couple of hours."

"Good." He kisses my neck, wrapping his arms around my midsection. "Get some rest, beautiful."

My eyes fall shut before the words finish leaving his mouth.

53

MISFORTUNE & MAMA DRAMA

LYDIA

"Okay, I have to head to the arena," Fletcher says as he puts on his jacket, lingering by the front door. "Are you sure you two don't want to ride with me?"

I'm sitting on the couch with my yarn in my lap, crocheting a hat for Dottie.

"Positive." Dottie leaves the kitchen to give him a quick hug. "We will be just fine."

"I'm not standing up," I tell Fletcher when he looks over to me. "She just got comfortable in there, and I'm not risking it." I gesture to my belly with my crochet hook.

Fletcher chuckles, striding over and bending over to kiss me on the lips. "Bye, baby. I'll call you in a bit."

I laugh. "You know, you don't have to call me before every game."

He always calls before a game, even on home games, unless I ride with him, and I never get why. It's not like we don't talk an hour earlier when he leaves home.

"Yes." He kisses me on the lips again. "I." *Kiss.* "Do." *Kiss.* When he pulls back, there's a gleam in his eyes. "Don't question the method to my madness, Lydia Ward."

"Alright." I caress his stubbled cheek.

He's going to shave it into a mustache once more before the playoffs start, since I love it so much, and at this rate, we're a shoo-in for the first round. "I'll see you for warm-ups. Love—"

I catch myself before saying it.

Yes, we used to say I love you, love you, or some variant of the phrase before, but now that we're together, it's different. It holds a new weight. Fletcher almost slipped up this morning, and now I almost did. It's only a matter of time before we say it for real.

I love him, I do. And as more than my best friend. As my partner. The man who has stepped up to be the father of my child, who has supported me every step of the way. I've never been so thankful we ruined our friendship to take this pathway.

After he leaves, Dottie and I settle in for a relaxing afternoon before we head to the arena.

"Are you ready?" she asks.

The baby kicks at the sound of her voice.

"As ready as I can be, I suppose." I shrug. "If I were doing this on my own, I'd be more of a mess, but Fletcher has made things so much easier." I hold her weathered hand in mine. "Thank you for raising an amazing man."

Her eyes shine. "I'm so happy you two finally found your way together. Watching you become parents will be one of the great joys of my life."

My eyes well up, too.

"You're in love with him, aren't you?" Dottie wipes away my tears.

I nod, words failing me. I am. I love him so much, and I can't wait for the moment I finally tell him. I need to tell him as soon as possible.

"He loves you, too, you know. He would move mountains for you and your little girl."

"I know," I say through a sob. "He's shown me that every day."

"Good." She wraps her arms around me in a tight embrace, and baby girl kicks when her grandma rests her palm flat over my stomach.

We talk for a while longer before we head to the arena, walking arm in arm to our section. There's still a bit of time before warm-ups, so we decide to get some popcorn before heading to our seats.

Something feels off as we step into the popcorn line. It feels like everyone is staring at me. There's a pricking sensation at the back of my neck, and when I glance to my right, two girls have their eyes locked on me as they glance between their phone and me.

When I look in the opposite direction, a couple is also staring at me—or rather, at my hand resting on my pregnant stomach. The more I look around, the more I see people pointing me out as they walk by, eyes catching me in every direction.

What the hell is going on? No one has ever paid me this much attention.

I reach into my back pocket to grab my phone.

There's a text from my mom on my home screen, and when I open it, there's a link to an article with a message below.

MOM

Thought you might like to see this! Those photos turned out wonderfully.

My jaw drops. The thumbnail image is a photo of

Fletcher and me from the baby shower, and not only that, but it's a photo my mother took.

I click on the link as my heart pounds and a clammy sweat breaks out on my brow. The heading reads: *'Baby Mama Snares Blue Herons Captain. He's the Father: Will Fletcher Graff leave it all on the ice in the playoffs? Or will the baby blues keep him down?'*

Swiping down, I see multiple images from yesterday's shower, all taken by my mother. The betrayal sinks deep into my heart, and I can hardly breathe.

"I-I need to go to the bathroom." I barely stay long enough to hear Dottie's response.

I rush to the nearest bathroom, ignoring the looks and gasps. I might as well have put a flashing red light on my head. I'm wearing the new, larger jersey Fletcher got me with his name on it, and my belly is like a homing beacon for attention.

Lurching into the first stall available, I shut the door behind me and open up the article on my phone again, skimming the words.

Fletcher Graff, Captain of the Minnesota Blue Herons, has a baby on the way!

A reputable source submitted these photos from the intimate baby shower yesterday, March fourteenth. The same source identified the woman in the photos as Lydia Ward, Graff's longtime best friend, turned girlfriend. We can't help but wonder what changed since one of Graff's post-game interviews this season (linked below). In the video, Graff states, "I don't foresee myself settling down or having kids."

Another source placed them together earlier last

month at a local daycare. The source says the couple were holding hands, but both appeared to be tense, and did not seem interested in the facility.

Was Fletcher baby-trapped by his so-called best friend? And what does this mean for the Minnesota Blue Herons as they prep for the upcoming playoffs?

I swallow the bile rising in my throat as I scroll down, skimming the rest of the article to get to the video they spoke about. I have to know if Fletcher said those words. The news loves to twist things, and something doesn't seem right about it.

Clicking the play button, I watch as Fletcher runs a hand through his damp hair, sweat still dripping down his face from the game. I can't place when this video was taken, but it's definitely from this season.

The interviewer asks him a few questions about the team and Trigg, citing their former goalie, who retired early to be home with his family. Then he asks, "Do you foresee yourself retiring early to start a family?"

Fletcher offers him a smile, one I recognize as his placating smile, the one he always gives the press when he's over the conversation. "I don't foresee myself settling down or having kids."

He says it flippantly, like he's unsure, but says them anyway.

The Fletcher on the screen nods, and the video cuts out.

My heart shatters. I don't even recognize the man on the screen. He doesn't want kids. If that's true, then what is he doing with me? Is this all an act? Is it all out of pity, or because it's me?

That doesn't feel right.

So many things are whirling through my brain, between the article, the images my mother shared, and that I have to go out there and pretend to act normal in front of Dottie. Meanwhile, my heart is breaking.

My phone vibrates in my palm, breaking me from my spiraling thoughts, Fletcher's name on the screen. I freeze, not ready to speak to him yet, knowing I'll break down. I can't have a conversation like that in a bathroom stall. Absolutely not. Not only that, but I don't want to do this while he's in the locker room. We need to talk about this at home. In private. Which, apparently, is the only place we can trust nowadays.

I let it ring, and when it goes to voicemail, he calls again. I watch it go to voicemail for a second time. A prickle of guilt builds in my chest, but I can't talk to him yet.

He doesn't call a third time.

Swiping out of the article, I text my mom back.

ME

We need to talk later.

MOM

About what? They loved the photos.

ME

I never gave you consent to share those.

And the article basically insinuated that I trapped him and he never wanted kids!

I can't talk about this right now. I'll call you later.

I turn my phone off, shoving it into my back pocket and taking a few more deep breaths. Heading out of the stall, I wash my hands, ignoring people staring me down. When I leave the bathroom, Dottie is standing by a pillar with two giant bags of popcorn. A grin lights up her face, and I muster up what I hope is a convincing smile.

"Everything okay?" she asks, passing me a bag.

I take a huge handful, shoving it into my mouth so I don't have to speak. If I say anything, I'm sure I'll break.

I nod and gesture toward our section. Dottie eyes me warily, but thankfully, she doesn't press it. We head to our seats, the blaring bass music thumping in my ears as the DJ announces the guys, and they fly onto the ice for warm-ups. Fletcher turns his gaze to the stands, but I chicken out, looking to the floor and slumping in my seat while Dottie stands and cheers for him.

I shovel bite after bite of popcorn into my mouth, doing everything in my power to keep my eyes off the ice.

"Are you okay?" Dottie asks.

I wave her off. "Fine. My back is kinda sore, so sitting feels better right now."

Hopefully, that's convincing enough.

"Ah, I remember those days," Dottie replies, rubbing my shoulder.

I smile awkwardly. Lying to Dottie makes me feel horrible, but I have to talk to Fletcher first.

When warm-ups finally end, Dottie sits beside me to settle in for the pre-game light show. The giant screen plays the video they show every game, and Fletcher's beautiful face illuminates the arena as he says a few things about the team and their motto.

I have no idea what to think. Have I been so oblivious to how he feels? Is he only stepping up because it's me? What does this mean for our future?

They announce the starting lineup, and the national anthem plays, but I'm so lost in my head. The puck drops. Dottie cheers beside me when Fletcher takes possession. I watch him closely, but his body is a blur. I can hear the sounds of the cheering crowd, the blaring music, but it's all muffled. It feels like everything is happening outside of my body.

It's a rough game. I haven't seen Fletcher—or anyone on the team for that matter—play this poorly in a long time. We are losing 1–5, and it's only the second period.

When the third period starts, Trigg is replaced by Filimonov, the backup goalie. Trigg sits on the end of the bench, the look on his face is pure defeat as he shifts his gaze down to his hands. Fletcher sits beside him, glaring at the ice.

Boston scores again within three minutes of the start of the period, and the arena starts to clear out as fans call it quits, leaving before the game is done.

The final horn blares, ending the game 1–7. I can't even bring myself to stand up and clap as the boys leave the ice, heading straight to the locker room.

Dottie rubs my shoulder. "Rough game." She grabs the empty popcorn bag and stands. "Do we want to meet him in the tunnel?"

I shake my head, knowing that's not a good idea. "Can you bring me home, actually? I'm not feeling well."

Dottie eyes me carefully. "Do we need to go to the hospital?"

"No, everything with the baby is fine. She's moving around like normal. I'm just exhausted." I rest my hand atop my bump. "I think I'm getting a cold or something."

I don't like lying, but I need to get out of here.

Dottie agrees, albeit warily. "I'll text Fletcher and let him know."

"Thanks."

We walk to the car in silence, dread eating away at my heart.

"Do you want to hang out at our apartment for a while?" I ask Dottie.

Normally, I'd love for her to come spend the evening with us, but tonight, I hope she says no. I had to ask; I'm sure she already suspects something is wrong.

"No." Dottie shakes her head. "You should get some rest. I'll see you both in the morning for breakfast before I head back home."

"Okay."

54

DISCONNECT

FLETCHER

nger courses through my veins as I stalk into the locker room. We haven't had that much disconnect in our team since fucking pre-season. I have no idea what happened tonight, but something was off.

First, Lydia didn't answer my calls, then she wouldn't look at me at all, not during warm-ups. If I caught her glancing at me while I sat on the bench, she'd rip her gaze from mine as fast as possible.

I don't want to blame the loss on my superstition, but it definitely didn't help me get in the right headspace for the game. Trigg takes his gear off as fast as possible, heading to the showers without a second glance at anyone. He's probably blaming himself, but we're a team. He's not the only one who stops the puck.

Clearing my throat, I wait for everyone's attention to shift to me. "It was a tough one tonight. We have a few things we can work on at practice this week, but it's one game. We'll get the next one."

The words are a bandage over a bullet wound, but it's all I have in me tonight. Coach tips his chin in my direction.

"You're on press tonight. Might want to prepare yourself after that article."

"Article?" I ask, confused.

"You didn't see the article about you and Lydia?" He raises his brow. "It's everywhere."

I clear my throat. "No, sir."

What could the article possibly be about? Is whatever it says the reason she didn't answer my calls? Why she ignored me?

I grab my phone from the shelf in my locker, quickly check for texts, and see one from my mother.

MOM

Lydia isn't feeling well, so I'm running her home. All is fine with the baby, she says. She thinks she's getting sick. I'll see you in the morning for breakfast. Love you.

I have a feeling Lydia isn't getting sick, and the reason she's going home has more to do with an article than illness. A sinking feeling settles in my gut. What did that article say?

There's another message, this one from Lydia's mom.

SANDRA

The photos are so beautiful. Enjoy!

Below it, she's sent a link.

I click it and skim through the article, each line making me angrier and angrier. What the actual fuck? Was Sandra the one who submitted those photos? She completely invaded our privacy by doing that, and now the whole world knows and is in our business.

When I get to the part with a quote from me, it all clicks. No wonder Lydia ignored me. If she saw this article, she's got to be losing her mind. I scroll to the end, clicking play on the video. They purposely skewed my words, cutting out the second half before I said, "But never say never."

I toss my phone into my locker. I want to run home. I don't want to speak to the press. They, and Lydia's mom, are the ones who caused this mess in the first place. I have to talk to her. She has to know what I said wasn't true. God, I can't imagine how stressed she is. I need to call her, need to get home, and make sure she knows they cut the video.

"Fuck." I groan, pulling at my hair.

"Whoa," Calvin says, stepping up beside me. "What's going on?"

"That article is bullshit," I breathe, running my hands down my face. I yank my jersey over my head, not caring about putting my gear away neatly. My life is falling apart.

"What article? What's happening, dude?" Calvin squeezes my shoulders and turns me to face him. "Breathe."

I take a sharp inhale of air, letting it out slowly. "Lydia's mom leaked photos of the baby shower to the press, and they used a quote I said a long time ago about not wanting to settle down and have kids, but they cut it off, so it sounds horrible. And I'm pretty sure Lydia saw it, and that's why she didn't answer me before the game. Now, my mom took her home."

Calvin's eyes widen. "Oh, *fuck*."

"Pretty much." My heart is threatening to burst from my chest. "I have to do press when all I want to do is get home to my girl."

"I'll go with you. We'll get it over with and then get you home."

Within a minute, we're walking to the press room, and my dread grows with each step. We've barely entered the room when they start asking questions, their words overlapping until they don't sound like words anymore.

Calvin holds up a hand. "One at a time."

I shake my head. "No. I need to make a statement first." I clear my throat. "The photos shared in that article were shared without our consent or knowledge. It's true that Lydia and I recently had a shift in our relationship, but I firmly believe a friendship is a perfect ground for a strong relationship. Yes, I will confirm that we are expecting our first child together. When I did that interview, things were different, and the video cut off one of the most important parts of my words—when I said 'never say never,'—skewing the tone of the video. I never saw myself having kids, but when you find the right person, things change. Now, I cannot wait to become a father and raise our child with my favorite person in the world."

The room is silent, and a few of the reporters smile.

Calvin chuckles to break the tension. "And here I thought I was your favorite person."

The reporters laugh, and Calvin claps me on the back, running his other hand through his damp red hair. "I think that covers everything. Do you need anything more from my boy, or can he get home to his family?"

The reporters shake their heads, and Calvin offers to stay and answer their questions about the game, which they take him up on.

I leave the room without another moment of hesitation, running through the halls to get back to the locker room to rinse off and grab my things.

Within ten minutes, I'm in my car, heading home. My skin prickles with fear as I worry about what's to come, but I need to stay calm and hope Lydia can see what went wrong.

55

I LOVE YOU

LYDIA

I sit on the couch, waiting for Fletcher. Part of me wants to burrow under my blankets and avoid it all, but I know I can't. We have to talk about this if we have any chance of saving this relationship.

The front door opens, and Fletcher strides in, looking as haggard as I feel. His hair is disheveled, his face contorted into fear, and his shoulders slumped.

"I'm sorry about your game," I say, making no move to get off the couch.

"I don't care about the game, Lydia."

A tear slides down my cheek. "You never wanted kids."

He sits beside me and tries to take my hand, but I pull away, and he winces. If he touches me, I'll crack.

"Did you watch the whole video?" Fletcher asks.

"Yes. When was it taken?"

"Did you watch the *whole* video, or the one they edited for the article?" He takes his phone out, swiping.

"I watched the video on the article, and it kinda seemed like it was the whole video, Fletch," I say, irritation seeping in. "Why didn't you say something sooner? No one said you had to step up and be her father or be with me. You could have let me do this on my own. You could have been the cool uncle, as I offered."

Anger flares on his features. "Don't *ever* call me the cool uncle again, Lydia. She's my daughter, and something I said once at the beginning of the season means nothing compared to all my words and actions since."

He tilts the phone toward me, tapping the screen to press play.

I shrink as he says the words that have been replaying in my mind for the last four hours. Except this time, the video continues, and a sly grin pops up on his face, like he's thinking of something—or *someone.*

"At least not anytime soon. But never say never."

I should have known that wasn't the whole story. Guilt creeps in as I look up at Fletcher, his eyes red-rimmed and full of despair.

"That video was taken out of context. Did I see myself settling down so soon? Honestly, no. But there was only one person I ever wanted to have that life with, and I didn't have any hope that you felt the same. I wouldn't change a thing about the way this evolved between us, and where our future is heading."

He takes my hand, while the other rests on my bump. The baby kicks and rolls.

"I reacted," I say sheepishly. "I should have stopped and thought, but it hit me so hard. First, that my mom sent those photos to the press, and then hearing you say you didn't see yourself having kids. It made me feel like I trapped you, like the article said. Or that you were doing it out of pity. My mom sent me the link like she was proud that she made my life go up in flames, all because it's my fifteen minutes of fame."

I let go of his hand to swipe at my cheeks. I'm so embarrassed.

Fletcher cups my wet cheeks. "Look at me. I want this. I want our relationship, the family we're making. She's my child, and I'll love her as my own, as much as I love you."

I inhale sharply. "You do?"

Fletcher nods, tears brimming in his eyes. "Of course, I do. I've been telling her for weeks, but I figure it's time I told her mama how much I love her."

"I love you, too." The words fall from my lips with so much sincerity, it strikes me. We're in this together. He's going to be by my side, and by my daughter's side, too. She'll have the best dad.

Fletcher leans in, kissing me deeply, pouring all his love and emotion into the kiss.

Before it goes too far, I pull back. "I need to call my mom. I'm done with our relationship."

"That's for the best. Do you want me here, or do you want to do it yourself?"

"I need you at my side."

He scoots in close, and I take a deep breath as I click on the call icon by her name. It rings a few times before she picks up.

"Oh, Lydia, it's so good to hear from you," she gushes. "What did you think of the article?"

"I hate it," I say forcefully. "You sent those pictures in. Pictures I wanted to stay private."

"Well, you never told me that—"

"I shouldn't have had to! I guess I assumed my mother would understand that I didn't want my private moments blasted all over the internet for the whole world to see. The article made me question my relationship with Fletcher."

"Oh, that's all made up. They always like to stir a little drama."

"Why did you do it?" I ask the question that's been gnawing at me. "What did you get out of this? Money?"

"They paid me for the photos, yes. But I think you'll thank me eventually. This is for your benefit. The opportunities that could come from this are endless. You could get brand deals for all sorts of things. Makeup, clothes, baby items, you name it."

"I don't want brand deals. Why don't you understand that I don't want some fancy lifestyle in the spotlight? We were keeping our relationship private for a reason." I let out a heavy breath. "I can't do this."

Fletcher squeezes my thigh.

"Can't do what?" Mom asks, confusion in her voice.

"I can't have a relationship with you if you're going to exploit my relationship with Fletcher and not treat me with respect. You never have, and things have gotten ten times worse since I told you I was pregnant. I've given you too many chances at this point."

"Lydia—"

"Are you going to apologize for this? For causing me pain?"

There's silence before she lets out a heavy sigh, which I recognize as one of irritation, not of sorrow or acknowledgment of wrongdoing.

"I'm done. If you don't see that the things you have done are wrong, please don't contact me." I hang up the phone and set it on the coffee table, turning my face into Fletcher's chest. He holds me close, rubbing my back in soothing circles as I cry. It hurts knowing my mom couldn't get over her vision of my life and focus on her relationship with me.

Knowing my daughter won't have a relationship with her grandparents. But perhaps it's for the better.

"I'm sorry," Fletcher whispers in between gentle kisses to the top of my head. "I know how much you wanted her to change."

"I did. But I don't need her or my dad if I have you. You're my family. Your parents, our friends. They're the ones who have proven they'll be there for me no matter what."

"You're right. We're your family. I love you."

"I love you, too."

Fletcher's phone starts ringing, and he glances at it. "It's my mom."

"You can answer it. I feel kinda bad, I wasn't exactly good company tonight."

"Understandable." He swipes his finger across the screen, and the moment he does, Dottie's shrieks come through the line.

"Fletcher Graff, what is this article!"

"Mom, breathe." He rubs an arm over my shoulder.

"No wonder Lydia was so off tonight," Dottie continues, barely paying Fletcher any attention. "And her mother. Those are the photos she sent me! I can't believe she sent those into the press and gave them a statement. Oh god, are you with Lydia—"

"Mom," Fletcher yells. "Yes, I'm with Lydia. We've talked it out. The video was taken out of context. I said more, but they cut the video to make it seem like she trapped me or something. And yeah, her mom is horrible."

"I would love to smack her upside the head. I mean, what a piece of work!"

"I know."

I hold my hand out for the phone, taking it from Fletcher's hand. "I'm okay. It sucks, but I talked to my mom and told her I'm done. She crossed the line too many times."

"Oh, honey." Dottie's voice softens. "I'm so sorry. I know how hard that must have been."

"It is, but I have a better family by my side now." I glance up at Fletcher.

There's so much love in his gaze and in his mother's voice that I know I've made the right decision for my daughter and me.

56

MUSTACHE RIDE

FLETCHER

After everything that happened, I don't want to be more than a few feet from Lydia at all times. In bed, we lie side by side, our bodies as close as physically possible. Her bump rests between us, and I rub soothing circles over her tight skin. I can feel our little girl rolling around in there.

"Does it hurt when she does that?" I ask curiously.

"Sometimes. She tends to kick my ribs and my bladder, so that is definitely not comfortable. She's running out of room in there, though."

"You're amazing."

A flush creeps up her cheeks. "So are you."

"I can't believe we're here. That this is my life. I've wanted you for so long, Lydia. I wanted more, but I couldn't rock the boat, and I was content. Truly, I was. If all I ever got from you was a best friend, that's all I needed. Now, though, I can't imagine it any other way."

"I love you," Lydia murmurs, smiling.

"I love you." Leaning in, I kiss her. Something shifts from sweet and tender to a frantic need between us.

Our clothes are pulled off in record time, and our bodies twine together until the need grows too strong.

"I need you to sit on my face."

"What?" she gasps breathlessly. "I can't do that."

"Yes, you can." I lie flat on the bed and pat my chest. "Come on, baby."

Sheepishly, Lydia straddles my chest, and I move until my face is level with her soaked pussy. I glide my hands up her thick thighs, gripping her wide hips and pulling her down until she tries to stop me.

"Fletcher, wait. I'm too heavy with the baby."

"No, you're not. I need a taste of this soaking pussy. I need it like I need air. Now, hands on the headboard, and sit."

I pull her down again, and this time, she lets me. My tongue slides through her pussy lips to find her sensitive clit, and she jerks as soon as I glide my tongue along it. I hum, letting the vibration on my lips add to the sensation as her sweetness hits my taste buds.

She tastes so good. I want to drown in her.

Lydia bucks, letting out a long, guttural moan as my tongue flicks and sucks at her clit. I dreamed of a life with Lydia, of the sweet moments and a future, but I'd be lying if I said I didn't dream of this, too. I've wanted her for a long time, wanted to taste her and fuck her senseless. This is a literal dream come true for me, and I'm going to savor every second of it. I massage my hands over the round globes of her ass, roaming every inch of her skin as my tongue works its magic.

I can feel her getting closer, her hips rocking at a staccato pace. I can't speak, can't spur her closer to an orgasm with my words, but I hum against her clit again, hoping that helps. I feel the moment she finishes, her body twitching as she gasps.

"Fletcher," she whimpers, and what a beautiful sound it is to have my name on her lips as she comes. Music to my fucking ears.

My hand flies to my cock; I'm so close to coming just from the sound of her that I have to grip the base tightly in an attempt to stave off my release. My tongue flutters against her clit still but stops when she shifts off my face. I miss the weight of her immediately.

"Did I kill you?" Lydia murmurs, falling to her side on the bed.

A goofy grin forms on my face as she pushes back my hair, taking in my soaked chin with a chuckle.

"I guess not."

"Nope," I answer. "I already look forward to the next time we do that again. As soon as possible, if I have my way."

"You're ridiculous." Her fingers tighten in my hair. "Your turn."

She moves to sit between my thighs, but I stop her. "I have something else in mind."

"Oh?"

"Lie on your side and face the wall."

She does as I direct, and I adjust our pillows, pushing her thigh up so she's open for me. I slide my cock in without any preamble. I need this. Need this connection and touch.

Lydia gasps, her hand gliding behind her to wrap around the nape of my neck. "Fletcher."

"Yeah, baby?"

"Keep going."

I do as she says, my hips rocking in and out of her at a

leisurely pace. I don't want a reckless fuck right now; I want to show her just how much I love her.

"I love you," I breathe, wrapping my arm underneath her breasts, keeping her close to me.

"I love you," she responds with a whimpering gasp.

"So much. You and me. We're in this forever."

"Forever."

My heart clenches. I have everything I ever wanted, and more.

Her second orgasm hits her just as my own does, and I thrust into her a few more times, letting our breathing slow as our hearts pound in synchronized beats.

We stay together again until my cock grows soft and I pull out of her. I watch as my cum slowly drips down her thighs, and again, I use my fingers to scoop it back up and push it back into her swollen cunt.

"Mine," I breathe, the possessive side of me coming out.

"Yours." She tilts her head back for a kiss, then rests back on the pillow with a heavy sigh.

57

FAMILY ARE THE
ONES THAT SHOW UP

LYDIA

THIRTY-TWO WEEKS PREGNANT

"Dude, did you see that goal Torman made on the Bulls last night?" Calvin asks as he screws a bolt into a rail of the crib.

"People underestimate him." Adam shrugs, breaking down another box across the room.

We're currently in what used to be my bedroom, setting up the nursery. The guys have some time off before heading into the playoffs in a few weeks, and Fletcher and I are beginning to get antsy over the upcoming arrival of the baby. It's hard to believe that in eight weeks or less, she'll be here.

She kicks at my ribs, and I rub my hand over my belly, wincing. I'm sitting on the floor folding clothes and blankets, and to be honest, I'm going to need a lot of help to get up.

"Do you guys only know how to talk about hockey, or is that really all your personality is?" Grace teases as she hangs up a tiny dress in the closet.

All of the guys chuckle before Adam speaks up. "Pretty sure you know the answer to that."

Adam winks at Grace, and she narrows her eyes. I don't think anyone else catches it, but I do.

Grace scoffs. "Fine, but all we ever talk about is hockey. Can we please change the subject?"

There's an awkward silence, and I glance across the room at Fletcher, who's trying to hold back his laughter.

"Our lives revolve around hockey, you know this," Calvin replies as he walks back in the room, shoving her shoulder.

Zoey chuckles. "We're all going to the cabin on Willow Lake this summer, right?"

Calvin nods enthusiastically and sits back down next to Fletcher to help with the crib. "Yep. My parents said we're welcome anytime."

The memory of what occurred between Fletcher and me the last time we were at their cabin flares in my brain, sending heat spiking through my body. Thoughts of his mouth all over my skin make my cheeks flush, and a pulse thump between my thighs.

Fletcher clears his throat, and I glance up, noticing his eyes on me. He must be thinking of the same thing. We hold gazes before Grace's voice breaks the moment.

"I'll be at the cabin all summer since I'll be working at Sweeney's all the time." She nudges Hattie. "Are you excited to start?"

"So excited," Hattie says. "I met with Mike last week, and he offered me a good number of hours."

"I hate that you have to work so much," I say as I fold another onesie. It's hard not to squeal every time I come across another cute pattern or design. Let's face it, they are all adorable.

Hattie shrugs. "Honestly, I'm used to it. Ever since I could work, I have been. It's been hard, but we are making it work. I want Dylan to have a good life. And he loves hockey, so I want him to be able to do what he loves."

Zoey rubs her shoulder. "You're so good to him."

"Thanks," Hattie says. "He's a good kid."

"He will do great things. He's a natural in the net," Trigg says affirmatively.

Hattie seems lost for words as she stares across the room at Trigg, the two of them in their own world.

"Alright, I think we're ready to screw these two pieces together," Fletcher says after there's a moment of quiet.

He stands, pulling the completed rail up with him. The boys put the pieces together until it finally resembles a crib.

Tears prick my eyes as the reality begins to sink in. Soon, my baby girl will be here. I glance around the room at my friends and all the hard work they are putting in for us. A single tear slides down my cheek. Before I can stop it, the floodgates open.

A constant stream of tears runs down my cheeks as I silently cry, so thankful for these people that it's healing a piece of my soul.

"Oh no," Calvin mumbles when he's the first to notice me crying. "Um, Fletchy baby, something's wrong with your girl."

Fletcher's eyes snap to me immediately, and he crosses the room, dropping to his knees in a heartbeat. "Hey, are you okay?"

His hands flutter over my face, then rest on my stomach, the fear in his face lessening when he feels our daughter kick.

I nod, covering my mouth to silence my sobs. From the corner of my eye, I see our friends silently leave the room.

Shaking my head, I rest my head on his shoulder as he wraps his arms around me. "I'm fine," I blubber. "Really."

"It doesn't seem like it," he whispers, rubbing a hand up and down my spine.

"I am. It all sort of hit me, y'know?" I take a deep breath—well, as much of a deep breath as I can with a baby pressing on my lungs. "Even though my mom and dad suck, I have these amazing people here to support me and our daughter. Watching you guys put up the crib, it sunk in. I mean, they're all spending their day off helping us put together the nursery. Who does that?"

"Good people. We've got lots of good people surrounding us, Lydi-bug. People who love you for who you are, and not what you can offer them."

I inhale a shaky breath. "Yeah, you're right."

Fletcher leans back, locking his green eyes with mine. "Feeling better?"

I nod, swiping away the tears. "We should probably call them back in. I think I scared Calvin."

"Apparently." Fletcher laughs and goes to open the door before I stop him.

"Wait!"

"What?" His eyes widen.

"Can you help me up off the floor? I have to pee, and I'm scared to stand up with everyone watching me. Movement is way too hard."

Fletcher chuckles, stepping back over to me. I hold out my arms for him, and he hooks his under my armpits, and without even trying, I'm on my feet in a second.

"Jeepers, that was much easier than when I did that myself yesterday."

Fletcher shakes his head. "No more sitting on the floor if I'm not here. I don't want you to get stuck down there."

"That's probably a good point." I waddle into the bathroom.

When I come back a few minutes later, the room looks totally different. They've pushed the crib up against the wall and put the mattress in. It has a light-pink polka-dot sheet, and the little crocheted ladybug I made sits in the corner of the mattress.

"Oh," I gasp, covering my mouth. "You guys, it's so cute."

Grace finishes folding the blanket Dottie made and hangs it over the side of the crib.

I step up to it, running my hands over the soft fabric. "Thank you."

She rubs my shoulders and points to the closet. "I think we have everything hung and organized we could for now, and Hattie and Zoey are putting all the onesies in the dresser drawers in order by size."

Fletcher stands in the corner with a wide smile on his face as Calvin, Trigg, and Adam bicker over a new box that's been brought in.

"What's that?" I point to the box.

The three men go quiet, shifting so they're in front of the box.

Fletcher moves forward, a shy expression on his face. "Remember the day we went and added a bunch of things to your registry?"

Nodding, I try to look around the men who are still blocking the box. "Yes, but I got all the things I added to the registry."

He shakes his head. "You didn't get the glider you wanted, because you weren't sure it would fit."

"Oh," I breathe, my heart swelling. "You got me a glider?"

"Of course I did." He pushes a curl from my face and kisses the tip of my nose. "I knew you'd never get it for yourself, or that you'd say you could just feed her on the couch, but you wanted it. And besides, it looks comfy as hell."

"It really does." I make a choked sound. "Fletcher, thank you. I love you." I reach up on my tiptoes to wrap my arms around his neck, twisting my fingers in his hair.

"I love you too, Lydi-bug." Fletcher's lips slant over mine as our friends hoot and holler around us.

When we break apart, Calvin is already tearing into the box like the chaos goblin he is. He pulls the back of the chair out, and I see that instead of the cream color they had in the store, Fletcher opted to get a pastel pink to match the nursery.

I clutch his arm. "It's perfect."

"It's not even put together yet." He laughs. "It could be horrible and not match at all."

I shake my head. "It's perfect. Thank you."

58

RUNNING THOUGHTS

FLETCHER

THIRTY-FIVE WEEKS PREGNANT

"Come on, Waffles!" I hit my hand on the outside of the boards as Shepherd skates toward the goal on a breakaway.

The crowd is on its feet, cheering him on.

He shoots, but the goalie catches it, and the crowd groans, dropping back into their seats. The whistle blows, and Waffles drops his head in a moment of defeat. He comes back to the boards, swapping out with Monroe.

I pat him on the head. "Hey, don't sweat it."

He nods, but I can tell he's beating himself up.

Play resumes on the ice, with Calvin winning the face-off. This is the last game before we head to the playoffs, and if we win this, we get home-ice advantage for the first two games.

I, for one, hope we get that advantage. I'm feeling antsy after Lydia's thirty-five-week appointment this afternoon. The doctor anticipates Lydia going into labor early based on how the baby is positioned or something. To be honest, I wasn't really listening after she said there was a potential the baby could come early. There's still so much to do, and my mom isn't coming up for another three weeks. I was making lists and plans in my head for the rest of the appointment. Lydia's totally chill about everything, but I couldn't be more anxious.

The thought of missing the birth of our daughter is too hard to bear. Not only that, but add in the stress of the play-offs, and I'm on a hair-trigger. The car seat bases are installed in both of our vehicles, and Lydia is packing her hospital bag at home as we speak. We're as ready as we possibly can be, but there's a niggling voice in my head telling me I need to prep for every possibility.

And one of those possibilities is that I could be halfway across the country when Lydia goes into labor.

If that happens, I'll have to rely on Grace, Zoey, and Hattie to be there for her until I can. And if my mom is here by then, she'll have to be the one to take care of her.

For now, the more time I can spend at home, the better.

We end up winning the game in overtime, thankfully giving us home-ice advantage for the first two games. I give a rousing speech and get the guys excited for the upcoming series, but inside, I'm trying not to spiral.

I shower, and when I head back to my locker, Trigg, Adam, and Calvin are standing around waiting for me.

"What's up?" I ask as I grab my phone, scanning the screen for any messages from Lydia. Thankfully, the only one is her congratulating me on the win.

A bag of popcorn rests on the bench in front of my locker, and I smile, silently thanking the social media girl, Vivi, for getting this for me. I texted her before the game today, asking if she could get me a bag since Lydia wasn't coming. Thankfully, she obliged.

"What are you doing tonight?" Adam asks, running a hand through his dark brown hair.

"Honestly, I'm probably going to head right home. With how close Lydia is to the end of her pregnancy..."

Trigg nods, resting a hand on my shoulder. "We get it. We were going to see if you wanted to come over for a celebratory drink, but you need to get home."

I nod. "Yeah. As much as I'd love to, I can't stand the thought of being away from her for another minute. Maybe when we're out of town, we can go out for one or something."

"We'll play it by ear," Adam says.

Calvin shoves his hands in his pockets as he glances at me.

"What?" I ask him when he doesn't say anything.

A huge smile breaks out on his face, and he gently punches my shoulder. "You're going to be a dad, man!" He pulls me into a long hug, slapping my back. "Fuck, I'm happy for you."

"Thanks," I reply, trying to swallow down the emotion in my voice.

"I'm totally not jealous at all."

"You want to settle down, Miller?" I tease, needing to make the moment less emotional.

When he pulls away, his expression is somber. Huh, I guess he really does want to settle down. I log that into my memory, knowing he might need someone to talk to about this later. Right now, I need to get home. Every moment I'm away from Lydia is giving me hives.

The guys and I walk to our cars together, and when I climb into mine, tossing the bag of popcorn into the passenger seat, I glance at the car seat in the back. This is all so surreal. Not even nine months ago, my life was completely different. Now, I have the woman of my dreams, and we're starting our life together and welcoming our first child in the next few weeks. It can't get any better than this.

Well, maybe if we win the Cup this season, but right now, I'm more than happy with where things are.

When I finally make it to our apartment, I breathe in the familiar scent of home, or rather, the familiar scent of Lydia. She's nowhere in sight, and though I know she's probably in bed, my heart pounds a little faster.

I creep walk down the hall, popcorn bag in hand. Pushing open our bedroom door, the lamp washes the room in warmth. Lydia is propped against the headboard, a pile of yarn in her lap as she works on her latest project. It looks like a black-and-white blob, and I can't figure out what it is.

"Hey, beautiful." I hold up the popcorn bag.

"Yay!" Lydia squeals, resting the project on her belly.

I bring the popcorn to her side, but instead of giving it to her, I lean in, slanting my lips over hers and stealing a kiss first.

"Hi," I whisper against her lips. "I missed you."

"I missed you, too." She peppers kisses all over my cheeks and face, distracting me as she yanks the baggie from my hand. Immediately, she digs into the buttery popcorn, shoving a handful into her mouth and moaning. "God, this is so good."

"You don't even make that sound when I eat your pussy," I tease, kicking off my shoes and rounding the bed to climb on.

"Shut up," Lydia mumbles through her mouthful.

I chuckle as I settle in next to her bump, running my hand over it. "Hey, my little ladybug." When she kicks my hand at the sound of my voice, my heart skips. I feel so much better already, just being here with them. "I missed you, too. Were you good to your mom while I was gone?"

She thumps my hand again, almost like she's acknowledging that I'm speaking to her.

"She wasn't," Lydia says. "She's been kicking my bladder every five minutes."

"That's not very nice," I say to Lydia's bump, wishing I could take away her discomfort for even a day. "I know you're running out of room in there, but you need to be good to your mom."

I talk to my daughter for a while, telling her all about tonight's game and how the playoff series works. By the time I finish, the weight that settled on my chest during the game has eased, and I'm feeling better.

Lydia has finished her popcorn and has been running her fingers through my hair.

"You okay?" she asks as I scoot up on the bed, resting my back against the headboard.

Shrugging, I lean in to rest my head on her shoulder. "I'm anxious."

"What about?" Lydia asks, resting her hand on mine over her stomach.

"Everything. Leaving you, the possibility of you going into labor when I'm across the country, you being alone with the baby, something happening during your labor."

She squeezes my hand. "I get it. It's a lot, but we'll just have to take it as it comes. And next time, we have to make sure not to have a baby in the middle of playoffs."

"Next time?" I lift my head, a smile tugging at the corner of my mouth as I stare into those blue eyes.

They widen as she realizes what she's said. "Um, no—"

"No take-backs," I shout, excited. "You're already thinking about having another."

With a resolved sigh, Lydia nods. "Yeah. I am. I always wanted a sibling growing up, and as uncomfortable as I am, this pregnancy hasn't been too horrible."

"So, when would we have to get pregnant for you to deliver in the off-season?" I question as I settle back in beside her.

Lydia picks up her crochet hook and resumes her project. I still can't figure out what it is, but I'm sure she'll show me later.

"Probably October or November? That would have me delivering mid to end of summer, which would work out well even if you make it all the way to the final round of the playoffs."

"Hmm," I reply, already thinking about what our life with two kids would be like as opposed to one. "I love you."

Lydia leans over, pressing a gentle kiss to my lips. "I love you, Fletcher."

"What are you making?" I finally ask when curiosity gets the better of me.

"A hockey puck." She shifts the yarn a bit. "See? Here's his little arms and his little legs with his skates."

"Oh my gosh, that's actually so cute. How did you do that?"

"I found the pattern on Etsy. I figured she could have this one to play with and bring to games, and then you could give her her first real hockey puck when we go to her first game."

"Can't wait."

My anxieties over the next few weeks are still present, and unfortunately, the only cure for them is time, but having my girl makes everything a bit easier.

59

READY OR NOT

LYDIA

THIRTY-SEVEN WEEKS PREGNANT

"I cannot get over how cute you are," Grace gushes as she brings me a bag of popcorn.

"I look like an avocado," I mutter. I've been in a mood all day today, and I'm so sick and tired of being pregnant. The worst part is, I still have three weeks left.

"An avocado?" Zoey laughs. "That's oddly specific."

"I have a pit sticking out of my center, so that's the only way I can describe it." I take a bite of popcorn, washing it down with my pop.

"I can see it," Grace says, running her eyes up and down my body. "Doesn't change the fact that you're adorable."

Groaning, I mumble out a thank you as she sits beside me. The arena is absolutely packed. It was close, but the guys have made it to the second round of the playoffs.

It's the first game of the second round, and my heart is already pounding in anticipation. This is probably going to be my last game before the baby comes, since getting here was a feat in itself. My body hurts so bad, and my lower back is killing me today. Grace was nice enough to pick me up, so I didn't have to leave when Fletcher did. I wasn't up to driving myself tonight.

My mom tried to call me earlier today, but I declined. She's left me multiple voicemails since the day the article came out. I haven't responded. Never once in any message has she apologized for the hurt she caused me and the way she used Fletcher and caused a rift in our relationship, no matter how brief it was.

I can't knowingly open myself up to any more hurt from them, and I definitely am going to do everything in my power to protect my daughter from it, too.

In an attempt to conserve energy, I stay in my seat for warm-ups. I've been napping often, too tired to function by the end of the workday.

Fletcher skates over, waving at me from his favorite spot on the ice, and heat floods my cheeks when he blows me a kiss.

Zoey plops down next to me, handing me a pop and swiping a handful of my popcorn.

"Hey," I scold. "That's mine."

She laughs. "There's plenty more in the back."

"Never take a pregnant woman's food, Zo." I gesture to the machine behind us. "You want some, go get your own." I narrow my eyes, daring her to take another handful of the popcorn Grace so kindly brought me.

"Jeepers, fine," Zoey says with a scared-sounding laugh. "You always used to share your popcorn."

"That was before a child inhabited my uterus and turned me into a popcorn fiend. I swear, this popcorn is the only thing that sounds good right now. Nothing else will live up to it, and believe me, I've tried."

She shakes her head dramatically. "And that is why I'm

scared to get pregnant. Don't get me wrong, I want kids. The pregnancy, though? No way. Too much discomfort, and I feel like I wouldn't even know my own body anymore."

An ache spreads through my back, and I groan. "Ugh, I have to adjust."

I pass my popcorn to Zoey with a glare, hoping she gets the hint not to take any more, and stand, stretching my body before sitting back down and readjusting.

"Are you sure you're okay?" Grace questions, her eyes filled with concern.

"Totally fine." I wave her off. "Just the end of pregnancy aches and pains."

Zoey hands me my popcorn back, and we chat about nothing and everything while we wait for the game to start.

Ten minutes into the first period, Calvin scores the first goal with an assist from Adam, giving us the lead.

I've had to shift in my seat no less than ten times, and I'm so unbelievably uncomfortable. I've been having some practice contractions this week, and tonight is no exception. These are a bit stronger than the ones I've previously had, but they aren't regular by any means.

"God, I'm so glad to have Adam back," Zoey says when the first period finishes. "It's been so nice having him around again. And now, he and Vincent can finally get to know each other, too."

Grace chimes in. "Calvin is absolutely loving playing with him again."

"Fletcher loves it too." I wince when an especially painful tightness spreads across my stomach.

"Okay, now what was that?" Grace pulls out her phone.

"It's nothing," I say through gritted teeth. "Just a practice contraction."

She types something on her phone. "Practice my ass."

I wave off Zoey's fluttering hands. "I'm fine. My doctor said if they aren't consistent, it's just practice. Besides, I can't leave the game."

Zoey glances over at Grace. "Are you timing these?"

"Yep." Grace nods, looking between me and her phone.

"Stop it. I'm not in labor." Except, there is a small part of me that thinks I may be wrong. This feels different than before, and it's still going.

The two lock eyes again, and when the contraction passes, I sit up a little straighter and take a sip of my pop to appear nonchalant. "See, it's done."

I should try not to be any more stubborn about this than I already have been, because if I really am in labor, I have no idea how fast this will go.

My mind whirs as time ticks down on the intermission clock. I don't have my hospital bag or car seat, Fletcher's in the middle of a playoff game, and Dottie isn't coming up for another week.

A short time later, another contraction hits. This one is stronger, the pain sharper. Grace starts a timer, and Zoey rubs my back as I breathe through it.

When the contraction ends, Grace stops the timer. "Seven minutes apart this time. When did they say to go to the hospital?"

I wave her off. "That was my first consistent one. I'm not going into the hospital yet. Not until they're consistently five minutes apart for an hour."

"I love you, but I am not a labor and delivery nurse. Pregnant women scare me. I don't want to deliver your baby in this suite, nor do I want to have to pull over on the side of the road," Zoey says forcefully, leaving no room for questions. "If they get to five minutes apart for over thirty minutes, we're going in."

I clench my jaw. "Fine."

I hope this isn't real labor.

The second period starts, and when I continuously have contractions every six and a half minutes, my nervousness grows.

I catch Fletcher watching me from the bench, and I offer him a half-hearted wave. He mouths something to me, but I can't catch it. I shake my head and smile, hoping to ease the worry I can see on his face.

Thankfully, he turns his focus back onto the game.

"Are you sure I can't take you home?" Grace asks me after the next contraction. This one was a doozy.

"Not yet. Let me try something else first." A restless feeling settles throughout my body, so I stand from the seat, stepping into the main part of the suite.

I lean against one of the high-top tables so I can still see the game and rock my hips back and forth. But I can feel her pressing down on my pelvis. This is happening, whether I like it or not. I thought I had more time.

Apparently not.

I rock while trying to focus on the game. Fletcher is playing a good game today. The stakes are high, and I can't stand the thought that I'm going to be a distraction to him, possibly pulling him away from the game. He'd scold me if he heard me say that, telling me there is nowhere he'd rather be, but I still feel bad.

I have to call Dottie. It's just going to be Fletcher with me in the delivery room, but Dottie will be there to help me when I get home, and I know she's going to want to be in the area to be here for us when she's born.

A fleeting thought crosses my mind as I think of my

mother. I wish things could be different between us, but they can't. She's proven to me that she won't respect my family or me, and I have to make peace with that.

"Zoey, can you grab my phone?" I ask.

She does, and I unlock it and call Dottie.

It rings twice before she answers. "Hi, sweetie. Are you watching the game?"

"Yep," I say through gritted teeth as another contraction starts.

Zoey motions to Grace, who taps her phone screen, marking the time. I already know there's been less time between the last contraction and this one.

"What's happening? Are you okay?" Dottie asks, concern fluttering in her voice.

"I think I'm in labor," I whimper through the waves of pain.

"Oh my. Are you at home?"

"Arena." My teeth clench over the words.

Grace snatches the phone from my palm, taking over the conversation. "Hi, Dottie. Do you think you can convince her it's time to go to the hospital?"

I can't hear what Dottie is saying, but Grace hums in agreement with whatever Dottie says.

"Yep. Her contractions are five minutes apart now. She's been contracting consistently for over an hour, they've just shortened in timing." Grace rattles off the timing of my most recent ones, then listens for a moment.

When this contraction finishes, I hold my hand back out for the phone. Grace slides it back into my palm, and I put it back to my ear.

"Hi, sorry," I say.

"I think it's time to go to the hospital. Even if it's a false alarm, it's better to go in than be stuck at the arena, or god forbid, hit the end-of-game traffic when you're too far gone."

Shit. I hadn't thought of that.

"Okay. You're right. I feel guilty, though. Fletcher's going to look up to the suite and panic when I'm not there."

The thought alone makes my heart hurt.

"He's going to be more stressed if you deliver the baby in the suite or in his car," Dottie replies.

"Can you come?" I ask, needing her here.

"I'm already packing, honey. Ron's getting the animals straightened away and calling the neighbor. That darn emu, Dave, is being a menace as always. We'll be there as soon as possible."

"Thank you."

A sense of peace washes over me. Dottie will be here soon.

We say our goodbyes, I promise to update her as much as I can, and I pass my phone back to Grace.

"Can you take me to the hospital?" I ask.

A heavy sigh of relief leaves both Grace and Zoey as they nod. "Yes, of course. I'll take you to the hospital, and Zoey can run to your apartment and grab your hospital bags."

Nodding, I exhale a heavy breath. "Thank you. Can you also text Fletcher and let him know? I know he won't see it until after the game, but I need him to know I'm okay."

"Already done," Grace says as she puts her phone in the back pocket of her jeans.

I can do this. I've been preparing for nine months, and now it's here. Am I ready? Honestly, I'm not sure, but I don't have time to think about it.

The second period is almost done, and we're up by one.

Adam gets a breakaway pass from Fletcher and flies across the ice toward the goal. Zoey shrieks as he shoots, the puck flying between the goalie's legs and into the net.

The crowd erupts as the horn blares, and another contraction hits me. The goal song plays, and I try my best not to curse every person in this arena. Now isn't the time to celebrate. It feels like my body is being ripped to shreds.

Grace puts pressure on my lower back as I breathe through the contraction. The pressure helps, but only marginally.

The goal celebration ends, and thankfully, so does my contraction. The girls help me stand up straight and lead me out. The walk to Grace's car is a blur. We have to stop twice while I have a contraction, but soon enough, we're on our way to the hospital, and Zoey is going to my apartment with instructions on everything she needs to grab.

This is not at all how I thought it would go, but all things considered, I'm glad I'm with the people I am.

60

ROOM SEVEN-TEN
FLETCHER

I breathe heavily as I climb over the boards, my heart pounding as I finish my shift. Adam scored a few minutes ago, but we are only up by one goal, so there is still a lot of work to do.

The horn blares, calling the end to the second period, and we make our way into the locker room. I glance up at the suite before leaving the bench. I don't see any of the girls, but they're probably getting snacks—and knowing Lydia in the last few weeks, she's probably in the bathroom.

Coach stands at the head of the room in front of the whiteboard, and we all focus on him for a few minutes as he discusses things we can work on in the upcoming period and plays we can make.

Adam sits beside me, his sweat-dampened hair falling in his face. "We need to keep on Montonen. He's getting sloppy as time goes on, less focused and making more aggressive plays, but it's not working."

"Agreed." I sip from my water bottle. "He's easy to rile up."

We talk for a few more minutes. Even though we're

winning, it would be easy for them to take over in the last period if we let them—but we're not going to.

The last few minutes of intermission fly by as we all hype each other up for the last twenty minutes of the game. As we make our way back to the bench, I look up to the suite once more, finding it empty again. Did something happen? Should I have checked my phone during the break? I don't usually do that, but with the impending due date, I should start.

Maybe they're walking around.

Something feels off, though. I can't exactly leave the bench to check my phone, but if they needed me, one of the girls would have gotten a message to Coach.

Calvin nudges me as the period starts, and we win possession of the puck in the face-off. "You good?"

"Where'd the girls go?" I tip my chin up to the suite. "They were gone at the end of last period, and they still aren't back."

He glances up. "Hm. I'm sure they're shopping, or maybe Lydia was craving something besides popcorn for once, so they went out of the suite to get it. If they needed you, they'd come find you."

"Right," I mutter, not sure I agree. I turn my focus back to the game anyway.

We score again with five minutes left.

When I glance up at the suite again, and it's still empty, I know something's wrong.

During a pause in play, I lean back, getting Coach's attention. "You haven't heard anything from Lydia, right?"

"No, why?"

"She left the game, I think."

"Once the game is done, go check your phone and do what you need to do," he says.

His blessing is the only approval I need. I play one more shift, but my head isn't in it. I know I should be more focused, but I feel it in my bones that something is up.

As soon as the final horn blares, I'm skating off the ice, ignoring the cheers of the crowd, not even giving Trigg a helmet tap or hug for a job well done. I run on my skates down the hall into the dressing room and straight to my locker. My heart is thrumming in my chest as I dig around for my phone, pull it out, and swipe it open to my messages.

There are two from Grace, and none from Lydia. The first message is from an hour ago, around the time the second period would have been ending.

GRACE

She's doing fine, but Lydia started having consistent contractions, so we are heading to the hospital. Zoey is running to your place to grab all your stuff. Come here as soon as you see this.

The second message is from only ten minutes ago.

GRACE

Here and checked in, they're going to check her cervix, but they think she's here to stay.

Instead of texting her, I click the call icon, putting it on speaker as I start taking my gear off, throwing it into my locker.

"Hey," Grace answers. "You on your way?"

"I just got off the ice. Changing. I'll be there as soon as I can. Is she okay?"

I can't miss my daughter's birth. I just can't.

"She's a stubborn girl. The only reason she agreed to come to the hospital was after talking to your mom. They're checking her now, so I'm not in the room. She's hooked up to the monitor, and baby is just fine."

I heave a sigh of relief hearing that. "Thank god." I'm dressed in my street clothes now, and already running down the hall toward the parking garage. "I'll be there as soon as possible. Call me if anything changes, okay?"

"You got it."

We hang up, and my panic increases again. I should have stayed on the phone with her, so I don't miss anything.

When I'm in my car, my phone connects to my Bluetooth, and I dial my parents.

"Are you there yet?" Mom asks, not even bothering to say hello.

"Not yet," I say through clenched teeth. "I'm pulling out of the arena now. Thanks for getting her to go in."

"She needed to. She wanted to watch the rest of the game, but I told her the last thing you needed was to find out she delivered your baby in the suite."

A forced chuckle breaks free from my lips. "Yeah, she was being stubborn."

"She is. Call me if you need anything, okay? I'm on my way, and I'll head to your house."

"Thanks, Mom."

I hang up without thinking and call Lydia.

"Hey," she answers, and her voice is tight, filled with so much pain it makes me want to cry.

"Hey, Lydi-bug. How are you doing?" It's a stupid question, I know, but I have to hear it from her.

"Hurts," she mutters, exhaling heavily. "Okay, it's over."

"Grace is with you?" I ask, even though I know the answer.

"Yep," Lydia responds. "They just checked me, and I'm six centimeters, so we're here to stay."

"We're going to have our baby soon."

The realization hits me like a brick wall.

"Are you on your way?" Lydia asks, her voice soft.

"I'm on my way, beautiful. I'll be there as soon as I can. I'm stuck in some of the post-game traffic, but I'll be there."

"I need you," she whimpers.

God, I wish I could teleport.

"I know, baby." I take a deep breath to try to calm my racing heart. "Are you getting the epidural?"

"Not yet."

Headstrong girl. I sigh, but I'll talk to her about it when I get there. Depending on how fast things move, she's going to be at this for a while, and she's going to need the rest. "Okay. I'll be there soon."

"Hurry."

"I will."

We say goodbye, and I end the call, tapping my fingers on the steering wheel as I sit at a standstill. I'm sure I reek of sweat and the locker room, but I have to hope Lydia doesn't notice, or that I can sneak a quick shower at some point.

A few minutes later, I arrive at the hospital and enter the Labor and Delivery Unit, pressing the button to have them unlock the door. I give them my name, they let me in, and I sprint down the hall.

"Whoa," a nurse says, holding up her hands and halting me. "She's fine. Waiting for you."

"Where is she?" I ask, out of breath.

"Room seven-ten. Come on, I'll bring you."

I follow close behind her, trying hard not to break out in another run. Finally, we're outside the door, and she knocks twice before Grace calls, "Come in!"

The nurse opens the door, and I walk in, not waiting another second to get to my girls.

Lydia is folded over the bed, dressed in a hospital gown. Her head is resting on her arms as she sways back and forth while Zoey rubs her back. Grace sits in the opposite corner, holding a cup of ice chips, and honestly, looking a little petrified.

I take Zoey's place at Lydia's side, rubbing her back through her contraction.

"Hey, beautiful." I push some of her curls off her sweaty face.

Lydia only lets out a low groan. I hate that I can't take away her pain. Once the contraction eases, she stands up straight, wrapping her arms around my neck and resting her head on my chest.

"Hi."

The proximity is exactly what I needed to feel marginally better. I hate that she's going to be in so much pain for an unknown length of time, but having her in my arms, in my sight, helps.

Then she says, "You stink."

"Sorry. I didn't shower. I wanted to get here as soon as possible once I figured out something was up."

"S'okay. Sorry we didn't tell you when we left."

"It's okay." I rub her back. "Scared me, but I'm glad you came here."

"I didn't want to."

I tilt my head down, slanting my lips over hers for a quick kiss. "I heard."

"Can you blame me? It's a playoff game." She sucks in a sharp breath.

I flutter my hands over her body, trying to help however possible. "What is it? What hurts?"

Lydia waves me off. "Did you win?"

I groan and rest my head on her forehead. "Yeah, Lydi-bug. We won. It doesn't matter."

"Of course, it matters—it's the playoffs! I have to have this baby tonight, so you can be back for the next game."

"Let's not worry about that now. Right now, our focus is on delivering this baby and making sure both of you are safe and healthy."

"I suppose that's a good point." Her grip tightens around the nape of my neck, and she lowers her voice. "I love you, but can you please shower before I send the girls home? You really stink."

Chuckling, I nod. "Yes. I'll be quick."

Lydia drops her arms from my neck, and I peck her on the lips. I glance at Zoey and Grace, who offer me a nod. I return the gesture, hoping I convey just how grateful I am.

Zoey points to my pre-packed bag in the corner, and I grab a fresh pair of clothes and my toiletries from it before heading to the bathroom. I start the shower, and while I wait for it to warm up, it sinks in.

I'm going to become a father.

61

THE NEXT CHAPTER

LYDIA

I'm so tired. My body aches everywhere, and I'm ready to give up. I've been holding out on getting the epidural, but it's past midnight now—nearly six hours after we got here—and I'm running out of steam. I need sleep, and my body needs rest. I wanted to hold off as long as I could, but I haven't progressed since I arrived, and I'm ready to have this baby.

"I'm waving the white flag." I'm lying on my left side, with a peanut ball between my legs.

Fletcher's sitting on a chair beside the bed, holding my hands in his and helping me through each and every contraction. "Time for an epidural?"

He's exhausted too, I'm sure, his gaze hooded. He's been my steady ground all evening into the night, and he was coming off a hard playoff game.

"Yeah." Another contraction tightens across my belly, and a low groan leaves my lips, my body curling in as I breathe through the pain.

I can barely hear Fletcher talking to the nurses, but I'm so grateful he's here.

SLEEP IS MUCH EASIER ONCE I get the epidural, and I wake up around six in the morning with an insane pressure in my pelvis. Fletcher is snoozing on the couch he pulled up beside my hospital bed, our hands entwined even through sleep.

I unlink our hands and press the button on the rail of the bed to call the nurse. When I tell them I'm feeling some pressure, they tell me they'll be right in. I jostle Fletcher, and he groans.

"What? Are you okay?" He bolts up, scanning me up and down. "What's going on?"

"I'm just feeling a lot of pressure. They're going to check it out."

He nods, standing up and pushing the makeshift couch bed back to the corner.

They come in a moment later and help me get situated on my back before performing the check. When the doctor nods, a knowing feeling settles in my gut.

"It's time," she says. "You're ten centimeters, and the baby is right there and ready."

"Holy crap." I glance up at Fletcher.

Everything happens fast. They get the room ready, helping me so I'm comfortable in the bed and making sure the baby warmer is on and good to go.

By the time they're ready for me to start pushing, the pressure is even stronger. My contractions are coming right on top of the other, it seems, and while I can't feel the pain as much, the tightness is still there.

They give me a few directions, and then my legs are

pushed up, baring my lower half to the entire room. I don't even have it in me to care. All sense of modesty is gone. I want to get my baby out, and if this is what it takes, so be it.

Fletcher takes my hand, pressing a kiss to the back of my palm. "You've got this, beautiful."

I tilt my chin, searching for a kiss. When he obliges, leaning down and cupping my cheek, it all locks into place. My heart belongs to him and our little girl. I never thought this was how we would end up, but I'm so glad we did. When he pulls away, he keeps one of my hands in his, while his other arm wraps behind my shoulders, helping to hold me up.

"Ready, Lydia?" the doctor asks, and I nod. "Great. Now, when your contraction starts, push."

It comes almost instantly, and I bear down, forcing all my energy into getting my baby out.

Time moves slowly as I continue to push, my body using every last molecule of strength through each and every push. I've been at this for over an hour now, and she's still not coming.

"Lydia, she's having some decels," Dr. Jones says.

No, no, no.

"We can give it a few more pushes, but she needs to come out as soon as possible, or we're going to have to do a C-section."

My baby has to be okay. I have to get her out, but I'm so tired. My muscles are mush, and my brain is running on fumes. *Oh, god, I don't think I can do this.*

"You can do this."

With a determined nod, I take a deep breath as I wait for the next contraction to start. I don't know where, but I find more strength.

"Good, good!" Dr. Jones says, and I hope that means I'm making some sort of progress.

A burning sensation hits, and I cry out.

"Don't stop," the doctor says.

I press on, screaming through the pain.

Fletcher pushes my hair back, his silent and steady presence helping the most. "Good job, baby. You're so amazing. We're going to meet our little girl soon."

His whispered words give me strength.

When the count ends, the pain stays this time, and I can tell she's moved farther down.

"Good job," Dr. Jones says. "If you keep up with that, you're going to have your baby in the next push."

I nod, flopping my head back. When the next contraction hits, I do the same as before, finding that last little reserve of energy I have.

"It's a girl," Dr. Jones shouts, placing my daughter on my chest as the nurses begin cleaning her off with blankets.

My beautiful girl screams, her lungs working as she announces her arrival. I brush my fingers over her face, tracing over the slope of her nose and the roundness in her cheeks. Right now, her eyes are blue like mine, but who knows if that will change. Her hair is dark, and the more the nurses clear all the goop off of her head, the more curls I see.

Fletcher leans in, tilting my head to kiss me as we both sob.

"She's here," I cry, my heart growing three sizes within only seconds. "Oh, my god. Fletcher."

"She's perfect." He kisses me and cradles her head in his giant palm. "You're incredible."

"Dad, do you want to cut the cord?" Dr. Jones asks, holding a pair of medical scissors.

Fletcher looks down at me, as if searching for permission. I nod. There's no question. His tears never cease as he cuts the cord, his gaze once again locking on me as soon as he's done.

Once I'm cleaned up, the nurses bring Baby Girl over to the warmer to wipe her off and wrap her in a blanket. I send Fletcher over to get some photos of her while I take a minute to breathe. The nurses help me get adjusted in the bed, and when they bring my little girl back, the tears begin again.

She's absolutely perfect, and everything I could have ever wanted. I *made* her. Every finger and toe, every eyelash and hair on her head came from me, and nothing will ever change that.

"Hi, baby," I whisper, unable to stop myself from tracing her face again.

Fletcher returns, taking his phone out. He snaps a few photos before flipping the camera and leaning in. He presses a kiss to my lips right as he takes a photo. It's the perfect moment, just the three of us as we begin the next chapter.

62

———————

NAMESAKE

LYDIA

"Fletch, can you take her for a moment?" I ask, shifting a bit. My whole body aches, the pain radiating through my pelvis.

"Of course." He stands from the reclining chair, coming over to my side to grab the little bundle from my arms. "Hey, Baby Girl," he whispers, easily lifting her into his embrace.

She just finished feeding, and I need to use the bathroom.

Dottie and Ron are coming to the hospital soon, along with all our friends, so I'd like to get cleaned up as much as I can.

I also want to decide on a name. We can't keep calling her Baby Girl, but nothing feels right. Fletcher helps me slowly stand, the baby cradled in his elbow, and walks with me to the bathroom, helping me sit on the toilet.

There's a different kind of intimacy in this moment. It's not sexy—I mean, I'm literally in a diaper—but he's here to support our daughter and me, even if it means helping me sit on the toilet and stand when I can't do it myself.

He leaves me alone while I relieve myself and do the process of cleaning up and putting witch hazel pads in my underwear. I call out to Fletcher when I'm ready for his assistance.

He comes back in, this time without our baby, telling me she's in the bassinet for a moment. Fletcher helps me stand, and I adjust my underwear before waddling over to the sink to wash my hands.

"Can you grab my robe from my bag, please?"

He leaves the small bathroom, returning with my light pink floral robe, and helps me out of the hospital gown and into this one. It immediately helps me feel a little refreshed.

I wash my face, brush my teeth, and make my way back to bed. Fletcher trails behind me, a hand on my lower back the whole time. Once I'm back in bed, Baby Girl lets out a squawk, letting us know she's no longer sleeping.

"I've got her." Fletcher rushes to her side and lifts her into his arms. "I think I'm going to do some skin-to-skin."

"Can I close my eyes for a bit while she's comfortable?" I ask, my eyes already drooping.

"Yep, I'll wake you if she gets hungry."

Not nearly enough time passes before Fletcher wakes me, but I was able to sleep a little bit. He helps me get her in my arms, and she thankfully latches onto my breast fairly easily.

While she eats, I stare at my daughter. "Do you have any other ideas for a name?"

Fletcher shakes his head. "I was doing some searching, but nothing has clicked so far."

When I think of the last nine months, a few people stand out the most. Obviously, Fletcher is the one who was there the most, but the second one is Dottie. Something rings in my chest. "What's your mom's full name?"

Fletcher quirks his eyebrow, and I can already see his eyes growing watery. "Dorothea."

"Dorothea," I whisper, running a finger over my baby's soft cheek. "What do you think of that?"

The name feels more and more right with each passing moment.

I look at Fletcher. His lower lip trembles as tears fill his eyes.

"We could call her Thea," I say, and it feels oh so right.

"I love it." He wipes the tears under his eyes. "It's perfect."

"Hi, Thea," I whisper to my beautiful daughter.

She doesn't have any of Fletcher's DNA or look like him, but she will always be a part of him and his family. Of mine.

"SHE'S ABSOLUTELY PERFECT," Dottie coos, rocking baby Thea in her arms. She and Ron just arrived about five minutes ago.

Dottie was more concerned about me at first, checking in and making sure I was okay before she even thought about holding my daughter. It's those things that matter, because while she loves my daughter, she cares for me too.

"Want to know her name?" Fletcher asks, and my heart pounds.

"Absolutely," Dottie replies, her eyes locked on our sweet girl.

"Her name is Dorothea," I say.

Dottie looks up to me with so much emotion that I start shedding tears.

"We'll call her Thea," I say, "but I wanted her to have a strong, meaningful name. A *family* name."

"Sweetie, are you sure?" Dottie walks over to me, resting her hand on my shoulder.

"The only thing I've ever been surer of was keeping her, and letting myself fall in love with Fletcher, so yes. You've always been like a mother to me and have been there for me more than my own. I love you, and I want her to know what a strong, caring, and amazing person her namesake is."

Dottie sobs as she holds Thea, and Ron wraps his arms around Dottie's shoulders and kisses her cheek.

"Thank you," he says, and I smile softly at both of them.

Now, the only thing left is to tell Fletcher her middle name. I decided not long after settling on her first name, but I'm waiting until we are alone again to tell him.

Dottie holds Thea for most of the time they're here, and we make sure to take a lot of pictures of her with her new grandparents.

We make plans for Dottie to meet us at the apartment tomorrow morning when we're discharged, so she can stick around and help me out since Fletcher has to be back at the arena tomorrow for another game. Thankfully, he won't miss any games, even though he's offered to skip the next one no less than three times. I won't let him. There's no reason for it, especially since it's the playoffs. His team needs him. Dottie will be with me, and I bet I could convince Grace, Zoey, and maybe even Hattie—depending on her work schedule—to come over too. We can have a low-key girls' night.

When the Graffs leave, Fletcher snuggles in next to me on the bed, holding Thea on his chest. He's been doing skin-to-skin any chance he can, and it makes my heart swell. He's already such a wonderful dad.

"I thought of what I want her middle name to be." I lean over to kiss his bare shoulder.

"Yeah?" he asks, running his hand over her soft curls. "What is it?"

"Sage."

"I like it. Dorothea Sage Ward."

"Dorothea Sage Graff. Sage, because of the color of her Dad's eyes. They're my favorite part of you, and I want her to have that piece of you, even if she doesn't have any part of your DNA. I also want her to have the Graff name, so she knows she always has a family with the people who gave me a family."

"Lydia." Tears brim in his eyes, the ones I love so much. "Thank you. I won't ever make you regret giving her my last name."

I kiss him gently. "I know you won't."

"I'll give it to you too, someday." His eyes lock on mine, and I know he means it, just like I mean my next words.

"I know, and I can't wait."

63

GOOD LUCK COMES IN TWOS

FLETCHER

Leaving Lydia and Thea is actually physically painful. Every block I drive away from the apartment hurts my soul. How do the other guys do this? I want to stay home with them, cuddled up and there to help Lydia with everything she needs. My mom and Grace are there with her, but it still doesn't feel right.

I'm leaving a piece of my heart behind.

How is it that less than forty-eight hours after Thea was born, I'm heading to play another game? The worst part is, we leave early tomorrow for the two-game away stretch of this series. I'll be gone for three days. Who knows how much Thea will grow in that time? I hate that I'm missing this, that Lydia will be without me. Yes, my mom will be there, but I won't be.

I get to the arena and head into the locker room to prep for warm-ups. I wave to Vivi as I walk through the tunnel, and she offers me a whispered congratulations. I nod, smiling.

Everyone on the team knows Lydia had the baby since I missed practice yesterday and this morning, but per Lydia's wishes, we are keeping her off social media. We've even asked that, at any family events, she either not be photographed or have her face covered. Admin was completely willing to abide by our request, and for that, I'm grateful. I want my daughter to watch me play and greet me at the plexiglass at warmups, but not if the team wasn't going to grant our request for privacy.

I know fans will probably photograph her, and there's only so much we can do about that, but we're trying to control what we can, especially after Lydia's mom sent private photos to the press.

When I walk into the locker room, a few of the guys are sitting around with their headphones in as they get their gear on, zoning in for the game. The playoffs are always a different kind of vibe in the locker room. Some guys are even more superstitious, but for me, I only need my good luck charm.

I sit on the bench and dial Lydia. She doesn't answer, but she might not be by her phone. I give her a minute before I call again.

No answer.

Something may be wrong. Lydia could have a delayed postpartum hemorrhage. She could be bleeding out, and I'm stuck here at the arena. So much could be going wrong, and I'm not there. Unbridled fear sinks deep into my bones.

I call my mom.

She answers quickly, and her voice soothes the anxiety right away. "Hi, honey. What's up?"

"Is Lydi okay?"

"Sleeping," Mom answers, and I sigh in relief. "Why? Is everything okay?"

"I talk to her before every game."

"You talked to her before you left."

"No, I mean like…" I rub my hands over my face. "I have to talk to her."

I don't know how to explain this to her, but hopefully she'll understand.

"Oh, I see," Mom says with a chuckle. "She went to rest for a while since Thea ate and is calm. Can it wait?"

I look up at the ceiling. I can't wake Lydia up, not now. "Can we FaceTime instead, and I'll talk to Thea? That will work."

A moment later, the call switches to video.

My beautiful baby girl's face fills my screen, and there's an ache in my chest, this time from missing her. "Hi, my little ladybug. Are you having fun with your grandma?"

She, of course, doesn't answer, but her blue eyes are wide. Thea is a near-identical copy of her mother, with the same eyes, nose, and chin. She's absolutely beautiful. I couldn't love her more if I tried. I talk to her for a few minutes about how much I love her and her mom, as her eyes droop shut, finally staying closed. Her mouth pops open into a little O-shape as she sleeps. I talk for another minute before saying, "Okay, I should get going."

When my mom pans the camera back to her, her eyes are welling with tears. "You're already a great dad."

My own eyes sting. "Thanks. Tell Lydia I'll call her when I am on my way home."

"I will."

We hang up, and I tip my head back. I wasn't able to talk to Lydia, and maybe it will mess up my superstition ritual, but I got to talk to a piece of her, and that's perfect.

WE WIN the game three to one, with me scoring two of the three goals. It was an incredible game, but I'm itching to get home. I do my cool-down exercises and shower quickly, heading back to my locker in record time.

"Heading out?" Trigg asks, his voice lilting.

"Yep. I don't want to miss any more time at home than I have to." I grab my phone and scan the screen to make sure I don't have anything important from my mom or Lydia.

"Makes sense. How is Lydia doing?"

"Good. She's an amazing mom already."

"I do not doubt that for a second," Trigg says. "Get home, we will see you in the morning. Tell Lydia I said hi."

"Will do." I turn to leave the locker room, waving to everyone as I do. As I walk through the tunnel, I click Lydia's name on my phone screen, putting the phone to my ear.

"Hi. Good game."

"Thanks, beautiful. How are you doing?"

"Sore but good. I finished feeding her a few minutes ago, and your mom is burping her now."

"Need me to stop and grab anything on the way home? Did you eat dinner?"

"Your mom made me a BLT. I don't need anything else besides you."

I walk a little bit faster. "I'll be there as soon as possible."

"Okay, I love you."

I can hear Thea begin crying in the background.

"I love you, too. I'll be there soon." We hang up, and I sprint to my car, climbing in and backing out of the spot immediately. Thankfully, most of the post-game traffic has cleared, so I make it home quickly.

When I open the apartment door, I hear the now

familiar sounds of Thea crying. My mom and Lydia are nowhere in sight, but I head down to the nursery, finding Lydia in the glider, rocking back and forth with Thea on her shoulder as she pats her back.

"Hi," I say, drawing their attention to me.

Lydia glances up, and a soft smile appears on her face. "She's cluster feeding."

"I have no idea what that means." I stride over to Lydia and lean in for a kiss. "Want me to take her?"

Lydia shakes her head. "No, she is going to want more, I think. Can you make a formula bottle? I don't think my boobs are doing it for her right now."

"Of course. Two ounces?"

"Please."

I kiss her one more time and head into the kitchen to make the bottle. A minute later, I'm back in the nursery, but instead of handing Lydia the bottle, I reach for Thea. "Let me. Go take a shower, or rest."

Lydia nods, passing Thea to me. I take my little bundle into my arms and help Lydia slowly stand. She winces a few times and walks slowly out the door while I sit in the glider. I put the bottle to Thea's lips, and she starts guzzling it down immediately.

Before Lydia leaves the room, she stops in the doorway, turning around to face me. "I missed your call before the game today."

I glance at her, furrowing my eyebrows. "You did, but you were sleeping. I talked to my little ladybug instead."

"Do you call me before every game for a reason?" she questions curiously.

A chuckle bursts through my lips. "You really never figured it out, did you?"

"No?"

"You're my good luck charm, Lydia Ward."

She scoffs. "No, I'm not."

"Yes, you are. I call you, or when you're at the game, I have to talk to you somehow before every game, because something about hearing your voice makes me play my best. I can't say goodbye, though. Only see you later or talk later. If I say goodbye, it messes it all up. It started back in college, and when I noticed a pattern, I stuck with it. Can't do a game without it. Well, until today, that is. Our little girl stepped in and did a phenomenal job, if you ask me."

"So, what you're saying is, I'm your superstition?"

"Yep. Not your average superstition, but it works for me."

"You still lose games, though."

"Yeah, but I play better if we talk. It's a thing, baby. Go with it."

"Alright." She laughs. "Well, if it works, it works. I'm going to shower."

She walks away, leaving me alone with our daughter. "I don't think Mommy gets it, but it's okay. You do, don't you, my ladybug."

64

ONE MORE CHANCE

FLETCHER

The locker room is silent tonight, a quiet focus and calm falling over the space. We lost the last two away games in overtime, and the game the day before yesterday. If we lose tonight, we're done. I rub my hand over my growing beard in an attempt to slow my racing heart.

I just got off the phone with my girls, and I need to get into the right headspace, but the only place I'd rather be is at home with them. Maybe Crowley was onto something when he retired early to be home with his kids. I shake off the thought before it takes root. I'm not ready to retire, no matter how much I want to be at home with them. I still have years left in me.

Do I want to win the championship? Of course. But it hurts being away from them. I'll never get these moments with Lydia and Thea back. She'll never be this small, and I dread missing even a second of it.

I turn my focus away from them and toward the men in the locker room. I stand, calling for their attention. "Alright. I know we've had a rough few games, but I wanted to say a few words. We are all ready for this game, and win or lose, we're a team, and we are in it together. Never forget that."

Each of my teammates nods and claps. Calvin lets out a whoop, and the rest of the team follows until everyone is on their feet, cheering and hollering. We all have a pep in our step now as we head out onto the ice for warm-ups.

Habitually, I skate to my favorite spot on the ice and glance up, a pang of disappointment sinking in my chest knowing that Lydia isn't in the crowd. She wanted to come tonight, but there was no way she could have. She's still in quite a bit of pain and isn't ready to bring Thea out into the germ-infested world quite yet. Neither am I, to be honest.

In the suite is Zoey with her fiancé, and Grace with her parents, Mabel and Stan. My mom is home with Lydia, of course. Trigg's family is watching at home in Norway. It feels good, knowing we have everyone's support.

Once the game starts, we're all focused on every single movement by our opposing team, fighting for possession of the puck and shooting every shot we can.

Three periods isn't enough. The game is tied one to one, and we go into overtime, playing three on three. The last couple of games have prepared us for this, even though they haven't ended in our favor, I still have hope.

Trigg is a machine, blocking thirty-nine shots on goal.

Overtime starts, and I take the ice with Calvin and Waffles. We pass back and forth, trying to find an opening to shoot, but nothing comes. My shift ends, but Calvin and Shep stay on, Adam taking my place.

Something isn't clicking. Adam isn't locked in the way he should be. Calvin shouts something at Adam, but I can't hear it over the roar of the crowd. There are two minutes left in overtime. Two minutes to secure the next game and stay in the playoffs.

Calvin slaps the puck across the ice to Adam, but it tips off his stick, straight into the opposing player's stick. The player takes off toward Trigg.

"Shit," I mutter.

The player passes to his teammate at the last second, and he shoots the puck over his shoulder and into the net before Trigg can stop it.

The lamp lights up red behind the net, and the crowd groans. Trigg slumps to his knees, dropping his head into his gloved hand. Calvin slides to a stop next to him, rubbing his back.

Adam stands before them, completely dejected. Shepherd skates off the ice, following the rest of the team down the tunnel to the locker room.

That's it.

Our season is over.

Coach lets out his frustrations in the locker room before sending us on our way. There's nothing left for us to do now, and I glance around the room.

"I know it was a tough loss, but I'm proud of each and every one of you. We fought hard this season, and we'll fight even harder next year." I tip my chin toward my teammates, noting that Adam is sitting with his head in his hands on the bench.

Calvin sits beside him, and I leave them to their conversation, knowing they need the time to themselves. They've known each other for a long time, and Calvin can comfort Adam better than I can.

I finish my cool down and grab my things from my locker, waving goodbye to the guys. I'll see them at some workouts and events over the summer, but it's always a little bittersweet to leave after the end of the season.

Zoey and Grace stop me in the hall, offering hugs, and I

show them a few photos I took of Thea this morning. She was smiling in her sleep. Lydia and my mom both said it was just gas, but I don't know. I'm convinced it was a smile.

Mabel and Stan are there too, offering me congratulations and telling me they expect to see us at their lake place this summer.

Heading out of the arena, I take a deep breath. On the bright side, I now get uninterrupted time with my girls. I drive home, and when I enter the apartment, Lydia is sitting on the couch, feeding Thea. She has a somber look on her face, and I shrug.

"I'm sorry," she says, her brows knitted together. "It was a tough game."

"It was." I sit beside her and give her a long kiss. "Missed you." Leaning down, I press a gentle kiss to Thea's forehead. "Missed you, too, ladybug."

"So, what now?" Lydia asks, tilting her head to lean into my chest as I wrap my arm around her shoulders, scooting in close.

"Now, we get to spend as much time as we want together, all summer."

"Sounds pretty great, if you ask me." I can hear the smile in her voice.

"Mabel and Stan want us to come to their cabin sometime."

"I'd love that."

"Maybe someday we could get a lake place there, too."

I already have a plan in mind to get a place there. It's a beautiful area, and I've always wanted a summer getaway.

"That would be fun, but anything with you sounds fun."

"Agreed." I kiss the top of her head. "I love you."

"I love you."

Thea squirms in her lap as she finishes eating, and Lydia passes her to me to burp.

"Hey, pretty girl," I say with a smile, smoothing the curls on the top of her head, resting her on my shoulder, and patting her back.

Here with my two girls, life feels pretty damn good.

EPILOGUE
LYDIA

FIVE MONTHS LATER

Thea shrieks with excitement in my arms, a giant, gummy smile spreading across her chubby cheeks when she sees her dad skating toward us. I hold her a little tighter as she tries to squirm away.

"Hi, ladybug," Fletcher says, taking off his glove and squishing her cheek.

She squeals in delight, kicking her little legs.

"And hello, my Lydi-bug." He pecks me on the lips, offering me a smile.

"I think she missed you," I say with a laugh.

"Maybe a little."

The coaching event he and Calvin were running today is nearly done, but Fletcher asked me to bring Thea out so we could have some time alone on the ice. We haven't been able to skate together since that date night at the arena, and I'm looking forward to spending some one-on-one time on the ice with him.

Fletcher takes our daughter in his arms, and she

squawks happily. She loves her daddy so much. I think he's definitely her favorite person, and I can't even be mad about it. He's my favorite person, too.

Fletcher adjusts her Minnesota Blue Herons hat so she can see better, and he shifts her so she's facing outwards while they skate. She has on the cutest pastel pink fleece snowsuit, one of my favorite things of hers. I get a wild amount of cuteness aggression when she wears it.

Calvin bends down to smile at Thea, who giggles at her uncle. She loves all of her aunts and uncles so much, and they adore and spoil her.

We're going to her first hockey game early next week for the home opener, and I'm so excited. The last five months have been so fun. Fletcher convinced me to take the whole summer off, and I went back to work only a few weeks ago. It's been a big adjustment, and I miss my baby when she's at daycare, but the daycare they have for the players is amazing. I feel good leaving her there every day.

Fletcher is the best dad. He's a natural, and sometimes, he's the only one who can get her to settle when she's crying nonstop. She started teething the week I went back to work, and it made the transition hard, but even though Fletcher was in the middle of pre-season, he was up with her in the middle of the night for feeds or comfort whenever she woke up.

I haven't spoken to my mom or my dad since that night in March, and I'm better off because of it. They were never going to change, and while I wish I'd realized it sooner, I'm glad I cut them off when I did. My mom tried calling a few more times, but eventually, I blocked her number. A small part of me is sad my daughter won't know my parents, but it's for the best. She doesn't deserve to feel the pain I did, and besides, Ron and Dottie more than make up for my parents' absence.

Thea squeals when Fletcher skates a little faster, but never too fast. They finish up the event, and I grab my skates from my bag, putting them on and lacing them up.

When all the kids are gone, Calvin skates toward me on the bench. "Have fun, Lydia!" he practically shouts as he races by me, not even stopping to say hi.

Weird.

Usually, Calvin will stop and talk your ear off or at least make some sort of joke. I wonder what he was in such a rush for.

With the rink empty besides Fletcher and me, I step onto the ice, the glide under the blade of my skates familiar and settles a piece of my soul. I skate toward my little family, my heart clenching when Thea gives me her gummy smile.

"Hi, baby," I coo, taking her little hands in mine. "Did you have fun skating with Daddy?"

She squeals, and I giggle. Being a mom is one of my favorite things in the world. The first month or two were super rough; the lack of sleep and breastfeeding took a toll on me, but once we switched to formula and she started sleeping better, it got much easier.

"We had lots of fun." Fletcher leans in for another kiss.

Our relationship has grown so strong, too, as we became parents. We always had a strong friendship, and when we started dating, it was natural, and while parenting brought different challenges, we took them in stride and leaned on each other to get through them.

We skate together for a while, passing our daughter back and forth. Fletcher gets me to teach him a new jump, and he lands it a few times, but only after many falls.

Thea yawns. "We should probably get going," I say, gesturing to her. "She's going to get fussy if we keep her up any later."

Fletcher nods, reaching out for her. "First, I have something I want to ask you."

I furrow my brows. "Okay? What?"

To my utter surprise, Fletcher sinks to one knee, adjusting Thea so she's sitting on his thigh. Reaching into the pocket of his pants, he pulls out a small velvet box.

"Fletcher," I breathe, covering my mouth. I can't believe this is happening.

He opens the box, but my sole focus is on him. Nerves are written all over his face, and his hand trembles as he begins to speak.

"Lydia, you are the love of my life. What started as a crush in our anatomy lab turned into a beautiful friendship I have never once taken for granted. I knew I wanted to keep you in any way I could, and now, I've never been happier that I took a chance and turned our friendship into more. I'm even happier that we have our little girl, and who knows, maybe someday we will have more. But right now, I need to ask you one thing."

I'm already nodding, tears streaking down my cheeks. "Yes."

Fletcher lets out a watery chuckle. "I haven't even asked you yet."

"The answer is yes."

He quirks a smile, shaking his head. "Lydia Ward, will you marry me?"

I continue nodding, getting down onto my knees on the ice in front of him. I take his cold cheeks into my palms, kissing him as we laugh, our excitement palpable as Thea giggles right along with us.

Fletcher pulls back, reaching down to get the ring out of the box. A silver ring with a round diamond set in the center, with two little diamonds on each side. It's exactly what I imagined. Simple, not too big, and absolutely perfect.

He slides the ring onto my finger, and I kiss him again through my tears.

"I love you, Fletch," I whisper against his lips.

"I love you, too, Lydi. I can't wait to see where forever takes us."

This moment was everything I wanted and more. Something special, just the three of us as we start the next steps to our future.

ACKNOWLEDGMENTS

If you've been a reader of mine for a while, you knew that the Minnesota Blue Herons have been a long time coming. Originally, The first book in this series was supposed to be released after the Cinder Valley Series was completed. Well, that didn't happen. I struggled with writing, and hit my first bout of writers block.

I'll dive into the details another time, but for now, I'm so excited to finally dig into this series that has been residing in my head for two years. And don't worry. Adam and Grace are coming soon. And this time, I really mean it. Adam is stubborn, but he's finally ready to let his story be told.

Fletcher was unexpected if I'm being honest. He popped up in In Plain Sight, and I just knew he had a story. His book was actually going to be book four in this series, but... well, he was loud, and wanted to get with his girl a lot sooner than planned. And of course, I had to bring back Ron and Dottie. We all need a Dottie in our lives, to be honest.

I hope you loved Fletcher and Lydia as much as I do. I couldn't have written this book without the support and help of the amazing people I have in my life.

Aria & Tiff- For constantly being there for me. I love

you two more than you know and I am so freaking grateful for your friendship.

The Fat Writers Space- I fucking love you all. I have so many reasons to thank you all, but I'll keep it short this time around. Thank you for being there for me and hyping me up every second of the day. Also, it's Duck, Duck, Grey Duck.

Willa- I don't even know where to begin. You helped bring this book to a whole new level, and it would not be what it is without you. Honestly, words cannot express how thankful I am for you. I love you. Trigg is yours, and no one else can claim him.

My Beta Readers, Emily, Abbey, and Jessica-your kindness and suggestions are so incredible. I appreciate you taking the time out of your busy lives to read and make this book better!

My ARC and Street Team- The fact that you are all so willing to take time out of your lives and days to read my books and hype me up will always be amazing. Each and every one of you mean more to me than you know!

My family and friends- for listening to me gush about my characters and stories, and being my biggest supporters.

Victoria- I'm doing it, Mr. Krabs! I love you. How many books do you think it will take for her to read the acknowledgments?

HBC- Thank you for your constant willingness to help me with events, whether local or across the country, for the way you are always there for me and scream in excitement whenever I share exciting news.

Cinder Valley Series

Tip Of My Tongue- Lainey & Colin

How Do I Tell You?- Mallory & Tyler

Give Me A Minute- Theo & Peyton

Ivy Ridge

Flowers in Your Hair- Andrew & Josie

Never Really Mine- Beau & Marley

Can't Let You Go- Jason & Fallon

In Plain Sight- Thomas & Hannah

Minnesota Blue Herons Hockey Series

Ruin The Friendship- Fletcher & Lydia

Dancing With Our Hands Tied- Adam & Grace

ABOUT THE AUTHOR

Alice Daniels is a born and raised Minnesotan who loves to write books based on the small town she grew up in. Her books are sweet, heartfelt, and sexy, with relatable characters.

As a child, she was an avid fiction reader, which evolved into a deep love for romance novels and the community surrounding them. She recently discovered a passion for putting her ideas into writing and decided to pursue her childhood dream of becoming an author.

She spends time with her family and friends when she's not writing, especially on the lakes or outdoors in the summer.

Follow Alice on Facebook, Instagram, and Goodreads for book updates, teasers, and future releases!

Join her Facebook Group, Alice Daniels Reader Group to get all the insider info, sneak peeks, and more!

https://alicedaniels.com/

amazon.com/author/alicedaniels

facebook.com/authoralicedaniels

instagram.com/authoralicedaniels

goodreads.com/authoralicedaniels

bookbub.com/authors/saylor-ann

www.ingramcontent.com/pod-product-compliance
Lightning Source LLC
Chambersburg PA
CBHW020900060726
47591CB00004B/1015